4.95
3.00



Hecht, Ben, 1893-
A treasury of Ben Hecht; collected stories and other writings. New York, Crown Publishers [1959]
397 p, 22cm.

I. Titl

# A TREASURY OF BEN HECHT

# *A Treasury of*
# BEN HECHT

*Collected Stories and Other Writings*

*by* BEN HECHT

CROWN PUBLISHERS, INC.

*New York*

Library of Congress Catalog Card Number: 59-9170

Printed in the United States of America

TO BILLY ROSE

# *Preface*

I RE-EDITED the five *Broken Necks* stories before handing them in to the publisher. They were written when I was young and full of complex reflections which seem to my present taste a bit silly. In fact, some of the paragraphs I snipped out of my early stories angered me at myself. I thought, how could I have been so bright a young man and also so pompous and nitwitted at the same time—in the same story?

I've known the answer to this rhetorical question for quite a time. There were always a surprising number of me's in operation. Sometimes they operated at the same time. In my youth, especially, I was likely to write a story full of contradictory moods, such as compassion and cynicism. My pity had ridicule in it and my finest outbursts of love were often prickly with sneers.

Much of the ambivalence remains in my early stories despite my editing. I could remove only a portion of the philosophical bric-a-brac that cluttered these youthful pages. And though I winced at some of my early intellectual ornamentations, I was not entirely displeased. My faults were not those of a bad writer, but of an overexuberant one.

Nor did I ever change, much. My sharp sensitivities as a young man are still my equipment as a writer. But aided by editors and critics, I learned not to put them all into one story.

My many attitudes toward life make a collection such as this seem more the output of a half-dozen different writers, rather than of one fellow with a single address. I am not too sure whether or not this is a boast. Being a many-sided writer has drawbacks. You achieve no easily admired mannerism. Critics cannot write illuminatingly of your "style." And "inconsistency" makes you seem to many no artist at all. An artist, it is believed, must have an unvarying embrace of life.

There is some truth in this notion. But there is also truth in its denial. My variability is, perhaps, bad salesmanship, but I have seldom written prose without putting my best into it. I have lived in a dozen worlds, as few writers do, and I have been different people in these worlds. I have enjoyed them as if I were a denizen and not a visiting exile. The stories I have included in this book represent most of these existences.

I have also included one of my plays because it is a play about a poet and because, unlike most of the plays I have written, it contains some of my favorite writing. The play *Winkelberg* was produced in New York, off-Broadway, by Lee Falk in 1958. It was mildly successful. Several adverse criticisms, a taxicab strike, and an unprecedented snowstorm isolated its fine actors somewhat in Bleecker Street. But it won a coterie of intense partisans. On rereading it before submitting it to the publisher, I felt a revived conviction that *Winkelberg* is one of the best of my works.

Missing from this volume are innumerable essays, fulminations, vignettes, and short stories of which I am equally fond. I hope some day to find a publisher demented enough to let me present all my works, maturely edited, in a score of fat volumes such as this. But until that notable occasion, I am content with the present book. It offers a good sample of most of my selves in prose and dialogue.

BEN HECHT

NYACK,
December, 1958.

# *Some Introductory Thoughts*

READERS are a much odder tribe than writers. They are much more fretful and egotistic.

The vainest of writers will often pause and ponder whether he knows anything about writing. No such humble moments afflict a reader. The reader knows everything—that is, about writing.

I imagine this is as it should be. It would be disastrous if a critic ever had any doubts about his opinions. He would cease to be a critic instanter and become something else, perhaps an artist, or worse—a man out of a job.

A reader is a critic with a very fine and important job—to please himself. It is, however, his job, not mine.

The stories that fill this book will undoubtedly fail to please a great many readers. I shall identify them in advance and thus save us both an unprofitable meeting.

Those readers who are fond of reading things that bore them, under the delusion that boredom is the mark of high class art, will find little profit in me. I have never tried to wheedle myself into their parvenu libraries by pulling a long face and putting lead in my sentences.

Those readers who pleasure themselves with reading things they can't quite understand so that they may seem to others smarter than they are will find no comfort in me; although I am not completely positive on this point. I may be given to occasional lapses of intelligibility and whilom rhetorical flights that wind up in a fog bank—for I began life as a poet. But such misty patches are infrequent in my prose and provide small manna for the enigma fanciers.

Those readers who like to read about very dull people who do and say and think very dull things under the delusion that they, the readers, are coming to grips with Real Life by such slumming, will waste their time on me.

I have my periods of dullness, but they are not deliberate. I was weaned on The Arabian Nights and Dickens—both of whom taught me that a man who aspires to dullness is following a line of least resistance.

Those readers who admire Slices of Raw Life—real human beings lying inanimately on a fictional platter like a collection of rutabagas and pineapples, will be irked by my opposite offerings.

I have disliked always stories in which, right bang in front of you, nothing happens. And I have disliked always stories which have for their plots the opening of a door, or the creaking of a rocker or somebody sighing at a soda fountain.

And I have disliked always stories that tried to make me feel what a subtle fellow I was to understand them. There is at present a rash of this pretentious and inept vignette-fiction—and all of it as subtle as a bad shave.

Those readers who fancy what they like to call a chaste style and demand that a love story or a great adventure be told in words that would not embarrass a tomato-can label, will find me not their dish at all. For I am, and always have been, a very clever fellow with words.

I have been often fiercely challenged by readers as being insincere and superficial because I was fond of adding wit to my lucubrations and sticking a verbal feather in the hats of my characters. I can understand their challenge well enough. People who sweat when they think and to whom an idea comes with all the impact of a toothache, refuse to believe that gayety and not pain may be the mark of intellect.

Those readers with bobby-socks minds who like to read only celebrities will automatically skip me, so I need not address them.

I have, alas, never been a celebrity. I have had a good mead of admirers, and my files bulge with enough flattering communiqués to keep me soothed for the rest of my life. But I have never yet won to that unreasoning and uncritical back-slapping that makes a celebrity—and leaves everybody happy to be seen shaking hands with him or his works.

I have in the above paragraphs dismissed quite a bag of readers, and my publisher who is investing his money in the production of this volume may wonder with a twinge whether there are any left. God knows. However, under the assumption that there are, I shall address my remaining comments to them.

The stories they will read in this volume were written out of a greater variety of moods than it is customary for one writer to have. This variety in my work, and the contradictions it involves, have inspired one critic of parts to identify me as a schizophrenic or split personality. As an authority on schizophrenia I can easily deny this.

There is a basic and never varying reason behind all my short story writing. It is this—I write to cheer myself up. I know the world well and it fills me with an ugly mood. The stupidity of humans and their horrid incompetence toward life is a theme with which I have wrestled in many of my books.

My short stories are my chief social effort to escape the gloomy pits of information in my mind.

One does this by entering the happy storehouse of the imagination. Here is a world not yet gone to pot, here are people and events still as dreamy and charming as filled the days of one's innocence. Sitting down to write of them, I enjoy myself.

Yet in my stories, after they are written, I find always that I have actually invented nothing, that the people I have written about are actually people I have known, and that the anecdotes in which I wrap them up are truly adventures which have befallen me or those around me at some time.

It becomes obvious to me, then, that the only fictional thing in my stories is my point of view. My point of view in most of my stories is that of a child who finds the world full of exuberant and engrossing matters, who dramatizes what he sees so he may enjoy it more, and who asks as a reward for his labors only the illusion that existence is a fine thing.

If you read the stories in this book, however, you will notice that my innocence and gayety are not constantly present. The folly and poison of life manage to unhorse my sturdiest efforts at cheer. I am full of contempts that my wit and Arabian-Nights plots do not entirely conceal.

And try as I may to cheer myself up with spanking tales and a jolly point of view, a moan lurks in the corners of many of my tales.

I apologize for this unseemly sound. It belongs in me and not my tales. For I have had always a picture of myself as a story teller. I have seen myself like those sunny and cackling fellows who once upon a time stood on the street corners of Bagdad and unfolded tales to the harassed citizens who paused to listen—and fling grateful kopecks at their feet.

BEN HECHT

Nyack, N. Y.,
April, 1945.

# *Contents*

# A TREASURY OF BEN HECHT

# *Some Slightly Crazy People*

MAX POLIAKOFF, theatrical producer (of what?) sat in a booth of Sullivan's Greenwich Village Cafe, and smiled on the woman he had loved eloquently for twenty-two years. She was Madame La Sylph, once prima ballerina of the Brussels Ballet, now teacher of the dance in New York City. Poliakoff's smile was his chief possession. It minimized and often removed entirely his record of thirty years of unsuccess on two continents as an entrepreneur.

The smile left Poliakoff's face.

"You do not believe me." He sighed into his teacup, creating an arresting sound effect. "My adorable, I am not blaming you. It is only what I deserve. Anybody who lives in dreams, like me, must look to the outsider like a liar. What else? O.K., my angel, I do not deny. I admit I have had to tell some lies. How else can a man live? But, dear princess, I ask you from tonight forward to believe in me. Conclusively."

Madame La Sylph ignored the confession. It promised to her only an outburst of new lying. At forty-eight, La Sylph had the waistline of youth and the sagacity of a seeress. Her aquiline features and tousled hair, dyed a Pompeiian red, gave her indeed the look of such an oracular communicant.

"You refuse to believe in me." Poliakoff shook his head in wonder. "O.K. I was going to hold off the announcement till the arrival of my author. But never mind. Now, in two minutes, you are going to say to me, 'Polly, you are a man who has spoken finally the truth, the holy truth, so help him God.' "

La Sylph hummed a passage from Glazounow's *Ramonda.*

"Here," said Poliakoff, "I am not relying on word of mouth. Read, if you please."

He removed a check from his wallet and held it fearlessly under the ex-ballerina's nose. She studied it as attentively as a federal agent. The date was correct. The recipient was "Poliakoff Enterprises, Inc." The sum was for "$12,000 and no cents." The signature was "Magda Callahan."

Poliakoff spoke in a zephyr voice: "One week ago I gave Mrs. Callahan to read the play *Study in Brown*. Last night she read the manuscript. Today she calls me up to come at once. When I arrive, she is still walking up and down in her penthouse, in the lace kimona, holding her heart with excitement. 'Polly!'—she could hardly speak—'You are only a genius!' "

"A lace kimona?" cried La Sylph. "How revolting! That amorous beanpole is still after you! And the check is probably a forgery!" She stood up and started to leave the booth.

Poliakoff flung his arms on the table and dropped his head into them like a dead partridge. La Sylph conceded the point and settled back into the booth.

"My princess . . . !" Poliakoff returned gently to the living. "I am expecting any minute the author of *Study in Brown*. I hinted to him the good news over the telephone. Because I would like to see his face when he hears in full. He is a genius, that sweet boy. Unspoiled yet by fame. I have here"—he patted a large brief case at his side—"the contracts for his signature. My beautiful darling, I am going to produce off-Broadway the most sensational masterpiece of drama yet on the American stage. And you, madame, will be my associate, fifty-fifty, in the profits. Do you know what the united profits can be in one year with an off-Broadway smash? As high as one-half-million dollars. . . . *Ah!*" Poliakoff added joyfully as he stood up, arms extended, "Franklyn Goodyear, my favorite genius! I am happy to see you!"

Two figures walked slowly toward Poliakoff. One was a blondish young man of twenty-five in a torn raincoat. He was tall, tie-less, muscle-less, and morose beyond his years. His head was tilted to one side and his chin tucked down as if he were in conference.

The other figure was a girl of nineteen in a black turtle-neck sweater, black skirt, ballet slippers, and black stockings. Her piquant features were without make-up or expression. She looked like a small boy who needed a haircut.

"Shoshana," said Franklyn Goodyear as introduction, and sat down, head tilted, in a corner of the booth.

"Ah, an Indian!" Poliakoff beamed. "I have always loved the Indians since Poccahuntus."

"She is not an Indian," Franklyn Goodyear said in a gloomy voice. "She is a Hebrew from Israel. A descendant of Saul and Solomon."

"And here," said Poliakoff, "you have my dearest friend and Belgian's greatest ballerina—Madame La Sylph."

The descendant of Saul, etc., squeezed in beside her sponsor.

Madame La Sylph flashed a curtain-call smile at the arrivals. Poliakoff spoke.

"Mr. Goodyear, my pal—no beating around the bush—we are in the bag! Your masterpiece *Study in Brown* is in production as of now. I have the check from the society leader Magda Callahan. Tomorrow we select an off-Broadway theater, seating capacity two-hundred-fifty minimum. The casting starts at the same moment from my office in Slavonia Hall on Bleecker Street, the heart of Bohemia."

He paused. Playwright Goodyear's look of gloom had only deepened.

"Waiter!" Poliakoff called, "a bottle of wine! The best in the house!" A depressed type in shirt sleeves, who had been hiding behind a clothes rack, exited reluctantly. Poliakoff continued. "This is the biggest historic moment of my life. And in your life, my pal. Believe me! It is the beginning of the new O'Gene O'Neill plus Tennessee William. Here, Mr. Goodyear, is the contract, approved by two lawyers and Mrs. Callahan. Please sign all five copies."

Poliakoff removed the documents from his brief case. Placing them in front of the playwright, he tendered a fountain pen like a sword in surrender.

"Mr. Poliakoff," said Franklyn Goodyear, "I don't want my play produced."

"I love you," said the descendant. "You are magnificent." She had an attractive accent and amazingly large eyes when she smiled. Franklyn Goodyear kissed her hand humbly and said, "Thank you."

"I understand," said Poliakoff, "You have made other arrangements. I understand." He closed his eyes in pain.

"No," the playwright began, but Poliakoff interrupted.

"Franklyn Goodyear, I discovered you. But that is not important to you or the world. It is important only that you are a great artist. You have written a top smash work of art which I also discovered and which I love as if it was my own baby. But, my pal, if you have made other arrangements, forget me. Forget also our verbal contract in front of witnesses. Forget everything! And I wish you the greatest success." Tears filled the Poliakoff eyes but the brave smile remained.

"We do not want the wine." La Sylph spoke to the waiter shuffling up.

"No. Leave the bottle!" Poliakoff cried. "I was going to drink with joy. I will drink with lost hope. It is Life—over again!"

The playwright sighed heavily.

"You don't understand," he said. "The point is I don't want my play produced by anybody. If I wanted it produced, I'd be glad to have you produce it. Because I basically admire your attitude toward my work. But as I said, I don't want it produced at all. By anybody. Ever."

"What is it?" Poliakoff stared at his genius. "Something deep is bothering you. I can feel it. Please forget I am a producer. Look at me like a father. Both of you."

Madam La Sylph sipped her tumbler of wine. A Poliakoff in defeat called for no comment.

"Haven't you noticed my head?" Franklyn Goodyear asked moodily.

"You are holding it on one side," said Poliakoff.

"I am not holding it," the playwright scowled. "It's that way by itself. It's locked. It happened right after our telephone conversation this noon. Three minutes after."

"My darling boy," Poliakoff trembled. "All I said on the telephone was I have good news for you tonight. You must have misunderstood."

"I didn't misunderstand," the playwright answered. "I understood perfectly. And that's what did this." He pointed to his tilted head. "The least movement is agony."

"I will send for a doctor," Poliakoff pronounced. "La Sylph, please call up a doctor for the neck."

"I don't need any doctor." The playwright scowled. "It's a psychological phenomenon. A conversion symptom."

"My boy, if you have changed your religion—" Poliakoff began with a pained look.

"A conversion symptom," Franklyn Goodyear went on, patiently, "is a sickness produced by an inner resistance to something. I thought everybody knew that."

Shoshana turned her headlight eyes on Poliakoff.

"He is very delicate inside," she said.

"The symptom will disappear," said Franklyn Goodyear, "the moment I remove the cause." He looked at Poliakoff sadly. "You, and your threat of production."

Poliakoff searched his memory for some disaster that might throw a light on the present one. The large troupe of perfidious ballet, stage, and concert geniuses with whom he had tried to do business offered itself quickly for his inspection. There was no previous claim of a broken neck by his hand.

"Don't blame yourself too much," the playwright added lopsidedly. "You were just the precipitating incident. May I explain it?"

Poliakoff decided to hold back his tears for a few minutes and nodded.

"I am a poet," Franklyn Goodyear said bitterly. "My play *Study in Brown* wears the capricious mask of drama. But it is a poem. It is myself—in play form."

"That is why it has life and blood," Poliakoff shouted.

"*My* blood," retorted Franklyn Goodyear. "I don't want it spilled by the critics."

Poliakoff came to life as if a spell had lifted. His face grew pink. His eyes sparkled. His rooster crest of graying hair jiggled over his scalp.

"My dear, dear Franklyn Goodyear!" He beamed. "This is the problem? That you are afraid of the critics? My dear pal, let me speak to you as my son on this point. Let me tell you what the critics are going to write about *Study in Brown*. The critics are going to state in their papers only one thing—that you have written the most sensational top smash work of drama since they can recall. Franklyn, my dear genius, I guarantee you this like a father."

A smile lighted Franklyn Goodyear's face, briefly.

"I've thought in that direction," he said. "But as a psychologist, I know too well what that means. Greater suffering in the reality. Every dream has to be paid for."

"Mr. Franklyn Goodyear—" Poliakoff began.

"Please. No more!" The playwright's voice rose. "I know those critics. I've read their lynching bees. No, thank you. I don't wish to be strung up on every lamppost in New York and set fire to!" The young man's voice grew heated. "Oh, how I know those critics! I am not going to offer them my soul to beat into a pulp with their schoolteacher wands! No, thank you! The theatre has nothing to offer me. I don't desire its barbershop fame and its passing belch of publicity! Or money. I have no use for money. All I want is to remain a poet and to continue writing poetry!"

The poet's head tossed with passion. A moan of pain followed.

"This is only the beginning." Franklyn Goodyear pointed to his twisted neck. "I know my subconscious."

"I quite agree with you." Madame La Sylph smiled suddenly at him. "Art is a great mystery. It does not belong on bargain counters."

"Thank you for understanding," Franklin Goodyear answered. "If I decide to have *Study in Brown* published, I'll send you several copies. Come, Shoshana."

"You are a great man," Shoshana said, and stood up.

Poliakoff ended his silence.

"One moment," he said huskily.

"I am not open to argument," the playwright scolded. "I have to get rid of this pain in my neck before it drives me crazy. And as I told you before, there is only one way."

"My dear Franklin Goodyear"—Poliakoff beamed—"I am not going to argue. Because you have convinced me one thousand per cent that you are right. Completely! To take a chance on injuring such a genius as yours—this would be a crime in which I would not allow myself to get involved. Franklyn!" He seized the poet's forearm and looked pleadingly at the lovely Israeli. "Please, my beautiful Scheherezade, I want you to be the judge. Kindly sit down." He waited until the oversized eyes had re-entered the booth. "I am going to produce *Study in Brown* only *after*—I repeat—only *after* your play has been hailed as a beautiful and sensational success by the combined drama critics of the city of New York.

"Please follow what I am going to say. Tomorrow, I make ten new typewritten copies of *Study in Brown*. This will take a full day. The next day, each copy goes by registered mail to each separate dramatic critic, with a letter attached, in which I say: Dear Mr. Brooks Atkinson (for example) et cetera . . . And you have my word of honor, if the replies from the critics are not one thousand per cent favorable, I tear them up. And I take my medicine."

Eight days later, Max Poliakoff stood on the stone steps of Slavonia Hall in Bleeker Street and scanned the sun-baked east and west distances for a mailman. He had stood thus yesterday. "Today they must arrive," Poliakoff said firmly to himself. "Today is a must . . . Ah!"

The mailman had suddenly emerged from an adjoining basement. Poliakoff was down the steps and standing beside him in the hot July sun.

"Max Poliakoff, Slavonia Hall, Floor C," he said. "I am expecting ten letters, mailed three days ago."

"Where were they mailed from?" the postman asked.

"From different parts of New York City," said Poliakoff. "Uptown, downtown."

"The mailman handed over a packet of envelopes. Poliakoff counted them.

"Nine," he announced. "One more, please."

"Maybe Numben Ten didn't write," said the postman.

"He wrote." Poliakoff was firm. "Look again, please."

"Here we are. Number ten." The mailman produced an envelope.

"Thank you, that is all," said Poliakoff, and re-entered Slavonia. He climbed three broad flights of stairs in the massive, darkened building, passing cavernous empty chambers. On the third floor, Poliakoff, his footsteps echoing as in a wilderness, entered his "office." This was a banquet hall and lodge headquarters, with towering mirrored walls, a theatre stage at one end, and some two hundred round tables standing stacked in acrobatic units reaching four high. In the distance sat Madame La Sylph on a wall bench seemingly several hundred feet long. It curved around the auditorium. A small card table was in front of her. She was knitting.

"They have arrived." Poliakoff placed the letters on the card table. "Notice the stationery. That was the most difficult part. You cannot go out and buy simply the authentic stationery used by *The New York Times*, the *Tribune*, et cetera. You have to go to each newspaper yourself and look from department to department until you find a stenographer who is not also a Sherlock Holmes."

"I am utterly horrified by your villainy," said La Sylph quietly. "I have always known you were a despicable liar. But this is really too hideous."

"What is hideous about it?" Poliakoff cried out, beginning to open the letters. "Franklyn Goodyear has a mental craziness. I am curing it. I am making it possible for him to have a play produced like every other human being. Please, my angel—there is one thing I know well: the path to failure. I am digging him out of this path and forcing him to the top. You call this hideousness?"

"Of course," said La Sylph coldly. "It doesn't matter to you if they kill him."

"Who kills him?" Poliakoff cried.

"Don't be cheap," La Sylph answered, "and pretend you don't understand. You heard him. You saw his neck. They had almost broken it already. But whether the critics kill him like they did Nijinsky is not really the point. The thing that is appalling is your character."

Poliakoff gathered up the opened letters and spoke gently.

"My sweet angel, I hate myself even more than you hate me. But not for this unimportant little business of forging a few letters. I hate myself because I am a failure who nobody can respect. I hate myself because my whole life I have tried to bring something beautiful into the world. And what have I brought? Nothing! You see in front of you a man fifty-one years old—with nothing to show. No money. No success. No hope." He placed the ten letters in La Sylph's hand and continued: "My princess, you are holding the letters which may bring me fame and fortune. Never mind. Tear them up. If I lose even the little feeling of love you have left for me—I don't want this half-million dollars. Tear them up, and I will remain, as always, Poliakoff, the nobody who loves you."

La Sylph was silent. She looked at the trembling, gray-crested orator, and she saw a small boy on the verge of tears. Slowly, with dignity, she lowered her head and began to study the letters. Poliakoff sat down, another crisis passed.

"Silly of me to have worried about it," said La Sylph. "These ridiculous letters aren't going to fool Mr. Goodyear. They sound exactly like you."

"How can they sound like me?" Poliakoff cried. "I copied every one, word for word, from ten different dramatic critics. Absolutely authentic ones."

La Sylph read aloud from one of the letters.

" 'The great throb of lost humanity runs through this play and lifts it out of the macabre and sordid relationships in it into the glowing realms of art. Franklyn Goodyear has, I am very much afraid, written a masterpiece.' "

"Atkinson from *The New York Times*," said Poliakoff proudly. "This is his review of the *Iceman* play by O'Gene O'Neill."

La Sylph studied the others. "But they are all alike," she declared.

"They can't be alike," Poliakoff pleaded. "You are now reading Walter Kerr's review of *The Glass Menagerie* from the *Tribune*. Word for word."

La Sylph read, in rebuttal.

" 'The delicate throb of human drama raises this lovely play out of its dingy setting into the effulgent purlieus of Art. I fear me there is nothing more to say about Franklyn Goodyear's *Study in Brown* than that he has written a masterpiece.' "

"And notice the different styles of signature, including the different colored ink," Poliakoff said proudly, as La Sylph leafed through the rest of the communiqués.

"There's been a slip-up," La Sylph announced suddenly. "This one isn't at all favorable."

Poliakoff smiled.

"You are reading exactly what Horace Bison, dramatic critic for the *Athenian Magazine*, wrote about Arthur Miller's drama three years ago," he said. "I copied out word for word. And why do I do this?

Because one little complaint in a symphony of praises—this is the touch which makes the situation superb and convincing. Out of ten critics, even if they are looking on something written by God, there is always one who has to object. Please, I am exhausted. My darling, call up and leave word at the delicatessen store to notify Franklyn Goodyear to come to my office at once."

It was raining outside of Slavonia Hall.

Franklyn Goodyear was bent silently over his reading matter—the Walter Kerr review.

"Hm. . . . 'I fear me—' " he quoted. "You see, I'm a threat to their egos."

"My dear pal," said Max Poliakoff, "I will turn on the lights so you can see plainer."

Two great chandeliers burst forth in banquet-hall splendor. Poliakoff removed the five contract copies from his brief case. The blazing banquet hall remained eerily silent except for the rattle of the rain on its front windows as the playwright peered into his future. Poliakoff removed a half-dozen small ink bottles from his brief case. Catching the playwright's momentarily lifted eye, he inquired respectfully:

"Which color ink do you prefer, dear boy, for the signing of the contracts?"

The inquiry went unheeded except by La Sylph, who shuddered and turned another thirty degrees away from the scene. Poliakoff opened the black ink. An old Hungarian dance tune came to his mind but he refrained from whistling it. Instead, he thought: As soon as he signs, I call up to notify the bank to accept my checks. Ah, yes, yes. The first thing I will buy is a summer fur like she used to wear once [he looked tenderly at La Sylph] a summer fur made of feathers. And for myself, a jacket with brass buttons like a sea captain. It will be distinctive. Then a small filing cabinet for plays. A typewriter I can rent. Ah, yes, yes. And maybe a stenographer. We will see.

An odd sound came from Franklyn Goodyear.

"What is it?" Poliakoff smiled.

"Did you read this one?" the playwright asked. He was breathing hard.

"Yes, yes," Poliakoff chuckled. "From that shoemaker, Horace Bison, on the *Athenian Magazine*. I thought it was very amusing."

"Amusing?" The playwright stared at him. "He says my second act is no good."

"My dear pal," Poliakoff beamed. "You cannot expect ten critics all to be geniuses. One has to be below average."

"He says 'It thins out.'" The playwright's voice shook. "And 'I don't realize myself or my characters.'"

"Dear Franklyn Goodyear." Poliakoff smiled. "I did not have to show you that letter. But I showed it to you because for two reasons. First, I want everything open and aboveboard between us. Second, this is a critic on a small magazine who nobody reads. A critic so unimportant that no producer quotes him in the ads even when he is good. My pal, this stuff which he writes is a joke to laugh at. Dear boy, the nine top smash critics of New York City are insane with joy over your play, and this little fellow, whatever his name is . . ."

"His name is Horace Bison!" the playwright cried out. "The only critic I respect!"

"Respect? How can you respect?" Poliakoff yelled. "He has proved himself a complete idiot. This is a man without a brain. A man who belongs sweeping the streets."

"Don't tell me about Horace Bison!" Franklyn Goodyear's voice filled the banquet hall. "Horace Bison's book *Poetry in the Theater* has been my bible for five years! These other so-called critics are—"

Poliakoff's voice drowned him out.

"Please, please!" he bellowed. "Look at the facts. The beautiful facts. Nine raves—nine supreme raves and one little confused remark about Act Two only. My pal, this is more than any playwright has received, dead or alive. Believe me, it is a world record, even for a genius."

"'Act Two is thin.'" The playwright brooded.

"We will sign the contracts"—Poliakoff lowered his voice—"and then we will discuss."

"My play isn't ready to produce," Franklyn Goodyear answered firmly. "I had an instinct all along about the second act."

Poliakoff dipped a trembling pen into the black ink bottle.

"Please," he held the pen out. "I have indicated the places to put your name with a small pencil mark."

"No," said Franklyn Goodyear. "Not now. I have to rewrite Act Two first."

"You will have plenty of time," Poliakoff pleaded. "Four weeks while we are casting. Four weeks while we rehearse."

"No," said the playwright. "Horace Bison has opened my eyes. It's amazing. I always knew inside that the second act thinned out. Is there a phone here? I want to talk to him."

"You want to talk to him?" Poliakoff repeated in a small voice.

"Yes," said the playwright. "I'll make an appointment with him to discuss the second act."

"Never!" Poliakoff cried. "This is absolutely the wrong thing to do."

"I can't start the rewrite till I talk it through with him," the playwright answered.

"Fine," said Poliakoff, "fine! But not on the telephone, for God's sake! For an important situation like this, you write a letter. A letter in which you ask for the advice, the suggestions, and whatever you wish to find out, et cetera. Please, I am a man of the world who understands critics. Look how they all responded to me."

He removed writing paper from his brief case and placed the sheets in front of the playwright.

"Use the black ink." He sighed. "It is the smoothest."

"Thanks." Franklyn Goodyear hunched creatively over the card table. The rain rattled on the windows. Poliakoff stood by in silence as the playwright's pen moved in rapid inspiration across the paper.

"When you are finished"—Poliakoff sighed—"I will mail it for you. I have a stamp left over."

Madame La Sylph entered Sullivan's Greenwich Village Cafe and walked slowly toward the booth in which Max Poliakoff waited. She sat down without a greeting and ignored the exalted, faraway look in her friend's eye.

After a pause, Poliakoff said tenderly, "My adorable, thank you for coming."

He reached for her hand.

"Don't touch me," La Sylph warned quietly.

"As you wish." Poliakoff turned his eyes from her and resumed his Lucifer-like stare into distances.

"Have you written the new forgery from Horace Bison to Mr. Goodyear?" La Sylph snapped.

Poliakoff removed three typewritten pages of *Athenian Magazine* stationery from his coat.

"Here it is," he said with an air of whimsy. "It is not a bad letter. I spent two days in the public library composing, and two days typewriting. Would you care to read, perhaps?"

"No," La Sylph answered. "I came here merely to tell you that we are through."

"Through?" Poliakoff closed his eyes.

"Yes, through," La Sylph repeated. "Max Poliakoff, you are a crook, a horse thief, and a common swindler on whom I have wasted my life and love. I say good-by to you!"

She paused as Poliakoff lifted both his hands in a slow gesture of humility that no ballerina could ignore, although she recognized it as borrowed from *Giselle*—the Lover pleading with the damsels of Death.

"May I speak?" he inquired huskily.

La Sylph waited as he dried the tears in his eyes with the heels of his palms.

"My princess," Poliakoff said, "at six o'clock this evening on the telephone I have confessed to Franklyn Goodyear in the delicatessen store all my crimes. The whole truth of this miserable *Affaire* Atkinson, Kerr, Bison, et cetera. Straight, without a single lie or mistake. Including this final criminal attempt." He waved the three pages of *Athenian* stationery. "I would have been happier committing suicide."

"What did Mr. Goodyear say?" La Sylph asked softly.

"It was impossible to hear," Poliakoff answered. "I was crying so loud. When I could recover my senses, he was gone from the telephone." Poliakoff paled. "Here comes somebody now," he said.

It was Shoshana, the large-eyed Israeli.

"You have killed him!" she cried, rushing at Poliakoff. "Assassin! Miserable Arab!"

"Please be seated," Poliakoff begged her politely.

"He ran out of Epstein's Delicatessen," the raging girl continued as La Sylph clamped a bear hug on her. "I couldn't find him. He is gone, my poet! He has drowned himself in the river!"

"I know. I killed him," Poliakoff admitted, his head lowered. "Go on, please. I deserve it."

"I have sworn by TelHai and Trumpeldor," Shoshana went on, straining in vain against La Sylph's muscles, "that you will follow Franklyn into his grave, Mr. Poliakoff!"

Her violence gave way to grief. La Sylph allowed the girl to collapse into a sitting position beside her. "Waiter!" she called out to Sullivan's invisible personnel, "bring the young lady a coffee with Irish Mist in it." She added to Poliakoff: "It's very good for this sort of thing."

Poliakoff said nothing. He was staring at the café entrance. A figure in a torn raincoat stood there.

Shoshana instinctively uncovered her face.

"Frankele," she sang out, "You are here!"

La Sylph slid a protective arm around Poliakoff as Franklyn Goodyear approached the entrepreneur.

"Give me that letter about my second act—the new letter you forged from Horace Bison," he demanded, looming over Poliakoff.

"Please—" Poliakoff groaned. "Franklyn Goodyear. Do not do this to me again. I have confessed once, confessed completely. I have told you already that I am no good. A rotten apple. A horse thief. A man who would betray his own mother—"

"Stop it!" La Sylph shook the penitent violently. "Let someone else talk!"

"Yes, stop it," said Franklyn Goodyear. "What are you trying to do —prove to me that you are a man, a human being? Everyone lies, everyone betrays his mother. It is a small flaw."

He sat down beside Shoshana and kissed her hand.

"Excuse me for upsetting you," he said. "I was excited and I took the wrong subway. It was an express, and I had to go to Brooklyn Bridge." He returned to Poliakoff. "Now kindly give me that phantasy from Horace Bison you concocted about what's wrong with my second act."

Poliakoff blanched.

"You want to give it to the police?" he asked.

"No," Franklyn Goodyear answered eagerly, "I want to read it, to study it. Because as a psychologist, I know it is something more than a forgery. It is a message from your subconscious, your own truthful opinion of what is wrong with my second act. It is Truth itself. The id cannot lie."

"Yes, yes, I understand you, of course, my dear genius." Poliakoff beamed and quoted from Lermontov: " 'Soul speaks to soul.' " He handed over the Horace Bison critique. "Here, Franklyn Goodyear," he said, his voice once again full of the benevolence of the entrepreneur, "if I have helped you, that is all I ask. To help a great artist is all that I have dreamed of and lived for."

*Study in Brown* opened three months later off-Broadway in the Rienza Theatre. It was a snowy night. A subway strike isolated lower New York from normal entry. A last-minute crew of union workers had failed to start the furnace of the building.

A rain-soaked audience sat in the frosty theatre like a little band of art commandos. At ten o'clock they were still staring at *Study in Brown* as if in a state of mass coma. All the major critics and their wives were seen to be present.

The reviews the next day were generally ecstatic. The critics hailed *Study in Brown* as a work of compelling beauty. They hailed the new playwright, Franklyn Goodyear, as the first genuine genius hatched by the off-Broadway theatre. They also hailed Max Poliakoff as a producer who had wrung the last drop of beauty out of the play's sordid milieu.

At 3:00 P.M. the next day, Poliakoff stood in the street and looked at the persistent line in front of the Rienza box office. Inside the office the phone was ringing like a bell of victory. Loath to leave this fairy-tale spectacle, Poliakoff finally moved away. Shoshana had been insistent over the telephone.

The newlyweds were huddled on the mile-long bench of his darkened fourth floor "office" when Poliakoff flung open the door.

"My favorite genius!" he cried in ornate tones. "They have hailed you as—"

"John Chapman of the *Daily News* hailed me as rotten!" the shadowed genius replied with a dark groan.

Poliakoff paused in his triumphant approach. In the gloom of the former ballroom, he could make out that Franklyn Goodyear's head was on a side, and a look of great pain was in his eyes.

"I have brought the other eight critics! I am carrying them—every one! Franklyn Goodyear, my darling boy, you are the new hero of New York. Shall I put on the light so you can read?"

"I know this one by heart," the head-tilted genius riposted. He began to recite, despite the desperate pleadings of Shoshana: " 'Toward the middle of Act Two, I was relieved to note that I was not the only auditor fighting against slumber. The entire audience yawned and fidgeted as if about to go beddy-bye. *Study in Brown* is an incoherent and pretentious bore. Its author, Fr . . .' "

But the unhappy voice was momentarily cut off in the fierce embrace of the black-clad bride. Poliakoff began to tiptoe quietly out of the room so as not to disturb the huddled lovers.

Playwright Goodyear's voice halted him at the door.

"Is there any chance of your closing the play?" he called.

Max Poliakoff discreetly opened the door. Before he could close it, he heard the moan of the playwright. "Very well. I'll just have to go on suffering . . ."

The bride's whisper echoed after Poliakoff.

"I will suffer with you . . . the rest of my life. . . ."

Poliakoff walked rapidly toward the Rienza Theatre and the miracle that waited him there. Many things, including John Chapman, puzzled him. But the United States was a noble land, and off-Broadway a paradise where a lifelong dream had come true.

# *Snowfall in Childhood*

I GOT OUT OF BED to see what had happened in the night. I was thirteen years old. I had fallen asleep watching the snow falling through the half frosted window.

But though the snow had promised to keep falling for a long time, perhaps three or four days, on opening my eyes I was full of doubts. Snowstorms usually ended too soon.

While getting out of bed I remembered how, as I was nearly asleep, the night outside the frosted window had seemed to burst into a white jungle. I had dreamed of streets and houses buried in snow.

I hurried barefooted to the window. It was scribbled with a thick frost and I couldn't see through it. The room was cold and through the opened window came the fresh smell of snow like the moist nose of an animal resting on the ledge and breathing into the room.

I knew from the smell and the darkness of the window that snow was falling. I melted a peephole on the glass with my palms. I saw that this time the snow had not fooled me. There it was, still coming down white and silent and too thick for the wind to move, and the streets and houses were almost as I had dreamed. I watched, shivering and happy. Then I dressed, pulling on my clothes as if the house were on fire. I was finished with breakfast and out in the storm two hours before schooltime.

The world had changed. All the houses, fences, and barren trees had new shapes. Everything was round and white and unfamiliar.

I set out through these new streets on a voyage of discovery. The unknown surrounded me. Through the thick falling snow, the trees, houses, and fences looked like ghost shapes that had floated down out of the sky during the night. The morning was without light, but the snowfall hung and swayed like a marvelous lantern over the streets. The snowbanks, already over my head in places, glowed mysteriously.

I was pleased with this new world. It seemed to belong to me more than that other world which lay hidden.

I headed for the school, jumping like a clumsy rabbit in and out of snowbanks. It seemed wrong to spoil the smooth outlines of these snowdrifts and I hoped that nobody else would pass this way after me. In that case the thick falling snow would soon restore the damage. Reassured by this hope I continued on my devastations like some wanton explorer. I began to feel that no one would dare the dangers of my wake. Then, as I became more aware of the noble proportions of this snowstorm, I stopped worrying altogether about the marring of this new and glowing world. Other snows had melted and been shoveled away, but this snow would never disappear. The sun would never shine again and the little Wisconsin town through which I plunged and tumbled to school on this dark storm-filled morning was from now on an arctic land full of danger and adventure.

When eventually, encased in snow, I arrived at the school, I found scores of white-covered figures already there. The girls had taken shelter inside, but the boys stayed in the storm. They jumped in and out of the snowdrifts and tumbled through the deep unbroken white fields in front of the school.

Muffled cries filled the street. Someone had discovered how faraway our voices sounded in the snowfall and this started the screaming. We screamed for ten minutes, delighted with the fact that our voices no longer carried and that the snowstorm had made us nearly dumb.

Tired with two hours of such plunging and rolling, I joined a number of boys who like myself had been busy since dawn and who now stood for the last few minutes before the school bell with half-frozen faces staring at the heavily falling snow as if it were some game they couldn't bear to leave.

When we were finally seated in our grade room, we continued to watch the snowstorm through the windows. The morning had grown darker as we had all hoped it would, and it was necessary to turn on the electric lights in the room. This was almost as thrilling as the pale storm still floating outside the windows.

In this yellow light the school seemed to disappear and in its place a picnic spread around us. The teachers themselves seemed to change. Their eyes kept turning toward the windows and they kept looking at us behind our desks as if we were strangers. We grew excited and even the sound of our lessons—the sentences out of geography and arithmetic books—made us tremble.

Passing through the halls during recess we whispered to one another about the snowstorm, guessing at how deep the snowdrifts must be by this time. We looked nervously at our teachers who stood in the classroom doorways stiff and far removed from our secret whispers about the snow.

I felt sorry for these teachers, particularly for the one who had taught me several years ago when I was in the Fifth Grade. I saw her as I walked by the opened door of her room. She was younger than the other teachers, with two dark braids coiled around her head, a white starched shirtwaist, and soft dark eyes that had always looked kindly at me when I was younger. I saw her now sitting behind her large desk looking over the heads of her class out of the window and paying no attention to the whispers and giggles of her pupils.

As for my own teacher, a tall thin woman with a man's face, by afternoon I had become so happy I could no longer hear what she was saying. I sat looking at the large clock over her head. My feeling on the way to school that it would never be light again and that the snowstorm would keep on forever had increased so that it was something I now knew rather than hoped. My eagerness to get out into the world of wind, gloom, and perpetual snow, kept lifting me out of my seat.

At three o'clock we rushed into the storm. Our screams died as we reached the school entrance. What we saw silenced us. Under the dark sky the street lay piled in an unbroken bank of snow. And above it the snowfall still hung in a thick and moving cloud. Nothing was visible but snow. Everything else had disappeared. Even the sky was gone.

I saw the teachers come out and look around them, frowning. The children of the lower grades stood chattering and frightened near the teachers. I waited until the teacher with the two black braids saw me, and then, paying no attention to her warning, spoken in a gentle voice, I plunged into the storm. I felt brave but slightly regretful that Miss Wheeler could no longer see me as I pushed into the head-high piles of snow and vanished fearlessly into the storm. But I was certain that she was still thinking of me and worrying about my safety. This thought added excitement to the snowstorm.

After an hour I found myself alone. My legs were tired with jumping and my face burned. It had grown darker and the friendliness seemed to have gone out of the storm. The wind bit with a sharper edge and I turned toward my home.

I arrived at the house that now looked like a snowdrift and ploughed my way up to its front door. My heart was beating violently. I stopped to take a last look at the storm. It was hard to leave it. But for the first time in my life an adult logic instructed me. There would be even more snow tomorrow. And in this wind and snow-filled gloom, and even in the marvelously buried street, there was something now unplayful.

I entered the house, calling for something to eat, but as soon as I had taken my coat off and shaken myself clean, I was at the window again. The way this storm was keeping on was hard to believe.

At the table I was too excited to eat. I trembled and was unable to hear what was being said around me. In this room I could feel the night outside and the storm still blowing on my face. It seemed as if I were still in the street. My eyes kept seeing snow and my nose breathing it. The room and the people in it became far away. I left the table, taking a slice of bread and butter with me, and ran upstairs to my own room.

There were a lot of things to do, such as making my leather boots more waterproof by rubbing lard on them, putting my stamp collection in order, sharpening a deer's-foot knife I had recently acquired, winding tape on my new hockey stick, or reading one of the half-dozen new books I had bought with my last birthday money. But none of these activities or even redrawing the plans for the ice-boat on which I was working was possible. I sat in a chair near the window, unable to think. The pale storm in the night seemed to spin like a top, and, keeping the window frost melted with my palms, I sat and watched it snowing for an hour. Then, becoming sleepy, I went to bed. I thought drowsily of how happy Miss Wheeler would be to see me alive on Monday after the way I had rushed into the storm.

There was no seeing through my window when I awoke. The furnace never got going until after seven, and before that hour on a winter's morning the house creaked with cold and the windows were sheeted thick with ice. But I knew as I dressed that the snowfall was over. There was too much wind blowing outside and the breath that came in from the snow-banked window ledge was no longer as fresh as it had been.

It was still dark. The bleak and gusty dawn lay over the snow like a guttering candle. The sky had finished with its snowing but now the wind sent the snowbanks ballooning into the air and the roof tops burst into little snowstorms.

I went outside and explored for ten minutes. When I came back into the house, I needed no warning against going out to play. My skin was almost frozen and the wind was too strong to stand up in. I settled down as a prisoner in front of the fireplace after breakfast, lying on my stomach and turning the pages of a familiar oversized edition of Dante's *Inferno*. It was full of Doré's nightmarish pictures.

The house bustled with cooking and cleaning. But these were the dim activities of grownups. I felt alone and took care of the fire to keep it from going out and leaving me to freeze to death. I carried logs all morning from the cellar and lay perspiring and half-scorched on the hearthstone. Every half-hour I went to the window to have a look at the enemy. The sight of the whirling snowbanks and the sound of the brutal wind as it hit against the houses sent me back to the fireplace to scorch myself anew.

In this way I spent the day until late afternoon. It grew dark early. The snow turned leaden. The wind stopped. The dead storm lay in the street and as far as I could see from the window there were no inhabitants in the world. The dark snow was empty. I shivered and went back to the fireplace.

A half-hour later our doorbell rang. Company had arrived for supper. They were the Joneses, who lived in the town of Corliss some eight miles away. They had brought their daughter Anna.

The lights went on in the house. Baked and dizzy with the fire's heat, I joined the two families in the larger parlor. They were talking excitedly about the damage done by the storm. Accounts of store windows blown in, roofs blown off, signs blown down, and wagons abandoned in the drifts were exchanged, and I listened happily. Later, when the talk turned to duller topics, I became aware of Anna.

She was sitting in a corner watching me. She was a blondish girl two years older than I was and she went to high school. I had known her for a long time but had never liked her because she was too calm, never laughing or running, but always looking at people with a sad smile or just a stare as if she had something important on her mind. But now that she was watching me that way, I felt suddenly interested in her. I wondered what she could be thinking of me and what made her smile in that half-sad way at me.

I sat next to her at the table, and after looking at her several times out of the side of my eyes and catching her eyes doing the same thing, my heart started beating faster. I lost interest in eating. I wanted to be alone with her so we could sit and look at each other without the others noticing.

After supper the two families let us go to the hall upstairs, where I kept most of my possessions, without asking us any questions. I found a deck of cards and a cribbage board for a table. Underneath the lapboard our knees touched.

She played cribbage better than I and smiled at me as I kept losing. But I was only half aware of the game. I kept looking at her, unable to talk, and the light pressure of her knees began to make me feel weak. Her face seemed to become brighter and more beautiful as we played. A mist appeared around her eyes and her smile became so close, as if it were moving swiftly toward me, that I began to tremble. I felt ashamed of being so tongue-tied and red-faced, but with a half-frightened, blissful indifference to everything—even Anna—I kept on playing.

We hardly spoke. I grew too nervous to follow the game and I wanted to stop. But I thought if we stopped, we could no longer sit this way with our knees touching. At moments when Anna withdrew her touch, I trembled and waited as if I were hanging from somewhere. When finally her knees returned to their place against mine, I caught my breath and frowned at the cards as if I were completely taken up with them.

As the hour passed, my face began to feel swollen and lopsided and it seemed to me my features had grown ugly beyond words. I tried to distract Anna's attention from this phenomenon by twisting my mouth, screwing up my eyes, and making popping noises with my cheeks as we played. But a new fear arrived to uncenter my attention. I became afraid now that Anna would notice her knees were touching mine and move them away. I began at once pretending a deeper excitement in the game, complaining against my bad luck and denouncing her for cheating. I was determined to keep her interested in the game at any cost, believing that her interest in what we were doing made her unaware of her knees touching mine.

Finally Anna said she was tired of the game. She pushed the cribbage board away. I waited, holding my breath, for her to realize where her knees were and to move them away. I tried not to look at her, but I was so frightened of this happening that I found myself staring at her. She seemed to be paying no attention to me. She was leaning back in her chair and her eyes were half closed. Her face was unsmiling and I felt she was thinking of something. This startled me. My throat filled with questions, but I was so afraid of breaking this hidden embrace of our knees under the lapboard that I said nothing.

The mist seemed to have spread from her eyes to her hair and over the rest of her face. Wherever I looked, this same glow rested around her. I noticed then that her hand was lying on the lapboard. I thought desperately of touching it, but there was something disillusioning in this thought. I watched her fingers begin to tap gently on the board as if she were playing the piano. There was something strange about her hand, as if it did not belong to the way her knees were touching mine or to the mist that rose from her eyes.

The minutes passed in silence and then Anna's mother called her from downstairs.

"I guess they're going home," I said, and Anna nodded. She pressed closer against me, but in my confusion I couldn't figure out whether this was the accidental result of her starting to get out of her chair or on purpose.

"Why don't you ride out with us?" she said. She leaned over the lapboard toward me. "We've got the wagon sleigh and there's plenty of room."

Before I could answer, she had stood up. My knees felt suddenly cold. I slid the lapboard to the floor, ashamed and sad. Anna, without looking back at me, had gone down the stairs. I kept myself from running after her. I was sure she was laughing at me and that she was saying to herself, He's a big fool. He's a big fool.

The Joneses were ready to leave when I came into the parlor. Anna's mother smiled at me.

"Why don't you come and visit us over Sunday?" she said. "There's even more snow in Corliss than here."

"More snow than you can shake a stick at," said another member of the Jones family. They all laughed, and while they were laughing, my mother hustled me off for my wraps. I was to drive away with the Jones family in the sleigh drawn by the two strong horses that stood in front of our house.

I pulled on my leather boots, sweater, and overcoat while the good-bys were being made. I kept trying to catch Anna's attention, but she was apparently unaware that I was in the room. This made me sad, and slowly my eagerness to go to Corliss left me. I wanted instead to go up to my room and slam the door forever on all the Joneses. Anna's gayety, the way she said good-by over and over again and laughed and kissed all the members of my family as if nothing had happened to her, as if she hadn't sat with her eyes closed pressing against my knees in the hallway upstairs, made me almost ill. I felt abandoned and forgotten.

Finally I stood muffled and capped and scowling as my family offered some final instructions for my behavior. I heard nothing of what was said but turned over and over in my mind what I was going to do on the ride and after we got to Corliss. Chiefly I was going to ignore Anna, neither speak to her nor show her by a single look that I knew she was alive.

At this point Anna, having said good-by to everybody several times, seized my arm unexpectedly and whispered against my ear.

"Come, hurry," she said. "We want to get a good place."

Without a word I rushed out of the house, slipping down the snow-caked steps and tumbling headlong into a snowdrift. I scrambled after Anna into the wagon sleigh. It was a low-sided farm wagon placed on wide, heavy wooden runners and piled with warm hay and horse blankets. There was room for only one on the seat. The rest of the Joneses, seven including me, would have to lie in the hay, covered by the robes.

Anna was already in the wagon half-buried in the hay, a blanket over her. She gave me excited orders to brush the snow from my clothes, to cover myself well and not to get out and run alongside the horses when we were going up hill.

"It doesn't help any," she said. "They can pull just the same if you stay in here. And besides, I don't want you to."

The rest of the Joneses came out and crowded into the wagon around us. Anna's father took his place on the driver's seat, assuring my mother, who had come out with a shawl over her head, that there was no danger because the state plow had cleared the road even to way beyond Corliss. I heard my mother ask where I was. Mrs. Jones answered that I was buried somewhere in the hay and Anna whispered close to me not to answer or say anything. I obeyed her.

The sleigh started off. I heard the horses thumping in the snow and the harness bells falling into a steady jingling. Lying on my back, I looked into the night. Stars filled the sky and a white glare hung over the housetops. The street was silent. I could no longer see the snow-covered houses with their lighted windows. My nose filled with the fresh smell of snow and the barn smells of hay and horse blankets, I lay, listening to the different sounds—the harness bells and the snow crunching under the runners.

The stillness of this winter's night was as intense as the storm that had raged for three days. I felt that all the wind and snow there was had blown themselves out forever and that the night as far as the highest star had been emptied by the storm. This emptiness as I lay looking into it was like being hypnotized. It was something to run out into, to fly up into, as the snowfall had been. I began to want to see further, and the star-filled sky that had seemed so vast a few minutes ago now didn't seem vast enough.

I had almost forgotten about Anna when I felt a now familiar warmth press against me. She had moved closer, as if joggled by the sleigh. I held my breath waiting for her to order me to move away and give her room, but she was silent.

My hand at my side touched her fingers. Now I forgot the sky and the great sprinkle of stars that seemed like a thin, far-away snowfall that had stopped moving. The night, the glare of snow, the jingling harness bells died away; only my fingers were alive.

When I had looked at her hand tapping gently on the lapboard, it had seemed strange, and the thought of touching it somehow disillusioning. But now under the horse blankets, hidden in the hay, this hand seemed more breathing and mysterious and familiar than anything about her. I lay unable to move closer to it, our fingertips barely touching. I grew dizzy wishing to reach her hand, but I felt as powerless to move toward it as to fly.

The minutes passed. Two of the Joneses started singing. The thump of the horses, the jingling of the sleighbells, and the crunching of the snow under the runners seemed part of this soft singing. I too wished to sing, to stand up suddenly in this sweeping-along sleigh and bellow at the silent night.

Then the fingers for which I had been wishing until I was dizzy seemed to start walking under the horse blankets, seemed to be running toward me in the warm hay. They came as far as my hand, closed around it, and I felt the throb of their tips against my palm. The night turned into a dream. I opened my eyes to the wide sprinkle of stars and a mist seemed to have come over them. The snow-covered hills over which we were gliding sparkled behind a mist, and suddenly the night into which I was looking lost its hours. It stretched away without time as if it were not something that was passing like our sleigh over the snow, but a star-filled winter's night that would never change and never move.

Lying beside Anna, her hand in mine, with the sleigh now flying in a whirl of snow down the white hill, I thought this night would never end.

# *Winkelberg*

Scene

ACT ONE. The present, and the 1920's and 1930's, in New York and Chicago.

ACT TWO. New York, the 1940's to the recent past.

## ACT ONE

### Scene 1

*A city street becomes visible in the dawn.*

*In the shadows at the end of the street, a* FIGURE *can be seen staring toward the coming light.*

*The* FIGURE *emerges from the shadows. It is a poverty-smitten looking fellow.*

*He wears an old army overcoat (First World War vintage). It is frayed and faded. He carries a worn, bulging brief case under an arm.*

*His face contradicts his Weary Willy get-up. It is a sensitive, mocking face.*

*Our* FIGURE *is a dead man, with fingers lifelessly curled, and a little stiff of gait as if he were still coffin cramped. This underground arthritis will leave him as he grows used to movement again. But there is no hint of Lazarus moan in his speech.*

*When he is done with this stare at the dawn and speaks, his speech will be lyric and precise, for he is a poet and utterance is his only riches.*

*The coarse cackle that punctuates his talk is the sign of his vagrant and muddy living. Mockery is nearly always in his tones, as if, despite himself, he must deride all he knows—to keep his tears in place.*

*The* POET *removes a flask from his seedy coat and takes a long swig. He restores the bottle to its pocket and gazes, with sudden pensiveness, at the audience.*

POET. The time is six-fifteen A.M. of a trivial morning in February. At this moment nine million naked New Yorkers are shifting on their pelvises and buttocks preparing to arise and turn into little dapper effigies of civilization. (*He looks at the audience with a mocking smile.*) O miracle of exquisite monotony called life, I salute you again. (*He takes a swig from his flask.*) I am Jonathan Winkelberg, a poet, who died a violent death not long ago at the hands of a bewildered sailor—with a gun. I haunt the broken bottles of the past. (*He cackles, pleased with his verbiage, and adds raucously as he slaps his overcoated flank*) O sun—O golden chicken of the sky—hatch out your brood of cockroaches and caesars, of brutes and brothers, starved eyes and fat behinds. (*He is delighted with his words, and removes a new bottle from his pocket and takes a swig. Whereupon he becomes aloof and serious.*) When the bullets fired by a bewildered sailor killed me and I was dead, I met a Black Man with a wreath of silver birds around his head.

"Are you God?" I asked pensively. "No, sir," the Black Man replied. "Then where is He? I am now in a position to speak to Him." "He is very hard to find," the Black Man replied. "Well, then," I said, "give me a hint as to his whereabouts." The Black Man answered, "God is a sweet dream." "I have no sweet dreams," I informed him.

"I'm very sorry, sir," he said, "but you'll have to go back and find one you may have overlooked. And call again, Mister Winkelberg."

I replied immediately, "My soul is a tiny rhyme written on the nose of a flea. Surely there must be room in heaven for so infinitesimal a visitor."

Whereupon the Black Man stated, "We have no accommodations called Heaven. Heaven is a dream the dead bring with them." "A sort of beautiful memory?" I grinned. "Precisely," said the Black Man. "No dice," said I. But the Black Man only repeated, "Go back, Mister Winkelberg, and find something nice—that may have escaped your attention. And call again." (*The* POET *turns a pensive smile to the audience and speaks softly.*) I was once a poet whose heart sang out of an ash can and who dreamed of an editor who would buy his work. And now I am honored with another rejection slip. (*He sneers triumphantly.*) It would seem I am unfit for admittance wherever there is a door. So I must prowl again among the hot coals of memory. (*He raises his eyes—now full of pain.*) Old Editor, old and elusive Editor, it was very nice of you to give me another chance. (*He grins at the street.*) Little world—where are your sweet dreams?

THE STAGE DARKENS

### Scene 2

*Music sounds in the dark—a piano, clarinet and drum. The stage brightens on the right. A small café is revealed.*

*The* POET'S *face is in the light.*

POET. Before I start my search for some little item of happiness I may have forgotten, I would like to see if any monuments are being erected to my genius—now that I am not on hand to enjoy them.

*The café becomes fully visible.*

*There are:*

LOUISE, *a girl out of Lautrec—gaudily dressed with bracelets, beads and earrings.*

ABRAMOVITCH, *a modern artist and dyspepsia sufferer.*

WILMA, *a plump, middle-aged woman with a boy's haircut—his wife.*

BERTHA, *an unsuccessful young actress.*

TONY RIGGS, *a critic of the arts, a Voice of Culture; and with the superiority of the pansy.*

WINKELBERG (*beams on the scene*). The Café of the Mildewed Spoon —the Coast of Bohemia—haven for runaway husbands, art-sipping tea lovers and nymphs out of a pawnbroker's window! Here where I reigned a little fitfully in my last year, I may find a slippery dream called fame. (*He raises his eyes aloft.*) An eternity of applause wouldn't be bad, Mister Black Man. The Milky Way echoing everlastingly, "Hooray for Winkelberg." I'd like that. (*The* EATERS *become active. They are eating soup.*)

LOUISE. For God's sake, what's the matter with everybody? Come on, I want to dance! We're sitting here eating soup like it was a contest.

ABRAMOVITCH. Contest or no contest, an artist likes a plate of soup once in a while. (HEINZEL, *a sloppy looking waiter-proprietor arrives at the table with a large tray of food. He starts distributing the dishes.*)

LOUISE (*during this*). This used to be a place! People used to climb on the table! Sweet God, what's happened to art? A stale bonbon. (*She smiles at* BERTHA.)

HEINZEL. O.K. Here we are! Hot from the stove. Everybody gets the finest from Max Heinzel.

LOUISE (*imitating Winkelberg's mocking tones*). Your goulash, Mister Heinzel, is a lethal masterpiece. (*To the others*) Recognize the imitation? (*She says as she starts to eat*) I miss Jonathan Winkelberg. It's not the same without him.

TONY (*eating*). Thank God.

LOUISE. He was a sweet boy.

ABRAMOVITCH (*eating*). He was a sweet boy—and my name is Pablo Picasso. No arguments.

TONY. Let's not ruin another evening over that dead bore.

LOUISE. My God, I keep thinking—who would want to kill Jonathan?

TONY. Let's ask an easier question—who wouldn't?

WILMA. The worst thing about Jonathan was his sex life.

ABRAMOVITCH. Whose isn't?

WILMA. My dear husband, a man shouldn't boast about sex in front of his wife.

ABRAMOVITCH. Who's boasting? I'm just trying to remember.

WILMA. I never told you this before. I invited Winkelberg to stay for dinner one evening. So he tried to rape me while I was cooking the soup. (*She snorts.*) I threw the soup in his face.

ABRAMOVITCH. I had to go out for supper.

WILMA (*indignant*). You should have punched his nose.

ABRAMOVITCH. A man who tried to rape my wife, I got to respect. It opened my eyes.

WILMA. Mine, too.

ABRAMOVITCH (*sneering back*). You ain't the only pebble on the beach. He tried with Bertha, too.

BERTHA (*a small shudder*). Please, don't remind me.

ABRAMOVITCH (*to* BERTHA). You have the floor.

BERTHA. I'd just met Mr. Winkelberg at a party.

TONY. To which he wasn't invited.

BERTHA. And I asked him if he would autograph his book of poetry.

LOUISE. It's your own fault—leading him on!

BERTHA. Oh, no. I was very polite. He asked me if I admired his poetry. Naturally, I said, "yes." And then—oh, it was too awful!

ABRAMOVITCH. Don't be bashful, Bertha. We're all artists.

TONY. The drunken clown tried to assault her under a Chippendale table.

ABRAMOVITCH. A connoisseur.

POET (*aloofly, as he puffs his corncob*). With some women, rape seems to be a minor caress remembered hopefully.

ABRAMOVITCH. The trouble with Jonathan Winkelberg was that he didn't match. He talked like Lord Chesterfield and he behaved like Jack the Ripper. (*The others laugh.* HEINZEL *arrives with a platter of food.* WINKELBERG *stands glaring at the hungry diners who coo over the food. The table dims. The* POET *stands in brightness.*)

POET. Just wait, you goulash eaters, wagging your wet tongues. Just wait! In a tiny while you will be dead—dead. And each of your tongues will curl up like an old lemon rind in a chalk-white jar of bones. Yes, sir! Before you know it, you'll be riding bareback on a worm! Oh, boy! (*The light goes up on the table again.*)

HEINZEL. Well, I gotta say Winkelberg was interestin' to have around. I loaned him plenty of money I'm never gonna see again.

POET. You are a dunghill of octagonal falsehoods, Mister Heinzel.

HEINZEL (*serving the rest of the food*). Yes, sir, I was a true friend to Jonathan.

POET. O cuspidor, straining to turn into a Loving Cup.

BERTHA. I'd like to hear what you think of Winkelberg's poetry, Mister Riggs.

TONY. I prefer Epsom salts.

POET (*gleefully*). Each man prefers the thing that moves him most.

LOUISE. He had more poetry in his little finger than T. S. Eliot has in his whole behind. When Jonathan died, the last lark fell out of the sky.

TONY. Good God!

LOUISE (*emotionally*). Remember how Johnny used to come in here, throw his coat on the floor and recite poems all night for a lousy meal? (*She mimics Winkelberg's tones.*)
The moon and an old man in a window—
Stare at each other.
Oh—

(*She breaks off.*) What the hell comes next?

POET (*finishing the poem*).
O, moon-staring old man,
Does the night sharpen its claws upon your heart?

TONY (*answering* LOUISE). I have no memory for hogwash.

POET. A strange lapse for a hog.

ABRAMOVITCH (*suddenly angry*). I can't eat my soup! For God's sake, I don't want to hear about a dead bum named Winkelberg.

LOUISE (*rising*). All right! To hell with him! He wasn't a poet. He's a dead bum. And he wore a dirty coat. To hell with all dead bums in dirty coats! (*The music has started a new tune.* LOUISE *speaks softly to* BERTHA.) Would you care to dance? I always like to dance with a girl. Less infighting. (BERTHA *rises. The two girls dance together gracefully at first and then with increasing gyrations . . . The diners watch them —and the light on them dims, as if they were out of the Poet's visionary thought. The light remains on the two dancing women and the mocking face of* WINKELBERG *as he watches.*)

POET (*pensively, as he watches Louise*). My sole admirer seems to be a lady jitterbug with an invisible goatee. Good-by, li'l dream of fame. You is not among those present. (*The scene darkens. A light remains on the* POET's *face as he addresses the universe.*) During the time in which I owned a pad and pencil and a breathing apparatus, I learned one sole and solitary fact—the world's a dirty dog. (*He looks aloft.*) I consider it exquisitely unfair to be asked to find this out a second time. (*He scowls.*) I shall skip the first nineteen years of my life. They were a barefoot promenade on a hot stove. (*He grins pensively.*) My father was a popular butcher on the South Side of Chicago. My mother expired giving birth to me—and thus I entered the world with the brand of murder on my tiny forehead. (*He chuckles.*) Papa didn't like me. When I was nineteen, I saw through all the silk-hatted absurdities of my time, from President Woodrow Wilson to Yellow Kid Weill. I had everybody's number, and only life could fool me. Here's to the field of daisies I may have failed to notice in little old Chicago where the wounds began.

THE STAGE DARKENS

## Scene 3

*A café in the Chicago lava beds.*

*A band plays a 1917 pop song.*

*At one of the tables sits* WINKELBERG, *arms on the table, head in his arms. He is in a momentary drunken coma.*

*Several couples are engaged in a gluelike dance shuffle on the dimly lit dance floor.*

*A colored waiter, named* WILLIE, *appears.* WILLIE *carries a tray. He arrives at Winkelberg's table. He removes a large white coffee cup from the tray, takes a whiskey bottle out of his pocket and fills the cup.*

WILLIE *shakes the slumbering bard's shoulder.* WINKELBERG *finally gets his head off the canvas. He gapes at the glued couples dancing to the long-ago music.*

WILLIE (*constructively*). How about a pot of black coffee, Mistuh Winkelberg?

POET. Which fly-specked grotto is this?

WILLIE (*grinning*). Sunset Number Two—no place else.

POET (*grinning*). You're my pal, Willie. (*He looks around.*) Yes, Sunset Number Two—run by a coy cutthroat named Mossy Enright.

WILLIE. Mister Enright's coming over to see you.

POET. When Mister Mossy Enright dies, his admirers will present him with a sewer pipe for a coffin. (*He cackles, pleased with his fine wit.*)

WILLIE (*frowning*). That ain't healthy talk.

POET (*eyeing the dance floor*). I see the revelry has not abated. The same jazz antechamber of sex. (WILLIE *fills the cup. The* POET *stares at the glued dancing couples.*) The same fumbling salute to Eros. Nymphs with balloon udders and pineapple knees. Pious daddies with tomcat libidos. The dance that saves room rent. (*His head droops.* MOSSY ENRIGHT, *a tough-looking dandy, comes to the table.*)

WILLIE (*deferentially*). He's able to talk, Mister Enright.

MR. ENRIGHT (*clipped and cold-voiced*). You are takin' up valu'ble space in my café, Mister Winkelberg, and consumin' valu'ble liquor. And you ain't payin' off.

POET (*aloofly*). I have handed you three full-length poems to enliven the back of your menus. What do you want for nickels, Mister Enright, the Iliad? (MR. ENRIGHT *waves three sheets of paper under the* POET's *nose.*)

MR. ENRIGHT. I tried this crap on the boys. Nobody can understand it. For Chris' sake, write something in English. (*He reads slowly with mounting ire.*)

Melisand, Juno, Fifi, Leonora
Prance nimbly in Mossy Enright's Gomorrah—
Where Beelzebub toots his epileptic horn
From hopeful midnight to hopeless morn.

POET. Beautiful.

MR. ENRIGHT (*throws the papers on the table and adds coldly*). Kindly write somethin' that makes sense, or haul your can out of here. (*He exits proudly.*)

POET (*softly*). Another editor begs to regret. (*Enter* JACK CALVIN, *a young man with a prize fighter's grace. He comes slowly to the table.* JACK *shakes the* POET's *shoulder politely.* WINKELBERG *raises his head wearily. The singing fades out. The dance music continues faintly.*)

JACK (*modest, boylike, polite*). Ain't you Mister Winkelberg, the poet?

POET (*sneering sleepily*). That is correct.

JACK. I'm Jack Calvin. You may have heard of me. I used to be in the ring—the lightweight division. (*Shyly*) I fought Packy McFarland.

POET (*sneeringly*). Your career is a matter of exquisite triviality to me. (*He glares at him.*) To what do I owe the honor of your attention, Mr. Jack Calvin, lightweight?

JACK. I want to give you some money.

POET (*sternly*). What kind of money?

JACK. U.S. currency. (*He grins apologetically.*) I usually hand it over and blow. But you bein' a poet, I'd like to talk to you, if I may, about the over-all philosophy that's part of my givin' money away.

POET (*indignantly*). You keep mentioning United States currency but I have yet to see a glimpse of any.

JACK. Excuse the delay, Mr. Winkelberg. Here. (*He hands him a fat wallet.*) There's two thousand dollars in there. Even. (WINKELBERG *snatches the wallet and then stares at his caller.*)

POET. This is some crude jest you are practicing.

JACK. No, I am very sincere.

POET (*scowling and unconvinced*). Why should anybody give me money? It is not a normal phenomenon. (*He stares at the wallet.*) I may not have heard you accurately . . . Is this money for me?

JACK (*shyly*). That's the idea, Mister Winkelberg. It's yours. (*The* POET *opens the wallet and starts feverishly counting the bills, piling them on the table.* JACK *continues softly.*) You see, we have the following situation. There are two sets of people in the world—the few who have and the many who got nothin'. Correct? So I have figured out a program that I call the Christification Plan for the Redistribution of Wealth.

The way it operates is like this. The first step is I steal a load of furs. On this occasion I concentrated on Marshall Field's. You may have read about it in the papers. They called it an inside job—which shows ya how smooth the operation was. Correct? Secondly, I dispose of the furs to a friend o' mine who is a fence. (*He gets more at ease in his tale.*) Now the reason I steal furs is that they are an unessential commodity doin' nobody any good—because in the Temperate Zone they are not needed to keep you warm and are strictly for showin' off. You can see women all the time in taxis and restaurants smotherin' to death with furs—and holdin' them in their laps like they was an undesirable pet, a nuisance. Correct? Of course, I appreciate that one guy stealin' furs by himself ain't gonna improve the world very far. That's why I'm interested in making converts. I got several fellas I'm teachin' the Christification Plan . . . (WINKELBERG *has finished counting the precious bills.* WILLIE, *the waiter, has been watching him goggle-eyed. He now walks away cautiously, his face ominous.*)

POET (*softly, ogling the piles of money*). This is my first contact with high finance. (*He inquires pensively*) It's mine?

JACK (*proudly*). All yours, Mr. Winkelberg. I selected you after hearing the speech you made at the Dill Pickle Club. (*He quotes with disciple ardor*) "Poetry is the impish attempt to paint the color of the wind." (*He shakes his head in awe.*) That kind of words do somethin' to me. After the conclusion, Jack Jones verified my impression that you were out of funds. Jack said you sometimes went for several days without eatin'. Correct? I was surprised, because I always thought poets made a lot of money—

POET (*smiling dreamily into space*). I'm going to take a ship to London and call on Ezra Pound and Wyndham Lewis and T. S. Eliot. And exchange capricious adjectives with them. Then I'll take a ship to Paris—Oh boy! And pay my respects to Jean Cocteau and James Joyce—two fellow steeple jacks. (*He groans.*) Wait a minute. First I shall pick up a ballerina in New York from the Metropolitan Grand Opera Company as a traveling companion. Oh boy! (*He grows haughty.*) From Paris I shall take a first-class train to Moscow where I shall deliver a series of lectures to the government officials . . . and possibly find a second ballerina of Mongolian extraction . . . (JACK *has been listening admiringly. He rises.*)

JACK (*eagerly*). Tell 'em in Russia I'm working for a common ideal. It's been a privilege talking to you. Good night, Mr. Winkelberg. (*He clasps his hands in a prize fighter's victory gesture and exits. The* POET *starts putting the same bills into the wallet, stroking them as he does.*)

POET (*murmuring*). Booful little fellas in green mother hubbards . . . (MOSSY ENRIGHT *has come quickly and quietly to the table.* WILLIE *is with him.* MR. ENRIGHT *grabs* WINKELBERG'S *wrist and tries to snatch the wallet from him.* WINKELBERG *jumps drunkenly to his feet.*)

MR. ENRIGHT. Gimme that money . . .

POET (*wildly*). Nothin' doin' . . . It's mine!

MR. ENRIGHT. It's thieves' money . . . (*He snatches at the wallet.* WINKELBERG *pushes him away.*)

POET. Get out o' here! It's mine! (MR. ENRIGHT *slips a set of brass knuckles on his fingers. It is now we see a resemblance between Mr. Enright and Tony Riggs, the acidulous critic, for it is the same actor who plays both parts.*)

MR. ENRIGHT. Gimme that or I'll bust you open.

POET (*loudly*). Let me alone. It's mine! (*The* POET *picks up a chair and starts swinging it.* WILLIE *pins his arms from behind.* MR. ENRIGHT *socks him in the face several times. For a few moments,* WINKELBERG, *spurting blood from his ripped face, fights wildly. Then he goes down —and out.* MR. ENRIGHT *picks the wallet out of the unconscious* POET's *pocket.*)

MR. ENRIGHT (*panting, to* WILLIE). The back way. Dump him in the alley. (WILLIE *starts dragging the limp figure off.*) And don't let the bastard in here again. (*The café is full of song and music, as the stage darkens.*)

WINKELBERG *is alone in the light. He mops a bloodied face with a bandanna.*

POET (*softly, mocking as he peers into the dark around him*). Sweet little world, don't be bashful. Don't go hiding your innumerable charms from this little traveler. (*He talks with a scowl as he fills and lights his corncob.*) A drunken sailor blew my head off. I'm rotting cozily in a pine box. Why send me back to ring red-hot doorbells again? But maybe you know what you're doing, Mr. Black Man with your wreath of silver birds. So I'll keep peekin' around. (*He stares around and smiles.*) There was a park in Chicago—a stone's throw away from the Dill Pickle Club—rendezvous of that ancient twosome "The Arts and Tarts." In this green acre I remember some dim companions. (*The stage lights up as he adds*) Come little Blue Bird of Bughouse Square—let papa see you—(*He stands looking at the scene revealed.*)

## SCENE 4

*A small city park is revealed. It is 9* A.M. *A few worn benches and sparse trees are visible. A large Refuse Deposit Can is beside a bench.*

WINKELBERG *stands looking at a white-haired, hatless, skinny crone called* BIRDIE *sitting on a bench.*

*There are three petticoats under her dress. Her shoes are ancient. She is milky-eyed. Her thin face is foolishly rouged. She carries an old purse. She removes a mirror and lipstick from it and coyly makes up her lips. She smiles childishly.*

*A buxom old wench waddles into the park. She sits down beside* BIRDIE. *Her name is* MAG THE BAG. *Her hair is white and carroty spotted. She wears a soiled, torn evening gown. She carries a white shoe box. She walks heavily.*

WINKELBERG *watches the two old ones.* MAG *sits down on the bench.*

MAG (*hoarse-voiced to the other bench sitter*). What ya doin', Birdie? (BIRDIE *giggles and doesn't answer.*) What's-a-matter? Ya drunk?

BIRDIE. I found a dead cat.

MAG. Yeh? That so? (BIRDIE *falls to work with the lipstick again.*) Aw, you're crazier every day. No good, goin' round crazy. (*She nudges her irritably.*)

POET. The children of Democracy enjoying the morning sun on Bughouse Square. Two elderly Loreleis still singing from their promontories. (WINKELBERG *joins the two women.*)

WINKELBERG (*he bows*). Good morning, ladies.

MAG. Look who's here.

POET (*smiling at her*). You are lookin' very seductive, Mag the Bag.

MAG (*croaking*). Ya?

POET. You, too, Birdie. (BIRDIE *giggles. Gallantly*) You wear a necklace of bedrooms.

BIRDIE (*giggles*). Yeh—Yeh—a beautiful necklace.

POET. Is it true, Mag, that you used to charge ten simoleons a night?

MAG (*hoarsely*). Not a night. A hour.

POET (*smiling at* BIRDIE). How much did Birdie charge?

MAG. Same t'ing. (BIRDIE *rises and starts to sing in a small girl's voice.*)

BIRDIE (*pirouetting slowly as she sings*). "Put your arms around me, honey—"

MAG (*pulling at her dress*). Si' down. Ya wan' the cops t'hear ya?

BIRDIE. I ain't singin' loud.

MAG (*opens her shoe box. She starts eating crumbs out of it. To* BIRDIE) Ya hungry? (BIRDIE *primps in her piece of mirror. She is too fascinated to answer.*) She can't eat nuttin'. I never see her eat nuttin'. Honest. (*A skinny* OLD MAN *enters. He is a washed-out, plucked chicken of a man. He moves to the empty bench.*)

POET. Hello, Mister. Mister Flea Belly. Mister Empty Guts. Mister Man. (THE BUM *sits down in silence. He twitches a bit. He needs a drink.*)

BUM (*shakily*). Anybody see in the papers what's new in the war?

MAG (*a little contemptuously*). Always showin' off.

BUM (*on the defensive*). I was in a war. China. We licked the Boxers. Big Chinamen wit' braids. (*Pleadingly to* WINKELBERG). Ya got a drink on ya, buddy? (MAG *is smitten with a sudden dream of whiskey.*)

MAG (*pleadingly*). Justa little snifter, huh? (*She shudders.*) I got the chills in me. My feet's always frozen. (*Smilingly roguishly at* WINKELBERG) Come on, let's have one.

BIRDIE (*suddenly eager and alert*). Yeh, yeh—me, too.

POET. The cupboard is bare. (MAG *resumes her eating.*)

BUM (*back to his first shaky query*). You see in the papers, what's new in the war?

POET. The military picture is unchanged since Nebuchadnezzar. Old men are winning arguments and young men are losing their lives.

BIRDIE (*sings*).

"Put yer arms around me, honey
Hold me tight—
Cuddle up a little closer
you're a sight."

MAG (*pushing her with an elbow*). Shut up! Ya wanna get in trouble? (BIRDIE *stops singing. She looks frightened and sniffles tearfully.*)

POET (*smiling at the sniffles*). I wrote a poem about you, Birdie. (*He opens his brief case and fishes among its load of papers.*) My virgin forest of poems—in which no alien eye has peered.

MAG. Ya write one about me?

POET. Yes, indeedy. All three are in it. It's called Three Saints Around An Ash Can.

MAG. I liked the one about the fire. The fire wit' the fellas workin'.

POET (*quoting as he searches*). "The fire made a golden fir tree in the street." (*He ends his search and adds dotingly.*) Here's our little baby.

BIRDIE (*sings again*).

"Cuddle up a little closer,
Lovely mine—
Cuddle up and—"

POET (*announcing the title from a sheet of typing*). Three Saints Around An Ash Can. (*The* BUM *leans forward to listen. The* POET *reads, looking first at* BIRDIE.)

"Her lips were a little red couch on which a child lay dead—
Beside her a cobweb face ate crumbs out of a shoe box.
Nearby, a discarded man hid in the sun.
Oh, dim companions,
You were born in houses that looked like teeth in an old man's mouth..
Your youth was a torn shirt flapping on an alley clothes line.
After awkward journeys, you settle like dust on a lonely bench.
(*He tilts his head back and closes his eyes as he recites the climax.*)
Underneath disaster's black debris
You sit and smile from all disasters free."

MAG (*croaks*). Nice.

BIRDIE (*sings softly*).

"Put yer arms around me, honey
Hold me tight—"

(*A uniformed* COP *appears.* MAG *tugs warningly at* BIRDIE—*who stops singing.*)

COP (*amicably*). Hello, Mag.

MAG (*formally*). What d'ya want, Officer?

COP. Remember me?

MAG. Ya. O'Shaughnessy.

COP. No. O'Malley.

MAG. Pardon me.

COP. You know a fella named Jack Calvin? Used to be a prize fighter?

MAG (*looking away, guiltily*). What about him?

COP (*smiling*). You know him, Mag?

MAG (*loyally*). He's a fine fella.

COP. Seen him lately?

POET (*sneering*). No siree. Her social engagements have not included Mister Jack Calvin. (*The* COP *studies* WINKELBERG *for a pause.*)

COP. You're Jonathan Winkelberg.

POET (*sneering*). My name is not exactly news to me.

COP (*quietly*). Keep out of this, y'screwball. (*To* MAG) You know where this fella Calvin lives, Mag?

MAG. He comes around sometimes.

COP (*patiently*). Where can we find him, Mag?

POET. Does the city pay you to harass old ladies with obtuse questions, Mister Officer?

COP (*ignoring him*). Ain't I your friend, Mag?

MAG. Ya, O'Shaughnessy. You used to run me in.

COP. O'Shaughnessy's retired. I'm O'Malley. Now be a good girl and tell me where this fella Calvin lives.

MAG (*moodily*). He gimme a present.

COP. Did he ever give you any furs? Fur pieces. Or a fur coat?

MAG. Ga-wan! You crazy!

POET. You don't have to answer this whimsical sleuth, Mag. The police are trying to make trouble for your prize fighter friend, Mr. Calvin.

MAG. He hit somebody?

COP (*smiling*). Where's he live, Mag? (MAG *is silent.*) Come on now, nobody's gonna hurt ya.

MAG. He gimme a present. Me and Birdie. A dozen stockin's.

COP. He had 'em in his room, didn't he?

MAG. Ya, in his room.

COP (*patiently*). Where's he live, Mag?

POET. Jack Calvin is your friend, Mag. Don't betray him to the police. It's bad to betray a friend, Mag.

COP (*quietly*). One more crack—I run ya in. (*To* MAG) Come on, baby, where can I find Calvin?

MAG. Whad'll ya gimme?

COP. A pint of whiskey.

MAG (*whispering*). Whiskey—

COP (*smiling*). Hot in the belly.

BUM (*suddenly*). I know where he lives.

COP (*turning to him*). Where?

BUM. Will ya gimme a pint?

MAG (*eagerly*). Ga-wan! He don't need ya to tell him. The prize fighter's got a room in Erie Street.

BUM (*eagerly*). It's on East Erie.

COP. What number?

MAG. I dunno the number. He took us for the present.

BUM. Me, too. On the third floor.

COP. What address?

BUM (*rising*). I know the buildin'. I'll show you. He gimme ten shirts.

COP. Come on. We'll give you a ride in our car.

MAG. Come on, Birdie. We're gonna ride in an automobile. (BIRDIE *rises.*)

COP. You'll get a pint each. Let's go. (*The* COP *turns away. The four start off.*)

POET (*looking after the vanishing figures, his voice soft and mocking*).

O my sweet sister, mother, brother—
How good you are to one another—

THE STAGE DARKENS

## SCENE 5

*A courtroom becomes visible. The* JUDGE *is hidden behind the elevated bench. He remains offstage, heard over loud-speaker.*

A COURT CLERK *stands beside the bench. At a table at right angles to the judge's bench sit* JACK CALVIN *and a lawyer named* CHARLES ERBSTEIN.

*At another table, ten feet away, sits the prosecuting attorney,* JIM O'BRIEN. O'BRIEN *is an Irishman with a temper. When we have had a good look at* O'BRIEN, *we see that, underneath an altered make-up, his is the same face that belonged to Tony Riggs and Mossy Enright. It is, again, the same actor.*

ERBSTEIN *rises and steps to the bench.*

CLERK (*bangs gavel*). The court will please rise. (*All rise.*) The Honorable Court of the City of Chicago, Cook County, is now in session. Be seated. (*All sit.*)

ERBSTEIN. Your honor, I wish to call a character witness for the defendant, Jack Calvin.

O'BRIEN (*quickly to his feet*). I object, your honor. The defendant has admitted he is a fur thief, a ruthless burglar. I see no point in wasting the court's time proving that this rapacious criminal, Jack Calvin, is kind to his mother and loves dumb animals.

ERBSTEIN. Your honor, the only defense in this case is the remarkable character of the defendant. Does the learned prosecuting attorney wish this court and jury to judge a man without hearing his defense?

JUDGE (*offstage. Quietly*). Objection overruled.

O'BRIEN. Exception.

JUDGE. Call the witness.

CLERK (*consulting a paper—calls out*). Bring in the witness, Jonathan Winkelberg. (*A* BAILIFF *leads* WINKELBERG *into the courtroom.* WINKELBERG *is in summer attire—a thin, wrinkled suit of unmatching coat and trousers, a frayed shirt, and an unexpected white tie, somewhat spotted. He carries his bulging brief case. The* CLERK *beckons to him.*) Up here, please. (*He indicates the chair beside the judge's bench.* WINKELBERG *mounts the step and sits down firmly in the chair.*) Stand up. (WINKELBERG *stands up.*) Raise your right hand. (WINKELBERG *does. The* CLERK *rattles off the oath.*) Do you hereby solemnly swear to tell the truth, the whole truth and nothing but the truth, so help you God?

POET (*firmly*). I shall do my best to capture the elusive factor of truth and—

CLERK (*sourly to the* JUDGE). The witness won't answer.

POET (*indignantly*). I am answering.

ERBSTEIN (*quietly*). Just say, I do, Mr. Winkelberg.

POET (*cautiously*). I do what?

ERBSTEIN. You do swear to tell the truth.

POET (*coldly*). I do that little thing.

JUDGE. You may sit down.

POET (*with a slight bow*). Thank you. (*He sits down.*)

ERBSTEIN (*standing near him*). State your name.

POET (*suddenly a man of terseness*). Jonathan Winkelberg.

ERBSTEIN. Your vocation?

POET (*firmly*). I am a poet.

ERBSTEIN. You are engaged in no other employment?

POET (*patiently*). Writing poetry is a full-time job.

ERBSTEIN. That brief case you're holding—what does it contain, Mr. Winkelberg?

POET. My poems.

ERBSTEIN. Nothing else?

POET. A can of tobacco and a pair of socks.

ERBSTEIN. Are those your only worldly possessions, Mr. Winkelberg?

POET. My only tangible ones, Mr. Erbstein.

ERBSTEIN. Are you acquainted with the defendant, Jack Calvin?

POET. Superficially.

ERBSTEIN. What do you mean by that?

POET (*patiently*). I mean by that—that I have met the defendant Jack Calvin only once.

ERBSTEIN. Will you describe the circumstances of that meeting, Mr. Winkelberg—and tell everything that was done and said at the time —in your own words.

POET (*aloofly*). I am not in the habit of using other people's words.

ERBSTEIN (*soothingly*). I am sure of that. Will you describe your meeting with Mr. Calvin?

POET. I was sitting at a table in the Sunset Number Two Café, in my capacity as resident poet. Mr. Jack Calvin came to my table and introduced himself as an ex-lightweight prize fighter and also as an admirer of my genius as a poet and lecturer at the Dill Pickle Club, where he had heard me deliver a lecture on the Impish Contortions of October Moonlight.

O'BRIEN (*pulled to his feet by this*). Your honor, is this necessary?

ERBSTEIN. If Mr. O'Brien will restrain his distaste for poetry—

O'BRIEN (*interrupting beamishly*). I have no distaste for poetry, Mr. Erbstein. I am an admirer of the poets—

JUDGE. Is there an objection before the bench?

O'BRIEN (*drawing a calming breath*). No, your honor.

JUDGE. The witness may proceed.

ERBSTEIN. You were saying, Mr. Winkelberg, that—

POET (*coldly*). I know what I was saying. After introducing himself, Mr. Jack Calvin informed me that he was a highly successful fur thief and that it was his practice to convert these ornate and useless skins of dead animals into mazuma—and—

ERBSTEIN. Pardon me, into what?

POET (*a little indignant*). Mazuma—moola—green lettuce grown in Washington, D.C.

ERBSTEIN (*smiling*). Money.

POET (*aloofly*). That is what some people call it. Mr. Jack Calvin explained that he thereupon gave the aforesaid money away to any poor or hungry people he encountered.

ERBSTEIN. Did he give you any money, Mr. Winkelberg?

POET. Mr. Jack Calvin gave me two thousand dollars he had obtained from the sale of some unessential fur coats, stolen from Marshall Field and Company's Department Store. (*He beams with satisfaction.*)

ERBSTEIN. Did the defendant say why he was giving you the money, Mr. Winkelberg?

POET (*firmly*). The defendant, Mr. Calvin, said he was giving me the money because he considered it more beneficial to the human race for a poet to eat than for a rich fat woman to waddle around like a perspiring Eskimo.

ERBSTEIN. Did Mr. Calvin have any name for his philosophical beliefs?

POET. Mr. Calvin referred to his activities as the Christification Plan.

ERBSTEIN. Did you understand what Mr. Calvin meant by that title?

POET. I deduced from the title that Mr. Calvin was following in the footsteps of Jesus Christ.

O'BRIEN (*red-faced, on his feet*). I object. The answer is a sacrilegious presumption.

POET. Does Mr. O'Brien consider it sacrilegious to follow in the footsteps of Christ?

O'BRIEN (*angrily*). For a thief and a burglar, yes!

POET (*beaming*). How about Magdalen?

JUDGE. Objection overruled.

POET (*with a chuckle*). Oh, boy!

ERBSTEIN (*to the* JUDGE). Thank you. (*To the witness*) And now, Mr. Winkelberg, what did you do with the money this modern Robin Hood, Jack Calvin, gave you?

POET. I did nothing with the money. It was a fleeting mirage.

ERBSTEIN. Will you explain to the court the details of this fleeting mirage?

POET. Yes, indeedy. (*He glares at the memory he relates.*) Shortly after the gentleman to whom you refer as Robin Hood left my table, Mr. Mossy Enright and one of his waiters appeared and beat me into unconsciousness and stole the money from me. And threw me into the alley—where I woke up, penniless.

CALVIN. That's a cruel miscarriage of my plan.

ERBSTEIN. Thank you, Mr. Winkelberg. That's all. (WINKELBERG *rises and starts to leave.*) Just a minute, Mr. Winkelberg—

POET. You said, that's all.

ERBSTEIN. The prosecution may wish to cross-examine you.

POET (*indignantly*). What for?

ERBSTEIN. Your witness, Mr. O'Brien. (WINKELBERG sits down.)

O'BRIEN (*on his feet*). I understand you are a poet.

POET. Are you asking a question or do you wish me to admire you as a man of unexpected understanding?

O'BRIEN. Where may one read your poetry, sir?

POET. An ideal place would be the top of the pyramid of Rameses the First, where you would be free from interruption. (*He beams.*)

O'BRIEN. You're quite a joker.

POET (*with a slight bow*). Thank you.

O'BRIEN (*smoothly*). I shall try again. In what periodicals do your poems appear?

POET. In the periodicals of the future.

O'BRIEN. You mean your poetry has not appeared in print, as yet?

POET (*coldly*). As yet.

O'BRIEN (*smiling*). In other words, you are an invisible poet.

POET. The angels are equally invisible.

O'BRIEN (*sneering*). But a trifle prettier, let us hope. (*Abruptly*) Are you a married man, Mr. Winkelberg?

POET. I have not yet achieved that moral eminence, Mr. O'Brien.

O'BRIEN. You sound as if you don't particularly care for morality. Is that true?

POET. Whose morality have you in mind, yours or mine?

O'BRIEN. I have in mind the morality by which decent people live.

POET. I presume you mean husbands who lie to their wives about their infidelities, and churchgoers who lie to God about their fondness for the Ten Commandments.

O'BRIEN (*quietly*). Is that your concept of decent people, Mister Poet?

POET. It is my concept of your kind of decent people, Mister Lawyer.

O'BRIEN (*abruptly*). Have you ever been arrested, Winkelberg?

POET. Yes, O'Brien.

O'BRIEN. For stealing?

POET. No, sleeping.

O'BRIEN (*sarcastic*). Did you fall asleep in a bank you were robbing?

POET. No, I fell asleep in a park while I was thinking of a poem.

O'BRIEN. The charge was vagrancy. Is that correct?

POET. Yes—the same charge on which Walt Whitman was arrested.

O'BRIEN. You testified that after the thief, Jack Calvin, gave you the two thousand dollars, he withdrew from the café.

POET (*coldly*). He left.

O'BRIEN (*sarcastic*). I must apologize if my language does not meet with your poetic approval, Mr. Winkelberg.

POET (*beaming at him*). Your language is the— (*He punctuates with a little whistle.*) —cat's whiskers. (*And chuckles.*)

O'BRIEN (*abruptly*). Isn't it a fact that you left the café that night in company with Jack Calvin?

POET. That is not a fact. That is a feeble lie.

O'BRIEN (*sharply*). Isn't it a fact that Mr. Enright did not assault you that evening—or maltreat you in any way?

POET. That is even less a fact and a more feeble lie.

O'BRIEN (*in for the kill*). Isn't it a fact that the two thousand dollars Jack Calvin handed over was your part of the swag as his partner in crime?

POET (*coldly*). Your insinuation is a pitiful red herring!

O'BRIEN (*sharply*). Answer yes or no.

ERBSTEIN (*on his feet*). Objection! The question is unfounded and unwarranted.

O'BRIEN (*on his feet*). Your honor, we are going to prove this supercilious clown is a criminal liar and perjurer!

POET (*pointing to* O'BRIEN). I demand an apology from this Hibernian cutthroat!

CLERK (*through the foregoing*). Order in the court. The court will come to order! (*He bangs a gavel.*)

ERBSTEIN. I move the question be stricken from the record.

O'BRIEN (*loudly now*). We have witnesses to prove this man Winkelberg is Calvin's partner in crime.

POET (*fiercely pointing at the prosecutor*). You are either a pensive idiot or you are on the payroll of a gangster named Mossy Enright.

O'BRIEN (*loudly*). Your honor, I demand this witness be held in contempt.

POET (*fiercely, on his feet and pointing*). I demand that man be arrested and sent to jail!

(*The courtroom darkens as voices continue out of this gloom—all at the same time.*)

JUDGE'S VOICE. Gentlemen—Gentlemen. (*Gavel bangs.*)

O'BRIEN'S VOICE. We'll prove perjury—criminal perjury!

POET'S VOICE (*above the others*). I'm a character witness for Jack Calvin! Jack Calvin is a decent human being! Put that in your pipe and smoke it. (*The tumult ends. The stage is dark.* WINKELBERG *alone remains visible.*)

POET (*scowling*). Mr. Jack Calvin was sentenced to five years in the State Penitentiary at Joliet. And I was convicted of perjury and locked away for three months in the local hoosegow. His Honor stated, while sentencing me, "I hope that the lenience of this Court toward your wanton crime of lying under oath will give you a new concept of the humanitarianism by which civilization is run." (*He chuckles sardonically and looks aloft.*) Yes, sirree! It done gimme that all right, all right! (*He takes a swig and grins into the dark around him.*) Shortly after my release from jail, Warren Gamaliel Harding became President of the United States. And Miss Harriet Monroe, editor of Poetry Magazine, returned my fifty-first unwanted contribution with a brief handwritten note confessing that my poetry was not quite intelligible to her. (A WOMAN'S VOICE *calls gently out of the darkness.*)

WOMAN'S VOICE. Johnny—Johnny Winkelberg—

POET (*moodily*). That sounds like a nice voice.

WOMAN'S VOICE. Johnny Winkelberg.

POET (*hopefully*). A voice of oddly pleasing quality.

WOMAN'S VOICE (*trailing off*). Johnny—Johnny—

POET (*his face eager*). What was nice—? (*He walks into the darkness.*)

## SCENE 6

*An attic room on a winter's night. Through its two small dormer windows we see snow falling heavily. It is a dingy room with a door to the right. In the room is a rickety kitchen table.*

*A broken Franklin stove, a number of grocery-store boxes usable as filing cabinets and guest chairs, a rumpled cot as uninviting as a scrap heap, a litter of empty bottles, magazines, newspapers, several piles of books, a large wire refuse basket stolen from the Park System (it is beside the table), a single, unshaded electric bulb over the table—these constitute the attic room.*

*A heavy-set man with a bad disposition is at work trying to tidy up some of the room's mess.*

WINKELBERG *appears. His overcoat is covered with snow. He stands looking with rueful smile at the long-ago attic room. The heavy-set man, whose name is* SIG SCHULTE, *becomes aware of him. He turns on him angrily. We become aware that* MR. SCHULTE *is a continuation of Messrs. Riggs, Enright, and O'Brien. He looks and talks much differently—but he is the same actor.*

SCHULTE (*at work*). No arguments! You're gettin' out o' here tonight, ten o'clock sharp. I got a new tenant. Paid in advance. At ten, you get out—

POET (*shivering*). It's a cold night.

SCHULTE. That's none of my business. Ya owe me seventeen dollars. You're out—unnerstand?

POET. Don't argue with me now. I thought of a poem while walking in the snow. (*He picks up a pencil and starts to write. His fingers are too cold. He blows on his hand to warm it. He glares at* SCHULTE.) My fingers are too cold to write it down. You will pardon me if I recite the first verse so as not to forget it. (*He recites aloofly*)

A great white leopard prowling silently
Over the roof tops, up and down the sky,
Trailing its ermine and its ivory
The sinuous snow glides by.

SCHULTE. For Chris' sake!

(*An odd-looking young man appears in the doorway. He wears a corduroy Norfolk jacket. His hair is long, like the haircut of a medieval page boy. He carries a heavy cane. He is* STANISLAUS SZUKALSKI, *a young Polish painter and sculptor of great ego, strength, and litheness. He stands watching the two in the room.*)

POET (*warming his hand with his breath*). I would like to offer you an autographed copy of my first book of poetry, *The Sardonic Caterpillar.* Retails for a dollar seventy-five cents. I can let you have it for half price—eighty-three cents—including the autograph.

SCHULTE (*he starts out*). Don't gimme no bargains! Just pack up and blow!

POET (*to the exiting one*). I shall put my possessions into a thimble at the stroke of ten, Mr. Schulte. And say my farewell to another table. (*The sculptor enters. He speaks in a quiet voice and a fractured English. He hasn't eaten for two days. A slight dizziness is in his strong stride and gesture.*)

STANLEY. I am here before. (*He looks at the window.*) Outside, like

Polish winter. (WINKELBERG *has thawed his fingers. He looks at his visitor for the first time. Then he starts writing slowly.* STANLEY *walks to the cot and smites it with his heavy cane.* WINKELBERG *remains bowed in creation over the table.*)

STANLEY. This is what I like to do to Mr. Hobart Hatfield, president Chicago Art Institute. You know my painting Man Under Water. I take him, just now, out of Art Institute Exhibition of so-called Chicago artists. (*He hits the cot again, glares at it and sits down on a box near it.*) I come to Institute eight o'clock. I look on wall of Chicago artists. My painting, Man Under Water, is only painting hung upside down. Other paintings hung proper way. Mine, upside down. I get step ladder and remove him. When they try stop me I say, 'Stanislaus Szukalski do not stand on head for pork packers and old maids with catarrh. I do not ornament home for sofa-cushion menders called Art Institute. I put Art Institute under my fingernail.

POET (*reading*).

A tall white odalisque
Sinks to her knees—

STANLEY. I am only living artist who can split sky and make night bleed. I put Rembrandt in one pocket and Tintoretto in other pocket—and I walk forward. (*He rises and slashes the air with his stick. He strides to* WINKELBERG's *table.*) Excuse me. Can you lend me dollar?

POET (*writing*). Uh-huh.

STANLEY (*sternly*). You have book published. You are rich man.

POET (*aloofly*). I shall receive my first royalty payment six months from date of publication, which is five months and four days from tonight—on July fifteenth.

STANLEY. You have half dollar?

POET. Guess again. (STANLEY *sits down. His dizziness has grown.*)

STANLEY. Maybe we have tea together.

POET. I never touch it. Perhaps there's a sweet bun in that box. (STANLEY *goes to box on the floor and searches its litter.*)

STANLEY. Only rags. (*He sits on the box and stares dizzily.*) In Poland artist is hero. In United States he is dog without bone.

POET (*sneering*). Bow-wow!

STANLEY. Artist is civilization. The rest is animal with itch.

POET (*sneering*). Civilization could do with a little old bite of food tonight, eh, baby? Boy, am I hungry! (*His hunger is, in his mind, an indictment of society. Therefore, he gloats when he mentions it—and all other misfortunes—as if he were winning an argument. He grins at the window.*) It looks below zero in the animal world. And all the businessmen curled up like pussy cats in front of their fireplaces. (*He chuckles.*) Where you living, Stanley?

STANLEY. In Polish Freedom Institute.

POET. Is there room in your basement for another occupant?

STANLEY. They do not let in Jews.

POET. Not even in the basement?

STANLEY. It is nothing personal. It is patriotic philosophy of Poland.

POET. Patriotism is the honeymoon of stupidity.

STANLEY (*calmly*). That is philosophy of Jew.

POET (*reciting pensively*).

How sad that in the warmest hearts I knew
Lurked always a little cold spot for the Jew.

(*He chuckles and adds formally*) In the winter months, from November through February, I lapse, defensively, into rhyme. (*He reads his writing:*)

The snowfall offers dramas in the dark—
A tall white odalisque, sinking to her knees
Expires in the street. And in the park
The snow paints ghostly summer on the trees.

STANLEY (*softly*). You are my brother.

POET. Yes, we are in the same dubious business—we make dancing slippers for monkeys. (*Takes bottle from pocket.*) Half.

STANLEY (*drinks*). Nos drovya not twoiye is drovi.

POET (*drinks*). Mud in your eye.

STANLEY. Sometime you will be a great man.

POET. It is very possible. (*He beams.*) One must avoid the pitfalls of riches and contentment. So far I have been very lucky.

STANLEY. Where you sleep tonight?

POET (*bowed over his writing again*). In the Polk Street Railroad Station. I shall pretend to be waiting for a train to sunny California.

STANLEY. I join you. (*A* WOMAN'S VOICE *is heard approaching.*)

WOMAN'S VOICE (*gayly*). Easy on those blankets, Maxie. This stairway is like a dirt road. (WINKELBERG *stiffens at the voice. A haughty air comes on him. The arrival is a sprightly girl. This is* LOUISE, *some 20 years younger than in Scene 2. She is pretty and gay and strong-mannered. Her arms are full of bundles. Following her is a* CABBY *carrying suitcases. Then* MR. SCHULTE *appears with a bundle of quilts, sheets, and oddments.*)

LOUISE. Johnny—

POET. Miss Louise Larnigan, the virgin of East Chicago Avenue. (*He bows stiffly.*)

LOUISE (*beaming and breathless*). The landlord told me, you told me, everybody told me—you'd gone to New York!

POET (*a battle of wits*). Your information seems to be—inaccurate, Miss Larnigan.

LOUISE (*laughing*). And it's so cold outside. Icicles on the moon. I can't bear it. Except it's not much warmer in here. (*To the* CABBY) Thanks, Max. We'll bring the rest of the stuff over tomorrow. (*She pays him.*)

MAX (*grinning*). Any time, Miss Larnigan. (*He exits.*)

LOUISE (*espying* STANLEY). Stanley Szukalski! (STANLEY *clicks his heels together and offers a curt bow.*) I tell everybody—you're the greatest painter alive today.

STANLEY (*another small bow*). It is true.

LOUISE. Did you and Stanley really have that debate in front of the ritzy Book and Play Club—Resolved "Are People Who Attend Literary Debates Fools?"

POET. Yes, indeedy. Stanley took the affirmative.

STANLEY. I am silent for thirty seconds, looking on audience. Then I say, "I rest my case."

POET. I arose and after studying the audience for another thirty seconds said to Stanley, "You win."

LOUISE (*laughing*). And they paid you a hundred dollars!

POET. In advance!

LOUISE. Those poor idiots!

STANLEY (*abruptly*). Artist and poet have important job. God makes souls. We improve them. (*He bows to her and adds to* WINKELBERG) Polk Street Station I am there. (*He strides out.*)

LOUISE (*smiling after him*). Isn't he thrilling? How I envy you two. (*To* WINKELBERG) Polk Street Station? Is he leaving town? What a pity! I'm terribly sorry, Johnny. (*She shudders.*) God, I feel like the banker in his silk hat foreclosing on the widow and her little ones. (*She imitates that malefactor, twirling a villainous mustache.* SCHULTE *exits.* WINKELBERG *starts packing. He crams a tobacco tin and a pair of socks into the bulging briefcase. He picks up five books and starts tying them together with a string. His movements are efficient and determined.*)

LOUISE (*removing objects from the big bundle*). Here's how it happened, Johnny. You remember my landlord, Mr. McGurk? With the red nose and the black derby? He started banging on my door at all hours of the night and yelling I'm his Mavourneen. I just simply had to move, or turn the villain over to the police.

POET (*sneering*). You seem to have an unfortunate genius for inflaming the male.

LOUISE (*laughing*). Me, and a quart of whiskey. (*She looks at him pensively.*) Johnny, I want to talk to you.

POET (*coldly*). About your virtue? Thank you, I am sufficiently informed on that subject. (*He adds his standard bow.*)

LOUISE (*flaring*). You make me so damn mad, I could hit you with that stove.

POET (*aloofly*). You have much the same effect on me.

LOUISE (*impulsively*). Johnny, I want to be friends.

POET (*coldly*). You had your opportunity.

LOUISE. Please—I'm sorry about our fight. I didn't mean half the things I said. You're a great poet. You are definitely not an insensitive oaf befouling everything you touch. (*She smiles.*) You see, I was so disappointed by your attitude. I thought I was somebody more important to you than a hit-and-run sexual case.

POET (*coldly*). Why should you think that?

LOUISE. Johnny, I'm apologizing.

POET. I'm not.

LOUISE (*laughing*). You're priceless! Honestly, you make other men seem hopelessly sane. Oh, how I despise those bond salesmen pawing their way to fatherhood. (*She has opened the straw suitcase and now removes rolls, cheese, and a bottle of wine.*) I brought some food. I didn't have time for a bite. That howling Casanova. With his derby caved in. There's plenty here for two. (*She holds out food to him.*) Here—

POET (*haughtily*). I don't happen to be hungry.

LOUISE (*softly*). Please eat with me. It's very good cheese. (*He accepts the food with a sneer. He stands holding it and his hunger wrestles with his hauteur.*) This could be very nice. A room far away from everywhere. (*She has opened a suitcase and removed a milk bottle. She holds it out to him.*) Have some. (WINKELBERG *takes it slowly and then drinks thirstily.*) I don't suppose I'll ever be a painter. Because I'm too scattered. Love too many things—poetry, music, philosophy—even bird life. My folks keep begging me to come back to Highland Park. Oh, how I hate that flossy world! Everybody living up to their butlers! You wrote it so well, Johnny—"their clothes and dreams as alike as the teeth of a comb."

POET (*mockingly*). Joan of Arc in Suburbia.

LOUISE. Must you sneer at someone who—who admires you? What

I'm trying to tell you in my rattlebrained way is I don't give a damn for anything in the world except beauty.

POET (*coldly*). And marriage.

LOUISE. I can't understand you, Johnny. If you're interested in me enough to want me sexually, why not marry me? I've heard there's some sex activity in marriage.

POET. Yes. The feast becomes a midnight snack.

LOUISE (*softly*). I've got a nice paying job. I could make this attic so nice. And I could love you—as I love your poetry. (WINKELBERG *has swallowed his last morsel. He puts a hand on her arm. She rises. He embraces her. They kiss. She continues tenderly after the kiss, as he holds her.*) I couldn't be angry with you after our fight. Despite the nasty things you said. You know, you've got a tongue like a cat o' nine tails. A woman isn't a Lesbian with a barbed-wire bosom just because she doesn't want to satisfy a man's lust for an evening. And that's all you asked. If you'd have asked for more, darling—

POET (*moodily, as he tries to get a hand under her waist*). Your body aches with melodies—

LOUISE (*pushing him gently*). Let go, Paderewski. I want to talk—as artist to artist. (*They sit down on the cot.*)

POET (*releasing her*). I never beg for sex. If the sexual animation isn't mutual it's like a horse race with one horse in it.

LOUISE. It isn't mutual, Johnny, because I don't know about sex. I told you. It's true. I'm a virgin.

POET. A virgin has to start somewhere.

LOUISE (*smiling*). Please take your hand off my leg. (*He does, haughtily.*) Thanks.

POET (*coldly*). Don't mention it.

LOUISE (*tenderly*). Your clothes need mending. Your hair needs cutting. You need feeding—and you need somebody on your side. And I haven't any illusions about your being faithful. (*She smiles at him.*) I'd never stand in the way of your freedom—much.

POET. A husband in another woman's bed isn't freedom. It's the prisoner—in the exercise yard.

LOUISE (*softly*). Tell me, honestly, Johnny—why you won't marry me.

POET (*quietly*). I don't love you.

LOUISE. Must there be love?

POET. Yes.

LOUISE (*staring at him*). I'm amazed. Who could ever imagine you were a romantic idealist? You're not Jonathan Winkelberg. You're

Lord Alfred Tennyson, or one of his white knights, dreaming of a daffy princess in the Tower. A dream girl in an ivory tower. Well, I hope you find her, Mr. Tennyson. And I hope she'll be able to cook and sew, as well as swoon, and I hope you'll live happily ever afterward! (SCHULTE *has entered. She frowns at him.*) What the hell do *you* want?

SCHULTE. It's ten o'clock.

POET. The witching hour— (*He gathers up his books and brief case.*)

LOUISE. You're not angry, Johnny—

POET (*smiling*). Do you wish to—reconsider?

LOUISE. No, thank you. Where will you go?

POET. My immediate address will be the Polk Street Station—where one of Mr. Tennyson's contemporaries will sing me to sleep.

"They shall fail as I am failing,
Dizzy, lost, and unbewailing."

(*The stage is dark.* WINKELBERG *alone is visible. He takes a swig from his flask—and then grins aloft.*) That, O Black Man, was my Chicago. While President Calvin Coolidge was taking cat naps in the basement of the White House, I said good-by to Chicago. A wide-awake chief executive would have passed a law prohibiting the migration of poets. For a poet who travels is like a fish who moves through the water on the end of a hook. He heads only for a pail on a pier. My pail of water was New York City. (*He grins. He quotes—mockingly*)

"I came to town like Galahad,
I wandered in like Don Quixote.
With a pencil and a writing pad,
A brief case and an overcoat—
Pensive, and a little mad,
And hungry as a nanny goat."

(*The lights come up on the next scene.*)

## SCENE 7

*Publisher's office where publisher* HORACE WILLIGER *presides behind a desk. He is a gleaming-eyed dandy. There is the sound of wit in his voice.*

*Beside the desk, in conference, is Horace's chief aide,* JIMMY JONES. JIMMY *is middle-aged and a refugee from High Society. He wears a pince-nez with a black ribbon attached. He is a man of culture who keeps the authors in their place by an air of social superiority.*

JIMMY. Here's the new season's catalogue, Horace. I note that Jonathan Winkelberg, that darling boy, is no longer one of our offerings to the reading public.

HORACE. Good God, Jimmy, he's given us more trouble than our entire list of egomaniacal scribblers. Insulted every critic in town—including the one on *Women's Wear*. Had fist fights with every bookstore owner. He steals liquor, umbrellas, tablespoons, and practices rape on the side. Distinctly not a feather in the cap of Horace Williger and Company. (ALICE CONNOLLY, *a shapely woman in her thirties, enters.*)

ALICE. Our Mr. Winkelberg is here.

HORACE. I'm not in. And not expected till doomsday.

ALICE. I'm sorry, Mr. Williger. Somebody else will have to tell him. At the moment, the waiting room isn't safe for an honest working girl. (WINKELBERG *appears.*)

POET (*accusingly*). An honest working girl who shows her lovely legs to their stocking tops, wears no brassière and reeks lewdly of perfume. (*Pensively*) I do not understand why an advertised product is indignant with a customer.

ALICE (*smiling*). Really—he's out of the Stone Age.

POET (*grinning after her as she starts out*). Drop into my cave sometime, O lady of mincing indecencies. (*He bows.*)

HORACE. After this, would you mind not coming into my office until you are sent for? I'm running a business, Jonathan, and not a Greenwich Village basement dive.

POET (*haughtily*). I am glad to hear you are running a business, Mr. Horace Williger. Your failure to sell more than thirty-six copies of my last volume of poems puts a strain on my faith in you as a businessman. (*He smiles condescendingly.*) However, I am willing to let bygones be bygones. (*He has opened his bulging brief case and removed a cardboard box. He covers it and speaks lovingly.*) Here is the new Jonathan Winkelberg book of ninety-nine poems entitled, *Microscopic Somersaults.* (*He pats the manuscript.*) The next time I see you, little poems, you'll be wearing the fancy dress of print. (*To* HORACE) You will please make out a check for five hundred dollars as advance royalties.

HORACE (*quietly*). I am not publishing your next book, Jonathan.

POET (*softly*). What? (*He stares for a moment.*) How can you decide not to publish a book you haven't even read?

HORACE. Very easily—your behavior is embarrassing to us as your publishers.

POET (*angrily*). You are not publishing my behavior, you are publishing only my poems.

HORACE. Unfortunately, we have also to sell them. You insult and alienate every human being who comes within earshot. And what's unforgivable—you're gauche about it.

POET. Yes, I know I am not well dressed enough to be a wit, so I must be regarded as something that rhymes with that word. (*He smiles with sudden gentleness.*) I'm willing to accept an advance of two hundred and fifty dollars.

HORACE. I'm very sorry, Jonathan. I can't afford to be associated with an author who insists on making every critic and book store owner in the city an active enemy.

POET (*quietly*). I am willing to accept one hundred dollars.

HORACE. There are other publishers, Jonathan. You are free to try them. (TONY RIGGS, *the flossy literary critic, enters.*)

JIMMY (*effusively*). Tony Riggs! My favorite critic! Welcome back!

HORACE (*beaming*). Hello, Tony. How was Bermuda?

TONY. Delicious—Saks Fifth Avenue primitive—

POET (*grimly*). Mr. Anthony Riggs, permit me to introduce myself. I am Jonathan Winkelberg, whom you have been maliciously attacking for five years.

TONY (*coolly*). Is it only that long since you graced the literary world, Mr. Winkelberg?

POET (*grimly*). It is exactly five years and two months since my work aroused your infantile displeasure!

TONY (*to* HORACE). Good Lord, Horace, you should keep him on a leash.

HORACE (*grimly, to* WINKELBERG). Will you wait in my outer office—

POET (*glaring at* TONY). This man has taken the bread and butter out of my mouth—and I intend to be avenged!

TONY. You might try avenging yourself by writing poetry that wasn't pure bilge.

POET (*leering*). Poetry such as Emanuel Stampanato writes—shall we say? (*He imitates Tony's flossy tones as he quotes.*) "Emanuel Stampanato whose poetry glows with phosphorescent despair." (*He sneers.*) Oh, how little Manny glows! (*He stares at* TONY *and continues fiercely.*) My worst poem is twenty times better than Mr. Stampanato's best one. But, of course, the only way I could convince you of that is by going to bed with you—on Mr. Stampanato's night off.

TONY (*in a fury—but cold*). You filthy Greenwich Village scarecrow—

HORACE (*on his feet*). By God, Winkelberg, I ought to knock your block off!

POET (*loudly*). Come on and try—Mister!

TONY (*fiercely*). I hold you responsible for this, Horace! (*He starts out.*)

HORACE (*at* TONY's *side*). Just a minute, Tony. (*To* JIMMY) Go with Tony, Jimmy. (*To* TONY, *pleading*) As a favor—please wait till I straighten this bastard out—Please wait, Tony. (TONY *and* JIMMY *exit.* HORACE *looks grimly at* WINKELBERG. *He speaks tensely and quietly.*) You hopeless ape. Somebody ought to really take you apart! Attacking the most influential literary critic in the country. Now, listen to me, Winkelberg—you're going to apologize to Mr. Riggs. You owe that much to me, if not to yourself. He can kill our whole spring list—every damn book we publish. (WINKELBERG *stands motionless and silent. He smokes his reeking pipe as he listens.*) Wait, Johnny—All right, I'll make a deal with you. Apologize to Tony Riggs—right here and now—and I'll publish your new book of poems—this spring.

POET (*quietly*). Cross your heart?

HORACE. Word of honor. (*Eagerly*) Now do this—for both of us, Johnny.

POET. You'll give me an advance, too?

HORACE. Two hundred and fifty dollars. (*He sits down and starts writing.*) I'll make out the check—myself.

POET. All right. (*He sighs.*)

HORACE (*quickly into phone*). Hello, Bee—tell Jimmy to bring Mr. Riggs in—at once. (*He hangs up.*) By God, Johnny—your apologizing to Tony Riggs revives my faith in you—as a human being—as well as a poet. (RIGGS *and* JIMMY *enter.*) Come in. Glad you didn't run off, Tony—as you had every right to do. Mr. Winkelberg has something to say to you. (*To* WINKELBERG *who stands silently staring.*) Go ahead, Jonathan. (*He frowns at the silent poet.*) You said you had something to say to Mr. Riggs, Johnny. Go ahead, say it. (*He adds cajolingly.*) Oh, come on now, Johnny. It isn't as hard as all that. (*He smiles winningly.*) A gentleman can make—as well as receive—an apology.

POET (*slowly*). On thinking the matter over, Mr. Williger, the only apology I can make is for allowing myself to be disturbed for five years by the mincing little boos of a ludicrous homosexual like Anthony Riggs. Mr. Riggs is a tin can tied to the tail of art. An empty, stinking tin can. (*His voice crying out of the darkness.*) I apologize to nobody! To nobody! (WINKELBERG *appears at one side of the stage. He is alone. He stands with the lights on him. He grins and removes his bottle from his coat and takes a long swig. Grinning aloft*) No hits. No runs. No errors. But whose, Mr. Heavenly Bones? Spare me your pious answers. I had a bellyfull of them—when I had a belly. (*He looks around at the darkness. The sound of a harmonica playing a tune is heard faintly. It grows louder as he talks.*) Onward, ever onward. I think it was around this time—under the administration of President Herbert Hoover, the great Engineer—that I decided to devote myself seriously to drinking, an ambitious career for a citizen devoid of mazuma. It was a time whimsically called The Depression—to distinguish it from the days of joyous bloodshed and happy massacres to come. Yes, sirree, I was one of the pioneers in that good old depression —(*He raises his bottle and toasts it gleefully.*)

Hail, little bottle, friend and wizard,
Paint me a rainbow on my gizzard.
Nice little bottle, help me keep
My bruised rump on the rubbish heap."

(WINKELBERG *vanishes and the stage lights come up on the next scene.*)

## SCENE 8

*A ten-cent flophouse. A bare, dimly lit room. Three kitchen chairs and a flat table are the furnishings. A window is at the back.*

*It rains. Rain bubbles on the window. Sitting at the table at one end of the room is a listless monitor of the bums. He is named* LARSEN.

*Three guests occupy kitchen chairs. They are* KENTUCK, CORKY *and* MIKE. *They doze . . .*

*Standing near the window is a ragged figure. His name is* TOM. *He plays a mouth organ. Its tinny music keeps going . . .*

*Three men are sleeping on the floor. Their feet rest on a rope that reaches across the room to the leg of Larsen's table. A pull at the rope can waken the guests. One of the three on the floor is an old man with a bearded face. His name is* BRUNO BENZINGER. *He coughs and turns in fevered sleep. His noisy slumber awakens the man next to him. This is a plump character called* BOBBY.

*The figures are shadowy lumps of clothes.*

KENTUCK *gets out of his chair, squats on the floor and starts shooting craps. It is a solo game between* KENTUCK *and Lady Luck.* CORKY *opens his eyes and speaks to the harmonica player.*

CORKY. You know "Shine on Harvest Moon"? (*The soft tinny music continues unchanged.*)

KENTUCK (*quietly to a nonexistent partner*). Come on, big boy, you're faded. (*He shakes and rolls out the dice. He beams.*) Sev-own! I win! (*He shakes the dice again and addresses them.*) Stay hot, babies! (BRUNO *wakes up with a coughing fit. The plump* BOBBY *beside him wakes up.*)

BOBBY (*calling*). Hey, Larsen! There's a fella sick. (LARSEN *walks over and stares down at the cougher.*)

LARSEN (*to the cougher*). You got a cold? (BRUNO *coughs and chokes.*) What the hell. It's worse outside.

BOBBY. Hey, Larsen, you want your fortune told?

LARSEN. Some other time.

BOBBY. The way you can tell the future is you work out first what sex it is. For example, the nort' pole is female. The same for the Western Hemisphere.

LARSEN. Some other time . . . (*He walks away to his table.*)

KENTUCK (*with his dice*). Come on—sev-own! Five and a two! Kiss me, babies! (*He rolls out the dice.*)

WINKELBERG *appears. He has been standing in the dark near Larsen's table. He is drunk. He sways a bit.*

POET (*to* LARSEN). Two fellas were shipwrecked in a rowboat. Eleven days without sustenance. Finally the first fella yelled, "Land over there!" The other fella says, "That ain't land, matey. That's the horizon." And the first fella says, "Pull for that. It's better than nothin'." (*He sways and chuckles.*)

LARSEN. You back again?

POET (*aloofly*). Yes, Hotel Horizon . . . (*He takes a swig.*) I am peddling Alcoholics Victorious—

LARSEN. A dime in advance. You vacate at 6 A.M.

POET (*dropping two coins on the table*). Here you are, Baron Rothschild . . . I note with some surprise that the cockroaches have not loaded your chateau on their backs and made off with it. (*He looks around at the bums.*) The poet's ivory tower. (*He moves toward the men. There is one empty piece of blanket on the floor. He takes a swig.*) Come on, little dream . . .

CORKY. Hey, you'll drop it! Gimme. I'll hold the bottle for you. (WINKELBERG *sneers at this and puts the bottle back in his pocket.*) You sonofabitch.

POET (*coldly*). Are the vermin still playing tag on your glazed hide?

BOBBY (*moodily*). I see a dame with big tits—All mine.

POET (*as he lowers himself to the blanket*). The Kingdom of scarecrows . . .

CORKY. Hey, pal. Gimme a drink. I gotta have a drink.

POET (*taking a swig*). This passport is not transferable.

KENTUCK (*softly to his dice*). Get hot, babies! Come on—sev-own! (POET *takes a drink*.)

CORKY (*pleading*). I gotta have a drink. Listen, pal, if I don't get a drink I start shrinking . . . I get smaller and smaller . . . I get small as a bug . . . Gimme a drink. Oh, brother, gimme something or I'm a bug . . . I'm a bug . . .

BOBBY (*dreamily*). Oh, Mama, I'll hide in them big tits . . .

KENTUCK. Come on, babies . . . be nice to me . . .

CORKY (*whimpering*). Don't nobody step on me . . . I'm right here . . . Don't nobody step on me . . . I'm crawlin' around . . .

POET. The rats chatter at the bottom of the night—(*The third chair occupant wakes. He is a sailor in a black turtle neck sweater—a hard and tough man. His name is* MIKE*—and he is the same actor who was Riggs, Enright, O'Brien, Schulte.*)

MIKE (*hoarsely*). Hey bo'sun . . . where's the bo'sun? (*He scowls at the room.*) Gimme a drink, somebody.

KENTUCK (*gleefully*). Five and a two—I win! Five passes in a row! I win.

BRUNO (*sitting up—his voice fevered and loud*). I'm dyin'. I'm gonna be dead soon. I wanna speak to somebody. I'm dyin' . . . I wanna make a will before I'm dead.

BOBBY. Jesus, he's gonna roll up his eyes. Look . . . look, he's rollin' 'em up already!

POET (*softly to the dying man*). The painting will fall out of the frame . . .

BRUNO. I don't wanna die without a will . . .

POET (*he has removed paper and pencil from his brief case.* SAILOR MIKE *stares at the two*). Proceed with your last testament. I'll write it out for you—(*He uses the brief case as a desk.*) What's your name?

BRUNO (*confused*). My name?

POET. Your real name, please—

BRUNO. Bruno—

POET. Last name.

BRUNO (*softly*). Bruno Benzinger . . . Bruno Benzinger . . .

POET (*talking as he writes the words*). I, Bruno Benzinger, being of sound mind and expecting soon to depart this happy vale, do hereby distribute my earthly riches as follows. (*He looks at the staring* BRUNO *who is still whispering his own name.*) What is the nature of the fortune you are leaving behind, Mr. Bruno Benzinger?

BRUNO. My shoes. They're good shoes—

POET. One pair of bootsies—

BRUNO. Almost new—

POET. Who is the lucky beneficiary?

BRUNO (*coughing*). My son. Sam Benzinger. For Sam.

POET (*as he writes*). I do hereby bequeath one pair of shoes, almost new, to my son, Sam Benzinger, hoping they will keep him neatly shod on his little journey to nowhere.

BRUNO. I wanna leave him my money, too. (SAILOR MIKE *and* CORKY *lean forward eagerly.*)

POET. Any particular sum?

BRUNO. Ten dollars. Under the mattress. For my son, Sam. Ten dollars—under the mattress. (BRUNO *coughs and sinks back feverishly on his blanket.* MIKE, CORKY, *and* BOBBY *get to their feet and move ominously toward* BRUNO.)

POET (*as he writes*). And I do hereby bequeath to my aforesaid beloved son, Sam, ten simoleons—

MIKE (*hoarsely*). Get out!

CORKY. For God's sake—fifty-fifty . . .

BOBBY. Yeh! Yeh! We're partners . . . (*They move toward the coughing man.*)

MIKE (*grimly*). Lay off! (MIKE'S *cry stops them. He frightens them.* MIKE *lunges at the dying man, grabs the pallet, jerks it upwards and rolls* BRUNO *off it.* MIKE *drops to the floor and searches on hands and knees. He cries menacingly*) Where's the dough? Some stinker grabbed it . . . You! (*He glares at* WINKELBERG. *The scene dims to the two men. The harmonica continues faintly.*) The dough . . . gimme the dough . . .

POET. All I got is nothing. (MIKE *starts feverishly searching the pockets of the coughing* BRUNO. *Action freezes.*) Well, well—if it ain't His Lethal Nibs, the Sailor who bumped me off. So this is where we first met! I'd clean forgotten. But you're not a new face, Mister Sailor. I've seen you before—the Face that doesn't like me. My papa wore it first. The Know It All Face. The Kick Your Teeth In Face. The Go Gazump Yourself Face. The Dirty Dog Face of The World—that barked me down the cinder patch. And now, little face, you've come to roost on a sailor's neck—(MIKE *is getting to his feet as* WINKELBERG *adds softly*) Welcome again— (MIKE *seizes* WINKELBERG *as action unfreezes.*)

MIKE. You junkie bastard, you grabbed it!

POET (*drunkenly grinning in the sailor's grip*). I do not admire your face. (WINKELBERG *falls to the floor.* MIKE *pulls a gun out of his pocket.*)

MIKE (*standing over the crouching* POET). Where is it? Come on, or I'll blow yer brains out. I'll spill your guts—

POET (*softly to the pointed gun*). Not yet, O bewildered sailor—not yet. (*He slumps drunkenly on the floor.* MIKE *stands motionless. The other figures are motionless. The harmonica player plays on. The rain beats on the window. Nothing moves. Nothing makes any sound. Then the stage begins slowly to darken.*

## ACT TWO

### Scene 1

*A street in Greenwich Village at midnight. One end of it is in shadow. At this end, a figure can be seen lying on the pavement near the curbing. Its head is partly pillowed on a hydrant. It is* WINKELBERG *in his old army overcoat. His bulging brief case is in the street. He is drunk and out.*

*A woman walks slowly out of the dark end of the street. She is young and dressed for summertime. Her movements are vague. She is a* STREETWALKER. *She stops and starts making up her lips. She has a childlike manner. She is a whore with a polite and kindly soul. She takes her "shopping" position in the middle of the street.*

*She looks over and sees the drunk with his head on the hydrant. Her heart is touched. She goes to the drunk. His hat lies in the gutter. She retrieves the hat and puts it on his head. She picks his brief case up from the gutter and puts it next to him. She looks at him sadly. Then she returns to her position.*

MIKE, *the sailor, comes out of the lighted end of the street. He wears his black turtle neck sweater—no coat. He walks with easy grace. He comes toward the* STREETWALKER. *She smiles at him.*

STREETWALKER. Hello, mister.

MIKE (*studying her*). Hello, kid.

STREETWALKER. It's a nice night.

MIKE. How's your health?

STREETWALKER. I'm all right.

MIKE. How much?

STREETWALKER. Two dollars.

MIKE. You gotta room?

STREETWALKER. Yes. (*They start walking toward the shadows.*)

MIKE. What's your name?

STREETWALKER. Dorothy.

MIKE. My name's Mike. Ya like sailors?

STREETWALKER. Yes . . . (MIKE *has stopped. He stands scowling at the comatose drunk.*)

MIKE. I seen that bum somewhere before—

STREETWALKER (*staring at* WINKELBERG). He ain't a bum.

MIKE. Ya know him?

STREETWALKER. He talked to me once—

MIKE (*grinning at her*). Just talked, huh?

STREETWALKER. Yes. That's all. It was snowin', and he stopped and talked to me.

MIKE. Yeh? What about?

STREETWALKER. About the snow fallin'—

MIKE (*scowling again at the figure in the gutter*). There's somethin' about this bum gets me sore.

STREETWALKER (*softly*). You comin' along, Mike?

MIKE (*taking her arm and smiling at her*). Sure. You're a nice, soft kid. (*They walk off. Two women enter the lighted street end. One is* LOUISE, *now the same age as when seen in the Café of the Mildewed Spoon. She is dressed in a flamboyant cape, turban, earrings. With her is a pretty girl in a black velvet suit, white Eton collar and boyish haircut. She is* BILLIE.)

LOUISE (*pausing*). Cigarette?

BILLIE. Yes, Louise. (BILLIE *fishes a cigarette and lighter out of her bag.*)

LOUISE. A rotten party. That social small talk drives me crazy!

BILLIE (*jealously*). You seemed to be having a lovely time, Miss Larnigan.

LOUISE. Lovely time, my ass. Those overdressed wives still waving their boobies at the world—with no takers. And their husbands! Half mad with the look of a new behind! My God, married people oughtn't to show themselves in public!

BILLIE (*looking off*). There's a taxi—

LOUISE. No. I've got to find Jonathan. Tony said he saw him lying somewhere in Bleeker Street. Imagine him turning into a bum! We almost got married.

BILLIE (*clinging to her*). Don't say that.

LOUISE. Twenty years ago. In Chicago. Before I went to Paris—

BILLIE. Did you love him?

LOUISE. How the hell do I know! Anything can happen to you when you're young—measles, smallpox, love. (*She walks to the hydrant.*) Well, good God! There he is!

BILLIE (*shuddering as she looks*). He's awful.

LOUISE. Sweet God—he was young and pretty—and with such an aristocratic look. (*She shakes* WINKELBERG's *shoulder.*) Johnny—(*He opens his eyes.*)

POET (*hoarsely*). O.K., Mister Officer—(*He groans.*) No rush.

LOUISE. Johnny! (*He looks up.*) Remember me?

POET (*in a half croak, as he stares at her*). The Virgin of East Chicago Avenue.

LOUISE. Louise Larnigan . . .

POET (*hoarsely*). It was a winter night. Snow—over the housetops, up and down the sky—

LOUISE (*helping him*). Come on, upsy daisy! Where do you live?

POET (*on his feet, his eyes closing*). I live in a boob-packed paradise of platitudes. (*He opens his eyes and looks around.*) What year is this—

LOUISE (*holding him erect*). Come on, before the dogcatcher spots you. (*She picks up his brief case.*) I remember this, too.

POET (*taking the case*). My little bag of toys . . . (*He grins wearily at her.*) Miss Louise Larnigan of Chicago looks a trifle mutilated.

LOUISE. Look who's talking. You're dirty as a pig.

POET. I am a tomb of slime . . .

LOUISE. All right, Tomb of Slime, what's your address?

POET. Potter's Field. (*He sways.*)

LOUISE (*holding him*). Stay on your feet, beauty boy.

POET (*as he sinks to the curb*). 'Tis better this way. (*He props himself against the hydrant.*)

BILLIE (*tensely*). Louise—let him be—

LOUISE. You can't leave a headful of beautiful words in the gutter.

BILLIE. I'm going home.

LOUISE. Go on!

POET (*hoarsely*). Do you care to join me in my love seat? (LOUISE *sits down beside him.* BILLIE *watches tensely.*)

LOUISE. Goddammit, you should have come to Paris. Instead of sticking to this dog of a town.

POET. The flea sticks to the dog . . .

LOUISE. But how the hell coulda brilliant man like you turn into this?

POET. It was not difficult. (*Searching his pockets*) My pipe! Some pickpocket stole my pipe! (*He finds his pipe, fills and lights it as they talk.*)

BILLIE. Louise!

LOUISE (*moodily*). Everything changes . . . rots . . . dies—Even in Paris. I turned into a dress designer. Invented a new bathing suit. Shows everything but the Magna Carta. I was a rich bitch for ten years. Then blew everything at Monte Carlo—because I wanted to be richer . . . My God, Johnny, I never thought you'd give up writing poetry—

POET. I did not give up writing poetry. The world gave up reading it.

LOUISE. Why turn into a drunken bum?

POET. Why not? (*He closes his eyes.*)

LOUISE (*shaking him*). Wake up!

POET (*suddenly loquacious*). In reply to your indignant question, may I state I had the chance either of destroying myself or destroying my poetry. Yes, sirree. Society says "Grow up. Put away your toys. Sit in an office. Become a respectable shadow cast by yesterday. Dream of mazuma. And forget everything else. Forget the little old land of enchantment. Forget, little moonbeam chaser, forget! Forget the bright words! Forget." Excellent advice. (*He makes a face.*) I ignored it.

BILLIE. I'm going! I'm going away!

LOUISE. All right. Get on your green pony and beat it!

BILLIE. You said you wouldn't touch a man! You swore! You promised! You're a liar! A liar! A liar! (*She runs off.*)

LOUISE. They get a haircut and they think they own you. Come on, on your feet, Lord Tennyson.

POET (*grinning*). So—with the assistance of little ladies on green ponies—you are still a virgin. (*He sighs.*)

LOUISE. You silly bastard, you turned me down.

POET. Did I? (*He stares at her.*) On second thought, permit me to change my mind. Give me a kiss.

LOUISE. No kisses, Johnny. (*He puts an arm around her.*) Forget that.

POET (*half-conscious as she removes his arm*). On top of a hill. We will lie like a tangle of roots under an apple tree. (*He smiles wearily at her.*) Drop a little coin in my heart, baby . . .

LOUISE (*rising*). Oh my God, Casanova. (*She raises him. He stands silent. She picks up his brief case and hat, and finally starts him moving. During this she talks. He remains silent, swaying, slipping into near dormancy.*) You don't need a bedfellow. You need a dry cleaner.

And somebody who believes in you, who knows who you are . . . I gave up art long ago. I sat in an office. And forgot. My God, the things I forgot. But you didn't, Johnny. Sweet Johnny, you didn't forget—the bright words.

THE STAGE DARKENS

## Scene 2

*The den of Horace Williger's town house. It is a small room. A large window is at the rear. A treetop is visible. The garden is six feet below. The den's furnishings include a large Chandler screen near the rear wall.*

*The door at the side opens. A flamboyantly gowned* LOUISE *and tuxedo-wearing* HORACE WILLIGER *enter.*

LOUISE. We have plenty of time, Horace. Madam Lemski won't cut loose on the piano for hours. So don't be fidgety.

HORACE. Louise, I have a house full of important guests—who are certain to make off with half my first editions—if neglected.

LOUISE. The hell with your guests. We're going to talk business: *Winkelberg.*

HORACE. Good heavens, Louise—you're behaving like a mobster.

LOUISE. Your sister adores Jonathan's poetry.

HORACE. A madwoman. Charming, but sweet bells jangling out of tune.

LOUISE. She's willing to put another twenty thousand into your business.

HORACE. If I publish this literary hooligan—Winkelberg! Again? Good God, I'm not a public official to be bribed! Never! (*He sighs.*) Always a weak word. How much?

LOUISE. Twenty thousand—

HORACE. My character's gone. (*He takes her hand.*) If only there were a bit of sex involved. Something to bind me to the horrid thing I'm doing. Are you sure you're—?

LOUISE (*smiling*). Quite sure.

HORACE. We're publishing a book—*The Couch of Sappho.* A fine piece of analysis. I'll send you a copy. Oh God, that idiotic sister of mine. What a man will do for money—I mean a man of integrity!

LOUISE. Darling, Johnny's changed. I've taken him under my wing. It's a new Winkelberg—totally remodeled. (*A good-looking woman in a dinner gown, with bare arms, enters.*) Leila Case! Darling! Horace, this is Miss Leila Case of *Review Magazine*. Does all their literary coverage.

HORACE. Very pleased you're here, Miss Case. Madam Lemski is a magnificent artist. We're bringing out her memoirs for Christmas.

LOUISE. She doesn't give a damn about music—or fat piano players.

HORACE. She had sixty-two lovers—including Kaiser Wilhelm. A remarkable psychological document.

LEILA. Psychology is such fun.

LOUISE. Leila's here to get a story of Winkelberg's return to the world of letters under your banner—so stop waving Madam Lemski at her. (*The* BUTLER *enters, carrying a bottle and glasses on a tray.*)

HORACE. A great poet, Winkelberg. The mantle of Verlaine and Rimbaud—(*To* LOUISE) Let me know when my sister arrives. We'll settle everything after the concert. (*To* LEILA) Forgive me for running off. I must go harass my guests a bit. (*To* LOUISE) I adore you. Love you madly. See you after the concert. (*He exits.*)

LEILA (*coolly*). What's all that, Louise?

LOUISE. Habit pattern. (*To* BUTLER) Leave the bottle here, Junior, and save your legs.

BUTLER. As you wish, madam. (*He exits.* LOUISE *pours two drinks.*)

LEILA. Rotten of you, Louise, throwing a poet at me. They're such a hellish waste of time—with their damn baby talk about how high is up.

LOUISE. Jonathan's different, sweet. He's full of ginger. (*She caresses* LEILA'*s shoulder.*) And, darling, please—don't stab him. (WINKELBERG *enters. He is in a cutaway and striped pants. He wears a silk hat, which he leaves on—and with the angle of which he becomes more and more preoccupied during the scene.*) Johnny! It fits beautifully. Just in time. I want you to meet Leila Case—my friend—and magazine writer. (WINKELBERG *bows slowly.*)

LEILA (*staring at him*). So you're Jonathan Winkelberg.

POET. In Christmas wrapping. Are you going to use that bottle?

LEILA. Not at the moment. (*He heads for it.*) Louise has told me so much about you, Mr. Winkelberg.

POET (*his drink poured*). A voice in the wilderness.

LOUISE. You can take off your hat, Johnny.

POET. Why? It came with the ensemble. Has Madam Lemski started her assault yet?

LEILA. Don't you like piano playing, Mr. Winkelberg?

POET (*firmly*). I am opposed to music. (LEILA *has poured herself a drink.* WINKELBERG *again pounces on the bottle, and fills a small tumbler.*)

LOUISE. Leila is going to interview you for a special magazine article.

POET (*bowing*). Enchanté.

LEILA (*taking out pencil and pad from her purse*). What have you got against music, Mr. Winkelberg?

POET (*drinks*). You may quote me as saying music is a hearing aid for the phallus.

LEILA. Even pure music?

POET. For pure phalluses.

LOUISE. Johnny, please—a little higher-minded. Leila writes for a family publication.

POET. The phallus is the basis of the family. But I apologize to Miss Case.

LEILA Thank you. (*To* LOUISE) No damage done, darling. (*To* WINKELBERG) You'll forgive me, I hope, but I haven't read you. What sort of poetry do you write?

POET. I fish with a cobweb over an invisible stream.

LEILA. Like Simple Simon.

POET (*as he drinks from the bottle*). To simpletons—yes.

LOUISE. Johnny!

LEILA. Don't worry, darling—I always throw the last punch. (*To* WINKELBERG) What do you think of T. S. Eliot?

POET. Mr. Eliot has a talent for making dullness fashionable.

LEILA (*as she writes*). And Carl Sandburg?

POET. A moonstruck bricklayer.

LEILA. And Keats?

POET (*as he drinks from the bottle*). Sweet bleats for garden-club meets.

LOUISE. Johnny, do stop sucking on that bottle. It'll distract you.

LEILA. He's terribly concentrated, Louise.

POET. Thank you.

LEILA. Shall we turn to prose, Mr. Winkelberg?

POET (*bowing*). By all means.

LEILA. What do you think of Henry James?

POET. I am not interested in constipation or any of its struggles.

LEILA. Not tiring you, am I?

POET (*beaming*). I am not even breathing hard.

LOUISE. I am.

LEILA. What have you got to say about William Faulkner?

POET (*in Southern dialect*). Mistah Faulkner makes people seem smarter than they are—just by pretendin' to understand him. But for me, ma'am, Mr. Faulkner is just a plain everyday bad writer.

LEILA. Isn't it a bit odd for a bad writer to become so famous?

POET. Fame is not even a symptom of merit.

LEILA. Someone wrote—failure takes refuge in epigrams.

POET. And success in clichés!

LOUISE. Johnny, try counting ten before your next answer.

LEILA (*smiling at* LOUISE). No help from the referee. (POET *steals spoon.*)

LOUISE. Hey, Raffles, may we hear what you think of Ernest Hemingway?

POET. An amateur.

LEILA. Just what do you consider an amateur?

POET. An amateur is a person who can't jump off a roof correctly.

LEILA. What a clever boy! With America out of it, are there any English writers worthy of your approval?

POET. Not that I can recall at the moment. The English literary mind is obscured by a fig leaf. Are you writing this down?

LEILA. Like mad.

POET. You may add that the English stiff upper lip about sex is a matter of misplaced firmness.

LOUISE. Time out, Leila. My boy needs a kick in the pants.

LEILA. Darling, don't interrupt our little massacre. (*To* WINKELBERG) Does your disdain for English writers include Shakespeare?

POET. Four nights ago I came away from *Richard III* wishing that Mr. Shakespeare had been more successful as a poacher. Does that cover it?

LEILA. Perfectly. (*She rises.*) Mr. Winkelberg disapproves of everybody except Mr. Winkelberg.

LOUISE. Come now, Leila—a poet is entitled to his opinions. They're about all he owns.

LEILA. Poor boy. (*She smiles at* WINKELBERG.) You're a very honest man, Mr. Winkelberg. A little nerve-wracking, but honest.

POET. What are you doing tonight, Miss Critic?

LEILA. Retiring to my cold little bed.

POET (*as he kisses her hand and wrist*). I would like to knit you a sweater of kisses.

LEILA. Never wear them. (*To* LOUISE) Don't worry, darling. I'll launder our little interview before using.

LOUISE. You're a dear girl.

LEILA. I have to tear myself away. Editorial powwow. You'll call me tomorrow?

LOUISE (*gently*). Of course. I'm free in the evening.

LEILA. Wonderful. I'll cook a nice steak for you—with huge mushrooms. The way you like it.

LOUISE. Sweet Leila. (*She walks* LEILA *to the door.*) Good night—and thanks.

LEILA. Good night, baby—till tomorrow. (LEILA *exits.*)

POET (*morosely*). One man left on base.

LOUISE (*returning*). What a little bundle of charm you are! You've got an ego like a dentist's drill! Do you have to insult everybody and everything from Pole to Pole?

POET (*firmly*). A man has to be fair-minded.

LOUISE (*laughing*). Forgive me, Johnny. I wouldn't have you any different. The only article of furniture you own is a throne. Stay on it. I adore you.

POET. Kindly adore me less indignantly. (LOUISE *drinks as a startling figure enters. It is* MADAME WILLIGER, *a woman in her thirties—dressed in a vivid sari. Her hair is piled on her head like a little black pagoda. She has a faraway manner, an expressionless voice.*)

LOUISE. Miss Williger! Your brother was inquiring about you. What a sweet outfit! Utterly chic!

MADAME WILLIGER. Has the piano playing started?

LOUISE. Not yet. You're quite in time.

MADAME WILLIGER. I was hoping it was over . . . I dislike occidental music.

LOUISE. Madam Williger, Jonathan Winkelberg, the poet.

POET (*bowing*). Enchanté.

MADAME WILLIGER. I have read your poems. So purifying. I was able to bathe in them.

POET (*bowing*). They float.

MADAME WILLIGER (*moodily*). Jonathan Winkelberg. The name is a perfect circle.

POET (*modestly*). I'm proud to hear it.

MADAME WILLIGER. You must reveal yourself to me. What sort of a poet are you?

POET. I am the sort of a poet who rides to work on a watermelon seed.

MADAME WILLIGER (*moved*). You speak like the *Ramayana*.

LOUISE. I've discussed your wonderful idea with your brother, Madame Williger. He's terribly eager to publish Jonathan Winkelberg.

MADAME WILLIGER. He should be. Such a relief from those deplorable books he puts out—all dealing with the crudities of sex. That is the failure of the Western world—its worship of the animal.

LOUISE. We are given to that.

POET (*a bit drunken but precise*). Your neck is like a white spear.

MADAME WILLIGER (*intensely*). The West needs you. We are covered with vulgarities. Only the poets can cleanse us.

LOUISE (*to* MADAME WILLIGER). I envy you, my dear—restoring a poet to the world. Such a rare and lovely thing to be able to do.

MADAME WILLIGER. I would like very much to speak to the poet alone.

LOUISE (*a mite tipsy*). Oh, yes, of course. And I'll go fetch brother Horace—and we'll relaunch Jonathan on the high seas. This sort of thing makes a girl feel like Napoleon. (*She exits. The Chopin piano piece fills the room for a moment as* WINKELBERG *downs a stiff drink. Then he stares at* MADAME WILLIGER *vis-à-vis.*)

POET. To what tribe do you belong?

MADAME WILLIGER. We are a disciple of Zen Buddha.

POET (*eyeing her fetching contour and smiling*). Zen Buddha is a very lucky fellow. (*He offers a bow.*)

MADAME WILLIGER. We have, however, succeeded in wedding Zen Buddha to the Cabala of the Hebrews. The combination increases the vibrations. And purifies them.

POET (*pouring a glass*). Have one?

MADAME WILLIGER. We never touch intoxicants.

POET (*a little drunken now*). Ah—the Wisdom of the East!

MADAME WILLIGER. Why do you stare at me? Am I strange?

POET (*wistfully*). Your hair is like a tortured midnight.

MADAME WILLIGER (*with a sigh*). I am a widow. I was married to a paint manufacturer who trifled stupidly with the Unknown.

POET. Husbands will always trifle with something.

MADAME WILLIGER. He was killed by Typhon, the evil spirit of the Egyptians described in the *Grimoire* of Honorius. I resumed my maiden name—and my maidenhood.

POET. Your face is whiter than a seraph's hat.

MADAME WILLIGER. Thank you. Do you believe in the Unknown?

POET. I would rather say I do not believe in the Known. (*Sighs.*)

MADAME WILLIGER. We see a man of sorrow. (*She closes her eyes.*) You are a third-vibration man. We would like to teach you the fourth vibration.

POET (*moving closer*). We are ready.

MADAME WILLIGER. Do you believe in the transmigration of souls, Mr. Winkelberg?

POET. In my last incarnation I was an infatuated glowworm exploring a rose named Madame Williger.

MADAME WILLIGER (*smiling*). Ah—the lute of Vishnu. We will be happy to instruct you. (*He steers her by the elbow toward the large screen at the rear of the room.*) Have you ever made contact with the great mysteries?

POET. A number of times. But never enough, O Queen of the Nile.

MADAME WILLIGER (*nearing the screen*). You desire seclusion?

POET. When available—(*He sways.*)

MADAME WILLIGER (*as they vanish behind the screen*). We will have to sit facing each other on the floor—and breathe in unison—(*They are behind the screen. The piano playing ends and an outburst of applause sounds from the adjoining room. The applause grows louder as the door opens.* LOUISE *and* HORACE *enter. Behind them are a couple and several men.*)

HORACE (*entering*). Awfully good in the fortissimo passages, don't you think?

LOUISE (*humoring him*). Divine, divine. (*Firmly*) We're going to settle everything with your sister right now.

HORACE. Strike while the iron's hot, eh?

LOUISE. She's just panting to invest twenty thousand—even more. (*A strangled cry comes from behind the screen.*)

MADAME WILLIGER. No! No!

HORACE (*confused, to* LOUISE). What did you say? (MADAME WILLIGER *rushes out from behind the screen in her underwear, screaming.*)

HORACE (*horrified, taking her to couch*). It's my sister! She's gone mad! I've been waiting for this!

MADAME WILLIGER. Sacrilege. Sacrilege.

HORACE. What happened?

MADAME WILLIGER. Him! Him!

POET (*emerging*). Where did she go? (HORACE *rushes at* WINKELBERG. *The* BUTLER *and guests join in the attack. They grab* WINKELBERG *and drive him toward the window.*)

HORACE. You monster! Throw him out!

POET'S VOICE. My hat—my silk hat—Give me my hat . . . (*The stage darkens . . . And* WINKELBERG *appears—in his old army overcoat, brief case under his arm. He stands in a light and meditatively fills and kindles his corncob as he speaks.*) From that night on I turned my back on High Society—the little flock of beribboned sheep huddled in the twilight of capitalism. Yes sirree—I began to question the blessings of Democracy of which I had not yet tasted a spoonful. And I enrolled in the Chicken Dinner for the Masses, the Communist Revolution. (*He looks aloft.*) O Black Man with your wreath of silver birds, I may have overlooked some enchanted moment among the Reds—

*The next scene becomes visible . . .*

## Scene 3

*A tenement room. A desk and some kitchen chairs are visible.*

JACK CALVIN, *twenty-five years older than when last seen, enters. With him is the* STREETWALKER *of Act Two, Scene 1. She is cheaply dressed. The* POET *looks tenderly at the girl. He remains in the shadows as the light illumines the two arrivals.*

GIRL (*shyly*). I can accomplish a number of duties for the Party, Mister Calvin. Before I took a position as a dishwasher at Newman's Café, I held a position as a typist. For the Owens Novelty Company. Then, to be frank, I was not employed for a time. Two years—or more, maybe.

JACK. I know. I checked. Two arrests for soliciting. (*He looks sternly at her.*) Anything else?

GIRL. No, sir.

JACK. So now you're a dishwasher. Got a union card?

GIRL (*eagerly*). Oh, yes, sir! (*She fishes it out of her purse.*)

JACK (*looking at it*). That entitles you to pay dues for the privilege of bein' exploited and underpaid. (*He scowls at her.*) Unions ain't the answer. (*He starts removing papers from a brief case.*) Now—why do you want to work for the Party?

GIRL. So I can do good for somebody.

JACK. That answer shows you are taking the first step in the revolution, which I call the sentimental step. Which it is necessary to outgrow. Take my case. I used to be a fur thief.

GIRL (*disbelieving*). You were a thief! Oh, no!

JACK. I used to sell the furs and give the money to the needy. This was strictly a sentimental concept of how to solve the economic injustices going on. Eventually I gave up my personal crusade as a fur thief and joined up with a bigger idea—the Communist Party. (JACK *busies himself with his desk papers.* WINKELBERG *stands beside the girl, invisible to her.*)

POET. I remember just how it was. Like this. I watched her in silence

—and love touched my shabby heart. (*He sighs.*) When I was young I lived for love. God was the lifting of a skirt and a woman's thigh was His lightning flash. When I was young I looked for Juliet and Isolde. (*He smiles at the* GIRL.) Now her. She came into my heart like a birdling scratching for a crumb on a winter road. (*Four men enter and take their seats.*)

JACK. Hello, folks. This girl is working for us. She's goin' to do typing.

FIRST COMMUNIST. What's her name?

JACK. I'm giving her a new name. (*To the* GIRL) How's Ellen Jones?

GIRL (*eagerly*). Oh, that's very nice. Thank you.

JACK. Ellen Jones . . . It's a good name. (WINKELBERG *comes to* JACK'S *table—and enters the light of reality. He is no longer invisible—but now a part of a once-lived scene.*)

POET (*busy opening his brief case*). Hello, Jack.

JACK (*looking up*). Hello, Johnny. As soon as the minutes are out of the way—you'll have your chance. (MORRIE, *one of the arrivals, is a noisemaker.*)

MORRIE (*to* WINKELBERG). Get this—we ain't interested in hearin' any cockerei poetry. (*He sneers.*) The moonlight on the factory chiminies. We ain't interested. We got woik to do.

POET (*sneering*). I shall limit my remarks to your subbasement level, Mister Morrie.

JACK. No personalities, please. (*The light on the men grows dim, as if they had slipped to the back of* WINKELBERG'S *mind.* JACK CALVIN'S VOICE *remains faintly audible as he addresses the meeting.*)

JACK'S VOICE (*out of the dimness*). Comrades, I want you to hear this following letter I have sent to Mister Newman, care of Newman's Café—Mister Newman, Dear Sir . . . (*Here* JACK'S VOICE *trails off into silence. During it,* WINKELBERG *and* ELLEN *talk, in the light.*)

POET. You kept your word. You came just as you promised you would.

ELLEN. You were right, Mr. Winkelberg. They didn't have any objections.

POET. Naturally not. We both belong here—for the same reasons.

ELLEN (*incredulous*). For the same reasons?

POET (*smiling*). Yes, we have a great deal in common, Ellen Jones.

ELLEN. Oh, how can you say that? I hardly ever read anything.

POET. We have the cruelty of life in common, and the anger of the world.

ELLEN (*staring*). You, too?

POET. Yes . . . It's because we hurt ourselves—and not others. When you hurt others, you become rich and powerful; when you hurt yourself, you become poor and wretched . . .

ELLEN (*staring*). How—how did you hurt yourself—?

POET (*sighing*). I don't know. It was a crime committed by a shadow in a hole.

ELLEN. I used to live in a room opposite a wall. I don't know why —it scared me.

POET. You won't be scared any more. The Party will see to that . . .

ELLEN (*shyly*). Do you believe in Communism, Mr. Winkelberg?

POET. Belief is the noisy partner of hope. (*He smiles at her and, as they talk, the lights begin to come up on the others.*) Your hair is like a friendly smile.

ELLEN. I like to hear you talk.

POET. Why?

ELLEN. Because you are very kind—and you wrote me a poem. Tell it to me again.

POET.

Her eyes are bright as petals after rain,
Her lips tiptoe towards a smile
That only virgins know—

ELLEN (*repeating slowly*).

Her lips tiptoe toward a smile
That only virgins know—

JACK CALVIN *and the others are fully visible again.*

JACK (*continuing his reading of the letter*). "Mister Newman, Dear Sir, we are giving you thirty-six hours to meet our terms after which period we will resort to a more direct approach to the problem—"

MORRIE (*calling out*). Point of order—

JACK. Comrade Morrie has the floor.

MORRIE (*on his feet*). Am I correct in assuming that by a direct approach you mean the use of pickets for Newman's Café?

JACK. That is correct.

MORRIE. Oh . . . then I got a fella comin' who is A-one for this kind of activity. A sailor from the West Coast by the name of Mike . . .

POET (*calling*). Point of order!

MORRIE (*firmly*). Kindly no interruptions till I'm finished. This sailor I'm referrin' to has been prominent in the West Coast situation. Five arrests for beatin' up waterfront finks.

POET (*calling out*). We don't need any pugilistic imports!

MORRIE (*sneering*). No! All we need is poetry! Poems wi' poetry! What are we runnin'—a revolution or a candy store!

POET (*calling out*). Point of order!

MORRIE (*charging on*). I urge we wait for this sailor to take over the Newman Café situation, as head of our picket forces . . .

POET (*loudly*). Point of order!

JACK. You have the floor, Johnny. You can sit down, Morrie. Mr. Winkelberg has the floor.

MORRIE. I ain't through!

JACK (*quietly*). You're through. Proceed, Johnny.

POET (*suddenly eloquent*). I do not know why others are Communists but I'll tell you why I am one. Because there are people who work without hope, who, in the midst of feasting, live on crumbs. Rubbish-heap people who own only the dusty breath in their noses—and nothing more. I respectfully offer myself as a picket on the barricades of Mr. Newman's café. And if I am honored with the task, I assure Comrade Morrie there will be no poetry on my picket sign, but I will proclaim the sins of Mr. Newman's café in simple prose.

*The stage darkens as cries of "Second the Motion," "Now we're talkin'!" and "That's the ticket!" fill the dark.*

## SCENE 4

*The light reveals, slowly, a street of people and stores at night. A tinny phonograph record plays out of a music-store loud-speaker.*

*In front of a façade labeled Newman's Café, two* MEN *are picketing. They walk slowly in a sidewalk circle. One is a tired* FAT MAN. *The other is the* POET, WINKELBERG. *They carry signs on sticks. The Fat Man's sign reads: "Newman's Café Is Unfair to Dishwashers." Winkelberg's sign reads: "Mr. Newman Wants Slaves Not Workers."*

*Two burly looking men stop and regard the pickets. There is menace in their stares.*

*After the pedestrians have gone, the first burly man speaks. He is* BILL. *The other is* LOUIE.

BILL (*to the slowly circling* FAT MAN). Hey, creep. (*The* FAT MAN *stops.* BILL *sneers at him and adds coldly*) Get out o' here. (*The* FAT MAN *looks nervously at his colleague—who continues his slow, aloof circle on the pavement.* BILL *moves nearer to the* FAT MAN *and inquires*) You want your head busted? Drop that crappy sign and get lost. (*The* FAT MAN *stands frightened but undecided.*) You take him, Louie.

(LOUIE *moves to the* FAT MAN *who drops his sign and runs off in panic.* LOUIE *picks up the abandoned sign and tears it in four pieces.* BILL *watches the* POET *who keeps moving aloofly in his slow pavement circle.* (*Quietly*) All right, ya commie rat—get out!

POET (*as he walks*). Are you here in the interests of Democracy? (BILL *and* LOUIE *stand still and glare at him.*)

BILL (*menacingly*). Did you hear what I said—rat?

POET (*still walking, and sneering back*). You have made yourself exquisitely clear, Mister Democracy. (*The two men stand glaring and motionless.* WINKELBERG *raises his voice in defiant announcement, calling above the music.*) Mister Newman's Café is unfair to its kitchen employees. It is also overrun with bugs, rats—and under the protection of thugs and lawless goons. Mister Newman's Café is unfair to—(*The two men move in quickly. One grabs the sign. The other punches* WINKELBERG'S *face.* WINKELBERG *puts up an odd struggle. He clings to his brief case and fights with one hand.* BILL *pulls out a blackjack and whips it across the* POET'S *face several times. The* POET *falls to the pavement and lies huddled and unconscious against the music-blaring store front. The men tear up his sign and hurry off.* ELLEN JONES *comes running up. She drops to the* POET'S *side and tries to revive him.*)

ELLEN (*weeping*). I saw them! Oh, the dirty bastards—the dirty bastards! (*She looks around wildly.*) Somebody help him! Help, somebody! (WINKELBERG *speaks as he lies on the ground. He raises his head and stares at the night. The street scene freezes into immobility.*)

POET. Yes, this is the way it was—the same night leaning over the street like a tipsy madonna. And music like hot ice cream. (*He peers into the dimmed, immobile street scene and elation comes into him.*) But there is something else. Something wonderful. Eyes watching me as if I were a soldier who had fought bravely in their cause, the cause of poverty. (*His elation grows.*) Yes, sirree! There is a sweet dream here, O Black Man. The caress of brotherhood touched my blood on the pavement. They loved me! (*The street comes back into light and activity. There is a chatter from the mob grouped around the fallen man. Papers flutter across the pavement from out of the fallen man's brief case. With a queer cry, the stricken* WINKELBERG *starts crawling clumsily after the papers under the feet of the crowd, wailing:*) My poems! I want my poems! My poems! (*As the* POET *crawls weakly toward the sheets of paper, the crowd begins to laugh. The laughter spreads through all the watchers, roars up . . . Then the scene once more dims down—its music, lights, and laughter fade into a vague background. His voice anguished*) They laughed! I didn't know they had laughed! They laughed! They laughed!

*Laughter as*

THE STAGE DARKENS

## SCENE 5

*A few benches in the park. It is late night.*

ELLEN *and* WINKELBERG *enter. They walk slowly. She holds his arm. A cross of adhesive tape is on his cheek. They sit down in one of the benches.*

ELLEN. It makes me sick how awful people are . . . When they were hitting you, nobody raising a hand to help you. (*She touches his bruised face gently and inquires hopefully*) It doesn't hurt so much now, does it?

POET (*smiling*). Hurts go away.

ELLEN. Why are people so mean? You were on their side—helping them—

POET. They have no side, Ellen. You have to invent one for them. (*He grins at her.*)

ELLEN. It's a little chilly. Would you care to go to a movie? There's one runs all night.

POET. I was there last year.

ELLEN. They change the movie every day.

POET (*smiling at her.*) No, they don't. The entertainment offered is always the same. The movies are a little peppermint heaven where all the platitudes sit like judges on jelly-bean thrones. And only justice reigns. (*He cackles elatedly.*)

ELLEN. I was in front of a judge once. A real one. (*She sighs.*) Not like in the movies. (*The* POET *nods and his eyes watch her with tenderness.* ELLEN *starts to cry as she talks. Her weeping doesn't enter her voice. She talks in an untearful monotone, broken by an occasional sniffle.*) I came to New York from Calava, Michigan. We had a farm there, and a lot of cows. (*She pauses, and wipes her eyes. He sits looking at her in silence. She resumes her monotone as her tears continue.*) It was very peaceful. I used to bring the cows home through the fields in the summertime. (*She pauses. They sit in silence.*) In the winter I went to school with the kids. We used to build a snowman after school . . . (*She pauses.*) I couldn't go back on account of the Judge. The Judge made me write my father a letter saying why I was arrested. Soliciting. I didn't want to. But the Judge said I had to. Otherwise he would send me to jail . . . So I wrote to my father and mother in Calava why I'd been arrested. The Judge said that after I told them the truth why I was arrested I could go back home and start over again—on an honest basis, he said. (*She pauses, weeps in silence. He watches her with a gentle smile. The wound on* WINKELBERG'S *cheek starts seeping through the bandage.* ELLEN *sees it. She wipes his skin carefully as she continues.*) They wouldn't let me come back after they read the letter—my folks. They wrote me just once they never wanted to see me again in Calava . . . (*She weeps.*) Don't you think the Judge was wrong? He was, wasn't he?

POET (*softly*). Justice is an undiscovered continent.

ELLEN. I don't usually cry. I don't know why I should cry now. I'm sorry.

POET (*softly*). Rain is good for the fields of Calava.

ELLEN (*she dries her eyes once more and looks at him*). Why does everything turn out wrong? (MAG *and old* BIRDIE *come into the park and they walk slowly and sit down on a bench together in silence.*)

POET. Luck. It's all a matter of luck.

ELLEN. Were you ever lucky?

POET (*smiling as she cleans his cheek with her handkerchief.*) Yes, once. When I was nineteen I found a dollar, a lone simoleon. I took the little fella to a dice game and made twenty straight passes, and let the bankroll ride each time. Thus I left the gaming table with roughly four million dollars in my pocket. (*He beams at the staring* ELLEN.) I invested the four millions in a building operation. I built a city for poets. In order to live in my city and enjoy its pleasures without cost whatsoever, you had to submit three rejected poems. No other credentials were necessary. (*He chuckles as* ELLEN *smiles at him.*) In my city there was a princess for every poet, and her heart was soft as the night and loyal as the sun. During the day, children played around the silver fountains and the summer sky lay like a mandarin coat over the rooftops. At night exquisite music sounded and the poets walked in sleeping gardens and recited their poems to their princesses leaning out of moon-painted windows. (*He stands up and holds out a hand.*) Come on.

ELLEN (*rising*). Where?

POET. We'll walk in my city. (*He takes her arm. They pass* MAG *and* BIRDIE. *The* POET *stops and bows to them.*) Good night, Princesses. (*He walks on.*)

THE STAGE DARKENS

## SCENE 6

*A dance rehearsal hall. A shirtsleeved man plays the piano at one end of the room. Two girls in practice tights are limbering up at the wall rail. A third girl faces a tall framed mirror and dances, her eyes raptly on her image.*

WINKELBERG *enters, seeming to melt through the wall. His ghost light is on him. He stands smoking his corncob and looking around.*

POET (*mocking*). If I recall correctly, my last night on earth began in this studio of la danse owned by Comrade Morrie. (*He chuckles.*) Yes, sirree! Here's where the exit music for little old Jonathan sounded its A. (*He looks around.*) Yes, it's all here . . . And there's the humdrum door through which murder entered . . . (*He eyes the door and sneers.*) You will call for me again, Mister Death, and we will go into our familiar waltz. (*He waltzes a few steps with an imaginary partner, speaking as he moves.*) What hollow eyes you have, Old Boy. And what a seductive rattle your bones make—(*His attention is taken by the mirror dancer who executes a few difficult movements.*) I had almost forgotten what a nimble contrivance the female can be. (*He recites tenderly to the dancer.*) Your legs are exclamation points in a literature of muscles. (*He drinks and chortles.*) I'm certainly hotsy-totsy at recreating the past—down to the last buttock. (*Street voices come through the opened window.*)

STREET VOICES.

Rags. Ole' I'on. Rags Oleion . . .
Water-melohn! Fi' cents a slice!
Fresh Feesh! Fresh Feesh!

POET (*softly, as he hears, the voices*). How sweet this dead hour seems, how much sweeter than when it was alive—as if it had a secret heart that I neglected to notice during its debut. (ELLEN JONES *enters. The* POET *is invisible to her. He stands looking gently at her.* ELLEN *watches one of the dancing girls. Furtively, she imitates her ballet movements. Her face is alight.* MORRIE *enters and* ELLEN *halts embarrassedly.* MORRIE *scowls at her and speaks to the dancers.*)

MORRIE. Your time is up, girls. (*He consults his wrist watch.*) Five-seven. After this, kindly stop on the hour as entitled. Somebody else may be wanting to use the facilities.

DANCER. O.K., Mr. Morrie. (*She calls to the piano player:*) Knock it off, Joe. See you tomorrow. Good-by. (*The piano stops. She turns to*

MORRIE. ELLEN *stands motionless, watching her raptly. The other two girls exit.* MORRIE *nods.*)

ELLEN (*softly*). Good-by, Madame Valenska. (VALENSKA *doesn't hear her.* MORRIE *frowns at* ELLEN, *who watches* VALENSKA's *graceful exit.*)

MORRIE (*to* ELLEN). What's this idea of quittin'? It ain't even close to six o'clock yet. (*He looks at his wrist.*) In fact, five-ten.

ELLEN. I started before eight this morning, Mister Morrie.

MORRIE. I don't like a clock watcher, Ellen. Believe me, that's the wrong approach.

ELLEN. It's almost done. I finished the first floor. And I did all the windows except in the basement.

MORRIE (*hurt*). I particularly stated I wanted the basement windows cleaned today. They're a disgrace from the street.

ELLEN (*nervously*). I'll do them tonight. I promised Mr. Winkelberg to meet him at five, here.

MORRIE. That drunken bum! A big mouth with nothin'! (WINKELBERG *enters the light of reality. He walks up to the two as if he had just entered the hall.*)

POET. Hello, Ellen Jones.

ELLEN (*shyly*). Oh, hello. I'll see you after, because Mister Morrie wants me to finish some work—

POET (*glaring at* MORRIE). He does, does he? I should think a ten-hour day without pay should satisfy any idealistic boss.

MORRIE. Ellen ain't workin' for me. She is workin' for the Party.

POET. A party named Morrie. Yes, indeedy! A greedy little party full of love for all the workers in the world except those he employs.

MORRIE. I don't reply to personal attacks.

POET (*fiercely*). May I point out impersonally, as a fellow member of the world revolution, that you are an odious hypocrite.

ELLEN (*quickly*). Johnny, please don't fight.

MORRIE (*angrily*). You don't fool me for a minute with your capitalistic leanings. Work is an education—for her especially. The Party believes in Comrade Stalin's doctrine of—

POET (*fiercely interrupting*). You have the brain of a parrot and you can stick Comrade Stalin's doctrine where it belongs—and I don't mean Tiffany's window!

MORRIE. All right! I am going to report you for this subversive talk! You are a fake Communist, hanging around for what you can get out of the Party.

POET. To date I have received three major beatings as my share of the Party's goodies.

MORRIE (*consulting his watch*). The executive meeting is at five-thirty. I have no further time to give this situation. (*To* ELLEN) As for you, I don't care to see you around here any more. When you finish the basement windows, you're through. (*He glares at* WINKELBERG.) Subversive, decadent and imperialistic—that's my answer to you! (*He marches out.*)

POET (*aloofly, to* ELLEN). I am going to write a letter to the Communist Party severing my connection with that two-faced organization. I shall point out to them that Communism is the new disease humanity has invented as a cure for its ills.

ELLEN. Oh please, it's just Mister Morrie—it isn't the Party that's wrong. (*She stares at him.*) Is it?

POET. Yes. Parties are always wrong.

ELLEN. But—it has such fine ideals.

POET. Ideals go one way—life goes another. (*He smiles at her.*) I suggest that we both retire from politics. (*He takes her hand.*) I wish I could take you some place you've never been. I am an elderly drunkard but I know the way to a sunny hilltop with a white bonnet of clouds. I own a key to a green forest and I have the address of a nightingale.

ELLEN. You're wonderful—(SAILOR MIKE, *in his black turtle-neck sweater, stands in the doorway watching.*)

POET (*frowning at the sailor*). Mister Death in person. He's coming through the door with an invitation which I would like to decline—this time. Because there is a hope in me now that tomorrow holds a nice hour—that I could wake up beside you content with failure and wretchedness. Who knows, if I had continued beyond ten-thirty tonight—(*He looks at the black-sweatered figure again.*) Mister Ten-Thirty has decided to accost me. (*The sailor comes slowly toward* WINKELBERG, *who speaks on in a lowered voice.*) I'll get away this time—and find my little dream. (SAILOR MIKE *has come up.*)

MIKE (*politely*). I'm lookin' for a fella named Morrie.

ELLEN. He isn't here. He left for the day.

MIKE (*smiling at her*). Thanks. I'll catch him some other time. (*He grins at* WINKELBERG.)

POET. The name is Jonathan Winkelberg. Both names unknown.

MIKE. Ain't I met you before?

POET (*formally*). I had that brief pleasure—in a Bowery flop. Nineteen forty-three.

MIKE (*quietly*). Oh yeh—a fella died.

POET (*formally*). That is correct.

MIKE. What d'ya work at?

POET. I am a carnival spieler for unhappiness.

MIKE (*grinning*). The real monkey-doodle, huh? (*Sociably*) You got anything special to do, matey?

POET. Just live.

MIKE (*grinning*). Same here. (*He looks at* ELLEN.) How about ya introduce me?

POET. Miss Ellen Jones—Sailor Mike. (*She smiles and holds out her hand nervously.*)

MIKE (*gallantly, as he takes her hand*). Happy to make your acquaintance. (*He grins suddenly.*) What's a little lady like you doin' runnin' around with a flophouse bum?

ELLEN (*pulling her hand away*). I don't wish to hear that kind of talk—(WINKELBERG *watches the sailor in silence—intent and plotting.*)

MIKE (*quickly*). I'm very sorry, Miss Jones. Kindly forget my remark. (*He grins an appeal at her.*) A couple o' years on an oil tanker and a fella forgets how to talk to a lady. (*To* WINKELBERG) What d'ya say, I pick up my girl and we have dinner together.

ELLEN (*softly*). Dinner—

MIKE. I'll do the buyin'—

ELLEN (*eagerly*). He said *dinner.*

POET (*looking at her*). On thinking it over, Mister Sailor, we'll join you in a bite of food. But I want it distinctly understood—after dinner I have an engagement elsewhere. (*He grins gleefully.*) I shall have to duck out on you.

MIKE. Anything you want, matey. (*He starts out.* WINKELBERG *lags behind;* ELLEN *holds his arm.* MIKE *turns and grins at them.*) Come on, Spieler, we'll have a big night.

*The stage darkens and jukebox music comes out of the dark.*

## Scene 7

*A Greenwich Village basement café is slowly revealed. Two dancing couples become visible. Then some tables appear. Men and women sit at them, drinking, talking, and laughing.*

*At one of the tables sit* WINKELBERG, ELLEN, MIKE, *and a flashy girl named* VICKY. *A bottle of whiskey is on the table.* MIKE *pours whiskey into a water glass at Winkelberg's elbow.*

MIKE. Come on, Spieler, you're fallin' behind.

POET (*smiling and conciliatory*). The less I consume, the more there'll be left for you.

MIKE. Get this bum! Bowing to me like a pansy. (*He scowls suddenly and hands* WINKELBERG *a filled glass.*) Drink that, ya monkey!

POET (*smiling*). To hear is to obey. (*He drinks slowly.*)

MIKE (*to* ELLEN). How about another for you, baby? Come on . . . (*He fills her glass.*) This'll put a smile in your kisser.

ELLEN. I'm not used to drinking.

MIKE (*grinning*). It's very easy. Just hold it to your mouth and swallow. (*He tilts the glass against her lips. She drinks and takes the glass. She continues sipping.*)

ELLEN. It makes me dizzy. But I like it. It's nice. I don't mind. This is a very nice place. I was in a café before but they didn't have music. (*She beams at* WINKELBERG, *after drinking.*) That was awfly smart what you said to Mr. Morrie. I'll never forget his face—he was so surprised. (*She giggles and adds*) I know that song. Oh, that's almost my favorite song. (*She starts to sing the words of the jukebox song in a childlike voice.*)

VICKY. I can't say I'm enjoyin' myself very much, Mike.

MIKE (*curtly*). Get lost. (*Studying* ELLEN) I seen ya before. Yah. I'll get it in a minute.

POET (*looking off*). Quite a gathering of notables tonight. Everybody with a tie on.

MIKE (*grinning at* ELLEN). I never forget a dame. Got 'em all up here. (*He taps his forehead.*) A head full o' dames. All shades, sizes and tricks. (*He drinks.*) And all alike. Cute bitches. Talk fancy. Act fancy. Keep their legs crossed. But soon as they take the dress off—it's the same old two dollars' worth.

POET. One more little snifter—(*He pours a drink.*)

MIKE. Now come on, baby—give. I seen ya before. Where was it? New York? Maybe Brooklyn?

ELLEN (*her voice small*). I don't know. I don't remember.

POET (*suddenly, his head clearing*). What time is it, Mister Sailor?

MIKE. Keep out o' this.

POET (*intently*). What time is it?

MIKE. Ten-fifteen.

POET (*half-drunk, and talking with added precision*). It is time to leave.

VICKY. Go on—and take your eye dropper with you.

MIKE (*To* VICKY). Shut up, ya gabby broad. (*To* WINKELBERG) What's the idea of leavin'?

POET. I do not wish to be here at ten-thirty.

MIKE. Listen to this mug! What's the matter with ten-thirty?

POET. Everything.

MIKE. How d'ya like that! We ain't good enough for this fancy puke.

POET (*smiling*). Nobody could ask for a more exhilirating or generous companion. (*He raises his glass.*) To our Ulysses of the oil tankers. Long may he decorate the Seven Seas. (*He drinks.*)

MIKE (*suddenly amiable*). O.K., Spieler. Ya wanna go—go. Cast off. (*The jukebox music ends. The dancers return to their tables.*) I'm not a fella who hangs on to nothing. So get the hell out, ya crumby bastard . . . (WINKELBERG *rises.* ELLEN *stands up. She is dizzied with drink.*)

ELLEN (*woozily*). Do we have to go now?

POET. Yes . . .

ELLEN (*smiling*). All right, I'll go. It's been very nice. I'm a little dizzy. But I feel all right. Good night everybody—it's been a pleasure —(*During her talk, voices call out from the tables:*)

MAN. Hey, Jonathan Winkelberg. Let's hear some poetry!

WOMAN. Come on, Jonathan—give us a hot sonnet.

MAN (*loudly*). Next on the program, the great Jonathan Winkelberg, poet laureate of Klein's basement . . .

VARIOUS MEN AND WOMEN. Come on, Johnny. Poetry! We want Poetry! . . . Let's go—Winkelberg.

POET (*as the cries begin, bows to his table*). My public wishes to sip of my lyric fountain. (*He pours himself a fresh drink and grins at* ELLEN.) Wait for me, Elaine of Astolat . . . (*The cries for* WINKELBERG *continue as* WINKELBERG *downs his drink and moves slowly and with hauteur to the center of the café . . . During his drink and walk* MIKE *has been staring at* ELLEN.)

MIKE (*while the outcries sound*). I'll be Goddamned! Bleecker Street. Yer the hooker who picked me up in Bleecker Street. Three years ago. And I stayed all night—remember? Come on, ya phoney little bitch, you remember. Dames don't forget me. Sit down, baby. (WINKELBERG *has reached the center of the café.* MIKE *pulls* ELLEN *back into her chair beside him—as the audience applauds* WINKELBERG. MIKE *pours two drinks and puts an arm around* ELLEN. *Staring and confused,* ELLEN *lifts her drink to her mouth.*) Down the hatch, baby!

It's a reunion! (*The lights dim on* ELLEN, *befuddled, and* MIKE *embracing her.*)

POET (*he holds his glass carefully*). Ladies and gentlemen, I shall honor you this evening by reciting one of my poems rejected by one hundred and seven editors, at home and abroad. The title of this universally unwanted masterpiece is "Who Are My Enemies?" (*He drinks. Coins are tossed by his audience. They fall at his feet. Holding his glass carefully, he picks up the coins as he speaks.*) Thank you. And please do not allow the delicate texture of my verse to inhibit your throwing arm. As a poet, I am at my best in a rain of gold. (*More coins are thrown. He picks them up, drinks again, and begins in a self-caressing and "important" tone.*) Who Are My Enemies? By Jonathan Winkelberg. (*He pauses—as his audience grows silent.*) Most potent of my enemies are the watchful ones who remain enthusiastically ignorant of my existence—But I have others—

The Moral Ones on whom Beauty
  exercises a corrupting influence—
The Successful Ones who gesture disdainfully from
  the depths of their ornamental coffins—
The Pious Ones who find their secret obscenities
  mirrored in every careless phrase . . .
The Prim Ones who fornicate apologetically—
The Radical Ones who crucify themselves on billboards—
The Conservative Ones who win battles in their sleep—
The Reforming Ones who find relief for constipation
  in forbidding their neighbors the water closet—

In the night when the new born cry,
  I count my enemies
And see myself a pale gray worm
  crawling across time and space to the stars.

*During his recitation coins have been falling around him, and he has picked them up without stopping the flow of his words or breaking the high-class tone of their utterance. His recitation over, he bows deeply, picks up coins.*

*During his walk, the table, which has been immobile and silent, becomes alive.*)

MIKE (*to* VICKY, *angrily*). Go on, go home, dog meat. Get out o' here. (*He puts an arm around* ELLEN *who sits stiffly silent.*)

VICKY. You said ya wanted me fer the night.

MIKE. I don't want ya fer nothin'! Get out! (*He pushes her viciously out of her chair.*) I like my new girl better. (VICKY *picks herself up and undulates off—and* WINKELBERG *is at the table.*)

VICKY. You bastard.

POET (*aloofly*). Miss Jones and I are now leaving.

MIKE (*drunk*). Listen to this puke! Miss Jones! Ya crumby bastard —tryin' to kid me.

ELLEN (*vague and dizzied*). I have to go now. Thanks very much.

MIKE (*holding her arm*). You ain't going, ya bitch. (*To* WINKELBERG) All that monkey doodle—poopin' around you got an engagement! I knew her long before you. Get out o' here. Goddamn cute little hooker. I like her. And you like me, don't ya, baby? (*He embraces her.*) Come on—ya ready to jump for two bucks?

POET (*grimly*). Take your dung forks off her.

MIKE (*grinning and drunk*). You ain't gonna let this bum come between us, baby. (*He holds up a bill.*) Look—sweetheart—five bucks . . .

POET. The bedbug financier . . .

MIKE. Get out o' here.

POET. Let her alone or I'll split your head open.

MIKE. Listen to the bum. (*He snarls.*) Get out! (WINKELBERG *seizes the whiskey bottle and brings it down on the sailor's head.* MIKE *is stunned for the moment.*)

POET (*To* ELLEN). Come, Ellen, quick. (ELLEN *tries to stand up. She is unsteady. She wavers and sinks down in the chair again.*)

ELLEN (*a wailing giggle*). Oh, my. I can't hardly walk. It's going round and round . . .

POET (*trying to help her up*). Come on, honey—quick . . . Please, Ellen . . .

ELLEN (*looking drunkenly at him and smiling, her voice tender*). You're so nice. You're nice, Johnny. You're so sweet and nice. Oh, thank you Johnny . . . thank you . . . (*During Ellen's words,* MIKE *has come to. He has drawn his gun.* WINKELBERG *sees and moves slowly away from* ELLEN *and she repeats her "Thank you . . ." as the stage darkens. Gun Shot.*)

WINKELBERG *alone remains visible. He stands in the light, motionless.*

POET (*looking aloft*). That is the way it was, O Black Man with your wreath of silver birds. The end of the cinder patch. One bullet in my forehead. A hot horror entered my brain. (*A second shot*) A second bullet investigated my lungs and red fireworks issued from my mouth. (*A third shot*) The third bullet was embraced by my digestive system. And I lay on a floor burning and crackling. And riding a red sled of pain, I swooped away. I ceased. The world was minus one Winkelberg.

THE STAGE DARKENS

## SCENE 8

VOICE. Winkelberg's a fool.

VOICE. A bum with a fancy snarl.

VOICE. Unfit for civilized society.

POET. You are correct.

VOICE. A dirty bore.

VOICE. A drunken clown.

POET. You are correct, ladies and gentlemen.

VOICE. Slobbering with vanity.

VOICE. He doesn't belong.

VOICE. Throw the bastard out.

POET. I was a loser with the wrong manners, I give me that.

VOICE. Give him nuttin'!

VOICES (*crescendo*). Jack the Ripper—Insensitive oaf—etc. . .

POET. I agree with the verdict. I was a dirty drunk. I robbed myself and blamed others. I wanted to be distinguished, and I wooed fame out of a booze bottle. I fouled myself. But that wasn't all! There was something more to me. I was a poet who tried to paint the color of the wind. I was a little kite of words in an enormous sky. I was a poet who sang of streets where poverty and despair perform their microscopic somersaults. I danced with rebellious elves in empty rooms. When I was hungry, I licked the moon and dined on the dawn. And I am a poet still. I need no other dream but the one I gave myself. You in Charge—whatever your debatable name is—you have your heaven of petulant clichés. And I have mine of words. I want no more. Let me stretch out in some celestial alley with hungry cats for angels—and my poems around me. (*The* BLACK MAN *appears. He wears a wreath of Silver Birds. He is in a sweat shirt, slacks, and sneakers. He is a strong black man with a gentle voice.* WINKELBERG *sinks into his arms.*)

BLACK MAN (*he holds* WINKELBERG *in his arms and looks aloft.*) Sir, we're goin' to have to figure out some place to put him—

CURTAIN

*Winkelberg* was first produced by Lee Falk at the Renata Theatre, New York, on January 14, 1958, with the following cast:

JONATHAN WINKELBERG............Mike Kellin
THE ENEMY: TONY RIGGS, MOSSY ENRIGHT, O'BRIEN, SCHULTE, SAILOR MIKE............James Mitchell
LOUISE............Frances Chaney
ABRAMOVITCH............Sorrell Booke
WILMA............Aza Bard
BERTHA............Shirley Smith
HEINZEL............Norman Budd
WILLIE............Harry Holsten
JACK CALVIN............Tom Clancy
BIRDIE............Aza Bard
MAG THE BAG............Louise Kirtland
BUM............Arthur Anderson
COP............Michael Lewis
ERBSTEIN............Sorrell Booke
CLERK............Ernie Austin
STANISLAUS SZUKALSKI............Norman Budd
CAB DRIVER............Ernie Austin
HORACE WILLIGER............Michael Lewis
JIMMY JONES............Sorrell Booke
ALICE............Jayne Heller
LARSEN............Harry Holsten
KENTUCK............Tom Clancy
CORKY............Sorrell Booke
BRUNO BENZINGER............Arthur Anderson
BOBBY............Norman Budd
ELLEN JONES............Sondra Lee
BILLIE............Shirley Smith
BUTLER............Robert Ginnaven
LEILA CASE............Jayne Heller
MADAME WILLIGER............Louise Kirtland
MORRIE............Sorrell Booke
FIRST COMMUNIST............Arthur Anderson
SECOND COMMUNIST............Norman Budd
THIRD COMMUNIST............Ernie Austin
FIRST GANGSTER............Michael Lewis
SECOND GANGSTER............Harry Holsten

MADAME VALESKA.......................................................Aza Bard
FIRST DANCER.......................................................Shirley Smith
SECOND DANCER.......................................................Jayne Heller
VICKY.......................................................Jayne Heller
BLACK MAN.......................................................Kenneth Whitlock
TOM, HARMONICA PLAYER.......................................................Bob Sugarman

Directed by Lee Falk

Scenery and lighting by Lester Polakov

Costumes by Don Jensen

# *The Little Candle*

On that dreadful July morning when we Jews opened our morning newspapers to see what kind of face the world had made overnight we expected to read the usual accounts of other people's troubles, and a few of our own. For the newspapers had lost their innocence for us Jews. Where to most of the readers the newspapers propped beside their coffee cups contained the legendary doings of those men-in-the-moon and their womenfolk who perform the daily stint of murders and marvels, for us Jews the journals had to offer a little more concrete excitement.

As we opened our eyes in bed on that July morning, we knew there would be present that cloud of anti-Semitism offered by the editors like some fascinating weather report as News of the Day. And out of this cloud would stare at us the faces of Hitler and his co-philosophers, informing us again of the latest measures for coping with the loathsomeness of the Jew. They had been staring at us out of our morning newspapers for a number of years and insulting us with a tirelessness that, however boring it may have grown to other readers, kept us Jews constantly grimacing as if we had a stomach ache.

We had grown used, by this July morning, to staring back at these philosophers who despised us so garrulously. And many of us had achieved the stoicism of our ancestors, that quality which in facing disaster is the least exhausting. Yet, callous as we had come to seem while regarding the cloud in our morning newspapers, at the sight of it there came always the feeling into our hearts of a momentary dreamlike illness, as if the smoke of the Dark Ages rising from the tormented figure of Israel still lay in the air.

The faces of those who hate us are bad for our digestion and for our thinking. There are many such faces in our history. But then in our history they are all dead. It is easier to look on them. However they gleam and snarl and however loaded with villainies their names, we have survived them and we may smile triumphantly, like all survivors, and think of them not as figures of evil, spreading terror among the helpless, but as poor little cadavers overrun with maggots. And we may read, for our solace, that they were Monsters and that Posterity has been pleased to verify the opinions of their many victims.

Yet with all this as part of our history and part of our daily breakfast we were unprepared for what we were to read on this July morning. We stared with nausea and disbelief at the print. For when we opened our newspapers we found that the cloud we had watched so long and, in a way, so aloofly, had grown suddenly black and dreadful and immense. It filled all the pages of the journals. The world had made, it seemed, but a single face overnight and this face thrust itself into our breakfast hour, ugly and hellish. Like a monster evoked out of the smoking pages of our history, it confronted us, exultant and with the ancient howl of massacre on its lips.

We learned that overnight some five hundred thousand Jews had been murdered in Germany, Italy, Rumania and Poland. Another million or so had been driven from their homes and hunted into forests, deserts, and mountains. Thousands lay wounded and dying everywhere. More thousands, having seen their loved ones butchered and decapitated under their eyes, had taken leave of their senses and were howling like animals behind the barbed wire of concentration camps into which they had been clubbed.

This great International Pogrom had taken place under the auspices of the four Nazi-Fascist governments and was the flower of a long and careful series of conferences among the thinkers of the countries involved. The need to purge these lands of the contaminating Jew—finally and forever—had become so urgent that to have delayed any longer would have been to endanger the racial welfare of all Germans, Rumanians, Italians, and Poles. So the mad face with the comedian's mustache, called the Fuehrer, informed us.

The extirpating of the Jews had been carefully planned. All places where the contaminating Jew lived, slept, ate, kept a shop or office, worshiped, sang, or labored had been noted down months ago. All the centers of Jewry had been slyly invested by well-equipped regiments.

At an hour agreed upon long in advance, the bayonet, musket, bomb, gas, shell, and cannon of the four nations had launched the Purge.

The first accounts of the five hundred thousand murders and million refugees still fleeing before the terror naturally contained a minimum of political and philosophical comment from those in charge of the mass executions. But Germany, whose propaganda division once hatched a victory on the North Sea before the battle was over, was ready as always. The sages in charge of creating world opinion did not neglect to let their public know at once the deeper significance of the work that had been done.

True, as the androgynous Hitler immediately announced, the bloodstream of Europe was now cleansed of the hobgoblin strain of Semitism. But it was apparent even in the first barrage of headlines and extras that something even greater had happened.

This was that a second Crucifixion had taken place. The Jews had been put to death merely as an accessory. On the Cross, looming above the half-million corpses, the True Victim was to be seen—the phantom Christ with His now muted cry of love and brotherhood. It was against the Christian philosophy that the dictators had risen, and the murder of half a million helpless men and women was the proof offered of their revolt.

The Jew was no more. His back had been broken. Like a dog run over, he would writhe awhile in the dusty roads of the world and then expire forever. Thus spoke one German theologian. Never again would the sly humanitarianism by which the Jew and other weaklings of the world had sought to drag the superior races down to their own level lame the soul of Europe. No more devitalizing internationalism, no more decadent peace talk, no more anti-power creeds masquerading as brotherly love. The Jews had been Christ-profiteers. So said another German theologian in their epitaph. No oriental Christ would rule in Europe any more. Jew and Christ had perished together.

Such was the message that bade the world rejoice over its deliverance. But for the most part the press, to which the currents of philosophy are but a tiny and confused trickle of ink in a hidden editorial page, confined itself to bloodshed rather than significance.

In its paragraphs the wounded still screamed, the maddened still tore their faces, and the corpses, piled high in home and highways, still lay with one foot in our hearts.

There were items of synagogue bombings and ghetto burnings, of the blind being put out of asylums to run before bayonets in the streets, of Hebrew school benches vacated forever by machine guns, of shopkeepers covered with kerosene burning noisily amid their wares, of doctors, lawyers, actors, teachers, scientists, and artists who, with clubs and steel, had been taught their new place, in the ranks of the dead.

There were tales and tales from north, east, west, and south, from great towns and small, from manufacturing districts, from places prettily famed for cathedrals, museums, universities, their history, or the beauty of their scenery. All those places were so scattered and so far-flung that the whole of Europe seemed suddenly to have become one vast trap whose thousand cities, like a thousand springs, had snapped off the head of Jewry overnight.

The tales continued in the afternoon press. Its columns took on a classic air. Out of the jumble of reported martyrdoms and sadistically related scenes of murder, there arose the strange and awesome picture of a race being put to death, of a great and ancient people in whose veins had lingered for so long the earliest words and image of God, dying like a single child on a single bayonet.

When the spokesmen for the Nazi-Fascist lands proclaimed that the back of the Jew had been broken (that back which had survived so many burdens), broken now finally and forever, they were not referring alone to those thousands of devastated bodies the crusaders had piled up in the streets.

By the broken-backed Jew they meant all of us—all of us who, like quicksilver under the ancient hammers of intolerance, had long ago, cringingly and yet defiantly, spread into the corners of the earth.

We had begotten and thrived in these corners into almost un-Jewish generations. The cringe of our souls had vanished or persisted only in those mysterious grimaces of fear which convulse the underworlds of our spirit. This handful of psychopathic hours we considered, thankfully, a small enough heritage of the evil centuries.

Thriving and learning the speech and even dreams of many lands, we had endured a vague but tenacious social obloquy with increasing unconcern. This discrimination against our presence in certain centers and the slight distaste for our persistently historic features on the part of those impromptu-faced races among whom we lived, were harmless enough ghosts of rack, thumb screw, and auto-da-fé.

Then slowly by our wits and our sometimes too facile talents, by the basic tenderness and sensitiveness of our bloodstream (inclined to turn the more timorous of us into toadies of those who liked us a little and hysterical disciples of any ideals that tolerated us a little), by these and many other of our racial charms, we had won a pleasant nod of recognition from the rest of humanity.

Thus, in the days preceding this July morning, we were in many parts of the earth making excellent progress in the rehabilitation of God's favored image. But we who had gone to sleep the night before on the borrowed pillows of civilization woke in the Dark Ages.

The echo of the great Pogrom crossed the seas and continents and sought us out in all the lands of the Gentiles. It came howling into our Long Island estates and New York penthouses. Its phantom bayonets charged into our offices and into all the high places we had won by our wits and talents. Its phantom bombs exploded in our humbler abodes, in our shops and stores and merry kitchens. And though none of our heads rolled from our shoulders, an ancient wound in our souls opened, and manhood, won through centuries of patience and struggle, drained from our depths.

It is folly to say that all Jews are related and that a mysterious umbilical cord ties us all together like a mob of wriggling Siamese twins. There is in us, however, a common denominator and a fraternalism curiously vital.

In our capacity for feeling each other's wounds we seem unhappily to resemble the growths of the lichen of which the biologists write. When in Norway a disease affects the lichen, causing its monocells to pale and wither, an exactly similar distress will overtake the lichen in Massachusetts and the Argentine. This gravely mystifies the botanists, who exchange cablegrams and later treatises on the curious kinship of the world's lichen, and who evolve, I am sure, the theory that the disease is carried not by swift-traveling bacilli, but is caused by the relation of all lichen to some force invisible, some reservoir of destiny that influences the entire species as the moon influences all the waters of the world.

Among us there is a similar relationship to such a reservoir of destiny. For we are, as a race, almost as old and unchanged a growth as the lichen and have had time, apparently, to evolve an extraneous soul to which we respond as the seas to the moon. This extraneous soul is not so mysterious as in the case of the lichen. It is, in the main, to be measured and identified, though it may own certain qualities beyond our psychological yardsticks.

Our extraneous soul is the attitude of the world toward us—the glint in our host's eye. Though among us there may be disparities of body, mind, and fortune—great barriers even, put up by culture and snobbery—in the eyes of our hosts we are all Jews. And in whatever guise we come to their tables we remain to them and to their servants, Jews. This unwavering classification, not in our own hearts but in theirs, is our kinship; and the most detached of us embrace it, more often in despair than in delight, as our pathetic racial strength.

On this July morning we were Jews again, whatever our previous conceptions of ourselves had been; Jews, battered and crushed and exiled once more from the pretense of fellowship. Not only was there in us that common denominator that echoed the cries of agony and death, that sent our spirits cowering beside the myriads of unknown

Jews in the shambles of Europe; but the eyes of our host, however compassionate, segregated us into sudden ghettos of grief.

There was, too, a great devitalizing shame. As always in the days of all our stricken history, we had no armies to move forward to avenge our murdered selves. Scattered and impotent we lay, refugees all. All our fortunes and talents were useless. Our egoism could blow no trumpets. With all our champions, all our heroes of prize rings and stages, counting rooms and tribunals, our veterans of many wars, our dead on others' battlefields; all our record of achievement, culture, genius, and humanity, we must stand idle and die without firing a shot or uttering a battle cry. It was this that helped to break our backs.

We knew that our impotence as a people, forgotten in the noise of our individual triumphs, would again react like a mysterious death on our separate souls. However loud the cry of sympathy from the Gentiles around us, their eyes turning to us demanded something we had not in our being; demanded we become as they—a nation—and make a fight of it; demanded we die valorously together who knew only how to die humbly and apart.

This demand made our heads hang as if before the swords of the Pogrom rather than the compassion of our neighbors. We knew that our souls, lacking battlefields on which to die, were drained even more deeply.

As news of the mass murders continued into a second July day we heard, under the cries of protest echoing from our host's church and state, a murmur that sickened us. We in New York lived in the brightest light of equality that had yet shone on us since our disinheritance. Yet here where our racial brand had been almost obliterated as a mark of obloquy, a mysterious anger began to light the eyes of the Gentiles.

It was the anger of the bully, the anger that weakness inspires—the ancient human impulse to stamp out that which is maimed and unable to defend itself. It is an anger, this anger toward the helpless, which mystically vivifies the egos of its owners. It improves their morale as if it were the glow of a battle they had nobly won. The presence of defeat arouses, however illogically, the victor in them. And in their contempt for those who have been vanquished they find a pleasing measure of their own superiority.

Our impotence, our pallor and tears that so stirred their compassion, appeared to reach deeper into them than their hearts and to release from the hidden places of their being an ancient sadism.

Then, too, there was another reason for many of them to turn against us. This was the need among the leaders of industry and finance for extricating themselves from the centuries of Christian morality which they had long found imcompatible with their economic war. Tolerance, kindliness, aspirations toward love of one's fellowman, and a belief in human equality and human brotherhood were a difficult credo for the money-weighted minority battling fearfully to retain its rights as exploiters and inheritors. How answer the insidious demands of the poor when the mouths of the strong were stopped with pious phrases and democratic proverbs sired by Christianity? By ridding themselves of the spiritual incubus of Christ and all his politicians, by overthrowing in their own souls the old ideals of Christianity, these industrial captains and their mercenaries could reach for mastership with no Sermons to weaken the arm of their Law. And this hatred of Jews was a heady exercise—a first vital step in the anti-humanitarianism the upper classes were finding more and more necessary in their struggle to remain on top. Thus in addition to the contempt our impotence aroused, and the sadism our wounds inspired, we offered the Fascist-minded of our countrymen a dumping ground for ideals they must discard, we offered them a honing stone for their cruelty and mastership. And we began to hear everywhere around us the unreason which, in our travail as much as in our palmier days, called us loathsome, and the mania which found us undesirable.

It was on the third day, with the newspapers crying out to us promises of English, French, and American reprisals, boycotts, state reprimands, leagues for our protection, that the Pogrom finished us. Swept by an exultation with which murder alone can light the spirit, the Nazi-Fascists brought their machine guns into the concentration camps and finished the work of the first night. Another hundred or two hundred thousand Jews (none kept count) tumbled like little archaic dominoes before an all-day shriek of bullets. And the Nazi-Fascist spokesmen, swooning with the power of their crime, raised priestly voices and thundered the holiness of their cause into the world. A marvelous eloquence lit their words. A sense of Vision and Obsession now came into the newspapers, and the intellectual side of the massacre dominated the mere physical drama of the event. These arguments became even more powerful against us than their regiments had been. Their Word ruined us.

They spoke of the world, afflicted for centuries by the Semite, being now delivered, being now rid of a stubborn malcontent and poison-bearing breed. There were Jews still alive, but let them tie their belongings into little packs to sling over their shoulders—and wander;

wander as the scum people of the earth and hatch in caves and forests; hide themselves as the condemned of the world and the repudiated of a new, fresh humanity.

We made no little packs of our belongings and we did not wander (not yet). But our souls crept into caves and forests and even in the streets of the new world which we half owned we moved condemned and repudiated. The strength of our finest egos was not sufficient to stand firm. There was none of our Champions who would ever raise his eyes again. We were again in gaberdine and yellow hat, again marked, again on that ancient trail of the oppressed that leads through the back of the world; again with furtive eyes for our fellowmen and defeat for our daily bread.

But even at such times the Jews, who have a tradition for every gesture and every bite of food, however bitter, are not without a prescribed pattern of action. It is written that when the Jew is about to die in droves, he must pray. They prayed now. They filled the synagogues with a chanting older than any fictions of the world. Covered with tallithes they wept and implored their Jehovah. They stood on their feet and bent their bodies backward and forward in a continuous rhythm and seemed, as always, when at their praying, trees being blown almost to the ground by a strong wind.

All the synagogues of all the lands were filled. In all of them rose the mad sing-song of Jewish agony. Many wise and holy men stood before many scattered altars and intoned and wept. But there was no congregation that prayed louder and sent their hearts climbing the stairs of Heaven more ecstatically than the fifty old men who filled the little hall called the B'nai Israel in the City of New York.

This was as tiny a tabernacle as Jerusalem had ever spawned. It stood in the lower East Side of New York. It was a one-story structure made of wood and hardly taller than a man's hat. Its roof sagged. Its walls bulged, and it faced the street with two dusty windows and a battered unpainted door. It seemed to crouch on its knees, in the midst of the tenements that surrounded it, like a beggar in rags peering cautiously out of an alley way.

It was an old synagogue and its importance as a center of worship had long vanished. Tabernacles of brick and stone had sprung up in the neighborhood and even temples full of elegant furnishings had blossomed in this East Side in the century since the B'nai Israel was built. But this shack of a synagogue, rakish and pathetic in its poverty, had persisted, seeming through the years to become more and more the symbol of a race whom Christ had crucified.

Mysteriously, too, it had always had enough worshipers to keep it occupied, not only on Saturday mornings and through the frequent holidays, but every day. This was because the members who contributed their few dollars toward its continuance were old men, released from the terrible toil in which their days had been passed and owing no duties to life other than those they observed in the synagogue. Some were very old, so old that they had been brought to this country as luxuries carried on the backs of their children, and some, after a middle age spent here in the service of their families, in small stores, over workbenches and over pushcarts of insignificant wares, had slipped into the skull caps and pious habits of their fathers, and were spending their last years as they had spent their first, in the study of God's Word.

At dawn they gathered to say the prayers said facing the east, and facing the west they sang the praises of the Lord at eventide, and hurt no man. Innocently, they divided their days in going back and forth between their homes and the synagogue, the very old among them sometimes forgetting to eat, spending whole days in a corner of the synagogue, turning the pages of a Hebrew book. In some homes they were revered, according to the refinement of their natures and of those among whom they lived. In others they were derided as aimless shuffling idlers, stupid and unworldly, though they were as wise as the professors of Alexandria. The old men no longer noticed these matters. They lived in a world of their own, save when occasionally they fastened their eyes and hearts on a child, the eternal small boy who is the hope of every Jewish home.

Their world was the synagogue. Seldom did they appear anywhere else. Occasionally, one of these elderly children was to be seen, lost on his way to a bookstore perhaps, deaf as an owl, and guided through traffic by a policeman. Or sometimes, their eyes far away, they stood with an umbrella over their arm at a funeral. But it was in the synagogue that they were alive. As other old men sit smiling in the sun, they sat happily in the decay and murky shadows of the ancient house of God. Some of them had grown a little foolish perhaps. Like old horses turned out to pasture they even frolicked a little in their fields of learning, they disputed loudly over some minor behavior at the Passover, they harangued one another about the Talmud, or spoke a contemptuous phrase for Alexander of Macedon, or an oath, accompanied by a sudden expectoration, for the name of Titus of Rome.

Some among them were scholars of religion, latter-day Scribes, who spoke only when properly addressed, and then only about the Mosaic law. It was old men such as they who had followed the True Candelabrum out of Rome, accompanied by a child, who might see it with his own eyes, so that its image might be preserved. It was such as they who through the long years of the disappearance of the Talmud had committed to memory the entire work. As long as they lived, or a child beside them to whom they could pass on a proverb or relate a custom, the Word would not be lost.

Had any honest Jewish ghost of fifth-century Vandalland or Gaul peered in through the dusty windows of this synagogue on this July day, it would have seen nothing new, nothing changed. It would have seen, too, faces as familiar as its own ghostly image, faces whose persistent historic look belittled now as always the garments they wore, and gave their owners the air of seeming in dingy masquerade. And on this July evening, it would have caught an even more familiar sound than the unchanging voice of prayer. This was the sound of grief, of agonized expostulation with the self-same Lord who was visiting the self-same trials on these, His orthodox children.

The old men, who had wept for all the personal griefs, who had labored, and flown in insect-like flights out of far-away lands; they, who had buried sons, and sat in vigil by sickbeds, and sorrowed without ending, now wept for Israel. With tiny grief-stricken eyes shedding sad tears, they sang high with their old shattered voices, and wept and prayed and bowed their backs before the altar of the Lord.

Prayer after prayer went up, called from the depths of their old bodies. The night came, hot and stirring the reek of decay in the old house of worship, but the Elders kept their feet. For their Rabbi, still clothed in his white tallith, held his back to them and his face to God as he bent and unbent in his service before the Ark.

This Rabbi was Ben Ezra, tall, lank-framed, aged, and bearded; long-nosed and with eyes wide apart; and feared by the fifty Elders beyond any power on earth; feared, indeed, as much as he was venerated. For Rabbi Ben Ezra was a great man. His greatness lay not merely in leading the prayers and knowing meticulously all the forms of faith. These all of them knew equally well. Their Rabbi was a great man because they felt behind his wide forehead the presence of God.

Other synagogues might boast of marbled walls and pillars and of beautiful columns and stone steps, of tall windows always cleaned and of fine carvings. But none could produce a Ben Ezra. None could produce a man so wise, so holy, and so modest.

And what made Ben Ezra even greater than this was that his greatness was known only to them. He shunned the light of the world and sought not beyond the sagging walls of his synagogue for admiration. Tales of his learning, long become legends with their constant telling, filled them with that wild, secret pride which is the hard-won treasure of the orthodox.

Where were the books Ben Ezra had not read? Where the philosophies he had not studied and mastered? Where in all the world was there an idea, a dream, even a heresy, their Rabbi had not tasted?

In the single room in which he lived alone and which the Elders took turns in cleaning and visiting, their Rabbi had sat for fifty years reading and contemplating and feeding his spirit as one might feed a sacred flame. What Temple was there in the world more beautiful than the all-knowing soul of their leader? And where was there a pulpit in all of scattered Israel over which such a hero presided as over their own worn and dingy block of wood?

Yet with all this, he asked for no subservience. His voice, since the oldest of them could remember, had been always gentle. He alone of the congregation had never been known to lose his temper, to scold, to complain, or to shame his flock. Beside him, the wisest of these Talmudists felt small as the sparrow before the eagle and unlearned as the child before the father. When he spoke, their minds, cramped by the swaddling theologies of their faith, felt a larger vision knocking for entrance.

So it was that on this black day they put their trust in Rabbi Ben Ezra. With souls grateful and humble they huddled before him, asking only to pray in his presence. True, their hearts were little and frightened. To some of them, so archaic were their old heads and so little sense had they of the nuances that made some Gentiles better than others, the Pogrom seemed already to have entered the streets outside. But had they not been led once out of Egypt and through the Red Sea?

Rabbi Ben Ezra was with them. What if a Power Invisible breathed on the sagging threshold outside? For so it began to seem to them after a long day of sorrow and terror. What even if this Power should come inside with sword raised and death grimacing beside it? Within their leader's heart the great and unwavering truth of God had its tabernacle. They were old men, but had he only signaled, they would have risen and uttered proudly the prayers to the Lord prescribed for the hour of massacre. Tallithes over their heads, their eyes turned inward, they would have died avowing their strange belief that they were the Chosen of God.

As evening deepened, the sound of prayer and lamentation increased. In the candle-lighted shadows waving over the suppliants' heads, the little synagogue seemed to drift further and further into the past. Finally the Rabbi straightened and turned slowly and looked down on the fifty old men swaying rhapsodically in the shadowed room, their white shawls flapping like the sails of little foundering ships.

He stood watching quietly. His eyes were opened wide but no light was left in them. He stood as if alone in a curious silence. Then he raised his hand.

The tear-stained faces ceased gradually their cries and movement. No longer did the book leaves rustle. The bent backs straightened.

Ben Ezra spoke.

Something shocking was happening. Impiously he addressed his flock from the altar in Yiddish. He said wearily that he wished them to leave.

"Be good Jews," he said, in the almost vulgar phrasing of the streets. "Go home. Go home at once. Don't loiter in the synagogue. Close the doors. Don't ask me any questions. Tomorrow you may return."

The fifty Jews stared at each other. They had prayed beside their leader in the divine language. When they stopped, it had been with exaltation in their hearts. Almost they had expected a miracle. They had waited for his message. And he had spoken to them as if they had been a bunch of fish peddlers. The sharp pang of embarrassment succeeded the historic grief on their features. The scholars hung their heads.

An old man, feeling suddenly lost, began to whimper in the mother tongue, asking querulously what God willed from them, only blood and blood? Suddenly he threw his book of prayer to the floor. Others led him away. In the doorway, some of the more timid, looking like tradesmen now and not Scribes, hesitated. Murder and torture seemed to wait outside the very door. If the Rabbi sent them from the synagogue, where were they to go?

The Rabbi remained silent.

And such was the habit of obedience and veneration among his followers that they went. Straight into the unwelcoming world outside, into the very heart of their fears, they stepped over the threshold and were gone. Among them were some so wise and so divining that they seemed to make a little circle in the doorway as they passed on with head bowed, as if they had made room for a ghost.

Doubt and coldness were in the Rabbi's eyes; coldness and indifference to his flock. He too had felt and seen the ghost and had not driven it from the door. It was not the ghost from Vandalland of the fifth-century Jew, not the ghostly curiosity-seeker who might have peered in through dusty windows to see who and what they were who prayed within. It was a ghost of many meanings, a ghost of the new dead, and the old . . . of the hatred that, like a foaming hound at Israel's heels, had pursued him down the centuries, of the heroism and faith that had wrung only deeper contempts and more humiliating punishments from all his enemies. It was a ghost of the tallith-covered Jew wading through his own blood to Where? Praying through his own agony to What? Standing exiled from the soul of humanity and turning for friendship to Whom?

The last ones to pass over the threshold turned and saw their Rabbi calmly lighting the seven candles in the altar candelabrum. But though they turned, no cry came out of the past in their Rabbi's heart, no tardy call to bring them back to faith and sacrifice.

In the night streets the old men dispersed. They dwindled to bent little figures shuffling through the ghetto shadows. In all the homes beside them, through open windows, they heard the weeping of the Jews. On the street corners the newsboys cried out in an unfamiliar language the news of the familiar horror.

When he was alone in his synagogue, Rabbi Ben Ezra stood looking at the empty little house of worship. Slowly, with calm fingers, as a woman might remove her finery after an overlong night of entertainment, he took from his shoulders the white silk prayer shawl and folded it neatly on the altar. His eyes rested a moment on the tassels of its edges which he had so often kissed. He tucked these tassels under the silk so they were no longer visible. He removed the black skull cap from his head. Bareheaded and rid of his holy vestments, he then turned toward the little cupboard above the altar in which lay the velvet-covered twin scrolls of the Torah whose every sacred word was known to him. In this Torah was written the definition of God that had exhausted the Jewish mind for a thousand years in its writing.

He stood thus for many minutes, his long thin bearded face gleaming like some medieval necromancer's in the light of the seven-branched candelabrum, symbol of the candlestick of Moses stolen from Jerusalem almost two thousand years ago. There was no fervor in his eyes, and his face lifted to the blessed Torah was cold. Because of the grace of his mind and depth of his wisdom, the old scholar neither scowled nor sneered in this great hour of his blasphemy.

In his heart the Rabbi was not questioning God or seeking to solve the mystery of His ways. He was judging Him coldly, out of the accumulation of wisdom reaching into the shadows of history. Since it was his habit to speak his thoughts aloud, the Rabbi spoke alone in the synagogue, eyes raised to the Torah. He spoke in Hebrew and addressed God, Whose Face was in the scrolls.

"I am an old man," he said. "I have served You as my fathers before me. I have studied the confusing words in which You have made Your Truth known. Since I was a child I have sought to see into these words and behold the spirit out of which they were crudely born. I have read much, thought much, and prayed more. My spirit is clean. My mind is informed. My heart, though heavy with the pain of my race, does not bid me cry out in anger. It weeps quietly in a corner of my being. For the heart of the Jew is a little child lost in a great darkness. It must cry, not because it is afraid, but because the father it loved has left it to flounder beside a lonely road. Though You hear its tears You ignore them. They are not for You. They are my own tears and I shed them within me."

The old Rabbi paused, for he thought he heard a sound as of winds blowing. Then he resumed.

"It is written that Your children shall stand for judgment before You," he said. "I, who am old and ready to appear for Your subtle decision, have no fear of that near hour. But before I go to Your glorious house to be judged, here in this little decaying house I have summoned You tonight for judgment. I, Ben Ezra, stand by the altar of my fathers and pass judgment on You."

Again the old Rabbi paused, for the sound he had fancied before came to his ears more loudly. A wind was blowing in the synagogue. It made the old walls creak. The candle flames around the walls one by one stretched eagerly and vanished. There were left only the seven candles in the candelabrum.

"It is a summer hurricane," said the Rabbi, and went on.

"I speak only for a little group of Your children . . ." he said, "a mere handful of all the creatures with whom You have covered Your earth. Jews, they call us. But of all the myriads who have sung Your name in different tongues, and perhaps in no tongue at all, and made offering to You in dreams as varied as the clouds of Heaven, this little group has been the most eager, the most loyal, and the most attentive to Your existence."

As he spoke the wind seemed to harass the doors and windows of the ancient structure. The walls fell to groaning, almost as if they had a voice.

"True, true . . ." the voice seemed to utter.

"When long ago we were the first to write Your Name in the Torah," said the old Rabbi, closing his eyes, "we did not offer ourselves vaingloriously as Your discoverers. We knew that You have always been in the hearts of men and even beasts, gleaming therein fitfully like a light that burns, exalts, and confuses. We did not discover You, but with Your help defined You a little better than many definitions of Your meaning already loud in the world. This Definition, however incomplete it may be, and however dimmed at times by the pride and stupidity of my people, we have preserved."

"True," the walls of the temple seemed to sigh around him.

"I hear Your Voice," said the Rabbi, "but You are an Illusion."

After a while he continued.

"In preserving this Definition," he spoke, "we have exhausted ourselves. We have preserved little else. The knowledge that we had the true Word in our keeping made us arrogant, divorced us from humanity, and set us apart as a curious and irritating survival of an epoch discarded. We are like the remains of a feast that refuses to be swept away.

"But arrogance, and the glow of sanctimony so repulsive to our fellow-humans, have not been our only crimes. We have committed a greater crime against ourselves. We have practiced and perfected an insanity, an insanity to preserve us against the evolutions of culture and history, against the influences of logic, science, and beauty, against the disintegrating forces of power brought into the world by braver and stronger people than ourselves.

"This insanity we have nursed in our bosoms," continued the old teacher, "until it became stronger in us than even the biology of our beings. We breathed, our lungs quickened, our sinews moved, and our blood flowed around a skeleton of faith. We taught ourselves gestures and rituals and inscribed them in books we called holy. We swaddled our daily movements in traditions and bound even our dreams with layers of linen as if to confine them in an eternal bed of invalidism.

"We invented miles of gibberish with which to celebrate the thousand and one fetishes we substituted for Life. So strenuously did we work at keeping intact our definition of You, at seeing that it did not leak out of a single crevice, that we became a freak among nations—an ancient mummy moving, to the distraction of mankind, through its outraged streets."

The Rabbi raised his eyes to the cupboard above the altar. Had he opened the two doors before, or did he look now for the first time on two opened doors, inside them the faded purple of the Torah? The scrolls shone as if under a strong light.

"I am an old man," he said apologetically, "and my senses are lost in dreams."

But now a voice seemed to speak through all his being.

"Look in your heart," it said. "It beholds Me."

"My heart," said Ben Ezra, "is a child dreaming."

Presently he resumed speaking.

"We moved with our fetishes through the outraged world. We attacked the egoism of races stronger than ourselves. We became a red rag to the sane. For however sane a man is, a little insanity held before his nose will flood his soul with the wild cries always hidden therein."

The light about the Torah seemed to him to be growing brighter. The Rabbi gazed long at the radiance.

"I am not surprised," he said at length to the Vision, "for I am a holy man who has often seen Your face."

Nevertheless he continued.

"There is a complex and mysterious quality in the human mind," he said calmly, "which doctors better than priests can decipher. Yet this quality is clear to me, for it has been given to me to understand much.

"There are underworlds of savagery that need but the miaow of a cat for their release. We have been that miaow," said the Rabbi.

"There are diseases of the ego, struggling always toward a sense of power and fulfillment, that need but the smile of a sage for their eruption. We have been that sage.

"And there is also in humanity a vital desire for conformity, a need for smoothing itself out into some final uniformed guise, that shudders always at the alien. We have been that alien.

"It is so that I have understood the curse of the Jew. Many of us have blasphemed against You because of it. I am not one of these. The minds that willed and planned our deaths throughout the lands of Europe today, as yesterday, are clear to me. I see into them. I do not turn and accuse You of their evil. I lay the blame of massacre at their feet."

So spoke the Rabbi in simple scholarly fashion. And yet, when he came to speak of the massacre of his brethren, his voice broke, sorrow overcame him, and he could not suppress one cry of pain to his Maker.

"Do You hear, O Lord, what they are doing to us, and how we die, calling out Your Name?"

"Aye, I hear, I hear," the Lord answered him.

At length the old man lifted up his head and went on in a gentle voice.

"It is this that I have thought," he said slowly, "that in order to have Your Name written in a book, You have driven a handful of Your children mad. And in order to have it remain in that book from which You shine at me, You have increased their madness and allowed them to be hunted like crippled children throughout the world without end.

"And this is my judgment, O Lord. It is that You have made a mistake. Even as You made many mistakes when You first filled the earth with monsters, even as You created animals too large, too malformed, too strangely hungry, or too ungainly for procuring food for their hungers—so You have erred in creating this sad little monster, the Jew.

"Now I will pray," he concluded, "for I still believe.

"O God," he prayed, calling Him by His Secret Name, known to the Jews, "let this little decaying house in which I stand, vanish. Let it not remain like a dark and battered little casket out of which rise the moans of the unburied. O Mighty God, recall Your error. Withdraw Your mistake from the earth. Unbind the mummy of Israel. Make him into a man, O Lord of Hosts. You need us no more. We are few, we are only a trickle in the great river of Life. Oh, let us then vanish. Reward us for our long piety by releasing us from it. You who freed us from the Egyptian, free us now from the bondage of Yourself. Lead us to freedom. No fire or sword of the enemy will free us. No humiliation, no torture. The more violent the enemy, the deeper grows our madness. Only Your Word can undo what Your Word has done. O Mighty Lord, let the heroic little monster, the sad little monster, the indestructible little monster of Israel pass from the earth and join the legend of history. This do I implore. Amen."

The Rabbi ceased. His hands, raised in supplication, came down. Only once more his eyes sought out longingly the sacred place, the beloved Holy of Holies.

"And forgive me for what, being God, You know that I must do."

It was his last prayer. Rabbi Ben Ezra was finished. For a while he stood leaning on the pulpit, for he was an old man and tired. And being only a man, and human, he looked around him at the edifice in which he had well-nigh spent his life. Beneath the beating of the wind, in the darkness, it seemed like a vast place, without outline. And one by one, he brought before his mind's eye the faces of the worshipers who daily filled it, the fifty noble old men whom he had hurt so unbearably today. He had not quaked before the Lord's face. And before the invisible ghost in the doorway he had not succumbed, nor wailed his pain in its presence. But the memory of the hurt old men before him touched him, and he wept. For a long time this awful sound continued.

Then he stepped down from the altarplace.

After a time, the summer storm again let fly its tumult. The door of the old house flew open. It banged several times, and remained open....

The night lightened into a color like lead. The street was empty when there appeared in one of its area-ways a shrunken, darting figure. It wielded a huge paper box, which it juggled to the sidewalk. Then it lifted out and deposited in the street a garbage can. For its nightly work, this figure had turned itself long ago into a sort of lever, with jerky springlike movements. Moving in this cavorting flealike fashion down the street, it slowly approached the synagogue.

Seen in the light of a near-by street lamp, this was a being of aspect so grimy, so wretched, and so inhuman that one could scarcely think of it at once as a man. If it did not inhabit the night and a neighborhood so sorry, it might have frightened anybody. Long ago, what with the tremendous leverlike work of the scavenger, and the scavenger's solitary life, this creature that was a man had probably gone mad. It never spoke. Its face that was like a dirty clenched fist never altered. Its eyes, like two bits of rubbish gone astray, reflected only dregs.

The synagogue was a place known to this man. Here, whether he knew it or not, he even had an identity other than that of rubbish man. He was the *Shabbes-goy*—the man who, for a few pennies, lit the Sabbath candles on the nights when it was forbidden for Jews to touch fire.

It was this man who found the body of Rabbi Ben Ezra hanging from a beam in the synagogue. Who knows what his thoughts were or what prompted him to do what he did? Perhaps he had done some such work in some former time or, more probable still, there was nothing lowly, nothing menial, that he had not done in his forgotten years. He cut the body of the Rabbi down. He removed the rope and stuffed it among the rubbishy treasures that he saved in the huge pockets of his coat. He levitated the body to the altarplace beside the cupboard where he had often seen it stand. He placed on its shoulders the white drape it was accustomed to wear, and on its head the velvet cap. With hands so roughened and clawlike that they seemed to be covered with scales, he straightened out the body's features.

If there was a gleam of compassion somewhere inside it as it worked, the dingy and witchlike figure of the old Shabbes-goy did not show it. His fistlike face did not relax during his labors, which seemed like those of an automaton. When he was through with the offices of death, he went to work in the synagogue. He straightened benches, he swept, he opened and dusted windows, he put the prayerbooks carefully away. At the end he did something else. He poured into a dustpan a packet of incense salvaged from the sweepings of a Catholic church near by, and lighted it. And then he took out of his pockets his chief item of rubbish—a candle, pure and white inside its wrappings. He cleaned out the center socket of the candelabrum, for the candles were all burned down and, placing there his little candle, he put to it the light.

Outside, a pallor came into the ghetto streets. The sun was rising. The tall buildings full of crowded human nests, whose furnishings erupted from windows like bits of straw, became gloomily visible. Summer dawn, like a defeated and weary magician, rose from the pavements, and regarded wistfully the rooftops of the ghetto. The sounds of the day began in a pizzicato of opening windows, vague cries, and the clatter of wheels and garbage cans.

Plodding through these dim and staring streets appeared a number of figures. They came quietly out of the tenements and moved in one direction. They were the fifty old men going to celebrate the Lord's new day.

None of them had slept. Their old eyes were tear-scarred, their faces collapsed with grief and something worse. Shame and disillusion were on the faces where recently security and noble thoughts of God had reigned.

The old men assembled outside the familiar building, for there is no singing the morning paean until there are ten men. And before the ten gathered, there were all the fifty converging with dawn into the little street.

The old one who had whimpered the night before appeared now to have lost his wits. He moved among the rest, mumbling and complaining, as if he would keep them from entering the temple door.

"Why do we stand here?" he asked, peering fearfully toward the synagogue. "Why are we here and why do we hobble up and down like old hens chirping for a crumb? Why are we not buried already? Who wants us? And where is God?"

The others ignored him and moved as always to the door. The one who had opened it gave a cry and then stood still. Behind him the others crowded forward and they, too, were rooted. Then slowly they crept forward into the dim little house of worship and, pressing against the walls, peering over each other's shoulders, remained staring.

The synagogue was still as in holy sleep. The benches stood erect and in order, and the dawn, glowing through the opened windows, revealed the swept floor and the tidiness everywhere. There was an odor, too, that clung to the old walls, an odor that seemed left behind by a feast. But who had feasted in this house of tears? It was so sweet and gentle an aroma that some of the old men closed their eyes and thought of the forests of their youth.

Slowly their hundred eyes moved to the altar. The sacred house of the Torah was open. Under it lay a body. Certain now that they were in the presence of something strange, the old men began to pray softly. They moved timidly forward and saw their Rabbi Ben Ezra. Within the drapery of the tallith, like a shroud, he lay smiling. As the echo of a bird's song lingers in the empty wood, so his soul departing had left behind a smile on the dead scholar's face.

And suddenly, as one, the hundred eyes beheld a Miracle!

On the altar stood the seven-branched candelabrum. Six of the candles had burnt out overnight. But the seventh candle in the center stood as fresh as it had been when it was lit, and from its top a little flame stretched in a point of blue and gold. The fifty old men stared at this candle that had burned all night and grown no less.

"A miracle—a miracle!" called out the wisest, and lifting their heads began to pray loudly.

"A miracle—a miracle!" the others cried, and their eyes overran with tears of joy.

Their Rabbi, the wise and good Ben Ezra, the great Ben Ezra had told them to return in the morning. And now he had given them the answer to their doubts, the word of hope for their agony. Here on the altar was the answer and the word—a candle unconsumed.

The fifty old men stood before the little candle and prayed and sang so loudly that their voices drifting into the morning street convinced passers-by that the B'nai Israel congregation had gone mad. But as the morning grew, word of the great singing going on in the battered synagogue began to draw people to its doors. Why on this black day should there be Jews who sang?

Boys and shawled old women came first. Then the sad-eyed peddlers arrived and then the little tradesmen who had had no sleep that night. And slowly the synagogue became so crowded that no more could enter. Wearied and embittered faces asked of each other what was happening, what new disasters had befallen Jews, and lamentations rose from the throng as if a sickness were wringing moans from them.

Slowly the news of the wonder came whispering out of the synagogue. God had placed His sign on the altar inside.

God had revealed Himself and spoken in some fashion to His people. A rabbi lay dead, but above him, unconsumed through the night of murder and woe, a flame had remained burning.

When the first awe had spent itself, a wave of exultation rolled through the streets of the ghetto. For such is the trusting heart of the Jew that the little candle dispelled the darkness of the great massacre. Not everywhere, of course, for there were those to whom no God could speak. But among the pious, and among those who had once been pious, the matter was plain. The rabbis of the city argued throughout the day and night, and out of their wisdom interpreted the meaning of Ben Ezra's little candle.

The Jew was such a light, feeble and powerless, but never to be extinguished. God had placed him in a world of cruelty and darkness and had bidden him to keep His image glowing. And the meaning of this miracle was that, when all the rages of man had spent themselves, and the world lay in an unholy chaos, gutted by hatred and greed and vainglory, out of the unconsumed soul of the Jew God's light would rise again.

Shuffling along the street in the dim morning of the next day, the old Shabbes-goy, bent and ragged as some alley scarecrow, paused in the half-light and wondered what holiday his old friends, the Jews, were celebrating, as the hosannas rose from various synagogues, large and little. He nodded his head and his mouth opened in a feeble grimace, for the sound of the singing pleased him.

# *The Mystery of the Fabulous Laundryman*

I WILL WRITE this story out as it was told to me with the hope that you will believe it, as did I, listening to the bibulous and rococo verbiage of Mr. Dick McCarey.

In the days when I was a newspaperman such a tale as my friend McCarey unleashed between his first and fifteenth drinks in that buzzing Harlem speakeasy would have sent me bouncing into the night to run it down, nor would I have rested till the last detail had been garnered and verified and the whole thing blazoned across a front page. (A statement, this, which such of my erstwhile editors as happen upon these words may very likely challenge with snorts. But what newspaperman, having quit that daft profession, does not remember himself as one of its heroes? And this is not so much a boast as an obeisance to a lost and glamorous vocation.)

The braves of the press today seem to me a less gaudy lot than those I once knew as colleagues. But that is perhaps due to the romanticism which distance and a thousand lies throw upon the past. This McCarey, however, who will in a moment take the floor, is of that species which rather egotistically I choose to fancy extinct. He is of that tribe that once practiced journalism as if it were Holy Orders.

Mr. McCarey was sitting by himself in a corner of the noisy, foggy barroom when I spied him this night and he was a man full of truculence and contempt, as I expected him to be although I hadn't seen him for a year.

"Hello," I said, "how's Parnell this evening?"

Mr. McCarey looked up and from the fact that his eyes failed to blaze at the name Parnell I knew that the highball before him was his first. For my friend McCarey, despite a dourness and cynicism derived from twenty years of newspaper work, is one who, having a sufficient number of drinks under his belt, will never fail to rise and do battle in behalf of that last most confused and ineffectual Irish patriot, Mr. Parnell.

Mr. McCarey grinned and beckoned me to sit opposite him.

"What are you doing in this foul town?" he said, laboring as always under the delusion that I was, despite five years' residence in Manhattan, an alien. But this was a rather general attitude held by Mr. McCarey toward men and women encountered in the secret barrooms that were his stamping ground—that they were all aliens, all wanderers with their hearts in faraway places. Such noble and romantic concepts are peculiar to the colleagues of my past.

"Still in search of fame and fortune," I answered him.

"Oho!" said Mr. McCarey and sneered.

His voice will bear mentioning that you may hear him. It was a husky, rushing voice whose most characteristic tones were those of boundless and derogatory anger. He spoke chiefly in sneers but the sneers, these, not of small frustration but of a large and tumultuous romanticism which found the world too dingy for its practice.

Then, looking me slowly up and down, Mr. McCarey remarked, "Same old suit of clothes, eh?"

I nodded and this brief confession of my unimproved estates appeared to lighten the McCarey mood. His swollen but still boyish face relaxed, his lip uncurled and his Celtic eye softened.

"How's the world been treating you?" I said.

"The world," said Mr. McCarey with an angry squint, "has seen fit to harass and bedevil me beyond the power of speech. You are looking upon a man who is one of the foul favorites of misfortune."

Turning his squint on the bartender some thirty feet to the leeward, Mr. McCarey cried out, "Here, you foul Corsican. Another glass of that peculiar liquor."

"I'll have one too," I said.

Mr. McCarey held up two fingers and the barkeep nodded.

"You are looking upon a man," then resumed Mr. McCarey, seemingly entranced by this locution, "who is one of the darlings of disaster."

He laughed cruelly as if he were a merciless spectator of his own distress and fell silent, making faces the while of deep inner meditation.

"What," I inquired, "is the general cause of your depression—women, debts or the ennui of a noble soul?"

"The cause of my depression," said Mr. McCarey, "is a laundryman. Oh, what a laundryman!" The Celtic eyes fluttered and a sigh shook the McCarey frame from head to foot. "You are looking upon a man," he added, falling after a pause into his favorite rodomontade, "who bears in his bosom a secret so fabulous, so heartbreaking as to render him speechless. Speechless!" he repeated loudly, and favored the coterie of drinkers draped around the bar in front of us with a carnivorous glare.

"Let's get out of this fish trap," he said after having sneered and squinted separately at a dozen of the customers. "Hey, you peculiar Aztec!" This brought the waiter. "Rechnung, bitte. Verstehen sie? The bill," he added, translating contemptuously. "Here are your thirty pieces of silver," he said with a high aversion for the whole transaction. "Count them, ingrate." To me he said, "Come on."

I started for the door but Mr. McCarey moved in an arc and, with an unexpected list, tacked into an unoccupied corner. Here, overturning a chair and kicking it savagely out of his path, he sat down in another.

"Ober kellner!" he bawled. "Hey, you foul Swiss! Some service here. If you please!"

Mr. McCarey would have fought for Parnell now.

"This place," he confided abruptly to me, "has one asset which distinguishes it among its horrible ilk. It is the watering trough of that foulest of all bipeds, Monsoor Gavin, my esteemed city editor."

"What paper are you on now?" I asked.

"None," said Mr. McCarey loudly. "I have tonight severed my association with the depraved press and as soon as Monsoor Gavin sticks his snout into this tallyho I am going to cool him off and lay him to rest."

Mr. McCarey, despite his scowl, seemed appeased by this pronouncement. He smiled sullenly and, ogling the doorway through which his enemy was to appear, lifted his glass and seemed to drink not his liquor but his foe's very blood.

"I would like to tell you about this laundryman," he said. "One reason being that it is slowly driving me mad. And the other being that Monsoor Gavin is a toad among toads, a snake and a varlet whom it will give me a great pleasure to betray. Foully."

This last word was a happy mouthful.

"The laundryman's name was Meyer," he went on. "What was that name that Mary Queen of Scots had written on her heart?"

"Calais," I said.

"Calais," repeated Mr. McCarey. "Well, the name Meyer is written on my heart. Meyer the laundryman."

Again Mr. McCarey laughed cruelly as if there were within him a Greek chorus cued to deride his hurt whenever he expressed it. Having ended his laughter, however, he looked at me with so sad and appealing an eye that I nodded sympathetically.

"May the angels guard his sleep," he said.

"Is this laundryman dead?" I asked.

"Yes, thank God," said Mr. McCarey. "Dead and under a slab in Potter's Field."

"What happened to him?" I asked.

"Words fail me," said Mr. McCarey and his eye, the one that wasn't squinting, clouded with tears. He swallowed his fifth drink in silence and then tossed his head in the manner of a bull entering the arena and glared about him.

"It's a foul world," he said.

"Let's hear," I insisted.

"Well, I can't tell you everything," he said. "My lips are sealed regarding certain matters. I'm sorry."

Mr. McCarey assumed the look of a sibyl and for several minutes he gazed at me darkly.

"I can tell you this much," he said finally, "Meyer died on a hot night a month ago, shot through the head twice. And his right hand chopped off at the wrist, for good measure. But I don't want you to misunderstand me. I am not one who sits in mourning for Meyer's death. It's his living, his ten years over the washtub in Harlem, that unnerves me when I think of it."

Mr. McCarey grew grave and squinted with both eyes.

"I can tell you this much," he said. "He was a short, thin old man with a thoughtful face and a weak chin. He came to Harlem ten years ago and moved into one of those putrid tenements on Troop Street—a hovel reeking with poverty and disaster. That's the kind of a home Meyer moved into," grinned Mr. McCarey as if in derision of his literary flourishes, "one of those edifices that seem built out of sweat and refuse. He took a single room, renting it off a monstrous wench named Mrs. Maum. An oily, sweating behemoth in a wrapper who tipped the scales at 314 pounds. One of those female hippogriffs that seem to thrive best, peculiarly enough, in districts where food and space are scarcest."

Another drink was directed with grace and thoughtfulness down the McCarey gullet.

"Meyer moved in with this unsightly piece of tenement fauna," he went on, "and started taking in washing. Yes, he pursued his career as a laundryman in the basement. You know what he did? He went around all day, soliciting customers. And then on the next day he presided at the tubs. Nobody ever looked at him or spoke to him. He just shuffled back and forth fetching his wash and carrying it in a basket—

on his head, by God. On his head in a basket," repeated Mr. McCarey. "Tie that!"

I nodded blankly at this challenge.

"Tie that," insisted Mr. McCarey, full of an odd excitement.

I changed my tactics and this time shook my head in impotence and Mr. McCarey was appeased.

"I thought so," he said and looked grim. "It's a foul world," he added, "full of horrible and fantastic things."

Again there was silence during which Mr. McCarey communed and debated the ways of life and washed down the secret results of his cerebration with another highball.

"Well, there's no use in hiding anything," he resumed. "Anyway I can tell you this much. This foul dinosaur, Madam Maum, was a widow with a weazened and half-idiot babe in arms, when Meyer moved in. And what attracted her beautiful ferret's eyes was the fact that Meyer spent all his hard-earned nickels buying new bolts for his door, putting steel bars across his windows and boarding himself in like some daffy old boy with a nightmare on his heels."

Mr. McCarey paused to ogle the door and his thoughts shifted angrily.

"Monsoor Gavin," he said, "is overdue. His dog sled is usually along by this time."

"What's wrong with the Monsoor?" I asked.

"Very, very many things," said Mr. McCarey. "He is a skulking ape that it will afford me considerable pleasure to cool off in seventeen shades of lavender. That's as much as I can say now."

True to his word Mr. McCarey lapsed again and fell to making menacing faces at his liquor glass. Then he laughed cruelly and said with a growl:

"He didn't have a friend. Not a friend."

"Who?" I asked.

"Meyer. Meyer," said Mr. McCarey. "Meyer, this fabulous laundryman. Not a human soul to talk to. Not one human being to take his hand."

"And why should they do that?" I asked.

"Because," said Mr. McCarey, "he was the loneliest, saddest creature alive in the world. What a life for him!"

"Who?" I asked.

And my friend McCarey shut his eyes and laughed with greater cruelty than ever this evening.

"There are some thing that can't be told," he said. "But this much I can tell you. He was up at dawn, washing in the tubs. In the afternoon he tottered through the streets, that foul basket on his head. He always showed up at six in a cigar store a block away and bought a package of cigarettes. One package a day. And then home and to bed and asleep behind his bolts and bars by eight."

"Not a very interesting regime," I said.

"Is that so?" said Mr. McCarey, ogling me as if I had been transformed into the mysterious foe, Monsoor Gavin himself. "Is that so!" he repeated. "Well, I beg to differ."

Rebuked, I beat to the leeward and inquired casually, "What happened to Meyer?"

"All these peculiar didoes on the part of this laundryman," said Mr. McCarey, "stirred the female curiosity of that horrible creature Mrs. Maum, who began to set her cap for Meyer. And there," he deflected himself with a snarl, "there you have the eternal feminine. Love coming to bud among the ashcans. Cupid bombarding this hippogriff with a battering-ram. This dismal squaw used to lie in wait for Meyer as he came shuffling home, puffing on a cigarette. Ready to make wassail she was. Primed for the kill, her five chins and three stomachs jiggling seductively. What a foul Cleopatra! But Meyer was proof against these blandishments. He chose to ignore them. He said good evening to her and so much for romance. But, mark you, there was a woman scorned and roundly."

"Come," I said quietly, "who was this Meyer?"

But Mr. McCarey appeared not to hear this question which had begun to aggravate me. A smoky look was on his face.

"Imagine this man," said Mr. McCarey, "living like that for ten years. Friendless and chained to a washtub like a Carthaginian slave. All sorts of fantastic things happened in the world during these ten years but none of them as fantastic as this that I'm telling you—Meyer at the washtubs. Meyer with a basket on his head. And nothing as heartbreaking. What a laundryman!"

I settled back in my chair, deciding on silence and indifference as the most effective measures. But Mr. McCarey was walking the ways of his secret and had no eyes for my tactics. He drank with dignity as I kept silent, and appeared to be toasting the dead and gone hero of his tale.

"Monsoor Gavin," he said, setting the glass on the table with ominous poise, "has heard that I am lying in wait for him and is shunning this horrible rendezvous like a plague spot."

"Let's hear of Meyer's death," I said.

"On a hot night," said Mr. McCarey wit han unexpected rush of words, "full of that summer steam which the dwellings of the poor begin to exhale no sooner does the foul sun go down; and in a darkness mixed with dust, cinders and disease that turned the shadows into pumice stones; amid these wretched and famine-haunted scenes Meyer was done to death and his right hand chopped off.

"I can tell you this much and no more," Mr. McCarey squinted cautiously at me. "The police arrived at ten o'clock and found Meyer's room locked, the doors bolted from the inside, mind you. The windows barred. The street agog with the news that there had been a murder done. Mrs. Maum, that dismal squaw, had heard two shots and come wallowing out of the house like a square rigger with her mouth full of screams. The foul police whacked away trying to get into Meyer's room and couldn't. They were thwarted. They brought axes and battered down the wretched door and there was Meyer, murdered and mutilated on the floor."

Mr. McCarey grew wistful. He lit a cigarette with a great deal of grace. And he stared morosely into the foggy air of the speakeasy, shaking his head and heaving three separate sighs.

"Let me tell you one thing," he said. "I have always looked on Gavin as a man of parts. He may be a rat and a varlet, as you say, but he knows more about the newspaper business in his little finger than all the foul geniuses on Park Row put together. But despite all this dazzling cunning which I am ready to admit in fairness, this Gavin has the heart of a snake. He is a craven and yellow thing that crawls. That's a very fair picture of the man."

"I've never met him," I said.

"He's a wizard," said Mr. McCarey. "Although I'm going to tear his heart out and stuff it like an olive, I give him his due. Let me tell you something."

Mr. McCarey wagged a wild forefinger under my nose.

"This bulletin of Meyer's death dropped on Gavin's desk was no more than two lines long," he said. "A stupid laundryman done to death in a tenement. One of those dull, poverty-ridden crimes. A bubble coming up from some dismal sewer revealing for the moment that there is life in those stale waters. That's all the bulletin showed. But not to Monsoor Gavin. Monsoor Gavin called me over and, with that peculiar sneer with which he addresses his betters, pointed at this dull, stupid announcement that some totally unimportant human being named Meyer had been snuffed out in some wretched hovel in Troop

Street and said to me, 'There's something in this. There's more in this than meets the eye.' So much for Monsoor Gavin's cunning."

Again my friend scowled and, ogling the door, dramed his foe's life-blood from his glass.

"Let me tell you another thing," he said and spat. "Lieutenant Neidlinger of the Harlem police is a bird of a similar ilk. A species of double-dealing cringing officialdom that I will cool off and lay to rest before yonder sun has set."

Mr. McCarey chuckled.

"What did you find when you got to Troop Street?" I asked.

"The usual blather," snarled Mr. McCarey. "Lieutenant Neidlinger was all agog when I descended on this tenement. He was hovering about the premises and perspiring like an African bride. I tackled him for the facts about this dull, stupid crime and he at once unburdened his vulgar heart to me. There was some wretched mystery about the business that filled this pretzel-headed police official full of confusion and alarm.

" 'Item one,' said this peculiar fellow, 'how had the desperado responsible for Meyer's death gained entrance into this laundryman's stronghold? Item two, having gained said entrance and committed the bloody deed, how had the same desperado made his exit, leaving every door bolted on the inside and the windows barred? Item three, the dastardly criminal could have pot-shotted Meyer from the street but how could he have chopped off his hand without coming inside the room? Item four, why had this peculiar assailant removed Meyer's hand and whisked it away?' All these nuances were rattling around inside that vast, empty policeman's skull on this hot night.

" 'There's some mystery here,' he said.

" 'We'll discuss that later,' said I. 'First I want to take a look at this dull corpse of a laundryman.' "

Mr. McCarey began to weave over the table and turn suddenly from left to right as if facing his enemies.

"Who was this Meyer?" I asked again and more soothingly than ever.

My friend was drifting through mists. Once more I could feel him walking the ways of his secret. He was beyond the prod of questions.

"I knew him at once," said Mr. McCarey. "I can tell you so much. I knew him. I took one look and I knew him. And I grabbed this dithering cop and fastened myself like a foul burr to his coat tails. I gave him no rest. I heckled and bedeviled him until he was panting like one of those horrible little Pomeranians. I drove him out of his mind.

I dragged that dizzy Teuton up and down this Pomander Walk where Meyer had lived. We pumped and blasted and burrowed, but not a ray of light. Nothing. There was less to find out about this strange laundryman than if he had never lived. He was a man with no more substance than a shadow on a screen. He was Meyer Nobody. We had at his customers. He was Meyer Nobody to them.

"And all the time this dull fellow Neidlinger kept mumbling, 'Why did he bar the windows and bolt the doors for ten years and how did they get away after killing him?'

"'Because,' your oratrix replied, 'he was afraid. Because there was some peculiar nightmare on his heels.' And I kept prodding this dismal bloodhound to redouble his efforts. To no avail."

"But you knew all the time," I said.

"Yes," said my friend and snarled.

"Who?"

Mr. McCarey stared at me. In the long pause that followed it became apparent that what kept my friend silent was neither drink nor reticence but a great desire not to cry. A series of symptoms showed that Mr. McCarey was overcoming the womanish crisis that held him spellbound. He brought his glazed eyes slowly back to reality until they encountered his cigarette, which hung in his fingers and trembled. He then carried this cigarette, which he held like the Prince of Wales, to his mouth and maneuvered it promptly back toward the table.

"We won't go into that now," he said. "This little thin, thoughtful-faced old man with a weak chin who slaved over a washtub for ten years kept his strange mouth shut and ended up cornered in his tenement fortress, murdered and wallowing in his own gore with his right hand chopped off."

I realized that Mr. McCarey's great secret was out on its feet but still fighting, and I summoned patience into my voice.

"Did they solve it?" I asked.

"All I am privileged to tell you," said Mr. McCarey, "is Yes."

His voice had thickened and grown angrier.

"But that worm of a man, Monsoor Gavin, writhes on the hook of his own cowardice. That foul Corsican trembles lest he hit a sunken road. He refuses to print it. Lieutenant Neidlinger refuses to open his dull mouth. He skulks in the bush. Three dithering cops who know what I know have been transferred and promoted and are full of a craven, foolish silence. You are looking upon a man," Mr. McCarey burst out, "who is slowly wilting under the bludgeonings of a conspiracy greater than St. Bartholomew's Eve."

"How did they solve it?" I asked, closing in on Mr. McCarey.

"By following Mrs. Maum," said he. "By shadowing that barely animate and faintly human mass of tissue to an office on Forty-ninth Street."

Mr. McCarey communicated with the waiter, ordered more drinks and issued a confused command that Monsoor Gavin immediately on his appearance should be haled before us for summary justice.

"What was she doing in Forty-ninth Street?" I asked.

"Who?" asked Mr. McCarey.

"La Maum," I said.

"Oh, that foul wench," said Mr. McCarey and spat.

"Yes," I persisted.

"My lips are sealed on that subject," said McCarey. "All I can tell you is that she went to collect the wages of her sin. She journeyed to Forty-ninth Street in quest of her share of the blood money. You see, it was she who had baffled that master mind, Lieutenant Neidlinger. It was this abnormal trollop that had hoisted her idiot boy in through the transom, barely large enough for a cat to crawl through, to bolt the doors inside after the murderers had left. This wizened and backward stripling had crawled in and out of the transom like some trained lizard."

"Why did she want the doors bolted from the inside?" I asked.

"For no reason," said Mr. McCarey, "just a foolish, silly female ambition to create mystery. She derived some species of deformed pleasure from her son's didoes in and out of that transom. But they had nothing to do with the case, per se. This dithering pachyderm of a female Macbeth had been hired only to get Meyer to unbolt his doors to the murderers. This she did by cooing outside his portal for an hour."

"Were they caught?" I asked, still closing in.

"No," said Mr. McCarey. "A thousand times, No. We followed Mrs. Maum into that Forty-ninth Street office but the dastardly crew we were after were wigwagged by some peculiar outpost—and escaped. Leaving behind," Mr. McCarey's eyes both squinted and his voice grew harsher, "leaving behind a package in the safe containing Meyer's right hand. It was addressed and ready to be mailed."

"To whom?" I asked.

Mr. McCarey was silent.

"To whom?" I persisted.

"To a man named Stalin in Moscow, Russia," he said. "It was being sent him with its fingerprints intact to verify the report already over the cables." "Who was Meyer?" I asked and this time with my hand on the McCarey arm.

He was silent again, his eyes glaring. I waited.

"Will you believe me when I tell you?" said Mr. McCarey softly and pulled his head erect with a lurch. "Or will you join this foul conspiracy against truth and justice led by Monsoor Gavin and his peculiar myrmidons? Will you believe me if I tell you I've got all the facts of this fabulous crime?"

"I will," I said.

"This laundryman," said Mr. McCarey in a soft voice, "was the Czar of Russia."

I regarded Mr. McCarey calmly.

"Nikolai the Second," he said with dignity, in a sad croak. Then he went on in a mumble, "Escaped from his executioners in Siberia in 1918. Shipped across the world, his royal mind fogged by the tragedy of his murdered kin. But enough of his brain left to know he was hunted and that murder waited for him around every corner on the globe. So he drifted into Harlem as a little laundryman with a Jewish name."

Mr. McCarey slowly folded up over his fifteenth drink and allowed his head to hang and his eyes to close.

"The Czar of all the Russias," he whispered.

I kept my hand on his arm.

"You said you knew the minute you saw him," I said.

"Yes."

"How?"

The McCarey heart came charging out of its torpor.

"How did I know?" he said. "Because when I looked down on this dead laundryman I saw a cross in his left hand. A Muscovite cross. And a look on that dead face I'll never forget. It was the look of a noble, graceful, royal soul. There were some people who knew who was on the middle cross." Mr. McCarey sneered, his face thrust close to mine. "They could tell by a light that hovered peculiarly in the air. There was a light on this laundryman—this Meyer. This little dead Meyer."

"What did Neidlinger say?" I asked.

But the McCarey was in the mists. Tears were slipping down his stiffened cheeks and his head was wagging loosely over the table.

A short, gray-haired man appeared beside him. He had a red, excited face and a pair of black bristling eyebrows. He began shaking the McCarey shoulder.

"Wake up, you lout," said this man. "Come on, quit your stalling, you lousy drunken bum."

Mr. McCarey opened one angry eye.

"Monsoor Gavin," he said and tried to rise, "you foul Armenian!"

"Pull yourself together," said Monsoor Gavin and stood trembling with an excitement even greater than Mr. McCarey's had been. Mr. McCarey slowly opened a second eye, glared and emitted a carnivorous snarl.

"I'm going to stuff your heart," he said, "like a foul olive."

The fearless Monsoor with the red face ignored this promise and hoisted the McCarey to his feet. He was pushing at him from behind with eager, almost frantic, gestures and steering him for the door.

"Pull yourself together," he whispered fiercely into the McCarey ear. He turned to me. "No, I can handle him. I don't need you." To Mr. McCarey he added, giving that brave a final shove toward the door, "You're going home and pack. I got it all fixed up. The boss has agreed. Do you hear me? Agreed, by God! You're leaving in the morning for Moscow."

# *The Bull That Won*

BEHOLD THE ANCESTORS of Pepe Santoyo, very prominent and spectacular people. Aztec priests and princes walking in gold shoes wearing mantles made of many-colored feathers; stately, child-like and sadistic. Gilden barbarians, say the historians, a race of murderous peacocks who once presided over an ornate little nightmare in the hills of Mexico. Grandfathers, these, of Pepe Santoyo.

Then come Cortez, the Great Captain, with his little group of helmeted cronies and earth shakers. A greedy, dauntless troop, say the historians, of Castilian Vikings; an iron-hearted crew called Conquistadores that hacked its way through the wedding-cake forts of Montezuma. These are also the grandfathers of Santoyo.

Then come the Colonial Lords, the Dukes and Hidalgos with their gibbets, bonfires and snickersnees. Horrendous bloodletters who vivisect an Empire and perform a hundred years' autopsy on its twitching cadaver searching for gold. And among these elegant monsters and Epicurean ogres of New Spain, more grandfathers for Pepe Santoyo.

And here our hero's lineage takes on complications. The sacrificial stone atop the Temple of the Sun no longer runs a river of blood down the pyramid steps into the gardens of Teotihuacán. The Aztec peacocks, plucked and scattered, chirp sadly in the hills. Pepe Santoyo's second crop of grandfathers rule but undergo mysterious alterations. Their skins slowly darken, their voices soften, their eyes grow velvety and a third yield of grandfathers enters the Santoyo lineage.

These are known as Mexicans, a moonstruck race of harlequins, heroes, and barefoot generals. Blood runs, death gallops the deserts and the purple hills; new flags and slogans fill the air—but the historians smile. These new grandfathers of Pepe Santoyo are full of glory and garrulity. They make war like happy children and die like stock company actors. They bow to firing squads, sing between volleys, fight like lions and argue like geese. They laugh at blood and weep at sunsets. But out of the hurdy-gurdy sounds of their battles and powwows the Republic is born. New government buildings rise and become full of statesmen in frock coats. And a lusty counter party known as The Revolution entertains the world with a mysterious series of Lost Causes.

And among these are the immediate forebears of Pepe Santoyo. They include a wagon-load of generals—General Inez García, grandfather and patriot who spent twenty-five years capturing people in the hills of Chihuahua and who in his dotage took to collecting the ears of his enemies; General Fierra, grandfather and patriot, who blew up the first, second, and third railroads between Monterrey and Saltillo as non-conducive of the honor of his country and the liberty of his people; General Manello, uncle and patriot, who seized the City of Vera Cruz and declared war on England, Germany, and America, in which unequal contest he died gloriously; General Santoyo—but the list is too long for detailing. Suffice that all these patriots who combined in the creation of Pepe Santoyo met death with a flourish, fell before the white wall smoking cigarros and smiling contemptuously upon the antics of their executioners. All, that is, with the exception of Santoyo père, whom destiny favored not only with a civilian temperament but an attack of the influenza, and who died (to the astonishment, no doubt, of innumerable ghosts) at the ripe age of forty-nine in a Louis XIV bed in the midst of more collateral than glory. Señor Santoyo, head of a Tampico oil company, was mourned by a board of directors, a widow aged twenty-eight, and a son turned eleven.

When he was eleven, Pepe was an undersized, sallow arrangement of skin and bones such as would have broken the heart of any Nordic mother. His manners seemed to hark back to a first-run ancestor, Ixtlxochitl by name and Lord of the Sun, who at the age of four fought and vanquished his nurse, drowning her in a deep well. When asked for an explanation the youthful Ixtlxochitl replied coldly that he did not relish somebody always telling him to blow his nose and that the defunct attendant had failed on the whole to treat him with proper dignity.

This same precocious sense of lordship had run in the veins of Pepe Santoyo almost from his birth. He had grown from a fragile but domineering baby into an egomaniac of eleven. At this age he conceived the world as revolving around him and its chief inhabitants—beginning with his mother, her fourteen servants and his three uncles—as slaves dedicated to his whims.

His father's death had made no impression on him. He had nothing in common with this puffy, methodical old gentleman and he received the news of his passing with a shrug whose heartlessness actually frightened the youthful and grieving widow. Some ancient impulse gave Pepe the impression at this moment that he had succeeded to some throne and after the funeral he worked quickly and ruthlessly in establishing himself. For a year the Señora Santoyo allowed herself to be bullied and harassed as his chief subject. But at the end of this year her brother, Felipe Ortiz, observing her rapid decline under the rule of her beloved tyrant, stepped in. Pepe, his four personal servants, his two wagon-loads of toys, devices, souvenirs and loot, were moved to the vicinity of Guadalajara and installed upon his uncle's extensive ranch. Uncle Felipe had expected this new and more primitive environment to curb the extravagances of Pepe's spirit and make a man of him.

"My men," said Uncle Felipe, in conference with his now hysterical sister, "are a very hard lot, half-bandit, half-centaur. They will soon take all this babyish nonsense out of Pepe and in a year he will change into a fine, healthy, sensible youth—like his father."

"But they may hurt him," the Señora protested. "They won't respect him and he suffers so. My poor little one is so proud."

Uncle Felipe snorted.

"They are honest, simple fellows, my men," he said, "and they will respect Pepe as much as is good for him. And no more."

"Take care of him," wailed the pretty Señora in farewell.

"I will, mucho," smiled red-faced Uncle Felipe, rancher and stock-breeder. And the train pulled out of the Tampico station.

None of the things Uncle Felipe had expected happened. Pepe, from the moment of his arrival, annexed the thousands of acres, crops, stock, bandits and centaurs, and set himself up as their new lord. Neither his spirit nor physique underwent a flicker of alteration. The bandits and centaurs struck no awe in him, and the boiling sun, the cold winds, the hard riding in the hills, trudging through deserts, hunting, sleeping under stars—all these numerous physical forces and activities left him as sallow as before, added apparently not a muscle to his undersized and spindly body.

But among these half-wild folk who worked the Ortiz ranch and defended it against other half-wild folk in the hills, Pepe Santoyo came into his own. They were of a race that had always responded to lords and heroes. In this arrogant, contemptuous little one, they perceived with a vision much more romantic than Uncle Felipe's, the blood of kings and captains. Nor were they misled, as Pepe's previous retainers had been, by the spindly legs, bony hips, flat chest and sallow face. They beheld under this anemic exterior a grace that delighted them, a mysterious strength that seemed to come from neither muscle nor sinew, and a courage that was noble. He would tire quickly, this little one; he would fall suddenly to the baking earth exhausted from his chasings, and there he would lie white and spent like a stunned fledgling. But he was up and on his feet in a few minutes, as good as new, as arrogant and contemptuous as ever and as ready for more hardships as the toughest of them.

Then, too, they admired his ugliness, his long nose and slightly malformed mouth and jaws. He was no pretty boy of the towns such as came to visit in the hills sometimes—but a muchacho who, with all his lordly airs and riches, bore the stamp of race on him such as their own ugly brats exhibited—the true mongrel look of one whose grandfathers came from thrones at different ends of the earth.

In the second month of his visit Pepe Santoyo discovered old Barrera, the ex-matador, and his stable of bulls. Barrera was an assistant overseer on the Ortiz ranch, but twenty years before he had worn the coleta in the bull rings of Spain and Mexico. Fame, riches and the love of many fine ladies had been his, he explained to Pepe. But he had been forced to retire and to turn his back upon glory because of a hernia. He could for that matter, he insisted, despite his gray hairs, and his hernia, go into a bull ring today blindfolded and with a penknife vanquish the kind of moth-eaten bulls with which the present worthless tribe of matadors engaged in Mexico City. Two years ago he had attended one of these disgusting exhibitions and wept over the collapse of the great sport.

"In the old days," said Barrera with a sad and modest snort, "there were matadors. Today there are little clowns in red and gold."

Pepe Santoyo, when he heard these statements, sneered and nodded. There was born in him immediately a great contempt for all modern bulls and all modern bullfighters.

Barrera from time to time had added to his staff certain cronies who came drifting through Guadalajara—toreros and picadors who had in the old days played the bull-ring circuits at his side. These joined in bearing out the tales of the hernia-ridden matador.

In the third month of his guardianship. Uncle Felipe, busy with a roundup and far from his hacienda, despatched messengers for Barrera and his riders. They were needed in the hills. The messengers returned in three days with word that Barrera and his men were deeply engaged by the little one who had refused to release them from their work. They were, said the messengers, training the young Señor to be a matador. Uncle Felipe fumed and rounded up his herds and galloped back for a showdown with Pepe. But on the long ride Uncle Felipe began to think this over. His sun-bitten bandidos riding behind him were already improvising songs of the future glories and triumphs of their muchacho.

> "The finest bulls will die of fear
> When they behold our boy come near,"

they sang:

> "Their eyes will roll, their blood will freeze
> Before the nephew of Ortiz."

And Uncle Felipe, for whom this nephew's charm had been always a waste product, mopped his red face and pondered as his saddle creaked. Never had he had so little trouble with these rascals behind him as since Pepe had come. Who knew but what it might turn out for the best? If not a matador what else in the name of many saints was this nasty youth good for? An ugly, irrational, and idiotic child, mused Uncle Felipe, but decided there would be no showdown.

The training of Pepe Santoyo was from the start an unconventional business. Before he had learned to tell a bull from a heifer Pepe demanded a matador's suit. After it had been constructed, he wore it on Sundays between the hours of three and six, parading the cattle pens so that his uncle's bulls, in case any of them ever found their way into some bull ring, might remember at such a time how a real matador looked.

Under the guidance of Barrera and his erstwhile troupe of toreros and picadors, Pepe chased young bulls with a stick, learned their mannerisms, studied the language of their eyes, hooves, and tails. Within nine months he had mastered the repertoire of Barrera and his cronies, learned in theory all the passes, gestures, and genuflections of the great art. Never had Barrera beheld such precocity. Never had he seen anyone, even in the great days, so at home with the cape, so graceful with the sword. But more than this was the thing that could not be taught—the courage that shamed the bull and filled his heart with despair long before the steel entered it. This his protégé possessed beyond all his predecessors in the arena.

Pepe listened to the praise of his instructors and nodded kindly at them. Praise, even then, did not embarrass or elate. It inspired a passing friendliness. But brilliant pupil though he was, Pepe became a great trial to Barrera. He disdained certain invaluable rules. He was indifferent to the play of the cape which makes a good show and delights the crowd. He was disinterested in the thousand and one ballet gestures and flourishes which are the pride of the matador. He refused to handle the banderillas and confined his practices more and more to lunging with his new sword at a mark and to chasing and being chased by bulls.

"I care nothing for all that other," Pepe explained coldly. "When I enter the ring, I will not act. There will be no make-believe. I will kill the bull, immediately."

"But," argued Barrera nervously, "the people will not like that. They like a good performance. Believe me."

"Good," argued Pepe, "then let them send in bulls clever enough to perform against me. For when I am matador the bulls will perform, not I. I will kill."

The bandidos and centaurs roared at these replies and Barrera grew thoughtful. This mania for killing in his pupil impressed him. It was a sign, he whispered to his cronies, of greatness. Not a day passed but Pepe brought down a half-dozen chickens and a stray dog or two with his agile sword. His marksmanship with this weapon delighted his admirers. One old Zapatista watching him one night climb the roof of the hacienda, sword in hand, and give battle to the bats swooping around his head, crossed himself and swore to his friends that there was devil's blood in this princeling.

The feats which most delighted Barrera and his cronies were those in the bull pastures. One bull did not suffice but he must venture with three and four. He would stand still, wooden stick in hand, staring calmly at the animals while the horsemen lounging in the vicinity looked on and held their breaths. Then he would approach one of the beasts, smiling almost lovingly into its eyes as he drew near. And when the animal charged, with that swift, head-lowered rush of a locomotive, Pepe's face would brighten, his eyes would glisten, his body would stand poised as if arrested in a dance measure. And with the death-dealing horns lifting to toss him he would move aside with neither leap nor scurry in his step. His manner at these vital moments thrilled the very stomachs of his tutors. His movements, as quick and unexpected as those of some fish, were a delight to watch, but more than these, for Barrera and his cronies, was the sense of mastery which stamped the performance. With two, three, and sometimes four of the beasts hurling themselves at this fragile and seemingly motionless figure, bellowing and thundering by him with their horns grazing his arm as they lifted for the kill, it was the bulls and not Pepe who appeared full of troubles. Uncle Felipe, observing Pepe's daily flirtations with death, noting how he delighted in teasing the most ferocious of the beasts, maliciously plucking their tails when they had failed to murder him, whacking them with his wooden stick as they wheeled to renew their goring efforts—noting these blood-curdling antics of this sallow whippersnapper of a nephew, Uncle Felipe would shrug his shoulders and observe calmly that he was witnessing either a great matador or a young corpse in the making—and that personally it was a matter of small importance to him which.

During the three years that followed, Uncle Felipe, at the insistence of the Señora Santoyo, engaged other tutors than his horsemen for Pepe —gentlemen of learning from the capital who were given the task of educating his ward. Pepe waved aside their theories of education, their books and their lessons and suffered them to remain on the ranch only as long as they had stories to tell him, historical tales to recite, or new and unforeseen facts concerning life in general to impart. As soon as they ran out of these pleasing informations Pepe dismissed them and waited coldly for their successors.

At sixteen Pepe killed his first bull and this was in the bull ring of Durango, a sun-baked town some hundred miles from the Ortiz ranch. Uncle Felipe and all his horsemen, friends, and neighbors were in the stands. Barrera, acting as sword valet for his pupil, was as nervous as a dog with a bone. The bull lumbered into the sun, the toreros turned him in circles, placed the banderillas; a picador's horse was gored, the trumpet sounded, and Pepe stepped forth in his gold braid and gleaming red silks. Nothing to speak of happened. He approached the bull disdainfully, for he had seen at a glance what a stupid beast it was. He stood looking into its eyes with contempt for a few moments and then with a single flourish of the cape lowered its head and thrust home with his sword. The bull's legs buckled. He sank and died. Pepe withdrew his sword, wiped it clean, and bowed first to the dead animal who, though unworthy of his steel, had yet the honor of sharing his début, and then to the President's box.

Uncle Felipe's horsemen cheered and old Barrera leaped up and down and was for rushing into the bull ring to embrace his pupil. But the crowd remained unimpressed. They saluted the youth of the matador with a few good-natured vivas. That they had witnessed the début of a great bull-ring hero never entered their heads. And leaving the arena, Pepe sensed his failure with the crowd and smiled.

"They are a pack of stupid fools," Pepe confided to his uncle that night.

To which Uncle Felipe answered, very pleased with his nephew's chagrin, "They are the audience you have chosen to impress."

"They are not," Pepe answered.

"Oho!" said Uncle Felipe, "you are already dreaming of Mexico City and Madrid and Lima. Hey! Hey! Hey! Well, let me tell you now, my young one, you'll find the same audiences there as in Durango."

"I am not dreaming of audiences," said Pepe.

"Then why," pursued Uncle Felipe, "why waste your time becoming a matador if you are so nobly indifferent to audiences."

"I do not need audiences," said Pepe. "I would just as soon kill bulls by myself. I am all the audience I need."

"You are a young fool," said Uncle Felipe, growing red. "You make me angry."

Pepe was silent and as his uncle's face reddened and his head lowered he regarded the rancher with very much the same look in his velvety eyes that he had turned on the stupid bull who had shared his début a few hours ago.

"You are not worthy my attention," Pepe answered slowly, which was also what he had said to the beast in the bull ring of Durango.

Two days later Pepe left the Ortiz ranch, taking with him his many swords, his dozen matador suits and Barrera. The bandidos and the centaurs rode with him to the railroad station, singing:

> "The palm trees will weep with every dawn
> When they wake to find our hero gone."

And prophesying to another clanking tune that within a short time the most beautiful women in the world would be groveling at the feet of their muchacho for one of his smiles:

"Farewell," they sang, "O prince of matadors. If you get into troubles call us, send for us and we will come and strangle your enemies with their own whiskers."

A few days later Pepe embraced his mother in Tampico, demanded an advance on his inheritance, listened politely to her maternal cries of love—and departed.

There are now many journalistic legends about Pepe Santoyo's beginnings in the bull ring, tales recounting his early prowess and fame. But these are, alas, apocryphal. Pepe's stubborn antics in the bull ring that first year almost finished him. For it was audiences he fought more than bulls, audiences and toreros, picadors and sport officials.

In the Puebla arena he stood regarding a knock-kneed bull by the name of Diablo for five minutes without moving, then walked up to the chicken-hearted beast, slapped its nose soundly and killed it with a single thrust—all this after the toreros had leaped about the ring in fine exhibitions of courage and agility in the face of this same death-dealing Diablo.

In Jalapa he tossed aside his sword at the signal for the kill, snatched a stiletto from Barrera's kit, returned to the wobbly and meditative beast and despatched it, exactly as he had seen it done in the slaughter house in Tampico.

In Monterrey he actually pulled a doddering old fake of a bull around by the tail, dragging the discouraged animal to the President's box and killing it while holding its nose to the ground with his foot.

Toward the end of the year, however, word trickled into the capital of a very youthful matador whose integrity was disorganizing the bullfights in the provinces. Disgruntled toreros helped launch the Santoyo legend. Barrera, who knew his way among the sporting groups of Mexico City and who was almost beside himself with the unrecognized genius of his protégé, finally secured the big managers. There was always the likelihood of news in a newcomer. The capital boasted a number of bull-ring favorites, fellows full of grace and daring. But since the retirement of Juan Belmonte, there had been no greatness in the arena, no one to release that curious ecstasy which lay in the public bosom for the true master of the bull.

Under Barrera's eye the fight was properly planned to show off his protégé at his best. First a noble bull, if there was such a thing left in Mexico; secondly, very little business from the toreros; thirdly, small business by the picadors. Señor Santoyo desired to reveal his skill against a ferocious and untired beast.

On the appointed Sunday, Pepe emerged, bowed, and walked across the glaring ring to engage the murderous attention of El Fino—and the stands beheld almost immediately their new idol. For there is in every type of champion the unmistakable signal of destiny—unmistakable, that is, to eyes trained for its existence. It is the inner strut of the hero, the aloofness and precision of the artist who offers not himself but his performance for the vivas of the crowd.

The fragile figure of Pepe Santoyo in its gold and scarlet silks, facing the bull on this first afternoon, filled the veteran spectators with that strange vibrancy which the virtuoso, known or unknown, must generate before he can perform as one. It is this pause before action, this arresting and secretive evolution of the human into the promise of hero under the very eyes of the spectators that raises their spirits and prepares them for doings on a higher key. In these first moments before El Fino, not all the ancestors of Pepe Santoyo marshaled around him could have added a whit to his boast of courage and prowess.

The stands applauded, the señoritas smiled excitedly, the newspapermen, who in Mexico resemble old-fashioned bartenders, nodded appreciatively to one another; the scattering of American tourists marveled unprofessionally at the youth of this gladiator and his lack of physique and his ugly face; and the occupants of the President's box leaned forward expectantly.

Pepe Santoyo's joust with El Fino passed into bull ring history that afternoon. For twenty minutes he stood without breaking ground, gliding and turning before the charges of the beast with the sudden, imperceptible agilities of a fish evading a blow. Time and again it seemed that El Fino, head lowered, horns tossing, had rushed right through him as if he were a phantom in red and gold; which is probably what the distracted animal complained about to its gods as it swung its empty horns and bellowed at the blinding sky.

One of the newspapermen described the performance as a thing of such exquisite beauty as to move the dullest member of the anti-administration forces to tears. It was, he wrote, superb, and restored bullfighting to the estate from which, owing to the confusion in Mexican life created by these same sinister forces, it had fallen in recent years.

The public that had actually witnessed the début of the new idol grew more mysterious and inarticulate as its raptures increased. It remembered the details of Pepe's performance through the haze of hero worship and was ready to proclaim each of his gestures a grace unknown before, and each of his movements a feat unparalleled. As for the young matador's courage, that was beyond the power of mere words—even Mexican ones—to describe. He had not fought but danced gravely with a bull more ferocious than any ever seen in an arena. He had waltzed the beast to death, never missing a step, and despatched it in a single gesture so rhythmic that El Fino himself must have felt its grace.

The cafés buzzed with the advent of this new hero. And of these matters Pepe Santoyo, dismissing the fawning and garrulous Barrera for the night, had only to say: "It was a fine bull, my friend."

The fame Pepe won this afternoon was his beginning. Within six months Lima and Madrid had enrolled themselves as captive cities. There too he inspired raptures and rode on the shoulders of idolators. But it was in Mexico that he was loved. Was he not descended of Cuauhtemoctzín, King of Kings; of Ixtlxochitl, Prince of Princes; of Captains and Generals, Heroes and Saviors too many to mention? It was truly as if all these potentates in feather mantles, all these conquerors in steel and silver, all these noble and spectacular sires of Pepe

Santoyo had collaborated to produce one supreme human being. And in these flourishes of adoration with which they surrounded his name, Pepe's countrymen were stating indeed a biological and racial truth.

For Pepe's secret in the bull ring was that he held himself not as matador but conqueror and priest. It was the smell of death that stirred his senses as he approached each beast and its blood that gushed after his sword was the symbol of a mysterious consummation. The battle with the bull became for him more and more a delicious ritual in which his pride was crowned not by the plaudits of the stands but the death of the beast. As his countrymen sensed he was in truth the perfection of a breed. Out of a double lineage drenched in blood, whose sadistic deeds and valor incarnadined two worlds, had been hatched this murderous little goldfish of a matador who loved to kill bulls.

Three years passed and Pepe progressed from the position of idol to that of national institution. He made his home in Mexico City, establishing himself in a great house surrounded by lovely gardens. He appeared weekly in the bull ring and made trips to Spain and Peru when the Mexican season was at an end. Despite the fabulous success that had come to him, he remained unchanged. His egomania was more than a match for his fame. As on his Uncle Felipe's ranch, praise failed to impress him. He had the air of one who wanted nothing, least of all the plaudits and ecstasies he inspired. Fame, his manner proclaimed, was an accident unnecessary to his greatness.

The caprice and cruelty, the fanatic pride in self and disdain of the world which his new friends mistook for the results of a turned head, the bandidos and centaurs of the Ortiz ranch had known years before. Uncle Felipe, after a brief visit to his nephew's palace in the capital, testified, in fact, that he had found the young man altered by not a hair, but the same bad-mannered peacock he had tried in vain to make a man of on his ranch.

The only change which distinguished Pepe, the national idol, from that spindly, sallow boy who had chased his Uncle Felipe's bulls with a wooden stick was his attitude toward the women who fell like exhausted moths at his feet. It was an attitude which would have stunned a moralist and outraged a lover. The señoritas who achieved his favors found themselves reduced in his arms to a species of toys. Their sighs, swoons, cries of love and fealty were to Pepe a very natural and pleasing form of play they had to offer. He was gallant and lavish. He returned vow for vow, kiss for kiss, fire for fire and passed from adorer to adorer with hardly a consciousness of change. He loved gracefully and at times his spirit softened to a kindly, almost childlike excitement.

But however ardent his arms and lips, his heart never dreamed of tomorrow or remembered yesterday. His heart, in fact, had no existence in his amours.

When he was twenty Pepe succeeded, with small effort on his part, to the affections of a vixenish nymph of the theater known to the public as Venida. The liaison contained a slight novelty for the national idol. Venida, scratched and dented from the hands of his predecessors, was still a brighter toy than Pepe had yet acquired.

She was to begin with a very odd creature to look at. A few inches less of height and she might have been classified as a dwarf, or rather as a miniature adult. Unlike so many undersized women, her head was small and perfectly proportioned, her body and features exquisitely related. She gave the impression of a full-blown, beautiful woman seen through the wrong end of an opera glass. Despite the jet coiffure and the high instep she was neither Spanish nor Indian to the eye, but that perfect neutralization of the racial atom which produces a breed identified in all countries as exotic.

Pepe, listening to her sing at the vaudeville theater one evening, felt the stir of interest which as a child he had always experienced before a rare toy. Her voice, full and robust, as it issued from so fragile a mold, delighted him, and never ceased to delight him for three months.

Barrera, now factotum to the nation's idol, was less delighted. The nature, name, and color of Pepe's conquests were matters which he regarded with the indifference they deserved. But this little doll woman who came hardly to the shoulders of the great matador was with all her airs of this and that a vixen, a bawd, and a wolf at heart. She filled the great house into which the amiable great man had introduced her with such yowlings as belonged in the fishmarkets. A strumpet, said Barrera, a female to be handled with a brass-studded belt. There was nothing in the world worse for a man than this breed of wanton, not even a diet of cactus or a pocket full of rattlesnakes.

"She's not for you," pleaded Barrera; "you can never understand such a beast as this. She is worse than a bull with six horns."

Pepe waved his factotum aside. He understood the grounds of Barrera's complaint. Venida was the first of his conquests who neither swooned in his arms nor sang hymns to his glory. But Pepe was tired of embracing señoritas with a matador's suit and bored with being embraced in return as if he were some public shrine on the loose. He preferred this, at least for the remainder of the bullfight season.

Accordingly, for three months Venida wheedled gifts out of the national idol as if he were a Tampico oil man with a roll; stole from him, lied, cheated, and indulged herself in such infidelities and hysterias as her position at the theater offered. And all this delighted Pepe. She had for him the mystery and charm of the heretic.

One Sunday night Venida came home in an astonishing mood. Pepe was in the garden awaiting her. He was half asleep. The bullfight season had closed that afternoon and he had been carried out of the ring on a thousand shoulders and almost murdered by adoring salutes. There was also Señora Morales, a proud and beautiful lady who was languishing with love for him; and her fifteen-year-old sister Teresa who had threatened to return home and hurl herself from the top of the highest pyramid in Yucatan unless he kissed her. The great matador had spent the evening in the home of these two admiring and swooning women. Thus he awaited the charming Venida under the tropical stars, with that good nature and detachment which only a rake can bring to the problems of love.

She arrived two hours late, walked the garden for fifteen minutes and then threw herself on the ground at Pepe's feet, embraced his legs and fell to sobbing. Pepe grinned in the dark. Such homage had never been his from Venida. And what pleasanter finale to a crowded day than this—the surrender of a heart that had so long mocked him? He listened, however, a bit dubiously. Venida was a talented actress. He listened and studied each note of grief, each arpeggio of pain and then closed his eye contentedly. The tune was perfect. He had never heard it better sung, or more sincerely. What a fool Barrera was. A bull with six horns, indeed! This little one with head lowered, as all the rest, for the coup de grâce! Ask nothing of a woman, be content to kiss, smile, and wait and her heart broke for you. He was pleased. It was in these moments of heartbreak that Pepe found, connoisseur fashion, the caress of pride he most desired. And surfeited though he was by the sighs, kisses, and hosannahs of the day, Pepe felt grateful for this exhibition in the garden. He stroked the grief-tumbled coiffure and felt very wise and gallant, even though no thoughts were in his head.

Venida's sobs ended but her tears continued to flow as she spoke, as if there were two voices coming from her. Pepe listened, his hand making tender comment on her hair. She did not expect to be believed, the poor little one insisted. She had been so wicked, done so many naughty things; even laughed at him in her heart. But look at her now. Weeping. She had never wept for any man before.

Briefly, Venida's tale concerned an American, Señor Lewis, a mighty theatrical producer from the city of New York, who had been swept from his feet and enchanted by her talent, and who had offered her a contract, three thousand pesos a week, her name in electric lights bigger than the Montezuma Beer sign opposite the Regis Hotel, to return with him to the States. Confronted with this golden opportunity, Venida had shuddered and found herself unable to seize on it. All this because she could not bear to be parted from her matador. She had never suspected it before, but the tragic incident had revealed to her that she adored him. She had refused riches and a career for love of a faithless man. But she was content. Love had made a fool of her, as she had so often done of men. This was justice. She asked no more than to be allowed to remain at the side of her lover until he tired of her and cast her away.

With this tale of sacrifice concluded, Venida, overcome anew by its significance, resumed her sobbing. Pepe, looking down on her in the silver-lighted night, considered her for the moment a creature of infinite charm.

There is a gallantry in heartlessness that lovers can never hope to achieve. To the lover, sacrifice is a reward for pains and desires. To the gallant it is a challenge to his pride. Pepe, receiving this unexpected gift, reached for his own superior pocketbook.

There were perhaps other forces that moved him to the gesture—the bullfight season was over, the capital was hot, Barrera was becoming a bore, Doña Morales and her juvenile sister had insisted he spend a month with them on their estate, and, as happens to all monarchs at times, his domain this night under the monotonous moon seemed to have grown small and airless. He thought, however, of none of these things. Speaking casually, as befits the bestowing of a truly royal and superior gift, Pepe pointed out that her grief and sacrifice were unnecessary since he had decided to go with her to the city of New York.

He was delighted with the result of his announcement. With a cry, the little one stared at him an instant and then sank to the ground quite as if she had fainted. Pepe accepted this gesture. He was, himself, pleasantly overcome by his own sense of largesse and with a tired and amiable grin he raised the little one to his side.

"Broadway—the heart of the world," sang the chorus boys who have rouged and asymmetrical faces. The chorus girls waved their bodies and squealed in unison of love and the summer moon.

New York, tall, glittering, and hot, drifted like a plate-glass galleon through the summer day. At night there was a Chinese actor full of grave and incoherent passions and a German pugilist with a promising right-hand wallop. At night there were Africans who leaped to a chant called Black Bottom, a Spaniard who strummed the guitar as if he owned four hands, an English lady with a Hamlet face who sang ribald Cockney songs. A cannonade of lights proclaimed these and other novelties in the Broadway dusk. Jazz bands played, clowns sobbed their griefs, courtesans bewailed their broken hearts. Semites moaned for the Carolinas, gigolos hurrahed for the Open Road, and from a thousand stages came the strut and whinny of the evening's makebelieve. New York, tall, daft, and cosmopolite, cakewalked with a Roman candle in its hand.

Pepe Santoyo, moving in these gaudy streets, felt a sting of desire in his heart. He was no longer an alien. New York colonizes its admirers quickly. Seven weeks had made Pepe a New Yorker.

He knew where the loudest bands played, where the prettiest girls danced, where the best liquor was sold, where the finest people went. He had learned the names of the funniest comedians, the most exclusive hostesses, the biggest gamblers, the best prize fighters, the leading baseball heroes and the current sophisticates. He was already a familiar and accepted figure in the whirligig of the town's night life. His name was inscribed in the shifting roster of celebrities that meet like some secret society in the cafés, theater lobbies and hotel suites.

He had learned to pass under the charging traffic without quickening his step, to drink ten cocktails without falling asleep or making arrogant remarks to strangers; to distinguish between the regulars and the upstarts, the Giants and the Yankees, the head waiters and the diners, the wives of Caesar and the cuties of Pan. He knew his way blindfolded from the Savoy Plaza to the Forty-fourth Street theater where Venida's name was raised in burning letters above the crowds. He spoke a broken but determined English and could whistle the chorus of the Maine "Stein Song." He had met the Mayor, week-ended on a magnificent yacht, raided the Fifth Avenue haberdashers, presented a tall, blond and internationally famous hetaera with an extravagant keepsake, been fêted by the Spanish-American Society and given a movie test at the Paramount Studios in Astoria.

These experiences and accomplishments, which had crowded the seven weeks in their acquiring, had generated a queer excitement in Pepe Santoyo, had disrupted that character which so many kings and captains, presiding over his inception, had bestowed on him; and had planted a nettle in his heart.

Amid these gaudy streets, surrounded by these pale, glib people,

Pepe felt the impact of a stronger land. Here, in Broadway, was that bull with six horns of whom Barrera had mumbled. And if his mind, never an instrument for analyses, failed to visualize the scene in the dramatic terms of the Great Sport, his spirit responded with an eagerness which reminded him of his early days in the bull ring. Ambition filled him, for what he did not know. Desire kept him awake, for whom he could not tell. He was, as he explained it to Venida, full of new life.

He was admired and sought after. He plunged from revelry to revelry, sporting his coleta amid Hindu turbans and Montparnasse haircuts. He offered side-splitting imitations of Venida, using a lampshade for a hat and a phonograph record for a fan. He laughed more in one night than he had in a year, and his gay, vibrant manner overcame, wherever he appeared, the handicap of his long nose, his prognathous jaw, his sparrowlike physique and his rapine tendencies. He was regarded by his new friends and hostesses as a distinguished youth of precocious poise and energy, as a dangerous satyr and an amusing type of Mexican.

Yet, with his blood tingling under this bombardment of jazz bands, cocktails, social and amorous triumphs, which seemingly made him master of this new and fantastic bull of the six horns, Pepe woke each noon clamorous and unsatisfied. There was too much fame, too many heroes, too many ballyhoos to drown out the vivas he won. It was a land that consisted of too much; of too much play and work, too much money, too much noise and light; a land that was lost behind too many. This was its lure for Pepe and the nettle in his heart.

He laughed at Venida's capers. Her infidelities, now signalled by the appearance of jewels and shining automobiles, amused him no less than in the capital. He reminded her ironically, during their infrequent tête-á-têtes, of how her great love for him had almost caused her to sacrifice all these delights. And arriving one night in her dressing room, sleek as a Pomeranian, ugly as a cuttle fish and bristling like a seltzer bottle, he told her he was returning to Mexico in four days for the opening of the bullfight season. He inquired, with mock tenderness, whether she could bear to stay in New York without him.

"Yes," said Venida, "I am no longer a child."

Sitting in her dressing room, watching her change from a Mexican into a Broadway cameo, he smiled coldly at her answer. He preferred the Venida who had burned and swooned at his feet in the silver-lighted garden a few months ago and for a moment this unruffled Phoenix angered him. She seemed suddenly part of that New York which one held and lost from day to day. Pepe studied her and whistled the Maine "Stein Song."

"I have called to take you to my party." He came out of his favorite musical practice with a smile.

"Your party," Venida laughed.

"Yes. It is in my honor," said Pepe, "to wish me good-by."

"Who will be there?" Venida inquired, for no less than Pepe, she was now a connoisseur of parties.

"Everybody," said Pepe.

Pepe had looked forward to this revel arranged in his honor by a visiting ambassador as a climax to his New Yorkhood. Very prominent people would be present, representatives from all the electric-lighted courts of fame that flourished in this land.

Pepe beheld them as he entered the buzz and glitter of the drawing room, the bull with six horns decorated for the coup de grâce. They had assembled to honor him with a farewell and he beheld them with a proud heart—sportsmen, financiers, aviators, aristocrats, journalists, gilded idlers, a renowned philosopher on a world tour, a British peer famed for his horses, a sprinkling of high-priced actors and opera stars; polo players, gamblers, and Casanovas all occupied like a well-trained chorus, bowing, nodding, chattering, drinking, laughing, and with an easy, unyielding egoism in their eyes; and illumining the corners and divans of the room the consorts, conquests, and courtesans of these assorted heroes.

Venida disappeared from his side. For a few minutes his entrance rippled the scene. Butlers balanced trays before him, celebrities turned bright welcomes on him. Journalists paused in their interminable anecdotes to shake his hand. Paunchy little men with tight red faces whom he recognized as members of the mysterious tribe called lords of industry offered him cigars and cigarettes and inquired with youthful winks after his friend Venida. For an hour he drifted from group to group swallowing another cocktail every time a butler caught his eye. He wandered into the room where the music played and made love to all the women he danced with but one. Her he treated to a whistled accompaniment to the orchestra playing the Maine "Stein Song."

But despite these familiar exertions the sense of revelry died in Pepe's bosom. Despite the music, liquor, kisses, and laughter, Pepe found himself being pushed by something very mysterious, out of the scene. It occurred to him that this farewell party in his honor had nothing to do with him. New York had nothing to do with him. He tried for several minutes to assemble his pride and greatness and he stood, as had one of his third-yield grandfathers, blowing a bugle to charge to troops that had fled.

He surveyed the scene, closing one eye to see it better, twisted his mouth into a remarkable sneer and spat at a passing butler. The servant paused and glowered. Pepe, as if challenger to a sneering competition, twisted his mouth, this time including his nose, into an even more horrible grimace. The butler gave up and hurried away.

What did these gringos know of bulls and the fine business of blood and death? What had he, Santoyo, been doing, wasting his time with such ignorant and lowly ones! (The troops, a bit disheveled, were shuffling back to the battlefield.) Did they think they were as fine and noble as Santoyo? Well, he would settle that matter right now. He was through with them. Closing one eye, he surveyed again the blur of gringos laughing and chattering around him with another fearful contortion of his face, this time abetted by a contemptuous noise half hiss and half belch, then he turned his back on them and moved to a corner. There he sat down and waylaid drinks whenever they passed, scowling until his jawbones stuck out at unbelievable angles. A stupid race, the gringos, who did not even know how to smile. Give him the hearty laugh of the bandidos.

Pepe opened his mouth wide and a sudden penetrating cackle rang out. A lady nearby dropped her drink and squealed. Pepe made a sickening face at her.

"Oh—but they're dangerous, these Mexicans," said the lady who was too old for kissing and moved hurriedly away.

Pepe fell to dreaming of better company. A smile hovered over his sour face and his eyes rolled up in a melting look as if he had drifted abruptly into a trance. Ay, Mexico! he was hungry for that Mexico whose dust lay white and tender on his heart. He began to fancy in the midst of this stupid gringo scene, the sun-baked roads of Jalisco. The acid sweat of bulls came into his nose. And over the deserts rode the black-browed, the strong-hearted, and ever-smiling bandidos. He saw them, himself in their midst, and heard them singing as he left them at the little depot, a matador on his way to the bulls.

"Farewell," they sang, "O prince of matadors. If you ever need us call for us and we will come and strangle your enemies with their own whiskers."

A cry broke from his mongrel, exiled heart.

"Ay—y, muchachos. Here I am. Pepe!" He held up his hand.

"Very good for killing bulls," someone laughed behind him, pointing at the fist he shook.

"Yes!" screeched Pepe. "No good for punch. No good for baseball, tennis ball, football. No good for here. But for keeling bulls, the best in the world."

A chorus of cheers stopped him. He looked drunkenly around, his heart sick for the little red and yellow kingdom of the bull ring, for the vivas of his empire. Now was the time to go. The muchachos had come and rescued him. He felt the calm and smiling faces insulting him for the last time. On the way to the door, staggering from figure to figure, he saw Venida. She was gringo scum. He was going back to Mexico. She would never go back.

"Good-by." He lurched past her, making a nasty sound under his long nose.

In the next three days Santoyo continued to drink and to grow more Mexican. In restaurants he demanded eggs with garlic and at the Savoy Plaza, where he lived, he required chili sauce on his chicken. He discovered a group of Mexicans in a Fourteenth Street speakeasy and dragged them with him for a new round of farewells to celebrities. He sought out also Cubans, Puerto Ricans, and Venezuelans as well as Spaniards. He slept without undressing, sang Mexican songs till his voice cracked, and on the fourth day, still drunk, was lifted aboard the New Orleans flier, embraced by a hurried Venida, deposited in a drawing room and started back for the land of his fathers.

On the second day, approaching New Orleans, his head began to clear. On the way to Laredo, he shaved himself three times during the day, drank several gallons of ginger ale and investigated the contents of his five suitcases. He recalled dimly the crew of flunkies who had attended his packing at the hotel and marveled at these Americanos anew. A strange people, in all ways. Not a shirt stud was missing. He alighted at Brownsville and telegraphed $300 to the Savoy Plaza to be distributed as tips.

And at Laredo, his face once more growing asymmetrically handsome, or at least dignified and purposeful, he presented himself to the Mexican customs for inspection and was recognized. The crowded station broke into cheers. "Santoyo . . . Pepe!" they cried. Men leaped to their feet and rushed to embrace him. Women smiled and clasped their hands and offered him their babies to kiss. He drew a deep breath and raised his arm to them in salute. He felt strange and confused—but he was going back to the bulls.

The three-day journey to the capital thereafter was a triumphal sweep through hills and deserts. News of Señor Santoyo's return preceded the train and produced mobs of ragged barefoot Indians and

Mexicans at the smallest depots. Bands played as the train pulled into the larger centers. Gifts were raised to the opened car windows. Scores of cooked chickens, pastries, bottles of wine, and silver ornaments poured into the drawing-room where the great matador sat, smiling and silent. Occasionally he emerged, let himself be seen on the steps of the train for a moment, and the bright air filled with shouts.

At Mexico City the national idol was greeted by a cavalry band, a troop of policemen, five senators in frock coats and silk hats, all the journalists the capital owned, and a mob estimated by the giddy narrators of the event as the largest ever seen in Mexico during a time of peace and plenty. Pepe was driven through the boulevards, cheered from thousands of windows and finally deposited in his home. Here Barrera wept on seeing him, kissed his cheeks, and screamed orders at the servants for an hour. It was Wednesday. The bullfight season was scheduled to open the following Sunday.

For three days Pepe lolled about his gardens, receiving the homage of admirers and answering the questions of the journalists.

His visit to the great capital of the north, they announced to their infatuated readers, had done more than a hundred treaties to cement the friendship between the two countries. Señor Santoyo had been fêted as a prince from the moment of his arrival to the moment of his departure, and the great sportsmen of New York had been filled with envy and chagrin at not being able to behold the beauty and skill of their Santoyo in the bull ring, since, owing to a complete absence of torero talent in the Anglo-Saxon, bullfighting had no home in the land of Washington. However, their idol had by his own personal magnetism, despite the handicap of the absence of bullfighting, won the hearts of the Americanos and the journalists felt certain that now that the Yankees had beheld this flower of Mexican manhood the immigration question would soon be satisfactorily settled. Señor Santoyo, modest as always under the new glories he had won, had returned eager for the bullfight season and had spoken with his old fire of his love of the great sport.

Barrera busied himself for the three days to insure a heroic opening for the season and return to the ring for the great matador. With the advent of this day, however, a nervousness came over the veteran. The lethargy he had smelled in the mood of his idol from the moment of their first embrace, appeared to have increased. Riding beside Pepe to the bull ring, he cursed himself for an old fool, stared desperately at the silent hero and grew heavy-hearted. He repeated to himself that he was father and mother to this young one, that it was he who had taught him every twist and move which had made him the greatest bullfighter in the world—and that he had a right to know what was clouding the Señor's eyes, what made his hand so listless, and what his thoughts were. But with high masculine insight for the dangers of such talk Barrera guarded his tongue and sat making angry faces at the chauffeur's head. Halfway to the bull ring his worry would no longer be denied.

"What are you thinking about?" Barrera scowled at the abstracted face.

Pepe's eyes glinted and a half smile came to him.

"The bull with six horns," he answered.

That was it! Barrera cursed silently. His warnings had been ignored and the Venida, snake of a woman with a pepper box for a heart, had crawled into his muchacho's soul and was devouring it. Let her show her face around him again. He would know how to deal with her this time.

"El Chico, your bull, is a fine one," he said.

El Chico was indeed a fine bull. The stands applauded as he came snorting into the ring. The toreros shrugged their shoulders and wished their part of the show over. The bulls Santoyo engaged were all of a stripe, cruel, swift, and unreliable. Fortunately the idol preferred to do his own cape-playing and the sooner they retired from the ring and the fresher they left the beast, the more pleased the President and all the officials. As for the stands, they had no eye for these preliminaries when Santoyo was awaited.

The band blaring gayly in the bright afternoon became silent. El Chico charged, wheeled, pawed the earth and charged again. The spectators smiled and, as if under a hypnosis, waited for Santoyo, their hearts remembering the incomparable spectacle of man, beast, and death he always provided.

A roar of delight greeted the familiar little figure in gold and scarlet silks as it stepped into the bull ring. They cried his name, threw their hats in the air, clapped their hands, and laughed joyously. Pepe heard these sounds of happiness and drew a deep breath. He had stood waiting like a man in a dream for the ovation—and for the first glimpse of the shining beast to awaken him. He saluted the President's box and moved forward slowly as was the tradition of his style. He took his stand in the center of the hot glaring ring and waited for El Chico to begin the performance.

With the first charge of the bull, a curious alien sense came over

Pepe Santoyo. His cape made a perfect flourish, his lean body turned gracefully and precisely from the thrust of the horns. But his heart had not experienced that quick throb of delight by which he knew himself master of the beast. He waited coolly for the return charge, his instincts warning him that this was another of his favorites—those bad ones who charged the smell of the man instead of the enticing swirl of the cape. Again the animal rushed, again the horns missed and again Pepe turned coldly and without elation for the next maneuver.

Now he knew that something had happened to him. He flashed the cape, pirouetted, kneeled and swayed before the plunging horns. The stands filled the bright day with shouts of joy. Their Santoyo was better than ever, quicker than ever and even more courageous. He was taking greater chances, allowing the horns to come nearer and nearer. But with each new burst of cheering that drifted to him Pepe felt this alien sense deepen. He had felt it first when his countrymen had cheered him in the little custom-shed at Laredo and the sensation had grown stronger as he had ridden farther and farther into the deserts and hills of his native land.

As if to shock himself into a livelier mood, he rose from his knee and approached the glowering beast, walking the path between its horns. El Chico rushed. Pepe did not twist aside. He remained in the path of the bull, stepping nimbly back before its charge. The horns framed his arms, the animal's head butted his thighs. Pepe slapped its nose and El Chico fell back with a snort. The stands rocked with excitement. There was no hero in the memory of the oldest and fattest of the journalists who had ever allowed this caress of death in the open. Señor Belmonte had let the beast pin its horns into the fence, standing between them. Never had this been seen in the open ring before.

Their Santoyo was greater than ever. Their Santoyo transcended all men's dreams of glory and courage. But these wild cheers coming to him in the glaring, lonely bull ring filled Pepe anew with that curious sense of alienism. He pirouetted, flourished the cape once more, and felt confused.

He was not frightened, his body moved with precision, his eyes were cool. There was nothing to be seen by even Barrera, watching with his heart in his mouth, that told of change or waver in the great matador. But to Pepe this always exalting dance with the beast seemed to have undergone a dismal disenchantment. He stood poised as if in a dream of himself. He saw the bull as an unreal monster and the very color and sounds around him, the blaze of sky and the burn of the sand were part of a phantom scene. There was no reality in this, no familiar ritualistic urge in his heart. His soul, it seemed to him, had changed and become a stranger to the spectacle he was contributing. He was viewing it with strange eyes, performing with a stranger's skill and senses. Reality lay elsewhere and, fronting the beast whose horns continued to graze him in their thrust, whose fetid breath burst again and again in his face, Pepe's thought wandered to that other Bull of the Six Horns, to the umbrellas of light that hung in the sky, to the clamor and throb of that greater land he had visited. The roars from the stands came to him like the murmur of a handful of children. The blur and flutter of faces that caught his eyes filled him with derision. He seemed suddenly engaged in childish antics before a group of nobodies. Even El Chico appeared a fool.

Amid those gaudy, far-off streets, surrounded by that pale glib and superior folk, Pepe had undergone a mysterious evaporation, as if the ghosts of Cuauhtemoctzín and Cortez and all the first, second, and third yield of grandfathers had departed his loins. The smell of death and the business of blood and sacrifice no longer delighted his soul. He had outgrown them. This was no longer an inner ritual that related him to the murderous peacocks, the Temple of the Sun, the helmets of the Conquistadores and the gibbets of the Colonial lords—but an alien and dangerous exercise. He stood now in the bull ring like some strangely disinherited one.

El Chico charged. Pepe smiled wearily at the persistent beast. The bugle signaled the kill and, drawing his sword, he approached, poised himself on his toes as if he were going to take flight, extended the glittering weapon and lunged. He felt the sword point sink and stop. Stupidly he pressed harder, refusing to believe in this vital moment that he had missed the mark. The ground suddenly swept away. He was on the horns. He fluttered a moment in the air like some flapping, ornate bird. He had been tossed. He came down on one of the points. There was a sickening burn in his groin. The horn sank in deep, wrenched at his flesh and thrust him high in the air. He had made no cry but from the stands came a high-pitched moan. Vanquished, that exquisite mechanism of courage, grace, and skill. There it was to be seen for another unbelievable moment, spinning like a broken plate on the sharp horns, falling to the earth like a bit of bright fabric. It lay without moving. El Chico nudged it with his reddened horn, sniffed, nudged again. It remained motionless.

The toreros were out, fluttering capes, and in front of them was Barrera. Tears poured from his eyes. He cursed as he ran. The stands were groaning as if in the midst of some slow disaster.

It was Barrera's cape that turned El Chico. The beast charged and the hernia-ridden veteran leaped clumsily from its path and rushed to the bleeding figure in the sand. Pepe moved. The stands bellowed their relief. Their Santoyo was up, his hands over his wound. Barrera seized him. Pepe squirmed loose. El Chico was running with the sword dangling from his neck and beating his sides like a silver drum-stick. Pausing, the beast tossed his head again and the weapon sailed through the air. It fell at Pepe's feet.

"Thank you," he cried. He picked up the weapon and wiped it on his dry side, waved Barrera and the toreros away.

"Go away—go away," he screamed. The stands drowned his cries.

Barrera wavered. El Chico had turned, his sides running blood, blood dripping from his mouth. But his eyes were still unclouded. He sniffed, trembled and gathered himself for the charge. Pepe stood swinging the sword at the toreros. They cursed him and sprang aside.

"Come on. Hurry if you want to be killed by Santoyo," Pepe cried to the beast.

His head was spinning. His groin burned. His stomach was heavy and faint. The sky was darkening for him. He could see only the black mass of the bull coming forward.

The stands saw him reel as the beast came on. They watched the point of his sword waver, the toes on which he tried to rise for the kill refuse their burden. Then, abruptly, as if a new life had been granted him, they saw their idol rise, stand in perfect balance, and thrust forward. Man and beast, both running blood, came together. The horns lifted, the sword flashed and vanished, disappearing to the hilt inside the body of El Chico. The beast stopped. Pepe Santoyo closed his eyes and the stands, screeching as if they too were under the horns of El Chico, saw bull and man go down together. They fell face to face and El Chico, as his legs buckled, slipped forward till his dead nose lay nuzzled like a dog's against the body of the matador.

The din continued as the figure of Santoyo was lifted over the fence by a hundred hands and rushed to the hospital a block away. He was dead! Santoyo had died. The horns had ripped his body to death! The band hesitated, started to play. A great wail silenced the musicians. The President's box was empty.

To the hospital! The spectators tumbling over each other rushed for exits. In the streets men and women seized each other to weep, cry out their grief and hurry on. Where was he? Dead in his dressing-room under the stands. No. In the hospital. Men came running toward the bull ring waving their arms. Santoyo was alive. The doctors said he would live. A bad wound but no arteries severed, no vital parts torn. He would never fight again. No five, ten such wounds could stop Santoyo. He would be out in a week, in two weeks. The crowds scurried the streets in panic. Police formed around the hospital doors. Throwing themselves tearfully against the guards, the crowd demanded news. Was he suffering, their little one, was he in pain? What were the doctors doing now?

The story of Santoyo's injury swept through the capital. Shops emptied. Stores closed. The streets filled with clamorous citizens hurrying to the newspaper offices, to the bull ring, to the hospital. People screamed to each other the details of his glorious deed as they ran, how he had stood dying, sword in hand before his murderer El Chico and with his own last breath sent the point home. What a man! What a matador! God save their idol, the saints give their glorious Pepe strength. The newspapers arrived. Santoyo lived, said the headlines. The prince of valor and idol of Mexico was undergoing an operation with every hope of recovery.

Inside the hospital six surgeons and a dozen nurses crowded the operating room. Pepe Santoyo lay on the white table. The wails of the crowd came dimly through the closed windows. The surgeon in charge nodded. Barrera, standing with half-shut eyes in the doorway, watched them wash the lean body of his pupil.

"Not a bad wound," said the head surgeon with a happy sigh. "Give him the ether a little."

The anesthetist placed the cone over the great matador's mouth. Pepe, closing his eyes, inhaled deeply. The cone was lifted. The surgeons studied him closely.

He was going under. A sleepy smile shone on his face. His lips pursed and he was whistling faintly the chorus of the Maine "Stein Song."

# *Broken Necks*

THERE WAS a group of us waiting patiently for the tall steel doors of the jail to open. After we had been admitted and our credentials examined, we were marched through barred corridors and told to enter a door and make ourselves comfortable inside. Within this door stretched the room which was to witness the hangings. It was a long and narrow room with towering walls. It could have been built for one purpose only—as a room in which to hang men. The gray plaster of its walls was unrelieved by any humanizing design. These walls formed a geometrical monotone unbroken by windows or doors except for the one through which we had entered, and another which opened on the high gallows. The floor was of stone.

Forty long benches such as picnickers use in groves had been introduced into this vault of a room. They seemed puny toys under the sweep and stretch of the towering, slotlike walls. We came walking slowly into the room. We were doctors, public officials, jail attendants, and newspapermen. We sat down on the benches and faced the gallows.

The timber of the gallows reached from the stone floor to the dark, forgotten ceiling. Fifteen feet above the floor was a platform. On this platform the men who were to be hanged were to stand until a part of its floor, which was on hinges, swung back and dropped them. Then they would be left dangling from the ropes. These ropes hung now from a crossbeam fifteen feet above the floor of the platform. They were two bright-yellow manila ropes. Each ended in a noose the size of a man's head. We on the benches stared at these ropes. In the gloom, our faces floated like little pale discs above the benches. The ends of cigars and cigarettes made red spots in the darkness, and above our heads, gray and violet parasols of smoke opened and vanished. They were eager and efficient ropes and they had personality. They became, when we had scrutinized them for a long space, the strange and attentuated furniture entirely suited to this room.

People do not think in these places. They sit with their mouths somewhat parted and smoke cigars and nod politely to each other as they talk. They stare about them as do children in a strange house, noting this and observing that.

Finally, there were two men on the scaffold platform. One, the sheriff, was a stout man with snow-colored hair. He was well dressed but we noticed that he seemed unduly conscious of his freshly shined patent-leather shoes. He kept moving them about and we watched them closely, like so many cats in the dark watching two bewildered mice. The other man was a jail guard.

Then we noticed simultaneously a boxlike shack which stood against the plaster wall at the rear of the gallows platform. It was just large enough to accommodate a man. We remarked to each other that the man who sprang the trap under the feet of the men about to hang was hidden in this enclosure. For a space we stared at a small circular window in the gallows shack. How did this man feel who actually did the thing which killed two men? As we stared, a face, vague and dark, appeared in the little window and then vanished.

Suddenly, as if greatly ahead of time, men started entering the room from the single door at the side of the gallows. Three public officials walked first. Behind them walked two priests in white-and-purple surplices. Between the two priests was a young man with a colorless face. He was in his shirt sleeves and without a collar. He looked as if he had been interrupted while washing dishes. Following these were several jail guards. We did not count their number. Behind the guards walked two more priests in white-and-purple surplices and between them walked the second man.

For the first man without a collar who walked between the two priests we had no eyes. There was about him a lack of interest which made him akin to us on the benches. He stopped and wobbled, and his head rolled and from his lips issued a moan.

"Oh, my Lord Jesus Christ," he said.

His lips as he walked were peeled back in the manner of a man suffering from nausea. We did not look long at him. But the other—we stared and watched and forgot to puff on our cigars. He was a man with gaunt features lined like the wing of a bat. He had a lean and muscular neck, and he walked high-shouldered, like an Egyptian. To the drooping lines of his mouth and chin clung a dark, curling covering of hair like the beard on the paintings of the adolescent Christ. He walked with his jaw thrust forward, a lean and hollow jaw like the jaw of a starving monk. His eyes were burning black.

We watched this man and shifted about on our benches. We knew what he had done in the world he was soon to leave. At night, gun in hand, he had gone after stray pedestrians, as a wolf might go after weaker creatures in the darkness.

Then he had changed from a thief into an enemy. He no longer wanted to rob people but only to kill them. He went out in the daylight with his gun. One afternoon he stood on a busy street corner shouting and shooting into the swarm of things about him until the street grew lonely and rid of all sounds but the whoop of his voice and the little bark of his gun. It was very sad, for the figures that lay dead in the emptied street might have been our wives and our mothers. Eventually a policeman pounced upon him from the rear and held him as he continued to shout and wave a useless gun toward the high roofs of the crowded buildings.

Now, here he was, walking up the slim wooden stairs that led to the gallows platform and here he was, standing under the looped rope that dangled at his ear and beside another man who continued to moan, "My Lord Jesus Christ, forgive me. Forgive us all." But we did not look at this one. The platform was now crowded with men, but we did not look at them. They came forward with the long black straps and proceeded to bind the man who was moaning. Then a priest came forward and stood beside the man who was moaning and rested an ivory crucifix upon his lips and opened a book under his rolling eyes. But our eyes remained on the gaunt, unbarbered face with its Christlike beard, with the mystic snarl in its eyes, of the man who stood under the other rope. Under our stares he grew and grew and became lopsided and out of focus and the features of his face swam apart into the grimace of a man laughing.

Then our eyes cleared and we saw that his arms were strapped flat against his sides and his legs strapped tightly together at the ankles and the knees, and that a priest in a white-and-purple surplice, with a pink startled face, was offering an ivory crucifix for him to kiss. We watched him look at the crucifix, his eyes becoming filled with yellow lights, and watched his lips peel back, and the teeth, exaggerated in their nakedness, shine in a grin. Suddenly he spat at the crucifix. Beside him the man under the rope was moaning, "Oh, my Creator. Let me see. Let me see." And his head wobbled toward the opened book the priest in front of him held to his eyes.

Of this we were conscious in an uninterested way. For a man had spat upon a crucifix and there was that in us which made us lower our heads and move uneasily. Other men stepped forward on the gallows platform and hung long white robes upon the two under the ropes. The robes fastened in a pucker about their necks and fell to the floor and were fastened in another pucker about their ankles. Then a man with unbelievable gestures slipped the rope over the head of the moaning one and drew the noose tight with unbelievable little jerks so that the knot fell under the man's ear.

"Oh, Lord Jesus Christ, my Jesus Christ, forgive me. Forgive us all," moaned the man, his face almost vanishing in the gloom.

About the neck of the other, whom we were watching as men watch something about to explode, the second rope was fixed and jerked into place. And then a voice came from the blur and flurry of men grouped behind the ropes.

"Have you anything to say?" it inquired.

A cry answered from the one who was moaning. His words, blurred and buzzing, filled the room. "Oh, my Creator, my Creator," he sang. "I am going to my Creator."

And the man with the face that was lined like the wing of a bat remained silent, gazing with his glowing eyes down upon our heads. In his puckered white robe he loomed out of the gloom like some ancient sage in masquerade. The faces above the ropes remained visible for several instants. Two men bearing white masks then approached them. The one who moaned was rolling his eyes up and down the towering, gloomy walls as if in frantic, helpless search. The other was staring down upon us in a strange, disinterested manner, his lips peeling back, his jaw thrusting forward. He drew a long breath and then vanished behind the white mask with a secret cry in his eyes.

Both men had disappeared. There were to be seen only two long white bundles, curiously shapeless. We were silent. The moaning of the man who had kissed the crucifix suddenly resumed. It filled the room. It came louder and louder from the depths of the long white bundle, crawling over us and along the towering walls that had no windows. From the other white bundle came silence. The feet under it stared at us without movement. The moaning burst into words: "Oh, my Creator—" and was lost in a crash. The trap had banged down.

A great, swaying howl rolled into the vaultlike room. It swept like a curtain between us and the two white bundles that had shot through the trap. The two men were hanging. The howling came from the prisoners in the cells beyond in the jail, a howling like the sustained cry of an army in panic.

The two white bundles that were hanging, stirred. One of them turned slightly, with a certain idleness. The other began to expand and contract. A curious animation gradually took possession of it.

Several minutes passed and the white bundles continued to bob and twitch. The one to the left which contained the man who had moaned began now to throb and quiver like a plucked violin string. The rope above it hummed, filling the room with the whang of its monotone. The other bundle remained turning idly. A group of men had risen from the benches in front. Several of them held black stethoscopes in their hands. They waited.

The rest of us stood to our feet. There was silence, and the moments passed with our eyes unwavering. The two bundles seemed mysteriously wound up, as if they would go on turning idly forever. Then they began to act as if someone were trying to blow them up from inside. Between the masks and the puckered tops of the white robes the necks of the two men hanging within the bundles became visible. Suddenly the turning ceased and the two bundles began to behave as if someone were jerking with violence on the ropes which supported them in mid-air. They executed a staccato jig.

The bundles hung motionless at the ends of the two ropes, limp, dead banners out of which the wind had died. A physician removing the stethoscope from his ears said something that ended with the words "twelve minutes." A second physician repeated what he had said.

We crowded forward from the benches, gathering about the two figures which had dropped their white robes. They were no longer interesting. A certain fascination had gone out of them, out of the ropes, out of the tall, spectral timbers of the gallows. We passed them a few minutes later on our way out of the door. They were lying on two wheeled cots. Their masks had been moved, and their faces, colored like stained glass, watched us with mouths opened.

I had forgotten my hat. We had moved into the lobby of the jail and I hurried back after my hat. I stood for a moment gazing at the towering gray walls, the wood structure, the two strands of rope that dropped from the beam. They had been cut. There was no one in the room. I seized my hat, which was on a bench, and ran awkwardly after the men who had gone.

# *Fanny*

WHY DID Fanny do this? The judge would like to know. The judge would like to help her. The judge says: "Now, Fanny, tell me all about it."

All about it, all about it! Fanny's stoical face stares at the floor. If Fanny had words. But Fanny has no words. Something heavy in her heart, something vague and heavy in her thought—these are all that Fanny has.

Let the policewoman's records show. Three years ago Fanny came to Chicago from a place called Plano. Red-cheeked and black-haired, vivid-eyed and like an ear of ripe corn dropped in the middle of State and Madison streets, Fanny came to the city.

Ah, the lonely city, with its crowds and its lonely lights. The lonely buildings busy with a thousand lonelinesses. People laughing and hurrying along, people eager-eyed for something; summer parks and streets white with snow, the city moon like a distant window, pretty geegaws in the stores—these are a part of Fanny's story.

The judge wants to know. Fanny's eyes look up. A dog takes a kick like this, with eyes like this, large, dumb, and brimming with pathos.

Sometimes in this court where the sinners are haled, his Honor has a moment of confusion. Eyes lift themselves to him, eyes dumb and brimming with pathos. Eyes stare out of sordid faces, evil faces, wasted faces, and say something not admissible as evidence. Eyes say, I don't know, I don't know. What is it all about?

These are not to be confused with the eyes that plead shrewdly for mercy, with eyes that feign dramatic naïvetés and offer themselves like primping little penitents to his Honor. His Honor knows them fairly well. And understands them. They are eyes still bargaining with life.

But Fanny's eyes. Yes, the judge would like to know. A vagueness comes into his precise mind. He half-hears the familiar accusation that the policeman drones.

Another raid on a suspected flat. Routine, routine. Evil has its eternal root in the cities. A tireless Satan, bored with the monotony of his role; a tireless Justice, bored with the routine of tears and pleadings, lies and guilt.

There is no story in all this. Once his Honor, walking home from a banquet, looked up and noticed the stars. Meaningless, immutable stars. There was nothing to be seen by looking at them. They were mysteries to be dismissed. Like the mystery of Fanny's eyes. Meaningless, immutable eyes. They do not bargain. Yet the world stares out of them. The face looks dumbly up at a judge.

No defense. The policeman's drone has ended and Fanny says nothing. This is difficult. Because his Honor knows suddenly there is a defense. An overwhelming defense. Since there are always two sides to everything. Yes, what is the other side? His Honor would like to know. Tell it, Fanny. About the crowds, streets, buildings, lights, about the whirligig of loneliness, about the humpty-dumpty clutter of longings. And then explain about the summer parks and the white snow and the moon-window in the sky. His Honor will listen bewilderedly and, perhaps, understand for a moment the dumb pathos of your eyes.

As it is, you were found, as the copper who reads the newspapers puts it, in a "suspected" flat. A violation of Section 2012 of the City Code. Thirty days in the bastille, Fanny. Unless his Honor is feeling good.

"How old are you?"

"Twenty."

"Make it twenty-two." His Honor smiles. "And you have nothing to say? About how you happened to get into this sort of thing? You look like a good girl. Although looks are often deceiving."

"I went there with *him,*" says Fanny, and she points to a beetle-browed citizen with an unshaven face. A quaint Don Juan, indeed.

"Ever see him before?"

A shake of the head. Plain case. And yet his Honor hesitates. His Honor feels something expand in his breast. Perhaps he would like to rise and, holding forth his hand, utter a famous plagiarism: "Go and sin no more." He chews a pen and sighs, instead.

"I'll give you another chance," he says. "The next time it'll be jail. Keep this in mind. If you're brought in again, no excuses will go. Call the next case."

Now one can follow Fanny. She walks out of the courtroom. The street swallows her. Nobody in the crowds knows what has happened. Fanny is anybody now. Still, one may follow. Perhaps something will reveal itself, something will add an illuminating touch to the incident of the courtroom.

There is only this. Fanny pauses in front of a drugstore window. The crowds clutter by. Fanny stands looking, without interest, into the window. There is a little mirror inside. The city tumbles by. The city is interested in something vastly complicated.

Staring into the little mirror, Fanny sighs and . . . powders her nose.

# *Nocturne*

THE NIGHT, like an army, possesses the city, swarms upon the buildings. Through the empty labyrinths of stone, the centuries sigh their desolation. Yellow and lonely advertisements burn here and there above invisible roofs.

The world was almost rid of its race. There remained only the figures like myself, the isolate and furtive figures of the night that move here and there in the shadows. What a melodramatic company we are! A few murderers and prostitutes standing like bold merchants on desolate street corners. And a little scattered army of the uncatalogued. The fat world sleeps with its window cautiously opened three inches, for it is autumn and chill, the while we move about adventuring on the treadmill.

I found myself before the entrance of a theatre. Its grimy façade lighted with innumerable yellow lamps strutted out of the darkness, a dirty and insolent gypsy in this funereal street. Gaiety and entertainment were here for the company that does not sleep at night. Gaudy lights and lithographs. Amid them, in a little round box office, sat a red-eyed woman offering tickets for the mysteries of Isis.

I felt chilled and wearied. I bought a ticket and walked through the carnival lobby into the movie theatre. Entering it, I felt as if I had suddenly thrust my head under the heavy dress of an old beggar woman. A rusty lavender light filled the place, and the uncoiling tinsel of tobacco smoke moved in the alien gloom. There was a sharp fishlike odor. Beyond the screen was the glare and sparkle of a movie. The click and whirr of the moving-picture machine came to my ears. I sat down with a feeling of relief and the theatre seemed to grow brighter. Heads of men and women grew out of the shadows. On the moving-picture screen, three horses with furious muscles were galloping over the crest of a sunlit hill. On the horses bounced three men, their heads stiffened and tucked down, their bodies reaching forward like claws in the wind.

We were distinct now in our seats, a silent company of heads sprinkled here and there. The figures sat in their seats as if they had been dropped from a great height. Their faces spotted the gloom with luminous patches of gray. There were snores and coughs. The darkness continued to lift as if some half-hearted dawn were approaching. Dog-faced men, old men with faces moulded out of phlegm, women with scarred, drawn skins—a shaggy, lifeless company.

Against the wall in my row sat an old man with a long bony face. His soggy hat was pulled down over his forehead and his hair stuck out in wisps from under it. His head rested against the wall, and with his mouth open, he slept. His coat was tied in front with a piece of yellow rope and his trousers were opened. The hands of this old man moved about as he slept. He was dreaming. His body twitched and his feet crawled timidly about on the floor. The odor which came from him was partially explained by the streaks of vomit on his clothes and the wetted look of his trousers.

On the movie screen a man with remarkable eyelashes was pointing a gun at a villain. In one arm this man held a clinging chrysanthemum-eyed girl. The moving-picture machine from somewhere behind me spurted forth its flickering, glazed moonbeam. I looked about me. Across the aisle, a row in front of where I sat, were two figures parted by several empty seats. The figure on the aisle was a woman. Her face seemed to be crudely carved out of stone. She had a wide mouth and a flat nose. She had decorously removed her hat, and her hair looked gray and green under the violet light of the moving-picture ray. A pair of fingerless black cotton gloves were on her hands as she raised them to scratch at the back of her neck. She stared with parrot eyes at the picture in front of her, chewing vigorously, swallowing with great excitement and rubbing her nose with a forefinger as a climax to her enthusiasms. It was evident that the picture was affecting her. I looked again at the screen.

The man with the remarkable eyelashes had come to grief. He lay on a white sunny bed and appeared to be dying. His hair was carefully combed. The chrysanthemum-eyed girl was kneeling at his bedside.

The old woman's chewing gained vigor and she began to weep. Her forefinger remained in position under her nose, and the tears lost themselves in the black cotton of her gloves. I became aware of a soft, deliberately spaced hiss. It came from the figure that sat several seats to the left of the old woman.

He was a stocky-shouldered man with a dark-haired leonine head and strong features. His flashing dark eyes were turned upon the old woman. He was hissing to her and making eager signals with his chin.

The old woman, noticing him through her tears, looked at him for several moments and screwed her hard face into a hesitant smile. The man's shoulders twitched, his massive head bobbed about. His mouth made clucking moist sounds. Twice his body dipped forward as if about to get up.

The old woman returned her eyes to the picture, but she appeared to have lost her enthusiasm for it. Through the corners of her eyes she observed the large-headed man at her left. He had become pleading. He was pouting like an aggrieved boy. He tossed his leonine head in little coquetries and then suddenly held up a single finger. The old woman, staring at this elevated finger, shook her head. Whereat two fingers appeared in the gloomy air like amazing words. The old woman's little parrot eyes turned full upon him and nodded.

There was a violent coughing in my row. The old man with the bony face had awakened. He sneezed, coughed, rubbed his eyes, and straightened. His body flopped about, and he began to scratch behind his ear. His face reminded me of the breast of a bird that had been plucked. As I looked at him, his eyes drifted across the theatre. He began suddenly to wag his head and blink with his dead lids, and his jaw rose on one side in a grin. The old woman across the aisle was looking at him and smiling. The bony-faced one sprawled to his feet, his clothes hanging stiff and shapeless from him. He moved by me. An odor of herring and medicine marked his passage. He walked up to the old woman and tapped her on the shoulder. The old woman cast a quick, contemptuous glance at the leonine head to her left, and rising with a chuckle, walked up the aisle after the shuffling, ragged figure. There was left the defeated one.

He sat biting his fingers. As his teeth worked in a growing ferocity upon his nails, a look of agony came into his eyes. His shoulders began to twitch. He lurched about like a man drunk. Then suddenly he disappeared.

Out of his row came crawling a stump of a man whose body was fastened with straps to a square board on four little wheels. The head of this man, black-haired and leonine, barely reached to the tops of the seats. He propelled himself by swinging two apelike arms back and forth. In his big fists he held two flatirons. Slowly he started up the aisle and came opposite me, his thick torso waving snakelike above the floor. He stopped and raised a pair of flashing eyes. His lips twisted and a dribble appeared at their corners. For several instants he eyed me, while his fury kept him silent. Then his voice burst forth, coming with a violent incongruity out of this half-man on the floor. It was the gruff voice of a towering man.

"Did you see that?" he demanded. His hands remained motionless, holding the flatirons to the floor. "Did you see it? I had her first. I got her eye first. And then that stew butts in. Didn't I have her first?"

The face lifted toward me twitched and its fury became a childlike grief. The legless man began to weep. He stared at me as the tears climbed out of his eyes and smeared themselves over his rugged face.

"She beat it with that stew," he said. "Say, honest t'God, didn't I have her first?" He rolled on up the aisle, swinging long apelike arms.

Outside, the night was vanishing. The chill morning air came like a scent of fresh water to my nose, dried by the odors of the theatre. People were moving in the gray streets. At the end of the block they moved in a thin procession across the car tracks, a string of dark figures without faces and shaped liked sevens. The city was waking. The rumble and the mumble and the bang, bang, bang had started again. From a corner came the shout of a man. I looked over and saw beside a stand heaped with fresh newspapers the heavy, dwarflike stump of the legless man. He was selling papers. He raised his voice in a shout as we of the little thin procession moved by.

"Extra here! All about . . ."

Evidently things had been happening in the night.

# *Decay*

HERE IN THIS STREET citizens give forth an odor. The rows of sagging little houses are like the teeth in an old man's mouth. From them arise the exhalations of stagnant wood, of putrescent stairways, of bodies from which the sweats of lust have never been washed, of ulcerous shadows, and soft bubbling alleys. The stench is like a grime that leadens the air. In this street live men and women whose hungers are not complicated by trifles.

The people who live in this street walk as if they were being pushed in and out of the sagging houses. Shrieking children appear and sprawl about. They roll over one another, their faces contorted with a miniature senility. They urinate in gutters, throw stones at each other in the soft alleys, run after each other cursing and gesturing with idiot violence. They bring an awkward fever into the street. Oblivious to them and to the debris about them, barrel-shaped women strut with protuberant bellies and flapping shoes over the pavements. They move as if unaccustomed to walking in streets.

It grows dark and the men coming home from the factories begin to crowd the streets. They walk in silence, a broken string of shufflers against the red of the sky. Their knees bend, their jaws thrust forward, their heads wag from side to side. They vanish into the sagging houses, and the night comes, an unwavering gloom pitted with little yellow glows from windows. The houses lie like bundles of carefully piled rags in the darkness. The shrieking of the children has died, and with it the pale fever of the day has passed out of the air. There are left only the odors, the invisible banners of decay that float upon the night. The stench of fat kitchens, of soft bubbling alleys, of gleaming refuse, and of the indefinable evaporations from the dark bundles of houses comes like a thrust into the nose.

Later, drunken men appear and lurch cursing into the darkness. The smoke of the factory chimneys is now visible. The chimneys, like rows of cylindrical minarets, make darker streaks in the gloom, and in the distance, blast furnaces gut the night with pink-and-orange flares. The figures of young women, not yet shaped like barrels, come out into the street and stand in the shadows. They move noiselessly into the depths of the soft bubbling alleys and vanish.

It was in one of these houses that I once lived. At night I now sometimes recall things that used to happen in this house.

There were eight children in Otto Muznik's family. They lived with Otto Muznik and his wife in three rooms. In summer and in winter these rooms were filled with a pungent bitter smell. There was much noise in them also. The eight children screamed at each other. Otto Muznik and his wife screamed at them and at each other. One of the rooms was a kitchen. The two other were bedrooms filled with cots. The screams and the stench in the three rooms, the littered floors and devastated furniture, told of activities.

Willy Muznik had a poisoned foot. A cat he had brought home had bitten him. It was night, and Mrs. Muznik sat in the kitchen. She was a woman with a spreading, phlegmatic body, and a round red-and-shining face. Her eyes were little. She went about with an unwavering stare, staring at this and at that. She sat in the kitchen now and stared at the stove, on which a black pot full of meat and soup was boiling. Willy was eleven. He sat in a corner, doubled up like a contortionist and sucking on his bared, grimy foot. Mrs. Muznik stared at him.

"What did the doctor say?" she asked in a husky voice. She had come home a few minutes ago from her day's scrubbing. Willy removed the foot from his mouth, and began to wail.

"The doctor says he'll maybe have to cut my foot off," Willy finally answered. His mother stared at the foot. Through the grime below the instep she saw a discoloration. She wiped her eyes and sighed.

"Your pa'll give it to you for bringing cats home," she said. "Does it hurt?" For answer Willy increased his wail and Mrs. Muznik looked at him, shaking her head. She moved into another room. The gaslight from the kitchen threw a faint glare among the shadows of this room. She sat down in a chair crowded between two cots. The sounds of someone gasping came to her and she stared about in the dark.

"Is that you, Joey?" she asked. The door leading into the street opened and Milly, a girl of fourteen with a round red-and-shining face and a pair of long thin legs rushed in screaming. In the dim light that dropped into the room from the street Mrs. Muznik saw her son lying on the floor. She hurried over and shook him .

"Don't have a fit," she cried. "Joey . . . Joey! Wait till your pa goes. He can't stand it." Joey stiffened and rolled over on his face. He was thirteen. His head was bent under as if he were trying to stand on it. A foam bubbled on his lips.

"Get the cold water," Mrs. Muznik ordered. Milly rushed out of the room, singing a song she had learned in the alleys. She returned with a pot of water and Mrs. Muznik threw it over Joey's head and shoulders. The voices of the two babies, suddenly awakened, filled the room with screams. The two babies were Munch and Sam. One of them, Munch, was sick. His fever-cry rose above his brother's complaint. Mrs. Muznik lighted a gas jet and the stench and disorder of the room came flickering out of the shadow. She leaned over one of the cots and picked up Munch. He was covered with a few rags. Through the cloth, the dry heat of his body burned against Mrs. Muznik's hands and bosom. She held the infant and cried to Milly, who was pulling a grimy cloth over the table in the kitchen.

"Where's Paula?" The screaming of the infants almost drowned the shriek of Milly's laughing, shrill answer. "Paula's in the alley. Paula's in the alley." Mrs. Muznik laid the hot child's body on the cot beside the other screamer and went to a window. She thrust it open and leaned out in the darkness.

"Paula," she cried, "you come in at once." She heard a boy's voice whispering below and made out two figures moving about against the dark wall.

"Paula, Paula," she screamed. "Come away. I'll come after you with a whip." There were more whisperings and then one of the figures detached itself from the gloom and floated into the depths of the alley.

"All right, Ma," a voice answered.

Mrs. Muznik sat down on the cot and stared at the two little bundles that wept and wailed on the other side of the room. The door opened and Paula entered. She was fifteen and had a ribbon in her hair. Her face was round and shining and as red as her mother's. Her dress was crumpled and covered with alley dirt. Mrs. Muznik stared. From the kitchen, Willy's wailing came to her.

"I can't walk, Ma, I can't walk." Willy came hopping into the room on one leg and fell across the floor. He lay screaming at Mrs. Muznik's feet. Mrs. Muznik turned toward Joey, who was sitting near her.

"How do you feel?" she asked. Joey's thin compressed face smiled. He shook his head.

"All right, now," he said. "Can I have some lemon drops?"

"Here, Milly," Mrs. Muznik ordered. "Go out and buy a penny's worth." Milly's thin legs flashed out of the room into the street. Paula had gone into the kitchen to look at the black pot on the stove. Mrs. Muznik stared out of the window as the babies continued to scream. The mother dropped her head and rocked slightly in her seat. The uneven floor about her was littered with clothes from which a heavy musty odor came. The walls were broken and smeared. The windows in front of her made two little gray clouds. The stench of the room came into Mrs. Muznik's head and made her sleepy. She drew a long breath and continued to rock her body gently back and forth. First the children would eat and then she would wake up Otto. Otto worked nights in a steel mill. He did not have to leave the house for two more hours. The stench and noise of the room drifted away from Mrs. Muznik as she sat and rocked. She was afraid she was going to have another baby. Willy's foot would have to be cut off. Joey was sick. Munch, little Munch, was sick. His hoarse fever-cry was growing softer. He lay whimpering, his hands moving over his face.

These things drifted through Mrs. Muznik's thoughts, keeping her awake as she rocked back and forth. She thought of Otto going to work in the darkness. He stood in front of an open furnace that roared with fire, and fed melted steel into it. She had seen him once. He was almost naked. The memory of his body, reddened by the glare which spread out of the open furnace, remained always with her. Otto's muscles stood out, and in his loosely belted trousers, he had seemed great and strong to her. The red light and the roar and the sputter of melted steel made him shine and changed him into a man with burning eyes and flaming skin. Whenever he left for work after that, Mrs. Muznik remembered this, and a vague shiver passed through her.

Milly burst in through the door. She handed Joey lemon drops. "Give me a little bit," said Mrs. Muznik.

"Ma," Joey cried, "there's a rat. It's wiping its nose with its feet." He looked eagerly into the dark alley. Mrs. Muznik ate lemon drops. A warmth spread over her, making her feet hum. This hour of the night was her leisure. She was used to sit like this and rock back and forth and let thoughts creep through her mind. Joey went into the kitchen and ate. He came back. Paula followed him, skipping from one foot to another.

"Going out, Ma," she cried. Mrs. Muznik raised an arm toward the girl.

"Wait . . . wait," she called.

Paula appeared, vague and dark in the alley below. Mrs. Muznik stared at her as she floated away into the gloom. She turned from the window and resumed her rocking. She heard, as from a distance, the voice of Willy wailing about his foot, and the voices of her two babies screaming again. Munch was sick. The doctor had said Munch might die. But Mrs. Muznik did not believe this. None of the others had died and they had all been sick. She sucked at the lemon drop in her mouth. The ache and burn in her shoulders were like hot voices bothering her brain. The hoarse fever-cry of the baby on the cot was another little hot voice in her brain.

"Oh, Ma," cried Joey from the window. "There's Paula with three boys in the alley." Mrs. Muznik rocked. "Never mind," she murmured. The hot voices made her feel swollen within. Her feet felt as if they were resting in flames. Joey came to her and looked at her face.

"Tired, Ma?" he asked. Mrs. Muznik lifted him into her lap. He was a thin, fragile boy. She put her arms around him and clung to him. He felt cool and sweet to her flesh beneath the dress. He was better than Willy, than Munch and Sam, than Milly and Paula, than Heine. Heine was in jail. He had done something. And Mary, her oldest, had gone away. Mary was wild, like Paula. Willy's foot would be cut off. Munch was crying too weakly. Mrs. Muznik kissed Joey and rocked. It was dark outside and in her head it was dark. The smell of the room was another darkness, and the burn of her body another. She sat hunched over Joey, clinging to him, and as she clung, a sweetness came into her. Her aches melted.

In a few minutes she would have to go to bed. It was wrong for her to sit up and hold Joey. She needed the rest in bed. The scrubbing was hard. It lasted all day. She rocked and the darkness in and around her grew deeper. Her ears fell asleep. She no longer heard the noises in the room. Milly was tugging at her shoulder and crying in a loud voice.

"If Paula can go out in the alley and play, why can't I? I can play if Paula can go in the alley and play."

Mrs. Muznik couldn't make out what Milly was saying. She rocked. Milly moved cautiously toward the door. She opened it softly.

"Ma, Ma," Willy cried. "Milly's gone. Milly's gone."

Mrs. Muznik nodded her head and rocked. She dreamed Joey was falling out of her arms and awoke, startled. Joey was asleep. She whispered to him, kissing his ears. Lifting him to the cot, she laid him down and knelt beside him, taking off his torn shoes.

Something impelled her toward little Munch, and she lifted him. The dry heat of his body struck through her dress at her heavy bosom and at the hard skin of her arms. He was whimpering and moving his hands slowly and aimlessly over his face. Mrs. Muznik stood and rocked him in her arms. . . . The baby stopped crying and lay quiet. She placed him next to Sam, who had also fallen asleep for the moment. It was time to wake up Otto, and she moved into the kitchen.

She leaned over the black pot on the stove, thinking. A voice called to her from another room. She turned and saw the door of the other bedroom had opened. A stale bitter smell drifted into the kitchen. The figure of her husband, dressed in a suit of long dirty underwear and a pair of thick, hard socks, appeared in the doorway. His face was smeared with sleep. A growth of hair hid his chin and cheeks.

"Ma," he called to her, stretching his arms, "come here a minute."

Mrs. Muznik stared at him. "What for?" she asked. A grin overspread her husband's face. His jaws thrust forward and his eyes began to shine. The grin passed and he remained glowering at Mrs. Muznik. Then he came, with his shoulders swaying, into the kitchen and seized her by the arm. Mrs. Muznik stared into the black pot on the stove. As Otto shoved her before him her mouth opened and her eyes turned to him.

"No, no," she whispered. "No, Otto. You go to work. Willy's having trouble with his foot."

Otto continued to drag the heavy figure of his wife toward the bedroom. A glowering playfulness was in his face and gestures.

"No, Otto, not now. Let me be," Mrs. Muznik cried. "You go eat."

Otto laughed and struck her on the shoulders. Stepping behind her he cursed, and with a guffaw pushed her violently into the dark, bitter-smelling bedroom. She staggered toward one of the beds and dropped into it. Through the open door she watched her husband. He walked back to the sink and drew some water in a glass and drank it. He was a short stocky figure in his dark tattered underwear. She remembered him before the furnace door in the steel mill, shining.

"Come on, Otto," she called. Her voice was hoarse and thin. She sat on the edge of the bed and waited. She rocked gently back and forth. The room floated before her eyes as if the darkness were moving. The little burns came again into her brain, and the stench creeping from the walls and the beds confused her. Through the window she became aware slowly of a great pink-and-orange glow in the distant night. It was from the factories. Her body leaned forward and she fumbled thickly with her shoe. Her lips mumbled sounds and she sat repeating the name of her husband, "Otto, Otto." Then her body tumbled to one side and she lay across the bed as if she had been flung there.

Otto her husband came at last into the bedroom. He was gnawing on a bone and a piece of meat. He glowered down at the heavy figure on the bed that mumbled, "Otto, Otto."

"Move over there," he called in a thick voice. Mrs. Muznik stirred and in the gloom her white teeth suddenly flashed in a grin. From the front part of the house Willy's voice, shrill and frightened, was calling, "Ma, Ma. Something's the matter."

# *Sergt. Kuzick and the Reporter*

"OFFHAND," said Sergt. Kuzick of the first precinct, "Offhand, I can't think of any stories for you. If you give me a little time, maybe I could think of one or two. What you want, I s'ppose, is some story as I know about from personal experience. Like the time, for instance, that the half-breed Indian busted out of the bridewell, where he was serving a six months' sentence, and snuck home and killed his wife and went back again to the bridewell, and they didn't find out who killed her until he got drunk a year later and told a bartender about it. That's the kind you want, ain't it?"

I said it was.

"Well," said Sergt. Kuzick, "I can't think of any offhand, like I said. There was a buildin' over on West Monroe Street once where we found three bodies in the basement. They was all dead, but that wouldn't make a story hardly, because nobody ever found out who killed them. Let me think a while."

Sergt. Kuzick thought.

'Do you remember the Leggett mystery?" he inquired doubtfully. "I guess that was before your time. I was only a patrolman then. Old Leggett had a tobacco jar made out of a human skull, and that's how they found out he killed his wife. It was her skull. It come out one evenin' when he brought his bride home. You know, he got married again after killin' the first one. And they was havin' a party and the new bride said she didn't want that skull around in her house. Old Leggett got mad and said he wouldn't part with that skull for love or money. So when he was to work one day she threw the skull into the ash can, and when old Leggett come home and saw the skull missin', he swore like the devil and come down to the station to swear out a warrant for his wife's arrest, chargin' her with disorderly conduct. He carried on so that one of the boys got suspicious and went out to the house with him and they found the skull in the ash can, and old Leggett begun to weep over it. So one of the boys asked him, naturally, whose skull it was. He said it wasn't a skull no more, but a tobacco jar. And they asked him where he'd got it. And he begun to lie so hard that they tripped him up and finally he said it was his first wife's skull, and he was hung shortly afterward. You see, if you give me time I could remember something like that for a story.

"Offhand, though," sighed Sergt. Kuzick, "it's difficult. I ain't got it clear in my head what you want, either. Of course I know it's got to be interestin' or the paper won't print it. But interestin' things is pretty hard to run into. I remember one night out to the old morgue. This was 'way back when I started on the force thirty years ago and more. And they was havin' trouble at the morgue owin' to the stiffs vanishin' and bein' mutilated. They thought maybe it was students carryin' them off to practice medicine on. But it wasn't, because they found old Pete—that was the colored janitor they had out there—he wasn't an African, but it turned out a Fiji Islander, afterward—they found him dead in the morgue one day and it turned out he was a cannibal. Or, anyway, his folks had been cannibals in Fiji, and the old habit had come up in him so he couldn't help himself, and he was makin' a diet off the bodies in the morgue. But he struck one that was embalmed, and the poison in the body killed him. The papers didn't carry much on it on account of it not bein' very important, but I always thought it was kind of interestin' at that. That's about what you want, I suppose—some story or other like that. Well, let's see."

"It's hard," sighed Sergt. Kuzick, after a pause, "to put your finger on a yarn offhand. I remember a lot of things now, come to think of it, like the case I was on where a fella named Zianow killed his wife by pourin' little pieces of hot lead into her ear, and he would've escaped, but he sold the body to the old county hospital for practicin' purposes, and while they was monkeyin' with the skull, they heard somethin' rattle, and when they investigated, it was several pieces of lead inside rattlin' around. So they arrested Zianow and got him to confess the whole thing, and he was sent up for life, because it turned out his wife had stabbed him four times the week before he poured the lead into her while she slept, and frightened him so that he did it in self-defense, in a way."

"I understand in a general way what you want," murmured Sergt. Kuzick, "but so help me if I can think of a thing that you might call interestin'. Most of the things we have to deal with is chiefly murders and suicides and highway robberies, like the time old Alderman Mc-

Guire—he's dead now—was held up by two bandits while goin' home from a night session of the council, and he hypnotized one bandit. Yes, sir, you may wonder at that, but you didn't know McGuire. He was a wonderful hypnotist, and he hypnotized the bandit, and just as the other one, who wasn't hypnotized, was searching his pockets, McGuire said to the hypnotized bandit, 'You're a policeman, shoot this highwayman.' And the hypnotized one was the bandit who had the gun, and he turned around, as Alderman McGuire said, and shot the other *un*-hypnotized bandit and killed him. But when he reported the entire incident to the station—I was on duty that night—the captain wouldn't believe it, and tried to argue McGuire into sayin' it was a accident, and that the gun went off accidentally and killed the unhypnotized bandit. But the alderman stuck to his story, and it was true, because the hypnotized bandit told me privately all about it when I took him down to Joliet."

"I will try," said Sergt. Kuzick, "to think of somethin' for you in about a week. I begin to get a pretty definite idea what you want, and I'll talk it over with Old Jim, who used to travel beat with me. He's a great one for stories, Old Jim is. A man can hardly think of them offhand like. You give me a week." And the old sergeant sank into his wooden chair and gazed out of the dusty station window with a perplexed and baffled eye.

# *The Champion from Far Away*

I AM VERY FOND of this story. Not because it's any good, necessarily; but because Vanya Kovelenko is my favorite hero. And Vanya's friend, Gaspodin Charash, is my favorite villain.

Whenever I get confused from reading too many books, or depressed by the return of an old insolvency trouble, or merely bored by the innocent reiterations of existence—in short about once every month, I look up Mr. Kovelenko (which must be done around 3:00 A.M.) and we sit down and discuss.

And listening to Mr. Kovelenko's slow and faltering saga filtering through as humpty-dumpty an accent as was ever brewed in the melting pot, a deep, philosophical calm takes hold of me. The hula-hula canyons of new Babylon, the electric hemorrhage of its Broadway, the fizz and pop of its nightmarish windows and Aladdinish geometries—these become phenomena of small import. Which is because my hero, for me at least, is a creature of such dignity, mood, and humor, of such Homeric troubles and earthly smell as restore man to his lordship of the Universe and reduce his handiwork—from the Battery to the Bronx—to a sort of mechanical little toy.

As for Gaspodin Charash, him I have never seen. I have only my friend Vanya's word that he exists at all. But the Charash cannot be doubted. He is as inevitable as the Wolf in *Little Red Riding Hood* or the strange gentleman in red tights who is known to have conferred with Dr. Faustus.

I shall begin long ago, skipping, however, many vital but unrelated incidents in Mr. Kovelenko's saga, and introduce you to my hero under the most conventionally heroic of circumstances—to wit, in battle.

Perhaps you will remember that famous German victory over the Russians in the Tannenberg marshes in 1915 when a hundred thousand Germans fought a million Muscovites and slew half of them. My friend Vanya was there, standing for three days knee-deep in mud, unarmed, as were seventy-five percent of his comrades (for owing to a certain confusion inherent in the Slavic character only one gun for every four men had found its way to this battle-front). Vanya was there, feeling a trifle conspicuous in this carnage, for despite his having settled a good foot in the soft ground, he still loomed over the heads of his fellow targets. At this time Vanya was twenty-three years old, weighed 235 pounds, and stood six feet three inches in his stockings.

For three days Vanya remained motionless in this shooting gallery, nibbling on a loaf of iron-like black bread, slapping his large hands against his sides to keep them from freezing off, and blinking with his pale deep-set eyes at the Witches' Sabbath in front of him. On the third morning most of Vanya's fellow targets were down—but our hero still stood munching on his bread and facing westward as he had been ordered.

He was rewarded for his long vigil by the sudden appearance of an enemy. The curtain of fire and shell broke, the ear-splitting din subsided, and streaming across the well-churned marshes Vanya beheld the myriads of Hell, all dressed in gray and heading for him.

A slight doubt as to his ability to stem this tide that was rushing forward to lay low his country, the beloved village of Shavarov included, must have crossed Vanya's mind. However, it in no way deterred him. He felt cramped from three days' inaction and not quite at his best. His head, too, was aching and his stomach (ah, what a stomach my hero has) grinding with a hunger which ordinarily would have brought tears to his eyes. Nevertheless he did his best.

He broke four Prussian heads, choked a lieutenant to death, kicked three jaws loose and bit off as many ears as came his way. Given firmer ground and a few minutes in which to recover his breath, Vanya might have turned the tide of victory—at least so it must have seemed to the wearied Uhlans who had flushed this snorting dinosaur in their drive across the marshes.

However, Vanya fell to earth, lay for a space staring up at a rain of boots, bayonets, and rifle butts, and then closed his eyes. When he opened them again the day had gone. He was lying on his back with a sheet over him, to distinguish him from the living. It was dark. Figures moved around him. Pulling the sheet below his eyes he counted them. Only six, and six were child's play for Vanya, provided his arms were still working and his legs stood up.

God was good, for Vanya found himself, except for a few sore places, still all in one piece and able to rise. So rise he did and a monstrous-looking figure he must have been, bloodied and caked with mud as he resumed the battle of the Tannenberg marshes where he had left off. Two more Prussian heads ceased to dream of victory, and Vanya galloped into the night. During the darkness he walked, crawled, and dragged himself through the bloody marshes in which his comrades lay imbedded as richly as raisins in an Easter cake. He circled and doubled on his tracks but continued to head always eastward. The day found him still moving, albeit he was hungry enough to eat his shoes—and toward dusk he smelled, as he put it, the ranks of his comrades.

A sentinel spied him and here the incidents grow vague in Vanya's memory. He recalls some talk of his being a deserter, and the anger of some officers and on the whole a great deal of confusion during which someone removed his coat and shirt and treated him to a hundred lashes—which had something to do with discipline as far as Vanya could make out.

But whatever happened was of no great importance, for a week later, Vanya, this time with an empty pistol in his hand (through an oversight his company had been given no bullets), was again playing target and facing the west as had been ordered.

Nineteen-seventeen found my hero very little changed. He has in fact a peculiarly personal memory of these years of disaster—for it is his hunger rather than the Prussians and all their hellish antics that he remembers.

"Oh, I was 'ongry!" says Vanya and recites a list of battles as if they were no more than fast days; recalls a series of campaigns that bled a dynasty to death as a time of dreadfully restricted diet.

"Before the war," says Vanya, "I eat five, seex times evrra day. I need lots food or I get seeck. The war come. No food. I am seeck all the time. I eat graas. I eat trees. I eat mud. Oh, I was verr glad when the war finch. But no. Et ees worse. Moch."

Worse it was, for Vanya's troubles began in earnest after Brest-Litovsk and the Bolsheviki. At first there was high talk and heroic singing as the proletarian sun burst over that bloody horizon. And Vanya reared his six-feet-three in the camp and sang of Bashkiria whose women were plump and whose skies rained kumiss milk.

For two weeks my hero, as far as I can make out from his modest confessions, inherited the earth indeed, drank vodka till his neck was bursting, pillaged, plundered, and ravished, fell off bridges and slept upside down in mud holes. Altogether an epic fortnight which the world watched holding its breath and which Vanya Kovelenko dimly mistook for a high-class wedding in Shavarov.

But all this passed and famine again descended on Vanya. With ringing head and shrinking stomach (which latter phenomena Vanya assures me is as painful as childbirth and, alas, more frequent) the marching began again. Back to Moscow with plenty of bullets in his pockets, for it was Russians he was now ordered to shoot—Russians who had a monopoly on the food supply (which was Vanya's simple idea of the revolution and at first an inspiring one); and from Moscow to Leningrad and from Leningrad through mountains of ice into Siberia—so my hero fared. But shooting Russians, even fat and noble ones, brought no more filling into Vanya's stomach than making faces at the Prussians had done.

And here the revolution began to lose some of its charm for Vanya. Twice he was arrested and beaten into unconsciousness for raids on the commissar provision depots and once, overheard mumbling about the pre-war glories of Shavarov in Bashkiria where you could get a gallon of kumiss for two kopecks and where there were whole cows to eat, he was shipped back to Leningrad as a Czarist.

And here there were more beatings and less victuals than ever. And there was such talk and yelling as kept Vanya dizzy from morning to night; there was a confusion for which he would gladly have exchanged the Tannenberg marshes. It seems that Vanya had only to open his mouth in some simple, heart-felt comment on the food situation and he was at once set upon by crazy men, gabbled at, beaten and threatened with death.

Vanya still marvels at how he ever kept body and soul together during the two years he was a red menace. He still marvels, too, over the way he was being continually rushed into the streets to shoot at people, sometimes in the middle of the night when he was just forgetting his hunger in a God-given hour of sleep. And over the way he was captured five times by the enemy (whoever they were) and gabbled at all over again and enrolled in a new cause and kissed on both cheeks and called Brother and shoved behind new barricades. It was impossible, says Vanya, to tell what was going on, everything got so mixed up, everybody going crazy if you so much as contradicted a sneeze, and Brother beating Brother over the head with vodka kegs even during moments of relaxation. In short it was something, says Vanya, which cannot be described or even imagined.

However, in 1919 Vanya belonged to some sort of Group concerning which he is rather vague. He remembers that this Group used to invade restaurants and throw people out of windows; and that sometimes it would hold meetings on the highway and wait for the peasants to come driving their produce wagons to town. This Group had some sort of a name and for a time Vanya had high hopes it would bring back those first happy days of the revolution and free Mother Russia of all the elaborate and complicated troubles that were slowly making life impossible—at least for Vanya.

But no. Various other Groups, including the Police, combined against Vanya and his comrades, harried them up and down alleys and finally, after a disastrous battle in which Vanya personally covered himself with glory (he was even mentioned in the enemy despatches printed that night in the newspapers as the dangerous Hooligan Giant), scattered and drove them out of town.

And here Vanya's troubles assume a classic outline. With Mitka and Chizhik, two surviving members of his Group who were soon to perish—not of hunger, says Vanya, for if anybody could die of such a thing as hunger he himself would have been dead a thousand times, but of grief, for Mitka and Chizhik were men with souls—with these two soulful comrades my hero in answer to some primordial urge endeavored to fight his way out of an absurd and civilized world.

He recalls such days of famine in this adventure as still make his eyes roll with terror, days when there were no houses to pillage; nights when there were no farms to raid; in fact not a sight or smell of food from one end of the world to the other. Nevertheless, moving steadily northward and eastward and hardly speaking to each other, these three Muscovite giants (for Mitka and Chizhik were men of stature) clawed their way toward the arctic regions. Man was their enemy and how many murders these three silent tow-headed stranglers committed in their queer climb up the end of the world, Vanya doesn't remember.

This whole passage is dim in my hero's mind quite as if it were someone else who had made this pilgrimage into the north. But his memory brightens with their arrival at the Pechora River, which is the leading river in Archangelsk, says Vanya, but in no way—either for depth, beauty, or comfort—to be compared to the Buguruslan that flows in Bashkiria.

Arrived at the Pechora and alarmed by the condition of his two friends, who were so done in by this half-year of sorties, murders, skirmishes, pitched battles, and forced marches that they could barely drag one foot after the other, Vanya built a large raft and the trio lay themselves wearily down thereon and were borne slowly toward the northern seas. Occasionally they anchored in the shadows of some sleeping village and Vanya, half frozen though he was, fighting his way in and out of the market place, would return to share his spoils with his companions.

Tragedy, however, overtook the raft. Mitka died in a snow storm, begging Vanya to play him some music on a fife which he fancied his friend was hiding from him, and Vanya, howling with grief, rolled him into the river. And a week later Chizhik the Giant began babbling like a child and took to reading aloud a letter received two years ago from his brother Parfim. And my hero, poling the raft slowly through the snows and ice of the Pechora, learned that this Parfim, favorite of fortune, now worked in a magnificent mill in a distant place called Gary, Indiana, or as Chizhik and Vanya pronounced it, Hary, Injani. Here, wrote Parfim, was the land of milk and honey and he himself was dressed from morning to night in the finest of colored silks and, what was more, lived in a beautiful cabin with three women to serve him and vie for his love.

Chizhik, grown sentimental as his last hours were on him, hoped only to survive long enough to see Parfim and share for an hour the bounties of faraway Hary. But he followed Mitka into the river, Parfim's tale of Canaan clutched in his huge, dead hand. And again Vanya howled with grief (for Chizhik even more than Mitka had been a man with a soul) and the raft moved more slowly through the ice and snows of the Pechora.

Now the sun went out of the world, Vanya tells me, and the night sat down on the dim white ground and an iron wind swung through the endless dark. And he was all alone and the hunger that came to him was a thing that made all the rest of his life seem like an unbroken feast day.

There was no longer a smell of man or life, and Vanya, pulling his raft after him—for though it had become useless on the frozen river it was yet his home and he had grown attached to it—Vanya (such is the mercilessness of fate) was forced to live on storks alone, and not many of them. In Archangelsk, says Vanya, the stork is the only variety of food accessible to the traveler. And day and night Vanya clattered after these half-frozen creatures, kicking them to death and devouring them sometimes feathers and all, so great was his hunger.

Thus drifting and sliding over the ice-choked Pechora into an ever emptier world Vanya came all unexpectedly and to his horror upon the land of the Samoyeds, a name which Vanya tells me means Eat Himself. And here, depressed by the increasing trials with which fate harried him, Vanya would have allowed himself to be set upon, roasted, dismembered and eaten (as was related in Bashkiria of voyagers who fell into the hands of these ice-bound cannibals) but for a curious hope that sustained his heart. This hope was the memory of the promised land of Hary, Injani, discovered by Chizhik's brother, Parfim.

It is doubtful, thinks Vanya, whether the Samoyeds would have found him to their taste if they had captured him, for his skin was leathery, his tongue bitter, his flanks stringy and he would not have yielded a mouthful of palatable food, however artfully cooked. Nevertheless, girding himself for battle, Vanya and his raft moved by the dim cabins of the Samoyeds whom he saw with his own eyes roasting a plump naked woman on a spit. As he was watching this spectacle horrified but, despite his Christian soul, almost fainting from the sweet, heady odors, he heard the sound of men on the river. Grimly he approached on his raft, the waters of the Pechora opening around him.

He saw a number of small craft, filled with men who were fishing, although what the Samoyeds wanted of fish when they had so much more substantial a dinner preparing for them on the shore was a matter that still puzzles Vanya. However, with a roar that must have stood the enemy's hair on end, coming as it did out of this arctic night, Vanya shot his raft into the very midst of these fishermen and there ensued a naval engagement such as the mouth of the Pechora had not witnessed since the days of the Vikings. Vanya fought for hours, drowning how many cannibals he does not remember, and with the last of their boats smashed to splinters and the voices of the women raised in a heathenish lament from the shore, emerged victoriously into the White Sea. And here my hero, bellowing with hunger, lay face downward on his raft while cakes of ice bigger than the hills of Bashkiria pelted him like stones from the hand of God and waves higher than the trees of Shavarov tossed him about like a feather in the dark.

These days, says Vanya, were like the end of the world and he would not have been surprised if the black skies had opened and all the beasts of the beyond had rushed down to devour the land and the water. Instead a much more unbelievable thing happened. A Norwegian freighter ran over him as it ploughed through the ice floes and he was hauled out of the sea, as shrunken as if he had been dead a thousand years. And two weeks later he was landed in icebound Spitsbergen.

As after a great storm all is serene and quiet, so Vanya found his succeeding days. At least that is his description of them. He was given a pair of overalls, dropped into the hold of a ship bigger than he had imagined it was possible to build. And for two months Vanya shoveled coal into its roaring furnace. The heat, says Vanya, was so great that at night his body smelled of burned hair and his eyes took fire when he closed them. The wind blew this ship, big though it was, until it tossed and spun like his Pechorian raft and Vanya, clinging to his shovel, fought to keep himself from bouncing into the blazing mouth of his furnace. But there was food, says Vanya, in small but never-failing quantities, and an instinct told him he was moving toward the promised land of Hary, Injani.

By what stages my hero in his seed-like passage from one end of the earth to the other was finally dropped on an Ojibway Indian reservation two hundred miles north of Toronto, he has not yet revealed. But summer found him deep in the affections of these redskins, a very nice but lazy people, says Vanya, with whom he would have been content to spend the rest of his days. My hero never speaks of this time without mentioning the Pickerel or as he calls it the Peek River on which his Indian friends lived and which in a few aspects compared favorably with his Buguruslan. But despite the semi-prevalence of meals now, two wives and the admiration of an entire Ojibway tribe, an instinct told Vanya that the food and women of the land discovered by Chizhik's brother, Parfim, were more palatable. So leaving his lovely Peek River, his wives, friends and red-skinned admirers, Vanya again placed himself in the wind and was blown back and forth, up and down, until he landed in New York. And this was on a spring morning four years after the signing of the treaty at Brest-Litovsk.

"Oh, I was 'ongry," says Vanya, asked for his first impressions of Babylon. "'Ongrier than I everr was in mine life."

Somehow in a manner he finds it difficult to detail and which I will not take the trouble to invent, Vanya encountered a Red Cross worker who spoke a little Russian and who secured him a job in a Brooklyn cemetery digging graves.

And here he stuck through spring and summer, inquiring as best he could of such preoccupied people as visited the scenes of his work, where lay the land of Hary, Injani—and receiving no information and even less attention. If not for the memory of Chizhik on the raft, reading aloud the elegant and inspiring words of Parfim, Vanya would have begun to doubt the very existence of this promised land of Hary. As it was, hope dimmed in his heart, and he dug graves day after day as if life itself had disappeared.

And here, after a long pause of time, Vanya, resting on his shovel, looks up from beside a newly made grave and sees in the dusk outlined against a tombstone a certain one whose name is Charash. This Charash is smoking a cigarette and has a very high-class way of leaning against this tombstone. And my hero, whose stout heart has never failed him, looks into the eyes of this man and something cold touches his stomach. No omens attend the one by the tombstone. No seven ravens circle his head. No dreadful lights play about his feet. But from the first Vanya is not deceived.

The stranger smiles and tosses away the cigarette, sighs, and steps forward, and Vanya, who stood motionless for three days and nights in the marshes while an army died around him, is ready to drop his shovel, turn tail and flee. But the stranger speaks, and in Russian too, and calls him by name. "One moment, my good Vanya. I desire very much to speak to you. You are a very interesting-looking fellow. I have noticed you several times. I have a friend who lies here. But today I did not come to visit her. I come only to observe you. I am Charash. This is my automobile. Step in, if you please. It is all right. You will not wish to come back here. So you may leave the shovel behind. All right, Victor, first drive us to the Piruzhnaya where we will have something to eat. My friend Vanya looks hungry."

This is a piece of pure invention, this monologue. For Vanya can no more recall the words of that first meeting than recite the Red Grimoire of Cagliostro. He trembled, perspired, felt strange prickly sensations, his ears grew cold, his throat burned as if an icicle had been thrust into it. And he sat beside Charash in this luxurious limousine as if he were riding on a broomstick with a black cat perched on his shoulders.

As I said in the beginning I have never seen this Charash. But so much the better. For, alas, it is not given to people such as I ever to behold a Charash in his true colors. We are too clever to see angels and our vanity is too great for the study of devils. We are too busy with disillusion to look up or look down.

Thus as I write I am tempted to steal Charash from Vanya and attire him in proper, sensible outlines with nothing more dreadful than a Broadway leer on his Muscovite lips. However, my respect for my hero restrains me and too, a slight, reportorial laziness. For if Charash is not the unicorn in the gray derby, the Aladdin, Jinn, Babayaga's son, dervish, Llama, and sorcerer to whom Vanya sold his soul, then who is he? A pock on the realities. This, after all, is still the twentieth century and not the thirtieth, and none of us will seem much keener or more sensible than Vanya when the archeologists come to exhume our doings and sayings. So I give you a Charash as improbable as a frog's dream, as absurd as a grasshopper's honeymoon, and as truthful as Vanya's simple heart.

When we sit down to discuss Charash, Vanya shakes his head and clucks with awe. I ask questions. What did he talk like? Like nobody, says Vanya. For Charash had no human voice. He squeaked. He uttered high-pitched, hoarsened sounds that frightened you. Did he talk Russian? What a question! All the languages—Russian, English, French, Turkish. But always in the same squeak. And very fast, as if he had no breath. He walked fast, too. He was bald-headed, with a head like a big egg. He had a long, purple face. He was not so tall but he had big feet and red hair on his hands. He wore a purple suit. Where did he come from? Vanya crosses himself and his wide cheekbones lift in a sad smile. The same place, says Vanya, to which he has returned.

But there was nothing in his smell to indicate this, says Vanya with a worried look. He smelled like a fine man, always perfumed. When he took out his handkerchief to blow his nose the air became like a garden. But when he got drunk he was very cruel. What did he do? He squeaked and gurgled like a flock of ravens and made sounds in the back of his throat enough to frighten a dozen priests. And he banged on the table and cried out in Russian, so that Vanya's blood ran cold, "Attention! ATTENTION, YOU!" Then Vanya, no matter where this occurred, had to rise and stand rigidly with his fingertips in salute against his perspiring brow while Charash lay back in his seat and squeaked with glee. But all this was nothing.

Vanya remembers this first week with Charash as almost worth the years of torment awaiting him when he appears before God minus his soul. A week of such eating as Vanya's hungriest dreams had never pictured. So many fowls, steaks, chops, soups; so many vegetables, concoctions, pies, pastries and puddings as nobody, not even in Shavarov, would have believed one man could devour, were Vanya's. Five, six times a day, whenever he woke up, a man opened the door and said, "What'll you have, sir?" And Vanya would nod and answer with the magic words Charash had taught him, "The same, please." And in less time than it takes to scratch yourself into a good, wakeful state, the steaming bowls, the crowded platters, all smelling like dreams of heaven, would be on the table before him. And beside this Paradise of dishes, one, two, three or as many bottles of vodka as one needed for a good stomach wash.

And when this enchanted week was done Charash revealed himself and his purpose. This week, he explained, was only a meager sample of what life had in store for Vanya if he would sign his name to a certain paper. So Vanya affixed his name to the document which made Charash his manager, or rather which made Vanya the tool, pawn, chattel, myrmidon and golem of Charash.

It was in this way that Vanya became a wrestler known as Kovelenko, the Mysterious Russian. What did Vanya know of wrestling? Oho, says Vanya, puffing out his cheeks and thrusting forth his lower lip, in Shavarov—my God, in Shavarov his name had been a household word as a wrestler. He had wrestled with Taras the miller, Oblomov the blacksmith, Sedukim the postman, with two farm hands whose names had slipped his mind, with Korolniki, a visiting soldier, and with a monstrous Turk named Sufi who had appeared out of nowhere and overrun Shavarov for a fortnight. All these he had conquered.

In his first month which followed, Vanya wrestled two and three times a week. At the start he was nervous. The shouts of people and the bright lights over his head confused him. Nevertheless these blubbery giants Charash sent into the ring against him were as easy to throw as so many chickens. In fact Vanya hardly needed to throw them; that is, pin both their shoulders carefully to the mat. What he would do was this—after several minutes he would embrace his opponent around the belly, lift him off his feet and hold him in a bear's hug until the man's toes became quiet. Then, at a nod from Charash in the corner, he would drop his opponent and roll him over and the opponent would lie still, like a dead man, and Vanya, at another nod from Charash, would lift his late enemy onto his shoulder like a sack of meal and carry him through the excited audience to the dressing room.

One after another they went to sleep, so to speak, in Vanya's arms. But in the few minutes which preceded each of these dénouements Vanya learned some of the more fanciful ways of the sport, such as seizing a man's toes and trying to break them off; or locking his head between one's thighs and trying to choke him to death, or spreading his legs apart and trying to split him in two, or seizing his wrist and trying to snap his arm as if it were a piece of kindling, or butting him in the stomach and trying to tumble him over so his head would crack against the floor. At first, learning these matters and hearing the crowd yell with delight as he felt his arms, legs, toes, neck and head being tormented in this picayunish and unscrupulous fashion, Vanya would bellow and curse and toss about like a stranded sea cow. However, the laughter he inspired by these antics annoyed him and finally shamed him into more restrained exhibitions of pain and rage.

But after the second month, realizing that all these bedevilments offered him in the first five minutes of his work were not as dangerous as they seemed, Vanya grew contemptuous altogether of them. He even allowed a few of his victims to amuse themselves and his public with this sort of childishness—the toe-holding, ear-pulling, and wrist-twisting—before shaking them loose and coming to serious, manly grips with them. Of what use all their nonsense when Vanya's arms closed round their middles and off the floor they went, their flesh in a vise, their ribs bending, their hearts, livers, lungs and alimentary canals slowly coming together in a jelly?

Vanya remembers them all—the Turks with handlebar mustachios, little eyes and flat cheeks; the Irish with short quick legs and stocky trunks like vodka barrels; the bullet-headed Germans with pale eyebrows and massive shoulders; the flabby, elephantine Greeks, the heavy-legged Indians, the tattooed men looking like a side of beef stamped for the market—he remembers all this bellowing, grunting, Neanderthalish race of ham-and-egg wrestlers as "verra" nice boys.

Twice and three times a week in various outlying towns Vanya applied his bear hug, received a slap on the back from the jolly, squeaking Charash and was returned by train or motor to his room above the café. At the end of the first month Charash presented him with a new suit and every Sunday morning Charash placed two ten-dollar bills in his hand and slapped him on the back again.

Thus for three months my hero, become Kovelenko, the Mysterious Russian, ate and drank to his stomach's delight; rode in automobiles; walked abroad in a suit as elegant and almost as purple as that worn by Charash; learned to carry a cane as big as a cudgel but much fancier; sat up all night in remarkable places where women sang and danced for his pleasure—and lived, says Vanya, like a lord.

His name and even photograph appeared in the newspapers. Men came to converse and drink with him. And my hero underwent changes which would have astonished his one-time raft mates, Mitka and Chizhik, hardly more than they did himself. As for the Promised Land of Hary, Injani, discovered by Parfim, that was a dream forgotten, pooh-poohed at by Charash, who would wave his hand at the glitter and rumble of Babylon and say, here, this, right around where we stand, my Vanya, that is the golden land.

But now in the sixth month of my hero's rise as a gladiator, I must intrude with sad truths and disillusioning asides. I shall be brief, for the subject is not a happy one. First, I wish it to be clear that nothing of this is known (even today) to Vanya. Vanya remembers these months with a simple and honest sigh for glories that are gone. There was a certain strangeness about them and Vanya was not without wonder and disquiet during their passing. But this was because his stout heart sometimes recoiled from the thought of Charash, the queer one. And because he knew with the sad theology of the poor that one does not receive gifts from a Charash without burning in Hell for them a thousand times. But the courage that had served my hero through his stormy Odyssey did not abandon him despite night sweats and evil dreams.

Having decided to serve Charash, he faced the loss of his soul with grim and truly heroic calm. And that was Vanya's only guilt in the matter—that he had made a pact with Charash.

But the truth, unknown to him, was that Charash had made many pacts vastly more evil—pacts with each of the blubbery giants who had melted in Vanya's bear hug, pacts with their managers, pacts with syndicates and fellow promoters. The truth was that my hero was being fed not battles but set-ups; that he was being coddled and stuffed with artificial victories and cunningly converted into a Great Impostor. All this was known only to the élite of the sport. Those who watched from in front beheld, to their delight, a mysterious Russian with murderous arms and a childish lust for battle—an invincible champion in the making.

Charash, squeaking and tireless, piloting his golem from state to state, his pockets always bulging with rolls of bills; Charash, maneuvering his merry troglodyte through more and more complicated skullduggeries, slowly converted Vanya into an important name. The sporting pages took note and began to babble about the Pleistocene mannerisms of this new boon to sport, Kovelenko, the Human Bear. And then, with some fifty bought-and-paid-for victories ornamenting the banner of my hero, Charash had suddenly catapulted him into the notice of that wider public known as the Million Dollar Gate.

The newspapers appeared one morning with the tale that Vera Nash, whose diamond bracelets, ex-husbands and vie d'amour were one of the gaudier legends of Babylon, had selected Kovelenko, the Mysterious Russian, to be the father of her Eugenic Baby. La Nash, in the throes of a maternal complex—so the tale went—had decided to mate with the Human Bear and enrich the world with a Perfect Offspring, etc., etc.

Vanya remembers this matter reluctantly. He speaks of it with his head lowered and a timorous look in his eyes. The first he knew of what was going on, says Vanya, was when they brought him to have his picture taken. And they stood him beside a Princess, so delicate, so beautiful, that he found it hard to breathe and he would have sunk to the floor in sheer bliss had not Charash supported him. As it was his ears trembled, his knees buckled and the roof of his mouth froze. For never had he smelled so delicious a morsel as this lovely woman. What nonsense to call her woman, says Vanya. Angel is the word, creature out of heaven, golden and sweet and more beautiful even than the dreams of a Turk.

The picture-taking done, my hero, still trembling, his heart beating so terribly that he was certain every step he took must be his last, was returned to his room. He spoke no word to Charash and Charash spoke no word to him. Food was brought but Vanya, miracle of love, failed to respond. How could he eat when his stomach was on fire? How could he taste anything when his soul was in his mouth?

The next morning Vanya learned from the man who served him his meals of the remarkable tale in the newspapers—that this Heavenly One had chosen him as a mate. And with his own eyes he beheld the pictures printed of himself and her. He listened, grew dizzy and then, says Vanya, "I try stand up. No. No use. My legs too weak. I try speak. No. No use. My tongue ees dead. I grab vodka. One, two bottle. I throw him in my mout. Then I stand up. I go find Charash. I grab Charash. I hold him, so. Till he grow purrrple like a squash. I kees Charash. I sing the songs of Bashkiria. I am so happy I dance. I am ready to go to this angel who waits forr me. But Charash—'No,' he say. 'No.' 'To Hell,' I say. 'No,' he say. 'What,' I say. 'Thees is my wooman. She love me.' Charash make terrible noise. 'Attention,' he say. 'Attention, you!' He bang the table. 'To Hell,' I say. I knock heem down. He roll over under the bed or I keeck him in pieces, sir. And I go out and find thees place where she is."

And here Vanya holds his head and moans with memories.

The tale of Vanya's wooing, though it lasted a short hour, filled the newspapers for weeks. How he broke down doors, cracked heads, kicked two elevator men unconscious and came hurtling into the presence of the terrified La Nash; how he sang to her, danced and bellowed around her and shattered a Sèvres chandelier and overturned an elegant Louis XIV bed in his courtship; how La Belle Nash, clad in gossamer, fled this Muscovite faun and collapsed in the arms of a Park Avenue policeman; how Vanya, realizing he had been tricked, remained behind and emptied La Nash's apartment out of its eighth-story windows, and how the police, arriving finally in sufficient numbers, clubbed the heart-broken grappler out of his misery—how all these things happened to the delight of hundreds of newspaper editors Vanya himself has never told me. His memory here is mottled. He recalls laconically that he woke up with his head bandaged and Charash beside him. And he lay with his face to the wall for two days. In vain Charash produced substitute goddesses. Vanya groaned and waved them off. And this might have been an end to all the pacts so skillfully made by Charash—for my hero had stomach neither for food, fame, nor females. But Charash persisted and was patient and set to work artfully luring his stricken golem out of his despair with bottle on bottle of vodka. And for two weeks Vanya drank himself in and out of comas. And Vanya slowly came back to sanity.

In the third week he was walking normally and ready to face the world again, the memory of the true goddess flooded out of his kidneys.

The incident, dangerous though its immediate results had seemed, swept the plans of Charash to a speedy climax. For Kovelenko, the Mysterious Russian, had by this gleefully chronicled affair of the heart become an exhilarating figure—one of the overnight celebrities of Babylon. And Charash, feeling his hour was striking, came forward with a challenge and the press responded enthusiastically. Kovelenko, the Mysterious Russian, alias The Great Lover, had challenged Hans Metzger, the world's wrestling champion, and this was news.

The ancient sport had long lain dormant. Metzger, conqueror of a hundred Slav, Greek, German, Indian, Chinese, and Anglo-Saxon champions, had been tossing palookas around for two years; finding none worthy his mettle (nor, what was worse, the price of admission), participating in dubious hippodromes, giving exhibitions of strength in the vaudevilles and praying (along with his troupe of hungry managers) for a Real Contender. Now one had risen, a fiery and passionate gentleman with a record as persuasive as Tamerlane's; with color, glamour and personality thrown in for good measure, and history was to be made for the sporting pages.

Oddly enough, the soothsayers rallied to a man around Vanya. And forthwith such a barrage of jabberwock was laid down by the oracles of the press that the public (always to be fetched by the prospect of the unhorsing of any sort of champion) began to take the forthcoming struggle to its nourishing bosom. All hands agreed that Metzger was a clever, tricky gladiator, full of science and experience, but of what avail, chortled the soothsayers, of what use this cunning against this Throw Back, this Primordial Force, this Uncle of Gorilla and Cousin of the Great Bear—Mr. Kovelenko?

And these were the days of splendor for my hero. He learned to speak English by slowly decoding the ravishing statements of his prowess, genius and marvelous characteristics. In fact he trained on these clippings. Charash, his challenge accepted, had installed his golem in a gymnasium under a considerate ex-wrestling champion with whom Vanya disported himself harmlessly for an hour each day—to the awe and inspiration of the smitten sport writers. The remainder of his time he devoted to his Greatness. He gave out interviews, posed for hundreds of cameras, laughed, blinked, would even sing if urged, grew dizzy and swallowed bottles of vodka to steady himself. These were the days of glory for my hero when he walked arm in arm with illusion and sat upon a throne.

Vanya was the favorite, the Invincible Force, yet the betting odds were against him. Metzger's record as a champion, ignored by the infatuated press, sustained his prestige in the face of the great Vanya ballyhoo. Colorless, scientific, unpopular and, compared to Kovelenko, unknown, Metzger remained a three-to-two and even two-to-one choice, and this served to increase the public's irritation with him. And the public, convinced that a cautious family man with two children and a house in Newark was no match for a Throw Back, a Rapist and a Friend of Glaciers and Mastodons, attacked this presumptuous German burgher in its own way. It bet against him.

And Charash, more active, more purple and more squeaking than ever, worked swiftly through a dozen agents gathering in all such wagers. For this had been the scheme which underlay all the connivings of Charash, and a week before the great Championship Bout, Charash and his syndicate had placed some million dollars in cash bets against their own Vanya. Through the formidable ballyhoo, through the clamorous and eloquent dissertations of the soothsayers, Charash smiled happily and knew he had builded well. Vanya, his golem, was entering the ring against a master wrestler and an honest one. Poor Vanya, whose fame was a fraud invented by Charash, whose victories were part of a carefully evolved hoax, whom Charash in the privacy of his own conclaves called an oaf, a hooligan and a palooka of the lowest order—this deluded and untutored ox of a Russian had as much chance against the brilliant Metzger as a stuffed bear.

So the night of the great doings arrived. Vanya remembers first the crowd outside the Garden, standing in a drizzle and fighting to get in. Like an army, says Vanya, besieging a fortress. Then overhead the lights of this Coliseum. And spelled out in letters of gold the legend—"Vanya Kovelenko Versus Hans Metzger. World's Wrestling Championship." What a thing to see gleaming in the rain! Like a phrase in a fairy tale. Who can forget such a thing? Vanya Kovelenko—spelled out in full for all the eyes of Babylon to read!

He grew dizzy, says Vanya, looking at it, and his attendants (ah, how many attendants Vanya had that night) had to pull him away and into the great Garden. And what shouts and cheers from the rain-soaked ones who recognized him—no King or Hero ever heard louder ones.

Vanya lingers on many details of that evening of which I will forego the telling. Such a buzz and hurrah and burst of lights, such a happy noise and wonderful sight Vanya is sure was never known in the world before. How they loved him when he came striding in his leopard skin to the ring. And how he loved them. He could have kissed each of the twenty thousand on both cheeks. And how they yelled and pointed and embraced him with their soul—him, Vanya, the peasant from Shavarov, the nobody, the hungry rider of ice cakes from Archangelsk.

And there, standing like a colossus out of another age, my hero waited in his corner. Six-feet-three, weighting two hundred and forty, and shaped like a bear. Several of the sharp-eyed ones at the ringside said later that he was drunk—but this was because they remembered tears in his eyes. It was not liquor but enchantment that dimmed Vanya's eyes during these moments.

Metzger, the champion, came and was booed and derided and quickly ignored. And the Coliseum hummed now as if full of millions of bees and crickets. The referee brought them together, spoke. Vanya remembered nothing of this, nothing of the minutes that passed from the time he entered the ring to the moment Charash slapped him on the back and whispered in Russian, "Farewell, my little dove."

Then he remembers seeing as if for the first time a man in purple tights moving toward him, with hands waving in the air like the paws of a cat. A German, says Vanya softly. A German of Germans. With a square head and a square face, pale eyebrows, wide mouth and the blond look behind which Germans disguise themselves. A shapely German, much shapelier than Vanya, with good shoulders and thin in the middle. And Vanya, watching him approach, grew angry. The cries of the Coliseum dimmed in his ears. There was something so evil and intense in the eyes of this German that Vanya grew confused. Not frightened, God forgive the word, but startled. For the weeks that had passed had been such a happy time that my hero had looked forward to this evening as an hour of superb delight. And if he had given thought to his opponent he had fancied another one of those blubbery, weak-backed creatures whom Charash was always producing for him to crush and fall upon.

But in this first moment, standing motionless and watching Metzger, the German, come toward him, Vanya's spirit cleared. There was one thing Vanya knew, one thing he had looked upon and studied in many places—and that was murder in the eyes of men. And murder in a German's eyes! Ah, there came a strange, marshy smell into Vanya's nose and he straightened up as once long ago when the smoke had lifted on the Tannenberg. A Russian curse broke from him and the crowd screamed with delight, but Vanya heard not a sound. He walked forward slowly to meet and seize this one, to choke this German sneer from his face. And his hands unaccountably missed their mark. He had instead slipped his arm into a vise that was bending it out of joint. Vanya let his arm stay in the vise to see how strong this man was. Yes, there was power in the vise, enough to bend him to his knees if he waited too long. And with a sudden growl Vanya ripped his arm free and the champion staggered away and sprawled against the ropes and the crowd boomed its joy.

And again Vanya came forward and again his hands missed their mark and this time the vise closed around his head, twisting it as if to unscrew it from his shoulders. Now Vanya, fully convinced about the general characteristics of this vise, did not wait at all. He flung his shoulders up and again the champion bounced off him like a rubber ball. Vanya pursued, as a bear lumbers swiftly, and reached out for his grip, the one grip he knew—arms around the middle, fingers clasped behind the back and then the feel of flesh and bone melting and cracking against his chest. Instead of all these pleasing events, a powerful hand smashed into his face, snapping back his head. And the champion was moving away, deliberately as if frightened, and the crowd was screaming for an early kill and Vanya, growling, his arms hungry and murderous, moved forward—just as the soothsayers had prophesied. Shamelessly the champion sidled out of his reach, keeping his body bent as if in the throes of an enormous cramp—and Vanya, puzzled at this pathetic exhibition of cowardice, cursed again and plunged. For a moment it seemed that his arms had found their mark. They were almost around this strangely elastic figure that heaved and twisted in his grip like an eel. But Vanya pushed forward, ignoring the head banging against his chin. And then, to his disgust, he found himself in another vise. The German had seized his head and was pulling it over his shoulders as if Vanya were a sack of meal he was going to carry somewhere.

Vanya tried to lock his legs in the German's, pawed furiously with his hands, grunted and thrashed but to no avail. He felt himself rising in the air as if he were a child being played with; rising, floundering in space and crashing to the ground. The champion had tossed him over his shoulder with a Flying Mare.

Vanya was on his feet. He roared with the crowd now and hurled himself forward. No man had ever done this to him. He crashed into Metzger, who gave way, who seemed to twist and slip like something made of rubber; who continued to retreat shamelessly across the ring, his arms extended limply, his hands waving slightly and Vanya after him snorting with rage. Then again the thing happened and Vanya was off his feet, bellowing and clawing the air through which he spun.

This time Vanya lay for a few seconds where he had been tossed and the champion pounced on him. The vise was on Vanya's legs now; now on the toes of his right foot. A pain brought a cry from Vanya and cleared his head. He struck out with his legs and the champion shot across the ring as if he had been tossed over a precipice. And Vanya leaped after him. He landed on an empty stretch of canvas, rose, leaped again, his arms waving before him like those of a man walking under water. But all that happened was that for the third time he found himself, as in a nightmare, rising from the ground, toppling helplessly through the air and crashing head down into the canvas. He heard a noise as he lay—a burst of human sound that shook his heart and brought him to his feet. Those who watched Vanya rise the third time knew from the clumsy way he had taken these falls that he was no wrestler; knew they had been sold again into witnessing Metzger, the scientist, toss another palooka to defeat. The champion, his opponent slightly dazed, would now begin playing medicine ball with him, would now begin bashing him methodically into unconsciousness with one Flying Mare after another, as one might club a giant fish to death by swinging his head against a post.

And these outraged ones, who a few moments ago had shouted themselves giddy with love of this Bear Man, now rose in their seats and demanded a speedy kill. Their hero had betrayed their hopes. The Invincible Force, the Throw Back, the Friend of the Saber-Toothed Tiger et al., was a delusion—and despite the millions wagered, they howled for his end and thundered for his death. And Metzger, still the cat, still sidling and waving paws before him, still crouching, leaped and landed and Vanya again felt the muscles of his leg tearing in the vise. But scissor holds and spread eagles, toe twists and hammerlocks were not invented for the defeat of such as Vanya. He tore himself free as he would have torn his leg out of a steel trap. He staggered, rose, loomed and lunged forward. As much chance to win as a stuffed bear, Charash had said, and this was true. But inside this stuffed bear was a heart that required more than science for its vanquishing. Through the air he sailed again. Crash to the canvas. Up, staggering, clawing—through the air once more. Whish, bang to the ground; dizzy, grunting. Up again and another sprawl, this time on his stomach so his wind went out in a shout. But still he rose and still the champion, leaping on him, bounced off like a terrier shaken from the flanks of a wounded bear. And Vanya, again on his feet, kept moving forward. The German was no German now but a thing of mystery that slipped and twisted continually out of his path and suddenly bent over and became an inhuman apparatus for shooting Vanyas through the air. But German or mystery, human or inhuman, Vanya reeled after it, with his heart bursting and oaths snorting from his mouth.

And now the howling ones standing on their chairs realized that they were witnessing not a wrestling match as advertised but something stranger and more diverting. They were attending the longest kill in the annals of the sport, a kill that promised to continue through the night.

Nine times, ten, eleven, twelve times this Mysterious Russian, in whom they had placed their illusions, sailed through the air, to rise again, to swing his arms, to reel murderously forward. Pounded seemingly to a jelly, tossed and twisted in vise after vise, his head lolling like a dead man's, his legs buckling under him, Vanya fought on though he could neither see nor sense where the battle was for the darkness was greater than any through which he had ever moved—even on that Pechora filled with cannibals.

There was no longer a question of victory. The arms that clutched at the champion were without power; the hands that pawed him were those of a child. All strength had been pounded out of Vanya, his bear hug hammered out of his sinews. Yet each time Metzger the champion leaped to turn him on his back the same thing happened. A mysterious strength that seemed to come from another and still untouched Vanya flowed into his shoulders, legs, and arms—and catapulted the dumbfounded Metzger continually across the canvas.

Twelve, thirteen, fourteen, fifteen, sixteen—the throng, jubilant with lust, counted the Flying Mares, watched the champion lift and smash the helpless Kovelenko to the ground with crotch holds, tumble him with leg tackles, until the scene became like some slow nightmarish murder; until a strange feeling crept into the shouting thousands that Vanya was cursed with some devilish immortality. But this was only Vanya's heart, long after the rest of him was finished, refusing to be hammered into silence.

The end came after an astonishing performance by Vanya. He had risen again, swaying drunkenly, unable for a moment to straighten his legs, his trunk, to lift his arms or open his eyes—a ruined man with a last totter in his marrow. Thus he had stood teetering on unconsciousness and then he had suddenly straightened, his eyes had opened and he had come charging into the champion again. This was unbelievable, to Metzger no less than to the screaming thousands.

It was now Metzger who felt an air of nightmare in that ring. This creature whom he had all but pounded to death, whose toes he knew to be broken, whose leg he knew to be wrenched from its socket, and whose arm he had felt snap in his grip, this Vanya was coming on again, arms swinging, Russian curses once more streaming from him.

And hardly crediting their senses the throng that had been shouting Vanya's requiem, beheld their Bear Man swing his tormentor off the ground, hoist him over his head and hold him aloft. Metzger squirmed and twisted, his feet beating a powerful tattoo against Vanya's face. And Vanya threw back his head and stared up at his inhuman tormentor and smiled and walked a few steps and then paused.

The Coliseum filled with a long roar. The Bear had him. The German was gone. One smash to the ground, one crack against the canvased flooring and Metzger was out. But Vanya, still holding the tossing champion in the air, stood motionless, a man with a strange burden. Then, waving the champion as if he were some mysterious kind of flag, Vanya lifted an agonized face to the roaring galleries and his knees bent, his head fell and he went down slowly under his burden and his flag.

Metzger lay sprawled over him, cautious and waiting. But Vanya was no longer moving. Vanya was still. And Metzger, the German, smiled and rolled him over on his back with a disdainful gesture. And on his back the Mysterious Russian lay while the crowd roared and laughed, while the referee, inaudible in the din, announced the time as twenty-four minutes and ten seconds. And Vanya's eyes were still closed when two men lifted him up and dragged him, hulking and limp, through the ropes, down the aisles and into his dressing room.

Here a doctor appeared and found a number of Vanya's bones to be broken—arm and toes broken, leg wrenched out of place, two ribs smashed, jaw dislocated and, said the doctor, finishing his examination, a serious concussion of the brain. An hour later, after the lights of the Coliseum had long been dark and newspapers carrying the story of his defeat were circulating through a hundred cities, Vanya opened his eyes.

This, in truth, is the end of Vanya's adventures. What followed has little to do with my hero. The scandal that simmered and exploded around Charash and caused him to disappear, the derisive story of Kovelenko's defeat which the press reprinted with increasing angers and accusations for almost a fortnight, the exposure one by one of the numerous set-ups by which Charash had established his palooka's reputation, the general attack on the sport of wrestling—all these epilogues were enacted with Vanya, so to speak, asleep in the wings. Charash in making his exit had sent a messenger to the room above the Piruzhnaya where Vanya lay bandaged like a mummy, and the messenger had handed Vanya five one-hundred-dollar bills. And when the newspapers learned that this paltry sum was all that Vanya had received as his share of the gigantic sport swindle in which he had so painfully participated, they turned their backs on him in disgust as an oaf and hooligan unworthy of their shafts. And in less than a month the name of Vanya Kovelenko had been buried in that limbo into which Babylon disgorges its Seven Day Wonders.

Today Vanya is the doorman at the Piruzhnaya. He stands on the curbing, a towering figure in an ornate Cossack uniform, a hetman's smock and boots, and a large flower-pot hat such as the heroes of eastern Europe affect. This finery pleases Vanya and he is sure that such another uniform is not to be found in all Bashkiria. Thus festooned and grinned at by the passing crowd, Vanya returns their amused stares with an amiable and childish gratitude and if they linger for a moment to wonder at his size he hands them a printed card, as he has been instructed to do.

Here I often come to discuss with Vanya, to hear in snatches his Odyssey and to listen over again to his account of that night of glory when Charash sent him in to fight with his Master, the Devil. And as he tells me of these and other matters, of Chizhik, Mitka, Hary, Injani, of the Pechora and its Samoyeds, and of icebergs, murders, songs and revolutions, of Homeric jaunts, great hungers and the beauties of Shavarov—as he relates these things standing ornate and idle on a curbing in Babylon, he often raises his eyes, grows silent and falls to studying the electric hullabaloo overhead with a critical and quite superior manner.

"My name," he says, "eet was beeger than that one. Beeg. Beeger than thees one. Oh, yes. Beeg as the whole night, sir. From here to there, the whole building, sir, it say, 'VANYA KOVELENKO.' I look all the time, sir, and I nevare see a sign so beeg as the one weeth my name—nevare. So beeg and so bright, people, evrrybody get deezy when they see heem that night. Yes, sir. Goo'night sir. I geev you this. . . ."

And Vanya for the tenth or fifteenth time hands me one of the cards of the Piruzhnaya on one side of which the cuisine of that excellent café is discussed in glowing terms, and on the other side of which is a full-length picture of my hero in a leopard's skin, his arms folded, his sinews abulge. And under this the rather enigmatic words:

"Vanya Kovelenko. Formerly The Mysterious Russian. Now under new management. Inquire within."

# *Miracle of the Fifteen Murderers*

THERE is always an aura of mystery to the conclaves of medical men. One may wonder whether the secrecy with which the fraternity surrounds its gathering is designed to keep the layman from discovering how much it knows or how much it doesn't know. Either knowledge would be unnerving to that immemorial guinea pig who submits himself to the abracadabras of chemicals, scalpels and incantations under the delusion he is being cured rather than explored.

Among the most mysterious of medical get-togethers in this generation have been those held in New York City by a group of eminent doctors calling themselves the X Club. Every three months this little band of healers have hied them to the Walton Hotel overlooking the East River and, behind locked doors and beyond the eye of even medical journalism, engaged themselves in unknown emprise lasting till dawn.

What the devil had been going on in these conclaves for twenty years no one knew, not even the ubiquitous head of the American Medical Association, nor yet any of the colleagues, wives, friends or dependents of the X Club's members. The talent for secrecy is highly developed among doctors who, even with nothing to conceal, are often as close mouthed as old-fashioned bomb throwers on their way to a rendezvous.

How then do I know the story of these long-guarded sessions? The answer is—the war. The war has put an end to them, as it has to nearly all mysteries other than its own. The world, engaged in reexamining its manners and its soul, has closed the door on minor adventure. Nine of the fifteen medical sages who comprised the X Club are in uniform and preside over combat zone hospitals. Deficiencies of age and health have kept the others at home—with increased labors.

"Considering that we have disbanded," Dr. Alex Hume said to me at dinner one evening, "and that it is unlikely we shall ever assemble again, I see no reason for preserving our secret. Yours is a childish and romantic mind, and may be revolted by the story I tell you. You will undoubtedly translate the whole thing into some sort of diabolical tale and miss the deep human and scientific import of the X Club. But I am not the one to reform the art of fiction, which must substitute sentimentality for truth and Cinderella for Galileo."

And so on. I will skip the rest of my friend's all-knowing prelude. You may have read Dr. Hume's various books, dealing with the horseplay of the subconscious. If you have, you know this bald-headed master mind well enough. If not, take my word for it he is a genius. There is nobody I know more adept at prancing around in the solar plexus swamps out of which most of the world's incompetence and confusion appear to rise. He has, too, if there is any doubt about his great talent, the sneer and chuckle which are the war whoop of the super-psychologist. His face is round and his mouth is pursed in a chronic grimace of disbelief and contradiction. You can't help such an expression once you have discovered what a scurvy and detestable morass is the soul of man. Like most subterranean workers, my friend is almost as blind as a bat behind his heavy glasses. And like many leading psychiatrists, he favors the short and balloon-like physique of Napoleon.

The last dramatic meeting of the X Club was held on a rainy March night. Despite the hostile weather, all fifteen of its members attended, for there was an added lure to this gathering. A new member was to be inducted into the society.

Dr. Hume was assigned to prepare the neophyte for his debut. And it was in the wake of the round-faced soul fixer that Dr. Samuel Warner entered the sanctum of the X Club.

Dr. Warner was unusually young for a medical genius—that is, a recognized one. And he had never received a fuller recognition of his wizardry with saw, axe and punch hole than his election as a member of the X Club. For the fourteen older men who had invited him to be one of them were leaders in their various fields. They were the medical peerage. This does not mean necessarily that any layman had ever heard of them. Eminence in the medical profession is as showy at best as a sprig of edelweiss on a mountain top. The war, which offers its magic billboards for the vanities of small souls and transmutes the hunger for publicity into sacrificial and patriotic ardors, has not yet disturbed the anonymity of the great medicos. They have moved their bushels to the front lines and are busy under them spreading their learning among the wounded.

The new member was a tense and good-looking man with the fever of hard work glowing in his steady dark eyes. His wide mouth smiled quickly and abstractedly, as is often the case with surgeons who train their reactions not to interfere with their concentration.

Having exchanged greetings with the eminent club members, who included half of his living medical heroes, Dr. Warner seated himself in a corner and quietly refused a highball, a cocktail, and a slug of brandy. His face remained tense, his athletic body straight in its chair as if it were poised for a sprint rather than a meeting.

At nine o'clock Dr. William Tick ordered an end to all the guzzling and declared the fifty-third meeting of the X Club in session. The venerable diagnostician placed himself behind a table at the end of the ornate hotel room and glared at the group ranged in front of him.

Dr. Tick had divided his seventy-five years equally between practicing the art of medicine and doing his best to stamp it out—such, at least, was the impression of the thousands of students who had been submitted to his irascible guidance. As Professor of Internal Medicine at a great Eastern medical school, Dr. Tick had favored the education-by-insult theory of pedagogy. There were eminent doctors who still winced when they recalled some of old bilious-eyed, arthritic, stooped Tick's appraisals of their budding talents, and who still shuddered at the memory of his medical philosophy.

"Medicine," Dr. Tick had confided to flock after flock of students, "is a noble dream and at the same time the most ancient expression of error and idiocy known to man. Solving the mysteries of heaven has not given birth to as many abortive findings as has the quest into the mysteries of the human body. When you think of yourselves as scientists, I want you always to remember everything you learn from me will probably be regarded tomorrow as the naïve confusions of a pack of medical aborigines. Despite all our toil and progress, the art of medicine still falls somewhere between trout casting and spook writing."

"There are two handicaps to the practice of medicine," Tick had repeated tenaciously through forty years of teaching. "The first is the eternal charlatanism of the patient who is full of fake diseases and phantom agonies. The second is the basic incompetence of the human mind, medical or otherwise, to observe without prejudice, acquire information without becoming too smug to use it intelligently, and most of all, to apply its wisdom without vanity."

From behind his table Old Tick's eyes glared at the present group of "incompetents" until a full classroom silence had arrived, and then turned to the tense, good-looking face of Dr. Warner.

"We have a new medical genius with us tonight," he began, "one I well remember in his pre-wizard days. A hyper-thyroid with kidney disfunction indicated. But not without a trace of talent. For your benefit, Sam, I will state the meaning and purpose of our organization."

"I have already done that," said Dr. Hume, "rather thoroughly."

"Dr. Hume's explanations to you," Tick continued coldly, "if they are of a kind with his printed works, have most certainly left you dazed if not dazzled."

"I understood him quite well," Warner said.

"Nonsense," Old Tick said. "You always had a soft spot for psychiatry and I always warned you against it. Psychiatry is a plot against medicine."

You may be sure that Dr. Hume smiled archly at this.

"You will allow me," Tick went on, "to clarify whatever the learned Hume has been trying to tell you."

"Well, if you want to waste time." The new member smiled nervously and mopped his neck with a handkerchief.

Dr. Frank Rosson, the portly and distinguished gynecologist, chuckled. "Tick's going good tonight," he whispered to Hume.

"Senility inflamed by sadism," said Hume.

"Dr. Warner," the pedagogue continued, "the members of the X Club have a single and interesting purpose in their meeting. They come together every three months to confess to some murder any of them may have committed since our last assembly.

"I am referring, of course, to medical murder. Although it would be a relief to hear any one of us confess to a murder performed out of passion rather than stupidity. Indeed, Dr. Warner, if you have killed a wife or polished off an uncle recently, and would care to unbosom yourself, we will listen respectfully. It is understood that nothing you say will be brought to the attention of the police or the A.M.A."

Old Tick's eyes paused to study the growing tension in the new member's face.

"I am sure you have not slain any of your relatives," he sighed, "or that you will ever do so except in the line of duty.

"The learned Hume," he went on, "has undoubtedly explained these forums to you on the psychiatric basis that confession is good for the soul. This is nonsense. We are not here to ease our souls but to improve them. Our real purpose is scientific. Since we dare not admit our mistakes to the public and since we are too great and learned to be criticized by the untutored laity and since such inhuman perfection as that to which we pretend is not good for our weak and human natures, we have formed this society. It is the only medical organization in the world where the members boast only of their mistakes.

"And now"—Tick beamed on the neophyte—"allow me to define what we consider a real, fine professional murder. It is the killing of a human being who has trustingly placed himself in a doctor's hands. Mind you, the death of a patient does not in itself spell murder. We are concerned only with those cases in which the doctor by a wrong diagnosis or by demonstrably wrong medication or operative procedure has killed off a patient who, without the aforesaid doctor's attention, would have continued to live and prosper."

"Hume explained all this to me," the new member muttered impatiently, and then raised his voice. "I appreciate that this is my first meeting and that I might learn more from my distinguished colleagues by listening than by talking. But I have something rather important to say."

"A murder?" Tick asked.

"Yes," said the new member.

The old professor nodded.

"Very good," he said. "And we shall be glad to listen to you. But we have several murderers in the docket ahead of you."

The new member was silent and remained sitting bolt-upright in his chair. It was at this point that several, including Hume, noticed there was something more than stage fright in the young surgeon's tension. The certainty filled the room that Sam Warner had come to his first meeting of the X Club with something violent and mysterious boiling in him.

Dr. Philip Kurtiff, the eminent neurologist, put his hand on Warner's arm and said quietly, "There's no reason to feel badly about anything you're going to tell us. We're all pretty good medical men and we've all done worse—whatever it is."

"If you please," Old Tick demanded, "we will have silence. This is not a sanatorium for doctors with guilt complexes. It is a clinic for error. And we will continue to conduct it in an orderly, scientific fashion. If you want to hold Sam Warner's hand, Kurtiff, that's your privilege. But do it in silence."

He beamed suddenly at the new member.

"I confess," he went on, "that I'm as curious as anybody to hear how so great a know-it-all as our young friend Dr. Warner could have killed off one of his customers. But our curiosity will have to wait. Since five of you were absent from our last gathering, I think that the confessions of Dr. James Sweeney should be repeated for your benefit."

Dr. Sweeney stood up and turned his lugubrious face and shining eyes to the five absentees.

"Well," he said in his preoccupied monotone, "I told it once, but I'll tell it again. I sent a patient to my X-ray room to have a fluoroscopy done. My assistant gave him a barium meal to drink and put him under the fluoroscope. I walked in a minute later, and when I saw the patient under the ray I observed to my assistant, Dr. Kroch, that it was amazing and that I had never seen anything like it. Kroch was too overcome to bear me out. What I saw was that the patient's entire gastro-intestinal tract from the esophagus down was apparently made out of stone. And as I studied this phenomenon, I noticed it was becoming clearer and sharper. The most disturbing factor in the situation was that we both knew there was nothing to be done. Dr. Kroch, in fact, showed definite signs of hysteria. Even while we were studying him the patient showed symptoms of death. Shortly afterward he became moribund and fell to the floor."

"Well, I'll be damned," several of the absentees cried in unison, Dr. Kurtiff adding, "What the hell was it?"

"It was simple," said Sweeney. "The bottom of the glass out of which the patient had drunk his barium meal was caked solid. We had filled him up with plaster of Paris. I fancy the pressure caused an instantaneous coronary attack."

"Good Lord!" the new member said. "How did it get into the glass?"

"Through some pharmaceutical error," said Sweeney mildly.

"What, if anything, was the matter with the patient before he adventured into your office?" Dr. Kurtiff inquired.

"The autopsy revealed chiefly a solidified gastro-intestinal tract," said Sweeney. "But I think from several indications that there may have been a little tendency to pyloric spasm which caused the belching for which he was referred to me."

"A rather literary murder," said Old Tick. "A sort of Pygmalion in reverse."

The old professor paused and fastened his red-rimmed eyes on Warner.

"By the way, before we proceed," he said, "I think it is time to tell you the full name of our club. Our full name is the X Marks the Spot Club. We prefer, of course, to use the abbreviated title as being a bit more social-sounding."

"Of course," said the new member, whose face now appeared to be getting redder.

"And now," announced Old Tick, consulting a scribbled piece of paper, "our first case on tonight's docket will be Dr. Wendell Davis."

There was silence as the elegant stomach specialist stood up. Davis was a doctor who took his manner as seriously as his medicine. Tall, solidly built, gray-haired and beautifully barbered, his face was without expression—a large, pink mask that no patient, however ill and agonized, had ever seen disturbed.

"I was called late last summer to the home of a workingman," he began. "Senator Bell had given a picnic for some of his poorer constituency. As a result of this event, the three children of a steamfitter named Horowitz were brought down with food poisoning. They had overeaten at the picnic. The Senator, as host, felt responsible, and I went to the Horowitz home at his earnest solicitation. I found two of the children very sick and vomiting considerably. They were nine and eleven. The mother gave me a list of the various foods all three of them had eaten. It was staggering. I gave them a good dose of castor oil.

"The third child, aged seven, was not as ill as the other two. He looked pale, had a slight fever, felt some nausea—but was not vomiting. It seemed obvious that he too was poisoned, but to a lesser degree. Accordingly I prescribed an equal dose of castor oil for the youngest child —just to be on the safe side.

"I was called by the father in the middle of the night. He was alarmed over the condition of the seven-year-old. He reported that the other two children were much improved. I told him not to worry, that the youngest had been a little late in developing food poisoning but would unquestionably be better in the morning, and that his cure was as certain as his sister's and brother's. When I hung up I felt quite pleased with myself for having anticipated the youngest one's condition and prescribed the castor oil prophylactically. I arrived at the Horowitz home at noon the next day and found the two older children practically recovered. The seven-year-old, however, appeared to be very sick indeed. They had been trying to reach me since breakfast. The child had 105° temperature. It was dehydrated, the eyes sunken and circled, the expression pinched, the nostrils dilated, the lips cyanotic and the skin cold and clammy."

Dr. Davis paused. Dr. Milton Morris, the renowned lung specialist, spoke.

"It died within a few hours?" he asked.

Dr. Davis nodded.

"Well," Dr. Morris said quietly, "it seems pretty obvious. The child was suffering from acute appendicitis when you first saw it. The castor oil ruptured its appendix. By the time you got around to looking at it again peritonitis had set in."

"Yes," said Dr. Davis slowly, "that's exactly what happened."

"Murder by castor oil," Old Tick cackled. "I have a memo from Dr. Kenneth Wood. Dr. Wood has the floor."

The noted Scotch surgeon, famed in his college days as an Olympic Games athlete, stood up. He was still a man of prowess, large-handed, heavy-shouldered, and with the purr of masculine strength in his soft voice.

"I don't know what kind of a murder you can call this," Dr. Wood smiled at his colleagues.

"Murder by butchery is the usual title," Tick said.

"No, I doubt that," Dr. Morris protested. "Ken's too skillful to cut off anybody's leg by mistake."

"I guess you'll have to call it just plain murder by stupidity," Dr. Wood said softly.

Old Tick cackled.

"If you'd paid a little more attention to diagnosis than to shot putting you wouldn't be killing off such hordes of patients," he said.

"This is my first report in three years," Wood answered modestly. "And I've been operating at the rate of four or five daily, including holidays."

"My dear Kenneth," Dr. Hume said, "every surgeon is entitled to one murder in three years. A phenomenal record, in fact—when you consider the temptations."

"Proceed with the crime," Tick said.

"Well"—the strong-looking surgeon turned to his hospital colleague, the new member—"you know how it is with these acute gall bladders, Sam."

Warner nodded abstractedly.

Dr. Wood went on.

"Brought in late at night. In extreme pain. I examined her. Found the pain in the right upper quadrant of the abdomen. It radiated to the back and right shoulder. Completely characteristic of gall bladder. I gave her opiates. They had no effect on her, which, as you know, backs up any gall bladder diagnosis. Opiates never touch the gall bladder."

"We know that," said the new member nervously.

"Excuse me," Dr. Wood smiled. "I want to get all the points down carefully. Well, I gave her some nitro-glycerine to lessen the pain then. Her temperature was 101. By morning the pain was so severe that it seemed certain the gall bladder had perforated. I operated. There was nothing wrong with her damn gall bladder. She died an hour later."

"What did the autopsy show?" Dr. Sweeney asked.

"Wait a minute," Wood answered. "You're supposed to figure it out, aren't you? Come on—you tell me what was the matter with her."

"Did you take her history?" Dr. Kurtiff asked after a pause.

"No," Wood answered.

"Aha!" Tick snorted. "There you have it! Blind man's buff again."

"It was an emergency." Wood looked flushed. "And it seemed an obvious case. I've had hundreds of them."

"The facts seem to be as follows," Tick spoke up. "Dr. Wood murdered a woman because he misunderstood the source of a pain. We have, then, a very simple problem. What besides the gall bladder can produce the sort of pain that eminent surgeon has described?"

"Heart," Dr. Morris answered quickly.

"You're getting warm," said Wood.

"Before operating on anyone with so acute a pain, and in the absence of any medical history," Tick went on, "I would most certainly have looked at the heart."

"Well, you'd have done right," said Wood quietly. "The autopsy showed an infraction of the descending branch of the right coronary artery."

"Murder by a sophomore," Old Tick pronounced wrathfully.

"The first and last," said Wood quietly. "There won't be any more heart-case mistakes in my hospital."

"Good, good," Old Tick said. "And now, gentlemen, the crimes reported thus far have been too infantile for discussion. We have learned nothing from them other than that science and stupidity go hand in hand, a fact already too well known to us. However, we have with us tonight a young but extremely talented wielder of the medical saws. And I can, from long acquaintance with this same gentleman, assure you that if he has done a murder it is bound to be what some of my female students would call 'a honey.' He has been sitting here for the last hour, fidgeting like a true criminal, sweating with guilt and a desire to tell all. Gentlemen, I give you our new and youngest culprit, Dr. Samuel Warner."

Dr. Warner faced his fourteen eminent colleagues with a sudden excitement in his manner. The older men regarded him quietly and with various degrees of irritation. They knew without further corroboration than his manner that this medico was full of untenable theories and half-baked medical discoveries. They had been full of such things themselves once. And they settled back to enjoy themselves. There is nothing as pleasing to a graying medicine man as the opportunity of slapping a dunce-cap on the young of science. Old Tick, surveying his colleagues, grinned. They had all acquired the look of pedagogues holding a switch behind their backs.

Dr. Warner mopped his neck with his wet handkerchief and smiled knowingly at the medical peerage. What he knew was that this same critical and suspicious attention would have been offered him were he there to recite the tale of some miraculous cure rather than a murder.

"I'll give you this case in some detail," he said, "because I think it contains as interesting a problem as you can find in practice."

Dr. Rosson, the gynecologist, grunted, but said nothing.

"The patient was a young man, or rather a boy," Warner went on eagerly. "He was seventeen, and amazingly talented. In fact, about the most remarkable young man I've ever met. He wrote poetry. That's how I happened to meet him. I read one of his poems in a magazine, and, by God, it was so impressive I wrote him a letter."

Dr. Kurtiff frowned at this unmedical behavior.

"Rhymed poetry?" Dr. Wood asked, with a wink at Old Tick.

"Yes," said Warner. "I read all his manuscripts. They were sort of revolutionary. His poetry was a cry against injustice. Every kind of injustice. Bitter and burning."

"Wait a minute," Dr. Rosson said. "The new member seems to have some misconception of our function. We are not a literary society, Warner."

"I know that," said Warner, working his jaw muscles and smiling lifelessly.

"And before you get started," Dr. Hume grinned, "no bragging. You can do your bragging at the annual surgeons' convention."

"Gentlemen," Warner said, "I have no intention of bragging. I'll stick to murder, I assure you. And as bad a one as you've ever heard."

"Good," Dr. Kurtiff said. "Go on. And take it easy and don't break down."

"I won't break down," Warner said. "Don't worry. Well, the patient was sick for two weeks before I was called."

"I thought you were his friend," Dr. Davis said.

"I was," Warner answered. "But he didn't believe in doctors."

"No faith in them, eh?" Old Tick cackled. "Brilliant boy."

"He was," said Warner eagerly. "I felt upset when I came and saw how sick he was. I had him moved to a hospital at once."

"Oh, a rich poet," Dr. Sweeney said.

"No," said Warner. "I paid his expenses. And I spent all the time I could with him. The sickness had started with a severe pain on the left side of the abdomen. He was going to call me, but the pain subsided after three days so the patient thought he was well. But it came back after two days and he began running a temperature. He developed diarrhea. There was pus and blood, but no amoeba or pathogenic bacteria when he finally sent for me. After the pathology reports I made a diagnosis of ulcerative colitis. The pain being on the left side ruled out the appendix. I put the patient on sulfaguanidin and unconcentrated liver extract and gave him a high protein diet—chiefly milk. Despite this treatment and constant observation the patient got worse. He developed generalized abdominal tenderness, both direct and rebound, and rigidity of the entire left rectus muscle. After two weeks of careful treatment the patient died."

"And the autopsy showed you'd been wrong?" Dr. Wood asked.

"I didn't make an autopsy," said Warner. "The boy's parents had perfect faith in me. As did the boy. They both believed I was doing everything possible to save his life."

"Then how do you know you were wrong in your diagnosis?" Dr. Hume asked.

"By the simple fact," said Warner irritably, "that the patient died instead of being cured. When he died I knew I had killed him by a faulty diagnosis."

"A logical conclusion," said Dr. Sweeney. "Pointless medication is no alibi."

"Well, gentlemen," Old Tick cackled from behind his table, "our talented new member has obviously polished off a great poet and close personal friend. Indictments of his diagnosis are now in order."

But no one spoke. Doctors have a sense for things unseen and complications unstated. And nearly all the fourteen looking at Warner felt there was something hidden. The surgeon's tension, his elation and its overtone of mockery, convinced them there was something untold in the story of the dead poet. They approached the problem cautiously.

"How long ago did the patient die?" Dr. Rosson asked.

"Last Wednesday," said Warner. "Why?"

"What hospital?" asked Davis.

"St. Michael's," said Warner.

"You say the parents had faith in you," said Kurtiff, "and still have. Yet you seem curiously worried about something. Has there been any inquiry by the police?"

"No," said Warner. "I committed the perfect crime. The police haven't even heard of it. And even my victim died full of gratitude."

He beamed at the room. "Listen," he went on, "even you people may not be able to disprove my diagnosis."

This brash challenge irritated a number of the members.

"I don't think it will be very difficult to knock out your diagnosis," said Dr. Morris.

"There's a catch to it," said Wood slowly, his eyes boring at Warner.

"The only catch there is," said Warner quickly, "is the complexity of the case. You gentlemen evidently prefer the simpler malpractice type of crime, such as I've listened to tonight."

There was a pause, and then Dr. Davis inquired in a soothing voice, "You described an acute onset of pain before the diarrhea, didn't you?"

"That's right," said Warner.

"Well," Davis continued coolly, "the temporary relief of symptoms and their recurrence within a few days sounds superficially like ulcers—except for one point."

"I disagree," Dr. Sweeney said softly. "Dr. Warner's diagnosis is a piece of blundering stupidity. The symptoms he has presented have nothing to do with ulcerative colitis."

Warner flushed and his jaw muscles moved angrily.

"Would you mind backing up your insults with a bit of science?" he said.

"Very easily done," Sweeney answered calmly. "The late onset of diarrhea and fever you describe rules out ulcerative colitis in ninety-nine cases out of a hundred. What do you think, Dr. Tick?"

"No ulcers," said Tick, his eyes studying Warner.

"You mentioned a general tenderness of the abdomen as one of the last symptoms," said Dr. Davis smoothly.

"That's right," said Warner.

"Well, if you have described the case accurately," Davis continued, "there is one obvious fact revealed. The general tenderness points to a peritonitis."

"How about a twisted gut?" Dr. Wood asked. "That could produce the symptoms described."

"No," said Dr. Rosson. "A vulvulus means gangrene and death in three days. Warner says he attended him for two weeks and that the patient was sick for two weeks before he was called. The length of the illness rules out intussusception, vulvulus and intestinal tumor."

"There's one other thing," Dr. Morris said. "A left-sided appendix."

"That's out, too," Dr. Wood said quickly. "The first symptom of a left-sided appendix would not be the acute pain described by Warner."

"The only thing we have determined," said Dr. Sweeney, "is a perforation other than ulcer. Why not go on with that?"

"Yes," said Dr. Morris. "Ulcerative colitis is out of the question, considering the course taken by the disease. I'm sure we're dealing with another type of perforation."

"The next question," announced Old Tick, "is, what made the perforation?"

Dr. Warner mopped his face with his wet handkerchief and said softly, "I never thought of an object perforation."

"You should have," Dr. Kurtiff smiled.

"Come, come," Old Tick interrupted. "Let's not wander. What caused the perforation?"

"He was seventeen," Kurtiff answered, "and too old to be swallowing pins."

"Unless," said Dr. Hume, "he had a taste for pins. Did the patient want to live, Warner?"

"He wanted to live," said Warner grimly, "more than anybody I ever knew."

"I think we can ignore the suicide theory," said Dr. Kurtiff. "I am certain we are dealing with a perforation of the intestines and not of the subconscious."

"Well," Dr. Wood said, "it couldn't have been a chicken bone. A chicken bone would have stuck in the esophagus and never got through to the stomach."

"There you are, Warner," Old Tick said. "We've narrowed it down. The spreading tenderness you described means a spreading infection. The course taken by the disease means a perforation other than ulcerous. And a perforation of that type means an object swallowed. We have ruled out pins and chicken bones. Which leaves us with only one other normal guess."

"A fish bone," said Dr. Sweeney.

"Exactly," said Tick.

Warner stood listening tensely to the voices affirming the diagnosis. Tick delivered the verdict.

"I think we are all agreed," he said, "that Sam Warner killed his patient by treating him for ulcerative colitis when an operation removing an abscessed fish bone would have saved his life."

Warner moved quickly across the room to the closet where he had hung his hat and coat.

"Where you going?" Dr. Wood called after him. "We've just started the meeting."

Warner was putting on his coat and grinning.

"I haven't got much time," he said, "but I want to thank all of you for your diagnoses. You were right about there being a catch to the case. The catch is that my patient is still alive. I've been treating him for ulcerative colitis for two weeks and I realized this afternoon that I had wrongly diagnosed the case—and that he would be dead in twenty-four hours unless I could find out what really was the matter with him."

Warner was in the doorway, his eyes glittering.

"Thanks again, gentlemen, for the consultation and your diagnosis," he said. "It will enable me to save my patient's life."

A half hour later the members of the X Club stood grouped in one of the operating rooms of St. Michael's Hospital. They were different-looking men than had been playing a medical Halloween in the Walton Hotel. There is a change that comes over doctors when they face disease. The oldest and the weariest of them draw vigor from a crisis. The shamble leaves them and it is the straight back of the champion that enters the operating room. Confronting the problem of life and death, the tired, red-rimmed eyes become full of greatness and even beauty.

On the operating table lay the naked body of a Negro boy. Dr. Warner in his surgical whites stood over him, waiting. The anesthetist finally nodded. The dark skin had turned ashen, and the fevered young Negro lay unconscious.

The fourteen X Club members watched Warner operate. Wood nodded approvingly at his speed. Rosson cleared his throat to say something, but the swift-moving hands of the surgeon held him silent. No one spoke. The minutes passed. The nurses quietly handed instruments to the surgeon. Blood spattered their hands.

Fourteen great medical men stared hopefully at the pinched and unconscious face of a colored boy who had swallowed a fish bone. No king or pope ever lay in travail with more medical genius holding its breath around him.

Suddenly the perspiring surgeon raised something aloft in his gloved fingers.

"Wash this off," he muttered to the nurse, "and show it to the gentlemen."

He busied himself placing drains in the abscessed cavity and then powdered some sulfanilamide into the opened abdomen to kill the infection.

Old Tick stepped forward and took the object from the nurse's hand.

"A fish bone," he said.

The X Club gathered around it as if it were a treasure indescribable.

"The removal of this small object," Tick cackled softly, "will enable the patient to continue writing poetry denouncing the greeds and horrors of our world."

That, in effect, was the story Hume told me, plus the epilogue of the Negro poet's recovery three weeks later. We had long finished dinner and it was late night when we stepped into the war-dimmed streets of New York. The headlines on the newsstands had changed in size only. They were larger in honor of the larger slaughters they heralded.

Looking at them you could see the death-strewn wastes of battles. But another picture came to my mind—a picture that had in it the hope of a better world. It was the hospital room in which fifteen famed and learned heroes stood battling for the life of a Negro boy who had swallowed a fish bone.

# *Specter of the Rose*

I HAVE TO MAKE up much of this story because it's something that happened inside of a man's head. I knew the man well. But knowing a man and knowing the inside of his head are separate matters.

A Russian once wrote, "The soul of another is always darkness." This is true about most people we know, even those close to us. The human mind, including the one we use ourselves, is an eternally unknown land.

But in writing of my poor dead friend I'm not dealing entirely with matters unknowable and unseeable. For there is a tribe of people whose secrets are more apparent than those of the rest of us, and whose mental underworlds are to be glimpsed by the veriest of strangers. These are the people who are medically identified as mad. My friend was one of them.

His name was André Sanine. He was young, he was handsome, he was a ballet dancer, and he was mad. He had the muscles of a tiger or a truck driver, the endurance of a sea gull, and the face of a smiling boy.

When I first knew him his madness had not progressed beyond the stage of charm. His character consisted seemingly of a single quality. He desired only to please people—not only people he knew, but everybody. A taxi driver, a waitress, a newsboy, a hotel porter, a property man, anybody's wife, mother, or uncle—André wooed them all as if he were a child plotting to locate the good graces of the world and snuggle in them. You would have sworn that this powerful and gentle youth owned a heart as innocent and overflowing with love as a valentine. You would have sworn it, and wondered why it was necessary to argue a thing that seemed so obvious. But that was always an interesting thing about André—he failed to convince you entirely that he was the André you knew. Yet my friend was so graceful, so reserved, and his eyes were so selfless and so full of a happy interest in everything they looked on, that people felt refreshed on meeting him, and when they got to know him better were ready to forgive whatever secret evil might lie hidden behind so pleasing a manner. For you could smell this evil.

There was about André's youth the faint and bitter smell of decay that you can detect in some flowers when they are at their prettiest. Long before he became mad and revealed the evil that was in him, it was to be sensed. It lay somehow coiled away in his boyish smile, and you could get a glimpse of it moving dimly under his very wooing of you.

I doubt if any one was bright enough to see through André when he was the talented darling of the ballet. I know I wasn't. I found him at times a little disturbing, as too much charm often is. And I wondered at times why it was that, if André loved everybody and everything, he had nevertheless managed to avoid falling in love with one particular human being. This was curious, since many exotic young women I knew were always swooning at the mention of his name. Yet no scandal of any sort had ever attached itself to that name. I thought this not only curious but surprising. For André inhabited a world where scandal was the rule, where passion, hysterics, and intrigue were the commonplaces of every hour. This was the world of the ballet—whose inhabitants seemingly devote themselves only to grace and disaster.

The people of this exuberant world are to be seen in the rehearsal halls toiling like the damned in the development of every one of their fifty-odd sinews, leaping about bathed in sweat, paling with exhaustion, breaking their toes, ankles, and kneecaps—a little race of men and women incredibly dedicated to the pursuit of ruptures, of heart enlargements, and of major bruises. All these exhausting rehearsals flower a few evenings a year into a dance. On these few evenings the toilers are to be seen drifting about in colored spotlights as rose petals, autumn leaves, sylphides, peacocks, and genii made of smoke and magic.

Yet these people who have learned to move as if music and not blood flowed in their veins engage in amours often as graceless as those of the most backward of savages. Their matings, infidelities, and reprisals are full of scream and cruelty. It may be there is a connection between their austere and backbreaking labors and their sadistic romances, but I will forego prying into it. I hint at all these matters only because they were André's background, and if you knew this background you could understand the glint of evil that touched his most boyish of smiles and the cruelty that seemed to sleep in his gentlest of words—and ignore it as only natural.

André's position as a dancer was, in these first years I knew him, more a matter of promise than fact. He was expert in all the leaps and sudden flashes of strength and balance the art of the ballet demands of its children as a matter of course. He knew the myriad steps and pantomimic movements that went with the various great tunes to which the ballets are performed—for these maneuvers are seldom left to the inventiveness of the dancer. They are usually a ritual handed down by the choreographers. André was alive also with that extra gleam of personality which, more than any other factor, ultimately separates the champions from the chaff in the ballet as everywhere else. And underlying all he did, even to the smallest of his day's details, was a love of dancing—a love so obsessive as to make him seem either less or more than human as do the yogis and lamas and the ancient saints.

Whenever I was with André where music played, were it only a barrel organ or a taxicab radio, he danced. He danced sitting still and with every muscle motionless. He danced inside himself, his mind moving about in leaps and convulsions. At such times André wore a sleepy and abstracted look and gave the impression that he had turned into a statue.

Thus equipped, this fragile-faced youth with the constitution of a truck driver might have made that skyrocket leap out of the ranks of promise but for the thing that happened to him—madness. It was a long time—a year at least—before I or anybody, except one person, had any idea of the mania that had come to roost like a vulture in André's head and to feed upon him, to devour his charm, his talent, and his bright smile. During this year that he had gone mad behind our backs, as it were, André worked hard and danced well, and continued to woo those he met, to beam upon and refresh hundreds of strangers. And the first rumor his friends had of his coming darkness was entirely unrecognizable as such an omen. Talk came to me that André was in love with a pretty dancer named Maria Ivonova, who was not nearly as foreign or exotic as her name, having been hatched in Trenton, New Jersey, and raised in the home of a warehouse employee and an ex-stenographer—her parents.

André finally achieving a love affair was, in fact, pleasant news to his many friends, all of whom immediately considered the girl lucky beyond her deserts, for she was neither particularly beautiful nor greatly talented. As the year progressed I saw André and his Maria a number of times. I saw always a smiling youth who treated his blond and rather innocuous sweetheart with the same grace and politeness he might have lavished on a dancing partner behind the footlights. But after several dinners with the couple I began to notice that André's Maria had acquired a wary look, that her manner toward my friend was too eager, too uncertain. And I began to suspect there was an André I didn't know at all, a behind-closed-doors André who was as far removed from a valentine as a war communiqué.

I read of this André one morning in the papers. He had choked Maria Ivonova to death in the middle of the night, and been found sitting quietly at her bedside in the morning and smiling to himself.

There was no doubt whatsoever from that morning on that André Sanine was a maniac. Even the police did not contest this fact. And André's trial as a murderer never got beyond his examination by the medicos. The doctors all agreed that André was insane, and supporting their finding was the diary poor Maria Ivonova of Trenton, New Jersey, had kept. In these almost childlike pages was found a record not of a lover but a monster. They revealed that since the first month of their marriage—a fact André had kept secret from his friends—he had been intent on only one thing: the murder of his bride.

He had begun with a series of jealous rages which had startled Maria into writing that André was unreasonable and that she would do everything she could to convince him that she loved nobody but him and was entirely true to him in all her thoughts as well as deeds. But apparently André's jealousy, so groundless and yet so necessary to him, was not to be reasoned with. It bloomed, it flourished on all of Maria's protestations and proofs of innocence. It grew big and dark and engulfed them both in something that could barely be written about—at least, not by Maria Ivonova. There were innumerable pathetic entries in the diary recounting nights of violence, screams and sobs.

She wrote in the third month a frightened cry of understanding. He was not responsible, she put down. He wanted to drive himself crazy, so that he could scream and mistreat her, because there was something in him that made this necessary. And after he had hurt her he would fall at her feet and weep and ask to be forgiven. Then his face, grown strange in the night, would become familiar again. In the fourth month she wrote that he had begun begging her to leave him and save herself from his craziness. But she had refused because she loved him. And he was trying hard to cure himself. He worked so long and so hard that when he came home he could hardly sit up. He would fall into bed and go to sleep scowling at her and trembling as if something were shaking him.

Toward the end of the year she wrote a dark little cry of love that I have never forgotten.

"How can he be so nice to everybody else?" she put down. "He must be two different men. I am afraid of him. I ought to leave him now. He cries all the time that I am ruining him with my badness. He says I am not to be trusted out of his sight and that I run after every man who looks at me. This is so untrue. But I can't tell him that any more. It only makes him worse. All he wants is that I should confess something to him. And when I have nothing to confess, he goes crazy and he loses control of himself. I know he will kill me, because that's what his craziness wants to do. But I can't bear to leave him even if he is a monster. Because sometimes he is still André. He still kisses me sometimes."

André was sent to a state institution as a man criminally insane. I visited him there occasionally, as did many of his friends. For a long time—years, in fact—these visits were more or less perfunctory. They were of no service to André—he was unaware of them.

I would come to his ward and watch him for ten minutes or so as he sat immobile before a long wooden table, his arms hanging limply, his head turned rigidly at an angle. He never moved. At such times I remembered how he had used to sit almost like that when music played and he danced inside. I wondered if this melancholy rigid figure were still dancing inside; for there was always music playing out of the ward's radio.

Many of his friends forgot André, for his fame had not been enough to make a legend of him. But a few of us continued to come to the institution to take note of his condition. And after five years we began to see that André's melancholia was loosening its violent fingers from his soul. André began to look at us and to remember us. He emerged slowly, as if he were afraid of the light into which he was moving again. He spoke and smiled once more—a little timidly. The doctors told me, however, that he had no memory of his crime and that the name Maria Ivonova was gone from his mind. It had sunk somewhere into the depths of his soul, together with the monster it had evoked.

I was glad about André's improvement. I called more often. And he took to showing me drawings he had made of dancing figures or of curious whirling patterns which he explained shyly were the essence of dance movements. He drew them always while the radio played.

The authorities finally allowed him a phonograph and I was permitted to bring him records of his favorite ballet music. He asked only for three—*The Faun, The Blue Bird,* and *The Specter of the Rose.* I was told that his condition had improved basically and that there was some chance of his being released. The doctor explained to me, however, that as long as his crime remained hidden from him and the name of Maria Ivonova out of his mind, André could not be considered sane, no matter how plausible all his speech and actions seemed

André's charm began to reassert itself. Every one who came in contact with him now began to feel, as of old, refreshed by his presence. Innocence was again returning to his smile, and the authorities grew eager to help him. Thus encouraged, he began to plan his return to the world. These plans consisted at first only of daydreams and drawings. He dreamed and he drew dances. He had selected the three ballets —*The Faun, The Blue Bird,* and *The Specter of the Rose*—to practice and to dream about.

"I am," he said to me, "going to be like Nijinsky was. I am going to dance his ballets. They are letting me practice now. My elevation is better than ever and my beats are a great deal improved. I am very good. I dance very well. I never get tired. And besides," he added, smiling sadly, "I have something else in me."

I asked him what that was.

"Atonement," said André. "I must atone for what I have done. I can only atone by dancing. I am unfit for living. I have learned this. I am fit only for art. I will atone for having been so bad by dancing better than anybody ever did in the world. Wait and see!"

When André told me this, I knew for the first time he had remembered Maria Ivonova.

He was thirty-six years old when the doctors, who had come to adore him, declared that he was sane enough to return to the world. And after fourteen years of exile André returned. Many things had happened in these fourteen years—among them the fact that the world had gone mad. Wars had swept nations out of existence and shaken the soul of man into a rage and a confusion almost unparalleled in all history.

But none of these things had happened to André. He returned to the world he had left. Neither politics nor cannon had touched it. It was an inner world so serene and pretty that André, living in it again, seemed madder than he had ever been. Still, it is unfair to consider a man a lunatic because he refuses to participate in the lunacies of others. Just the same, I was worried about André from the first night we dined together in our once favorite restaurant. I watched him go to work in the rehearsal hall and went to concerts with him, and tried to assure myself that André was sane. Nothing had aged in him except his smile. His face was still a boy's, his body still leaped like a cat and a sea gull and seemed full of smoke and magic.

But his smile appeared to wear a little crutch. It appeared to lean on his mouth.

"You mustn't worry about me," he said one night. "I am entirely better. I understand myself. There was something bad in me. But it's gone. Or anyway it's buried so deep it will never rise again. I won't let it."

Then he leaned over and whispered with a smile, "I won't let it."

André delayed his return to the ballet. He rehearsed constantly, bought costumes, and spoke of nothing else. But I began to feel that André, with all his rehearsing and planning, was never going to dance again. It is that way sometimes with artists who dream too deeply and aspire too high. They outstrip their talents. They sit like birds dreaming of the moon which is too far away to reach, and their wings, accordingly, remain folded. I don't know if there are any such birds, but there are such artists—rehearsal halls and attics full of them. André had become one of this tribe of "not good enough yet to start" geniuses. Other dancers dropped in to watch him practice. They clucked with excitement over his work, pronounced him head and shoulders above all his contemporaries, but seemed to understand perfectly his need for more practice.

After five months André turned up one evening at my studio with his new partner. Her name was Nina. She was young, blond, shy, and shapely. We sat for an hour trying not to show our nervousness. I was nervous because Nina reminded me of Maria. André was nervous because he knew what I was thinking. And Nina was nervous because she was obviously entranced with André and hoping that his oldest friend would approve of her. I didn't. I wouldn't have approved of Genêt or Pavlova as a partner for André. I would have preferred never to see him smiling gracefully on any woman again.

"Would you like to see a performance?" André said, after we had talked for an hour.

I turned on the phonograph. It played *The Specter of the Rose*. This is a ballet in which a young girl returns home from a ball, falls asleep in a chair, and dreams of a beautiful man dressed like a rose who arrives through the window and dances for her. She rises in her dream, dances with him, and returns to her chair. And the beautiful man spins and soars about her, and then, to a final burst of music, leaps out of the window and her dream.

I was full of admiration for the performance. There was no question about it—André was that thing apart, a body made to dance. His technique was invisible. He leaped as if he were floating, and he still seemed to float as he returned to his feet. He gave you the confusing impression that his body was so light it had more difficulty remaining on the ground than capering in the air.

That was the last time I saw André dance. It was also the end of my friendship with André. After this visit he became fugitive and mysterious. He took to rehearsing in out-of-the-way halls. Tracked down in one of these, he vanished again. He moved from his small hotel and his address became unknown. He was to be seen occasionally dining or making a purchase in one of the special shops dear to the ballet people. He had not disappeared out of the dance world but removed himself to its edge. And here he hovered like a shade—but not a lonely shade, for Nina was always beside him.

I thought several times of notifying the doctors who had become so fond of André about his new love affair. But I knew that André saw them every month. If he had lied to them about Nina, my uncovering the lie would mean his return to the asylum. This stopped me. I remembered also André's whispered promise that he would not let anything happen.

This is the part of the story now that must be made up—the part that happened in André's head. He married Nina as he had Maria—in secret. They were married the night they danced in my house. And Nina loved him even more than had Maria. For she was simpler and had no inkling of the inside of André's head. She failed to see the vulture return and the darkness come again.

She has told me since of how deeply André loved her. She remembers his love as something rather mad but wonderful. She lived with him as if they were two people alone on the moon. And to the end she never knew that it was not love but murder that lay beside her.

He used to spend the night trembling and weeping, with his body curled into a ball beside her and his hands clinging to his strong ankles. When she asked him why he wept, he answered her always that it was because he loved her.

All day he danced in various dusty rehearsal halls. She danced with him, performing over and over again the three ballets he was forever preparing. He wore out dozens of phonograph records, bought new ballet shoes, went into debt for fresh costumes, and sat up half the night drawing pictures of figures leaping and of whirling patterns. And when he was so tired that his head fell forward, he came to bed and curled himself up in a ball and lay trembling beside his bride. And of all this struggle with the vulture come to feast again on his sanity poor Nina had only one memory—a memory of being loved.

André was keeping his promise. He was not letting it happen again. But why did he remain with her when the thing began? Why did he keep her at his side when he knew that murder was again in his hands?

He must have seen the strangeness of his face in the mirrors before which he practiced constantly. He must have felt the evil back in his heart, and unreason, like a goad, tormenting him. His need to cry out the hatred he felt must have eaten at his throat.

The answers to why he remained are difficult to make if you think of André as he seemed—a smiling, eager lover of life, full of charm and gentleness. But there was another André. This other André lay for months locked away in a ball, and the André I knew wept and trembled with the agony of keeping him there. The André I knew lay in the dark, night after night, saying to himself that he was a dancer and not a murderer, that he was meant to dance and not to kill.

And dance he finally did. I have the story of his performance from Nina.

Due to a lack of money, they had moved into the servants' quarters of a large midtown hotel. André knew one of the managers. The room they occupied was small and furnished with only a bed and a dresser. It was directly under the roof and forty stories above the street.

They lived here on the management's bounty for a month. During this month André's nights had increased in horror. Even Nina had begun to feel there was something wrong with him; for, though he still loved her and wept at her side and trembled, he no longer spoke to her. He had fallen into a silence that nothing could break, not all her pleas and kisses. And, what was worse, he had stopped practicing.

On awakening each morning now, André would dress himself in the costume of the Rose, and he would remain sitting all day on the edge of the bed in his tights, his flower jacket, and his ballet shoes. Nina found a job clerking in one of the small stores in the neighborhood. She would leave André in the morning costumed for his ballet. At six o'clock she would return to find him still sitting in his lovely costume. The phonograph stood on the floor at his feet, but she learned from the people in the next room that it never played while she was away. It never played when she was at home.

But its music was in André's head. It never went out of his head. It played constantly to him, and he danced constantly to it—as I used to see him doing long ago—sitting still without a muscle moving and dancing inside himself.

It was on a spring night that Nina came home with the news that she had spoken to a doctor about André. The doctor was coming to visit him in the morning. André looked at her with tired eyes and said nothing. He sat motionless beside the silent phonograph.

Nina was weary that night. She sighed herself to sleep, dropped some tears silently on her pillow, and managed to sleep, although she knew *he* was still sitting on the edge of the bed. Something woke her—a sound, a sense of danger.

She opened her eyes and saw André standing over her. He was still in his costume—otherwise she would not have recognized him. His face was contorted, his eyes were another color. His mouth was stretched wide open and a strangling sound came from his throat. Nina's heart almost stopped as she saw the figure leaning over her. She saw the hands rise from his sides and reach toward her throat. She was unable to move or cry out. The hands came slowly around her throat. Their fingers tightened—and her terror was such that she was able only to whisper, "André."

The fingers remained, but their grip grew weaker. They remained for a number of minutes, and during these minutes André's face bending over her did not belong to him. Then the hands fell away and André stood up straight. He held his arms out rigidly. He raised one foot, bent his knee, and spun in a pirouette. Watching him from her pillow with eyes still terrified, Nina saw that André was dancing.

There was barely space in which to move, but André danced in it. And she recognized each of the long practiced turns and leaps of *The Specter of the Rose*. She recognized even the part of the ballet he was dancing. It was the part where she had returned to her chair and her dream was leaving her.

André's face was his own now. She recognized the gentle gleaming smile with which he had always performed the finale, and although the room was silent she knew he was dancing to music. It was a smile only music could bring. And then Nina's heart grew cold. For Nina knew the finale, the famous leap to be made out of the room—and out of her dream.

André was spinning like a top beside the bed. He came out of the spins. His eyes smiled gently on her. They were the eyes of a lover who was a rose, a dream, a thing of smoke and magic. And suddenly, coiling himself into a ball, he made the leap. His body crashed through the window.

Nina was on her feet. She rushed to the broken glass. She looked and saw him. He was falling straight as an arrow, his arms lowered, his hands folded in front of him, and his feet were making entrechats. His head was tilted gracefully to one side.

She saw him only for a second or two, but she was able to tell me this: He was dancing as he fell.

# *Crime without Passion*

MR. LOU HENDRIX looked at the lady he had been pretending to love for the past six months and, being a lawyer, said nothing. Mr. Hendrix was a gentleman who could listen longer to female hysterics without unbending than was normal. This, he would have said, was due to his aloof and analytical mind. Then, also, the events which were taking place in this boudoir at the moment were of a familiar pattern. Some eight or nine times Mr. Hendrix had been the hero of just such climaxes as this, when new love had entered his life, and necessitated similar farewells.

The young lady who, this time, was doing the screaming was a nymph of the cabarets known as Brownie. Her full name was Carmen Browne. She danced, and very effectively, at the El Bravo Club where, devoid of plumage as an eel, she led the Birds of Paradise number. In this she was ravishing as a Dream of Fair Women.

Why so young and delicious a siren as Brownie should be so disturbed over the amorous defection of Mr. Hendrix would have confused anyone who knew this gentleman or merely took a one-minute look at him. He was not Romeo nor was he Adonis, nor was he even such a male as one associates with the general practice of seduction. He was a little man with that objectionable immaculateness which reminds one, instanter, of sheep's clothing. He was one of those popinjays of the flesh pots with the face of a tired and sarcastic boy. His sideburns were a wee too long, his smile unduly persistent (like a ballet dancer's), his voice far too gentle to have deceived anyone, except perhaps a woman, as to his spiritual composition. But one can always depend on the ladies to misunderstand the combination of gentleness and sideburns.

Brownie, who among her own kind was considered not only quite a reader of books but a sort of practical authority on masculine characteristics, had misunderstood Lou Hendrix amazingly. Carry on as she would now, she was no match for this caballero of the law who, out of a clear sky, was engaged in giving her what she called "the go-by." As her monologue of screams, epithets and sobs progressed the lovely and muscular girl understood it all. She perceived, much too late for any use, that she had to do with as purring a hypocrite, rogue and underhanded soul as one might flush in a seven-day hunt on Broadway, which, according to the chroniclers Brownie most admired, is the world's leading water hole for human beasts of prey.

Looking around at the pretty apartment in which Mr. Hendrix had installed her and in which she had lorded it over her friends for the six months and from which she must now exit, love's dream being ended, Brownie spread herself on the couch and filled her Sybaritic diggings with a truly romantic din. From the more coherent utterances of this tear-stained beauty it seemed that she was innocent of all dallyings with a certain Eddie White, an ex-college hero, and that since leaving this same Mr. White, whose love interest she had been before the Birds of Paradise number was staged, she had never once permitted him to lay a finger on her. She was, wailed Brownie, being wrongly accused. Then, sitting up, her greenish eyes popping with rage until they looked like a pair of snake heads, Brownie laughed, as she would have said, scornfully, and declared that she could see through Mr. Hendrix and his so-called jealousy. He was getting rid of her because he didn't love her any more. He was tired of her and putting her on the escalator—that was all there was to it.

To this, Mr. Hendrix, thoroughly seen through, made no reply and Brownie, announcing that she was not going to be made a sucker of, fell back on the couch, beat some cushions with her fists and shook with grief. The telephone rang. Brownie straightened on the couch.

"It's probably for you," she said.

"More likely it's Mr. White," said Mr. Hendrix.

The taunt brought Brownie to her feet.

"If it's for me, by any mischance," said Mr. Hendrix, "say I'm not here."

Brownie spoke into the phone.

"Who?" she asked. "No, he's not here. No, I don't know when he'll be here. No, no, I don't expect him." Hanging up, she looked bitterly at Mr. Hendrix. "Your office," she said. "Always making me lie for you."

"You might have been a bit more polite," said Mr. Hendrix.

The heartlessness of this suggestion sent Brownie back to the couch and her grief. She resumed her sobs. Mr. Hendrix continued to regard her with creditable, if villainous, detachment. His heart was in the highlands with another lassie. But even discounting that factor Mr. Hendrix felt he was pursuing a wise course in ridding himself of so obstreperous an admirer as lay howling here. He had no use for overemotional types.

They were inclined to drive diversion, which was Mr. Hendrix' notion of Cupid, out of the window with their caterwauling.

Mr. Hendrix' soul, in fact, was a sort of china closet and he was firm in his aversion to flying hooves. He belonged to that tribe of Don Juans, rather numerous at the Broadway hole, who never hang themselves for love. Tears he regarded as bad sportsmanship and heartbreak was to him plain blackmail. Beauty—and by beauty Mr. Hendrix meant chiefly those delicious and agile Venuses of the cabaret floorshows—beauty had been put into Broadway (if not into the world) for man's delight; certainly not for his confusion and despair. And this little barrister lived elegantly, if rather villainously, by this conception.

A number of things, all obvious to the analytical Mr. Hendrix, were now operating in Brownie's mind and making her wail—Eddie's vengeful delight at her getting the go-by from his successor; the tittering of the little group of columnists, hoofers, waiters and good-time Charlies whom she called the World; the lessening of her status as a siren—she might even be demoted from leading the Birds of Paradise number, and through all these considerations—the Nerve of the Man, throwing her down as if she were some Nobody! As for the more passional side of the business, the pain in her heart at losing someone she had so stupidly loved and misunderstood and at losing the foolish Broadwayish dream of wedlock she had cherished for half a year, Brownie chose not to mention these in her ravings, being too proud.

Mr. Hendrix, still preserving his finest courtroom manner of Reason and Superiority, watched on in silence and fell to wondering what he had ever seen in this red-headed, almost illiterate creature with her muscular legs and childish face to have ever considered her charming or desirable. But he was given small time to meditate this problem of idealization. Brownie, with a yell that set the base of his spine to tingling, leaped from the couch, stared wildly around and then, emitting a series of shrill sounds, had at the furnishings of the Love Nest. She pulled a portière down, hurled two vases to the floor, swung a chair against the wall and smashed it, beat Mr. Hendrix' framed photograph to bits against the edge of the piano, seized a clock from the mantelpiece and bounced it on the floor and was making for Mr. Hendrix' derby, which he had placed on a chair near the door, when he, with an unexpected shout, headed her off.

The barrister, defending his derby, received a blow on the side of his face that sent him spinning. A thrown object caught him behind the ear. Brownie's pointed shoes belabored his shins. He retreated. But the hysteria to which he had been coolly and analytically listening seemed suddenly to have been injected, like a virus, into his bloodstream. It had started with the tingling in the base of his spine. Smarting from blows and full of some sort of electric current which gave off oaths in his head, the little lawyer began to outbellow his now ex-paramour. He came at the lady and in his hand he held, almost unaware of the fact, a large brass candlestick.

What it was that made this popinjay, so renowned for coolness, strategy and cynicism in his twin professions of amour and the law, so completely shed his character, God alone, who was not at Mr. Hendrix' elbow at the moment, could have told; and perhaps a psychiatrist or two might also have made a guess at. But here he was much too far gone for analysis, his own or anyone else's, charging at the lovely Carmen Browne like a bantam cave man, screaming and swinging the heavy piece of brass in the air.

There was no precedent in Mr. Hendrix' life for such a turn of events and no hint in any of his former love doings that passion could so blind his faculties and hate so fill his heart. Yet blind he was and full of a clamorous hate that demanded something of him. From the oaths which escaped Mr. Hendrix during this preliminary skirmish with the brass candlestick, it seemed that what he hated was women; loathed and hated them with a fury out of the Pit. Announcing this he swung the piece of brass and the second swing exhilarated him more. It had struck squarely against Brownie's head dropping her to the carpet. Mr. Hendrix, out of breath, stood cursing and grimacing over her like a murderer.

Slowly the little lawyer's rage melted. His heart swelled with terror and the nape of his neck grew warm. Brownie lay as she had fallen. He leaned over. Her skull was cracked. Blood was running. Her eyes were closed. Her legs, exposed in an incongruously graceful sprawl, were inert. He put his ear to her bosom. There was no heart beating. He stood for several minutes holding his breath and listening automatically for sounds outside the door. The choking sensation in his lungs subsided and the cool, analytical mind that was Mr. Hendrix returned like some errant accomplice tiptoeing back to the scene of the crime.

Carmen Browne lay dead on her hearthstone. No more would she lead the Birds of Paradise number at the El Bravo Club. But Mr. Hendrix wasted no time considering this sentimental phase of the matter. He had committed a murder, without intent, to be sure; even in self-defense, looked at factually. But no, self-defense wouldn't hold, Mr. Hendrix was thinking swiftly. There rushed through his mind all the angles, holes, difficulties, improbabilities and prejudices of his case and in less than a minute the little lawyer had put himself on trial on a plea of self-defense and found himself guilty.

Since a young man, Mr. Hendrix had always been close to crime. He had had that unmoral and intellectual understanding of it which helps make one type of excellent lawyer. In action, defending a criminal, Mr. Hendrix had always been like some imperturbable surgeon. Guilt was a disease that could be cured, not by any operation on the soul of its victim, but by a process of mental legerdemain which convinced a jury that no guilt existed. Mr. Hendrix might have said that he served a cause beyond good and evil, that of extricating the victims of fleeting misadventures from the unjustly permanent results of their deeds.

Thus, far beyond most men who might have found themselves confronted by the strange and ugly dilemma of having unexpectedly committed a murder, Mr. Hendrix was prepared for his new role of criminal. He knew all the ropes, he knew all the pitfalls of the defense of such a case as this. He knew the psychology of the prosecution. And with an expert, if still slightly fevered mind, he knew the perfect details by which his guilt might be cured, the ideal evidence, persuasive and circumstantial, by which a jury could be cajoled to the verdict of not guilty.

In less than a minute, Mr. Hendrix had a full grasp of his case, seeing far into its convolutions and difficulties. He set about straightening these out.

But like some dramatic critic who, after observing plays for years with subtle and intimate understanding of them, is summoned suddenly on the stage and with the strange footlights glaring in his eyes told to perform the part whose words he knows, whose ideal gesture and intonation he has always dreamed about, Mr. Hendrix felt the panic of debut. To know and to act were phenomena surprisingly separate. This was what delayed the cautious barrister for another minute, a minute during which Mr. Hendrix' client, with beating heart and white face, mumbled for speed, chattered even of flight.

But at the end of this second minute Mr. Hendrix had elbowed this ignominious client into a far corner of his mind, seated him, as it were, at the counsel's table with orders to keep his mouth shut—and taken charge of the case. He leaned over and looked at the clock on the floor. The dial glass was broken. The clock had stopped, its hands at two minutes of four. Mr. Hendrix' thoughts were rapid, almost as if he were not thinking at all but knowing. He could move the hands forward to five o'clock. He could leave the premises undetected, if possible, and attach himself for the next two hours to a group of prospective alibi witnesses, remain with them during the hours between four-ten and seven and this would be the proof he had not been in the apartment at the time of the murder. Mr. Hendrix examined the watch on Carmen Browne's wrist. It too had stopped. It registered one minute after four. The two timepieces, evidently synchronized by their owner, told a graphic and substantially correct tale. At 3:58 the struggle had begun. At 4:01 the woman had been killed. He would have to set the wrist watch forward a full hour to preserve this interesting discrepancy in the stopped clocks.

The telephone rang. Mr. Hendrix straightened, not having touched either of the hour hands. He had actually anticipated a telephone ringing, and in this anticipation known the ruse of the forwarded time hands was stupid. At 3:50 Carmen Browne had answered a phone call, a record of which was with the switchboard man in the lobby. Now at 4:03—he consulted his own watch—she failed to answer. Other phone calls might likewise come before five o'clock, all of which Carmen Browne would fail to answer, thus establishing an important series of witnesses against the fact that the murdered woman had been alive between four and five o'clock; thus rendering his alibi of his own whereabouts during that time practically futile. There was also the possibility that the neighbors had heard their quarrel and noted the time of the screaming. And more than all these the chance that someone, a maid or the building agent (Carmen Browne had been consulting him about sub-letting her place) might enter the room before five o'clock.

It was the hour preceding 4:01 for which Mr. Hendrix needed an alibi. He already knew its vital ground work. At 3:50 Carmen Browne, alive, had told someone on the phone—probably Tom Healey of his own law firm—that he was not in her apartment. Mr. Hendrix' eyes had remained on his own wrist watch as his thoughts slipped through these pros and cons. It was 4:04. He glanced at the sprawled figure on the floor, shivered, but stood his ground. Another phase of his case had overcome him. He smiled palely, shocked at what had almost been an oversight. He must not only provide an alibi for himself but fortify it with evidence tending to prove someone other than he had done the deed. He must invent a mythical murderer—leave a trail of evidence for the sharp eyes and wits of the prosecution leading to Another—a never-to-be-found another, but yet one always present in the Case.

Carmen Browne's fingerprints were on the broken clock, the

smashed chair, the battered photo frame. This was wrong. It would reveal that it was Carmen who had been in the rage, smashing things, demanding something that had resulted in her murder—and this sort of a situation, brought out by the prosecution, might easily point to Lou Hendrix, known to have been her lover. No, said Lawyer Hendrix swiftly, it must have been her assailant, demanding something of Carmen Browne, who had been in the rage and done the smashing and struck the fatal blow. Mr. Hendrix established this fact circumstantially by wiping Carmen Browne's fingerprints from the objects in question with a silk handkerchief. He wiped also and more carefully the brass candlestick. The absence of fingerprints pointed to a certain self-consciousness on the part of the assailant after the deed but that was both legitimate and normal. Men of the deepest passion, and there was precedence for this, remembered to obliterate evidence.

At the door, Mr. Hendrix, in his hat, overcoat and gloves, paused. He repeated to himself carefully, Carmen Browne had been attacked by some suitor, jealous of her real sweetheart, Mr. Hendrix, as witness the destroyed photograph of the latter. But why hadn't she used the gun the police would find in the desk drawer two feet from the spot where her body lay? There were of course normal explanations to be put forward. But Mr. Hendrix did not admire them legally. For fifteen precious seconds Lawyer Hendrix balanced the issue. During this space Mr. Hendrix listened rather than thought. He listened to the prosecution pointing out to the jury that the reason Carmen Browne had not reached for this available weapon with which to defend herself was because she had not expected an attack from the assailant, because the assailant was one familiar to her against whom she had no thought of arming herself; and even further, because the assailant, all too familiar with the premises, knew where this gun was as well as did Carmen Browne, and prevented her from reaching it. All these values pointed shadowly, Mr. Hendrix perceived, at his client. He removed the gun from the drawer and dropped it into his coat pocket. He must be careful in disposing of the weapon and Mr. Hendrix' mind dwelt stubbornly on a dozen cases in which an attempt at post crime evidence disposal had been the connecting link with guilt. But Mr. Hendrix assured his client firmly that he would be more cautious in this regard than any of his previous defendants had been.

With the gun in his coat pocket Mr. Hendrix stepped out of the apartment. Now he was, he knew, purely in the hands of luck. A door opening, a neighbor appearing, would ruin his case instantly. But no untoward event happened. He had three floors to descend. He listened at the ornamental elevator doors. Both cages were going up. Mr. Hendrix walked quickly down the three flights and coolly, now, like a gambler rather than a lawyer, rehearsed the possible permutations of Luck.

He had entered the apartment at three o'clock that morning with Carmen Browne. But because it was his habit to preserve a surface air of respectability toward the attendants of the place, though he fancied they knew well enough what was going on, he had walked up to the apartment with Brownie. The switchboard operator concealed in an alcove in the lobby had not seen them come in, nor had the elevator boy on duty, as both were out of sight at the moment. If now he could leave the building with the equal but vitally more important luck of not being seen, his case would be more than launched.

The lobby was empty, but Mr. Hendrix did not make the mistake of slipping out too quickly, and coddling the presumption that no eyes had observed him. He knew too well the possibility of the unexpected witness and he paused to study the premises. The switchboard attendant, half hidden in the alcove, had his back to the lobby and was reading a newspaper. Both elevator cages were out of sight. There was no one else. Mr. Hendrix stepped into the street.

Here again he stopped to look for that unexpected witness. How often, he remembered grimly, had the best of his cases been tumbled by the appearance on the stand of those aimless, incalculable human strays who had "Seen the Defendant." Mr. Hendrix saw two of just that type. Two women were walking, but with their backs to him and away from the apartment. A delivery truck was passing. Mr. Hendrix noticed that the driver was talking to a companion and that neither of these passers looked in his direction. There was no one else. Mr. Hendrix turned his attention to the windows across the street. Only the first three floors mattered. Identification was impossible, or at least could be sufficiently challenged, from any greater height. The windows were empty. As for the windows of the building directly over him, if he kept close to the wall none could see him from these.

Satisfied with this rapid but concentrated scrutiny, Mr. Hendrix started walking toward the corner. If the triumph of intellect over nerves, of reason over the impulses of the senses, may be called heroism, then this smiling, casually moving little popinjay in the black derby and snug overcoat might well be called a hero. Innocence, even aimlessness, was in his every movement; and in his refusal, despite a driving curiosity, to look at the time on his wrist—a tell-tale gesture were it recorded by anyone—there was something approaching the loftiness of purpose which distinguished the ancient Ascetics. As he turned the corner, Mr. Hendrix, still unruffled, still amiably rhythmic in his movements, looked back to make sure no taxicabs had entered the street. None had.

He was now on Sixth Avenue and he moved more briskly. He had four blocks to walk and habit sent his eyes looking for a taxicab. But, alert to every variety of witness, he shook his head and stayed afoot. He smiled, remembering that his own bed in his own apartment was unmade. He had just turned in the night before when Brownie had telephoned and asked to meet him. Thus his housekeeper, who never arrived before noon, would establish simply the fact that he had slept at home. This was unnecessary, to be sure, unless some passerby had seen Brownie and a man enter the former's apartment at three this morning.

Mr. Hendrix arrived now at a Sixth Avenue cinema palace. He looked carefully over the small crowd waiting for tickets and then joined the line. In a few minutes he was being ushered into the roped enclosure at the rear of the auditorium. He slipped away quickly, however, and walked in the dark to the other side of the theater. He approached one of the ushers and demanded to know where he could report the loss of a pair of gloves. After a brief colloquy he was led to the office of the Lost and Found department and here Mr. Hendrix, very voluble and affable, explained his mishap. He was not, he smiled, usually so careless with his belongings but the picture had been so engrossing that he had forgotten all about his haberdashery. Then Mr. Hendrix gave his name, address, a description of the missing gloves and watched with a glow of deep creative satisfaction the time being written down on the blank form used for cataloguing such matters. "Four-eighteen," the man wrote and Mr. Hendrix, consulting his watch, pretended to be startled. Was it that late? he demanded. Good Lord! he had had no idea of the time. It was quite a long picture. And the Lost and Found official, drawn into chumminess by Mr. Hendrix' affability, agreed that the film was a little longer than most, but well worth sitting through—to which Mr. Hendrix assented.

Emerging from the movie palace, Mr. Hendrix rehearsed his case to date. The main body of his alibi was achieved. He had spent the time between two-thirty and four watching a movie. His continued presence at four-eighteen in this theatre was written down in black and white. He had also taken care that it should be a movie he had already seen so as to be able to recite its plot were he questioned in the next few hours. And he had also provided a motive for seeing this particular movie. The film had to do with the character and career of a mythical state's attorney, and a newspaper friend of Mr. Hendrix who conducted a gossip column had asked him to contribute a few paragraphs from a legal point of view carping at the improbabilities of the scenario.

Mr. Hendrix' next port of call was an elegant speakeasy. Here he had a drink, engaged in an exchange of views with the bartender, who knew him, asked the correct time so he might adjust his watch. At 4:50 he stepped into a phone booth in the place and called his office. He inquired whether anybody had been trying to reach him that afternoon. The law clerk on duty for the firm, Tom Healey, answered as Mr. Hendrix had expected. Mr. Healey said he had been trying to find him in relation to a disposition but had been unable to locate him. At this Mr. Hendrix feigned a light anger. Where had the incompetent youth called? He had, said Mr. Healey, tried everywhere, even Miss Carmen Browne's apartment.

At this bit of information Mr. Hendrix, in his mind's eye addressing one of his future star witnesses, changed his voice. He grew angry and very obviously so, for he knew the laziness of people's memories and their slipshod powers of observation. He inquired sourly if Mr. Healey had spoken to Miss Browne. On hearing that he had, Mr. Hendrix said:

"Do you mind telling me how she seemed when you asked if I was there?"

"Well, I don't know," Mr. Healey said.

"Try and think," said Mr. Hendrix. "I'd like to know."

"Well," said Mr. Healey, "come to think of it, she struck me as a little curt or upset about something."

"Ha!" said Mr. Hendrix and, to the surprise of his office underling, called the young lady a villainous name.

"I don't want you to call me up at her place any more," he raised his voice. The clerk, Mr. Healey, said he would never do it again, but Mr. Hendrix, as though too enraged to notice this promise, continued, "I'm all washed up at that telephone number. Understand what I mean? You can just forget about it. Any other calls?"

"No," said Mr. Healey.

"O.K.," said Mr. Hendrix and hung up the phone with an angry bang.

He walked from the speakeasy with the light step which to Mr. Hendrix' office colleagues always characterized a Not Guilty verdict in sight. Now that the tingling at the base of his spine as well as the annoying warmth on the nape of his neck, as if a Prosecuting Staff were actually breathing on him, had gone entirely, Mr. Hendrix was beginning to feel not only relaxed but even amused. He could hear the Prosecution falling into this little trap he had just laid.

Question: So Mr. Hendrix told you that you needn't try to reach him at Miss Browne's apartment any more?

Answer: Yes, sir.

And Lawyer Hendrix looked winningly at the jury that sat in his mind's eye. Gentlemen of the Jury, consider this. As if, having committed a crime, the defendant would be so gauche as to give himself away by some such oafish remark to a law clerk—a type of person trained to remember what he hears. Not a casual stranger, mind you, but a man with sharp and practiced wits.

Mr. Hendrix, skittering happily along the street, cleared his throat, beamed and felt a desire to laugh. He had never quite so enjoyed a case. What subtle and yet vital psychological proof of his innocence was the fact that he had just said to Tom Healey what he had; what perfect proof of the fact that he had been the victim of an obvious coincidence in saying he was washed up with Carmen Browne when she lay dead in her apartment. No guilty man would ever have said that.

From a drug store he was passing, Mr. Hendrix made another telephone call. He called Carmen Browne. Inquiring for her of the apartment switchboard operator a sharp excitement stirred him. Before his eyes the image of her body, sprawled gracefully and awfully on the floor at his feet, swayed for a moment. He hoped the crime had been discovered, although there were still chances to improve his Case. But the switchboard man calmly plugged in for Carmen Browne's apartment.

"She doesn't answer," he said after a pause.

"This is Mr. Hendrix calling," said Mr. Hendrix. "Has she been in at all? I've been trying to get her all day."

"Hasn't come in while I've been here," said the man.

"How long is that?" said Mr. Hendrix.

"Oh, about three hours," said the man.

"Thank you," said Mr. Hendrix and hung up.

He had told Tom Healey he was washed up with Carmen Browne and now he was trying to reach her, and Mr. Hendrix considered this paradox, in behalf of his client, with a smile. It revealed, Gentlemen of the Jury, a distracted man; a lover full of confusion as a result of —what? Of the fact, gentlemen, Mr. Hendrix purred to himself, that my client was jealous of the attentions he had found out someone was paying to Carmen Browne; that he did not believe the poor girl's protestations of innocence and, driven from her side by suspicions, was yet lured back to her by his deep love. Jealous, Gentlemen of the Jury, of the attentions being paid to Carmen Browne by this creature who that very afternoon had entered her apartment and against whom Carmen Browne had defended herself until struck down and killed.

To augment this phase of the case, Mr. Hendrix returned now to the apartment building in which Carmen Browne lay murdered. He approached the switchboard operator, who greeted him by name. Here Mr. Hendrix controlled a curious impulse that whitened the skin around his mouth. He felt impelled to ask this man whether he had noticed Mr. Hendrix in the building before, whether he had seen him during the few moments he had walked from the lobby an hour ago. Astonished at this impulse, Mr. Hendrix held his tongue for a space, aware that the switchboard man was looking at him with curiosity.

Question: How did the defendant seem?

Answer: Confused.

Gentlemen of the Jury, and how would a man consumed with jealousy seem while inquiring, against all his pride, if the woman he thought was wronging him, was home?

"Has Miss Brown come in since I called?" asked Mr. Hendrix.

"I haven't seen her," said the man. "I'll try her apartment again."

There was no answer.

"Give her this note when she comes back," said Mr. Hendrix.

He wrote on the lower part of a business letter from his pocket:

"Darling, if you are innocent, don't torture me any more. Give me a chance to believe you. I'm willing to forget what I heard or thought I heard over the phone. As ever, Lou."

He placed this in a used envelope, scribbled her name on it, and sealed it.

Gentlemen of the Jury, can you imagine any man who had killed a woman he loved or had loved, so lost to all human reaction, so fiendishly wanton as to have written that little plea when he knew she was lying dead at his hands?

That was merely a rhetorical overtone, the human rather than evidential side of the note, but Mr. Hendrix filed it away in his memory as a bit of decoration. His alibi, Lawyer Hendrix murmured to himself, was now complete. But the secondary phase of the case needed further effort. The beauty of a case lay always in the elaborateness of diverse but corroborating detail—as if the world were crying the defendant's innocence from every nook and cranny. And happily at work, Mr. Hendrix had lawyer-like so far forgotten the human existence of his client as to whistle cheerily the while he turned over and re-turned over the major psychological problem in his mind.

Defense—Carmen Browne had been murdered by a man to whom she refused, after perhaps leading him on, to surrender herself. Also it might be that the killing had been one of those passional accidents which the sex instinct, run amok, precipitates. It might be that Carmen Browne had led a double life and was discovered in this double life by her slayer.

Ergo—Lou Hendrix, sharp-witted, observant, a veritable connoisseur of women, must suspect the existence of this other man. And Defendant Hendrix must also be jealous of him.

Witness to this—his talk to Tom Healey; his note to Carmen Browne now in the hands of the switchboard operator.

And Lawyer Hendrix, with the thrill of a gambler rolling a third lucky seven, remembered at this point a third witness—a veritable star witness, beautifully, if unwittingly, prepared for her role a few days ago. This was Peggy Moore.

Miss Moore danced at the El Bravo Club as a member of the ensemble. She had been Brownie's confidant for a year. Mr. Hendrix smiled blissfully recalling his conversation with Miss Moore less than a week ago and recalling also her general character, one made to order for the part he was to assign her.

This young lady was a tall, dark-haired Irish lassie with slightly bulging eyes and an expression of adenoidal and not unpleasing vacuity about her face. She was, as Brownie had frequently confided to him, a veritable love slave, a dithering creature incapable of thinking or talking on any subject other than the emotions stirred in her bosom by love or jealousy.

Some days ago Mr. Hendrix had selected this almost congenital idiot as the opening pawn in his decision to rid himself of Brownie. He had confided to Miss Moore's ears, so perfectly attuned to all tales of amorous agony, that he suspected Brownie of being still in love with his predecessor Eddie White. Miss Moore's eyes had bulged, her mouth opened as if to disgorge a fish hook and simultaneously a shrewd, if transparent emotion, had overcome her. Miss Moore, the victim of so much perfidy, had been convinced instanter of her chum's guilt and had launched at once into a series of lies, all defending Brownie's integrity and offering idiotic details of her devotion to her lawyer lover. Mr. Hendrix, intent on laying some foolish groundwork for his subsequent defection, had persisted, however, and, for no other reason than that he delighted in playing the human fraud whenever he could, had feigned sorrow and talked of woe.

Now Mr. Hendrix summoned Miss Moore on the telephone to meet him at the speakeasy he had recently quitted. He spoke guardedly, hinting at a lovers' quarrel, and pretending he needed her to verify some evidences of Brownie's guilt, just unearthed. Miss Moore, full of a laudable and loyal ambition to lie her head off in Brownie's behalf, as Mr. Hendrix had foreseen, arrived in a rush. And the two sat down at a table in a corner, Miss Moore to invent innocent explanations and alibis for her chum, at which like all over-tearful addicts of passion she was amazingly expert; and Mr. Hendrix to weave her artfully into his case.

But first Mr. Hendrix, aware of the lady's sensitivity toward all matters pertaining to love, proceeded to get himself drunk. He must be the lover stricken with jealousy and seeking to drown his pains in liquor, a characterization which this simple child and student of amour would remember only too vividly on the witness stand. Three drinks were consumed and then, honestly befuddled from such an unaccustomed dose, Mr. Hendrix launched into cross examination. And despite his thickened tongue and touch of genuine physical paralysis, Lawyer Hendrix remained as cool and analytical as if he were in a courtroom. He was not one to betray a client by any human weaknesses.

He put himself at Miss Moore's mercy. He must know the truth and she alone could tell him. Otherwise with too much brooding and uncertainty he would be sure to go out of his mind. His law practice was already suffering. He would lose all his money. Miss Moore nodded tenderly and understandingly at this saga of love woes. In reply she could assure Mr. Hendrix that he was being very foolish to be jealous of Eddie White because Mr. White wasn't even in town and besides Mr. White was engaged to marry a society girl in Newport. Mr. Hendrix sighed appreciatively at this walloping lie.

"It's not Eddie," said Mr. Hendrix; "it's somebody else. You know that as well as I. You're in her confidence. Don't try to lie to me, dearie. I caught her red-handed, talking over the phone. She hung up when I came into the room. She was making a date—and not with Eddie White."

Miss Moore paled at the thought of this dreadful contretemps, but kept her wits. Her chum's guilt frightened her but at the same time she saw through Mr. Hendrix' effort to lead her astray. Of course it was

Eddie White of whom he was jealous. Miss Moore was certain of this and Mr. Hendrix, listening to her somewhat hysterical defense of Brownie, sufficient to have convicted that young lady of a hundred infidelities had he been interested, realized exactly what was in his companion's mind. He considered for a moment the plan of involving Eddie White in his case. He had thought of it before—Brownie's previous lover, a known hot-headed young gentleman given to nocturnal fisticuffs in public places. But for the second time he dismissed this phase. Eddie would have an alibi and the establishing of Eddie's physical innocence, however psychologically promising his guilt might have looked, would embarrass his client's case.

For the next hour Mr. Hendrix drank and discussed his jealousy, pleading with Miss Moore to be kind to him and reveal what she knew; and hinting at gifts in return for such service. But Miss Moore only increased the scope of her lies.

"Have you seen Brownie today?" Miss Moore finally broke off, winded.

Mr. Hendrix weaved in his seat and looked at her with bleary drunken eyes.

"No," he said. "I don't trust myself to see her. God knows what I would do—feeling this way."

"You're just worked up about absolutely nothing," said Miss Moore and rose. She had to toddle off to the El Bravo where she performed during the dinner hour. Mr. Hendrix accompanied her to the door.

"Tell Brownie," he whispered, "I'll be over to the club tonight. And . . . and give her a last chance to prove her innocence."

"I'll give her the message," said Miss Moore and sighed.

Alone Mr. Hendrix returned to the phone booth. He sat down heavily and put in a call for Carmen Browne. His case was ready. He desired to hear the news of the finding of the body. An annoying tingle touched the base of his spine as he waited for the apartment switchboard to answer. He wondered how drunk he was. Drunk, to be sure, but sober enough to know exactly every phase and weigh every nuance. The moment he heard of the crime he would rush over, be detained by the police and with the aid of his intoxicated condition act thoroughly irrational and grief-stricken. He would hint at no alibis, reveal not a shred of his case until the coroner's inquest.

The switchboard operator finally answered. Mr. Hendrix inquired thickly for Miss Browne. He was told Miss Browne was not in. He hung up. Rising and swaying for a moment, Mr. Hendrix, thoroughly at peace with the world, except for this intermittent tingle, decided on the best course. He would go to the El Bravo Club, order his dinner and wait there till Brownie's absence was noticed and a search started.

The El Bravo orchestra was rendering a dance number. The dance floor was crowded. Mr. Hendrix looked dizzily at the circling figures. He had selected a table far to the side, one of those at which the performers and their friends grouped themselves during the evening. The stuffiness of the air made Mr. Hendrix feel drowsy. Looking up, he beheld a familiar figure approaching. It was Eddie White, whom he had pleased to style the ignorant drop-kicker. Mr. Hendrix smiled. He noticed tiredly that Mr. White seemed a little drunk.

The ex-college hero, still a sturdy tanned and muscular product of the Higher Education, greeted Mr. Hendrix calmly. He dropped into a chair at the table and inquired, with an eye roving over the place, how tricks were. Mr. Hendrix said they were fine.

There was a pause during which the music filled the café with glamorous and exciting sounds.

"Didn't know you were such a movie fan," said Mr. White apropos of nothing and Mr. Hendrix felt himself sobering up as if in a cold shower.

"Just what do you mean?" Mr. Hendrix managed to inquire and very casually.

His companion was busy looking them over on the dance floor and offering a roguish eye to a few of the tastier numbers. Mr. Hendrix stared at him in silence and felt the tingle return to his spine.

"Saw you going into the Roxy this afternoon," Mr. White resumed.

"You did," said Mr. Hendrix and then added, as if he were looping the loop, "What time was that?"

"What time?" Mr. White repeated, looking at the little lawyer with a dull, athlete's stare. "Oh, a little after four, I should say."

"You're crazy," said Mr. Hendrix, "if you think you saw me going into the Roxy after four. Why, I came out about twenty after four, after seeing the whole show."

"I don't care what you saw," said Mr. White. "I saw you going in at about a quarter after. I was gonna say hello but I thought the hell with it. How'd you like the picture? Ought to be in your line—all about one of those crooked legal sharks."

In the brief space during which Mr. Hendrix was now silent his thoughts were very rapid. Mr. White, God help Mr. Hendrix, was that most objectionable of all humans known to a legal case—the aimless stray that the Prosecution was wont to drag, rabbit fashion, out of its hat with which to confound the guilty. And Mr. Hendrix knew without thinking the full significance of this witness, Eddie White. If the defendant had been seen entering the movie theater after four, he had been seen entering after the murder had been committed. But that was the least damaging phase. The defendant had left the movie theater at 4:20, having lied to the attendants and told them he had spent an hour and a half in the place. With the fact of this lie established, the prosecution could take apart piece by piece the obvious mechanism of his alibi. There was no alibi. There was no case. In fact, to the contrary, Eddie White's simple statement of the time of day—after four—revealed all of the defendant's subsequent actions as those of a thoroughly guilty man, and Mr. Hendrix leaned across the table and put a hand on the athlete's arm.

"It must have been somebody else you saw," he purred.

"Listen, don't tell me," said Mr. White. "I saw you looking around, buying your ticket and ducking in."

Mr. Hendrix winced at the damning phraseology.

"I know it was about a quarter after four," pursued Mr. White, "because I had a date outside. And don't get so excited. It wasn't with Brownie."

The tingle at the base of the Hendrix spine was almost lifting him out of his seat.

"That's a lie," said Mr. Hendrix thickly.

"What's that?" Mr. White demanded.

"I said you're lying," Mr. Hendrix repeated slowly. "You didn't see me."

"Oh, that's what you said, is it?" Mr. White was unexpectedly grim. "Listen, I never liked you and I don't take talk off a guy I got no use for. Get that."

And for the second time that day an unprecedented mood overcame the little lawyer. He made an effort to stop the words which suddenly filled his head but he heard himself saying them and wondering confusedly who it was who was drunk—he who was listening or he who was speaking. He was telling Mr. White what a liar, numbskull and oaf he was and Mr. White stood up. Words continued, Mr. Hendrix aware that he and Mr. White were both talking at once. But the music made a blur in his ears and the El Bravo Club swayed in front of his eyes. Then Mr. Hendrix realized, and darkly, that the towering Mr. White's hand was on his collar and that he was being lifted out of his seat. The El Bravo orchestra was rolling out a jazz finale and nobody seemed to have noticed as yet the fracas taking place at this side table. As Mr.

Hendrix felt himself being hoisted to his feet, a sense of nausea and helplessness overcame him. He thrust his hand into his coat pocket.

"Calling me a liar, eh?" Mr. White was growling in the Hendrix ear. He added a number of epithets.

The little lawyer saw for an instant a fist pull back that never landed. Mr. Hendrix had removed a gun from his coat pocket, a gun of whose existence in his hand he was as unaware as he had been of the brass candlestick. The gun exploded and Mr. White with a look of suddenly sober astonishment fell back into a chair. The music at this moment finished with a nanny goat blare of trumpets. No heads turned. No waiters came rushing. Shaking as if his bones had turned into castanets, Mr. Hendrix stood looking at the crumpled athlete and watched his head sink over the table. The mouth was open. The athlete's fingers hanging near the floor were rigid.

Music started again and Mr. Hendrix turned his eyes automatically toward the dance floor. Blue and pink floodlights were shining on it and out from behind the orchestra shell came a line of almost naked girls. White legs kicked, smiles filled the air. Leading the chorus line Mr. Hendrix saw Carmen Browne. She was dancing.

The little lawyer grew sick. He shut his eyes. Then he opened them. They were full of pain and bewilderment. It was no hallucination. It was Brownie. Extending under her ear at the back of her head he saw strips of court plaster. She was alive and restored.

Mr. Hendrix knew exactly what had happened. The last time he had called her apartment, the switchboard man, failing to recognize his liquor-thickened voice, had withheld the information he might have offered Mr. Hendrix—that Carmen Browne was alive, that she had summoned a doctor, that she had left the apartment.

And even as he was thinking of this tiny detail, a hundred other details crowded into the Hendrix mind. He remembered his accusations to Brownie that she still loved Eddie White; his statement to Peggy Moore last week and this afternoon that he was too jealous to trust himself; his attack on Carmen Browne, his subsequent drunkenness, his idiotic antics in the movie theatre—as if he were shadowing Eddie White—what else could his rushing in and rushing out mean? Everything Mr. Hendrix had accomplished since 4:02 this afternoon pointed only at one conclusion—that he hated Eddie White, that he had almost killed his sweetheart out of jealousy over White, that, still burning with this emotion, he had tracked White down and murdered him in cold blood.

Mr. Hendrix, during these brief moments staring at the crumpled athlete, wanted to scream, so macabre did all these events strike him, but his voice trailed off into a moan. What was this insane thing he had done for his client! Exonerated him! Mr. Hendrix, still shaking, slipped down into his chair. He, Lou Hendrix, the shining legal intelligence, had like some Nemesis convicted himself—and not of manslaughter, which might have been the verdict otherwise—but of premeditated murder in the first degree. There was no case. No defense was possible. There was nothing left to do but to flee like some thug.

Mr. Hendrix looked at his wrist. He had twenty minutes to make the ten o'clock train for Chicago. From Chicago he would travel to New Orleans and thence into Mexico. He had a wallet full of bills. The side exit of the El Bravo was ten feet away. But Mr. Hendrix, struggling to get to his feet, swayed and fell forward. The dozen drinks he had so shrewdly tossed down his gullet to help him act his part joined the hideous plot he had hatched against himself. He was too drunk, too dizzy to stand up and move quickly.

They found the little barrister hunched in his seat staring at the murdered athlete. The gun was still in his hand. Mr. Hendrix was mumbling passionlessly:

"Guilty. Guilty. Guilty."

# *The Rival Dummy*

I WAS DINING in a place where vaudeville "artists" congregate to gossip and boast, when my friend Joe Ferris, the booking agent, pointed to a stocky little man with a gray toupée, alone at a table and said:

"There is, I think, the strangest, weirdest, craziest man in New York."

I looked a second time, and noted, despite this identification, nothing more unusual than the aforesaid gray toupée, a certain bewildered and shifty manner about the eyes, and a pair of nervous sensitive hands. He reminded me—this solitary diner—of some second-rate Hungarian fiddler worn out with poverty, alcohol, and egotism.

"That," said Joe Ferris, "is the man who ten years ago used to be known as Gabbo the Great—the world's most famous ventriloquist. I guess he heard me"—the booking agent lowered his voice—"but it doesn't matter. He'll pretend he didn't. We're not supposed to know who he is, you know. That's what the toupée is for. Disguise. Mad—madder than a cuckoo. It gives me the shivers just to look at him.

"I'll tell you his story," continued Ferris, "and maybe you can figure it out. That's more than I can. But being a newspaperman, you won't call me a liar. I hate to tell stories to people who are always certain that anything they never heard of before is a lie.

"This particular yarn"—Ferris smiled—"began way back before the war. He came over from Belgium, Gabbo. That's where a good percentage of the best performers come from. God knows why. Jugglers, contortionists, trapeze acts, strong men, and all that kind of stuff. Belgium and Lithuania, sometimes.

"I booked Gabbo when he first landed. The best all-around ventriloquist that ever played the big time—if I do say so. And nuts, of course. But you got to expect that from the talent. I never see a first-rate act that wasn't at least half nutty.

"The first time I met him I ask him what his name is.

"'Gabbo what?' I ask.

"'Gabbo the Great,' is the answer. And then he adds very seriously, 'I was born Great.'

"I thought at first this was the foreign equivalent for a gag. But there was less humor about Gabbo than a dead mackerel. He used to sign his letters G. G. Imagine. And—to give you a rough idea of what kind of a loon this baby was—he always opened his act with the *Marseillaise.*

"He used to come out in the middle of it, stand at attention till it was finished, and then, in a low, embarrassed voice, announce: 'Ladies and Gentlemen: I have the honor to present to you tonight the world's most gifted ventriloquist—Gabbo the Great.'

"And he would take a bow. That's pretty cuckoo, ain't it? But it always went big. You'd be surprised at what an audience will swallow and applaud.

"Well, the first time I came to the conclusion that there was something definitely cockeyed about Gabbo was when I called on him one night after his performance at the Palace. It was up in his room at the hotel. He'd just got in and was taking his dummy out of its black case. It had velvet lining in it, this case, and was trimmed in black and gold like a magician's layout.

"Let me tell you about this dummy—if I can. You've seen them. One of those red-cheeked, round-headed marionettes with popping, glassy eyes and a wide mouth that opens and shuts.

"Well, Jimmy—that was the name of this wooden-headed thing—was no different than the rest of them. That is, you wouldn't think so to look at it. That thing haunts me, honest to God. I can still see its dangling legs with the shoes painted on its feet and—let's forget about it. Where was I?

"Oh, yes. I go up to his room and stand there talking to him, and just as I'm making some remark or other, he sits Jimmy up on the bed, and all of a sudden turns to him—or it or whatever you want to call the thing—and starts holding a conversation.

"'I suppose,' says Gabbo, angry as blazes and glaring at this nutty dummy, 'I suppose you're proud of yourself, eh? After the way you acted tonight?'

"And Jimmy, the dummy, so help me, answers back in a squeaky voice, 'Aw, go soak your head. Listen to who's talkin'.'

"Then this nutty ventriloquist speaks up kind of heatedly. 'I'm talkin',' he says. 'And I'll ask you to listen to what I have to say. You forgot your jokes tonight, and if it happens again you get no milk.'

"Well, I thought it was a gag. You know, a bit of clowning for my benefit. So I stand by, grinning like an ape, although it don't look funny at all, while Gabbo pours a glass of milk and, opening Jimmy's mouth, feeds it to him. Then he turns to me, like I was a friend of the family, and says coolly: 'This Jimmy is getting worse and worse. What I wanted to see you about, Mr. Ferris, is taking his picture off the billing. I want to teach him a lesson.'

"I've had them before—cuckoos, I mean—and it didn't surprise me. Much. They come pretty queer in vaudeville.

"Remind me to tell you sometime about the prima donna I had who used to come on with a dagger and throw it on the stage. If it stuck, landed on its point, she'd go on with the act and sing. If it didn't she wouldn't. Walk right off.

"She was pretty expert at tossing the old dagger, so it usually landed right—they ain't ever too crazy. And on that account of the dagger always landing right, I never find out what it's all about for weeks. Until one night she up cold and walks out on herself. On an opening night at the Palace, too, where she's being featured. And when I come galloping back, red in the face, to ask her what the hell, she answers me very haughty: 'Go ask the dagger. He tell you.'

"Well, that's another story, and not so good, either. About this night in Gabbo's room, as I was saying. I took in Gabbo's little act with the dummy, and said nothing.

"But I started making a few inquiries the next day, and I find out plenty. I find out that this nutty give-and-take with the dummy is just a regular routine for Gabbo. That he keeps up a more or less steady conversation with the dummy like he was a kid brother. And not only that, but that this idiotic dummy is the only human being—or whatever you call him—that Gabbo ever says more than hello to. Barring me, of course.

"Look"—and Ferris snorted—"can you imagine him sitting at that table now and looking at me and pretending he don't know me? And, what's more, that I don't know him? On account he's got a nine-dollar toupée on. Well, that's part of the story, and I'll come to it.

"The way I figured it at the time—and I may be wrong—was that Gabbo was such an egotist that he could only talk to himself. You know, there's lots of hoofers, for instance, who won't watch anybody but themselves dance. They stand in front of a mirror—for diversion, mind you—and do their stuff. And applaud it. That's vaudeville for you.

"So I figured Gabbo that way. That he was so stuck on himself he got a big kick out of talking to himself. That's what he was doing, of course, when he held these pow-wows with Jimmy.

"As you can imagine, it kind of interested me. I got so I'd always try to drop around Gabbo's dressing room whenever I had time, just to catch this loony business with the dummy. I didn't think it exactly funny, you know, and it never made me laugh. I guess it was just morbid curiosity on my part. Anyway, I sort of become part of the family.

"The fights they used to have—Gabbo and this crazy dummy; fighting all the time. Usually about the act. Gabbo sore as the devil at Jimmy if anything went wrong with the turn—if one of the gags missed fire, for instance, he'd accuse him of stalling, laying down on the job, and honest to God, once he sailed into the damn thing because he was sure it wasn't getting enough sleep. Believe me or not, they were as quarrelsome as a team of hoofers.

"And after I got used to these spats—you know you can get used to anything—I got to thinking of Jimmy almost the way Gabbo did. I got to imagining it was him answering back—squealing, kidding, and swearing. And not Gabbo talking with his stomach—or whatever it is ventriloquists talk with.

"But with all this fighting between them, you could see that Gabbo had a soft spot for Jimmy. He fed him milk. There was a can or something fitted up inside. That's where the milk went.

"For instance, just to show you the pretty side of the picture, about three months after I change the billing and take Jimmy's name off the one-sheets, Gabbo arrives in my office with a demand that I put the picture back and the name too, in twice as big lettering as before.

"And one other time he comes to me, Gabbo does, and says Jimmy isn't getting enough money. Well, as you can imagine, this sounds a bit phony. There's such a thing as carrying a gag too far, is my first reaction. But so help me, he meant it. And he won't go on with the act unless I come through.

"Well, I learned long before that it don't pay to win arguments with the talent. It's worse than winning an argument with your own wife. Costs you more.

"So I finally control my temper and asks, 'How much of a raise does Jimmy want?'

" 'Five dollars a week more,' says Gabbo. And Gabbo was pulling down four hundred dollars for the act; so you can see the whole thing was on the square—asking a raise for Jimmy, I mean. Then he explains to me that he has been paying Jimmy ninety-five dollars per week right along, and he wants to make it an even hundred because Jimmy has been working very hard and so on.

"So much for that. Here's where the plot thickens. About three weeks or so after this conference, I get wind of the fact that Gabbo has fallen for a dame; and that the thing has become quite a joke among the talent.

"I can hardly believe my ears. Gabbo never looked at a dame ever since he was on the circuit. The loneliest, stuck-up professor I'd ever known. He used to walk around like Kaiser Wilhelm. Grand, gloomy, and peculiar. And with a mustache. Don't look now—he's shaved it off. Part of the disguise. But in those days it was his pride and joy.

"Well, the next thing I heard about his love's young dream is from Gabbo himself in person. He comes back to New York, and comes walking into the office with the information that he is adding a woman to his act; Mlle. Rubina. I look at him and say, 'What for, for the love of Pete? What do you need a jane in the act for, and why Rubina?'

"'For the water,' he answers. 'To bring on the glass of water which I drink. And take it off.' And he scowls at me as if to say, 'Do you want to make anything out of it?' And when I nod sort of dumbly, he goes on: 'She is willing to join me for a hundred dollars a week.'

"Well, this is pretty nuts. Rubina was a bowlegged wench working in a juggling act. Fetched plates and Indian clubs for Allen and Allen. And worth all of fifty cents a year as talent. Not even a looker. But go argue with Gabbo. I tried a little taffy about his going over so much better alone—that is, with his pal Jimmy to help him out. But he waves his hand at me, pulls his mustache, and begins to jump up and down with excitement.

"So I agree, and he then becomes the gentleman. He'll stand for a fifty dollar cut in his salary—that is twenty-five dollars out of his take and twenty-five out of Jimmy's. That's the way he puts it. And I should kick in with the other fifty for Rubina's graft.

"That's how this Rubina joined the act.

"I went over to catch it three nights later and see what was going on. I came right in the middle of Gabbo's turn. There he stood, with Jimmy sitting on the table, and this peroxide Rubina all dressed up in red plush knickerbockers with green bows on the sides of the knees, hovering around and 'acting'—registering surprise and delight every time the dummy made a wise crack. It almost ruined the turn.

"But what I noticed most was that Gabbo was a changed man. His whole attitude was different. He wasn't making his usual goo-goo eyes at the audience or shooting over personality—which had been his long suit.

"He was all wrapped up in Rubina, staring at her like a sick puppy with the heaves. And calling her over every half-minute, between gags, and demanding another glass of water. And bowing like an idiot whenever she handed it to him. He must have drank fourteen glasses of water during the act.

"And that, my friend, was just the beginning. The circuit thought it a big joke—Gabbo's crush on Rubina.

"And what everybody considered the funniest part of the racket was that Rubina was as fond of Gabbo as if he had been a rattlesnake. She never had anything but a sneer and a wise crack for him, and, when he got too fancy with his bow, just a low-down scowl. She would have none of him. Why, God only knows. Except perhaps that he was a little too nutty even for her. And she was no picker, believe me.

"In about two months things begin to grow serious. It seems, according to reports which come in from every town on the circuit, that Gabbo has carried his anger against Jimmy to such lengths that he'll hardly talk to him on the stage, mind you. Keeps sneering at his jokes and trying to trip him up, and bawling him out in front of the audience.

"And then, after the act, he sits him up on the table in his dressing room and starts in hurling curses at the dummy and screaming. It scares people out of their wits. The actors back-stage, I mean. You know, it's kind of woozy to pass a room where you know a man is alone and hear him yelling at the top of his voice. And, what's more, answering himself.

"And all this excitement, it seems, is due to jealousy. That was the whole point. It seems that this Rubina valentine had tumbled to the fact that Gabbo treated Jimmy like a living person. So, out of sheer cussedness, she had taken to patting Jimmy's wooden cheeks on the stage. Or winking at him during the turn. And the blow-off came, I learned, when she slipped Jimmy a caramel as he was sitting on Gabbo's lap in the dressing room. This was just downright morbid viciousness on Rubina's part.

"After that there was nothing could straighten the thing out. As soon as Gabbo lands in town, I go back-stage with him. He's in his dressing room, and he stands there—the turn being over—just motioning me away and raging at this maniac dummy of his.

"'That is the kind of a one you are,' he screams. 'That is the way you show your gratitude. After all I've done for you. Trying to steal the woman I love from me. The woman I love above everything.' And then I listen to Jimmy answer, and, so help me, for a minute I thought it was that damned wooden image speaking.

"'My life is my own,' says Jimmy, squealing wilder than usual. 'I can do what I want. And I'll ask you to mind your own business, you big tub of lard.'

"At these words Gabbo jumped into the air and pulled his hair out in handfuls.

"'Viper,' he howled at the dummy.

"'Idiot,' Jimmy squeals back at him.

"What could I do? I just sneaked off and left them calling each other names like a pair of fishwives. I crossed my fingers and hoped that the act wouldn't split up—that's where I was chiefly concerned, you understand.

"Then came the second stage. I don't know whatever got into this Rubina dame. She'd never pulled down more than thirty dollars a week in her life. And here she was getting a hundred. For doing nothing. And yet she writes me a long misspelled letter, that she's quitting the act on Saturday and for me to find someone to take her place.

"I was of course tickled silly. Fifty dollars is fifty dollars. And, besides, I sort of liked Gabbo and I felt this Rubina was dangerous to him. It's best for lunatics to steer clear of women—or for anybody for that matter.

"But my satisfaction didn't last long. I get a telephone call the following Monday to hurry over to the Bronx where Gabbo is opening—being starred, mind you. My great ventriloquist, it seems, has gone out of his head.

"I get there just as the bill has started. Gabbo has just told the manager he won't go on. He won't act. He knows what he owes to his art and his public, but would rather be torn by wild horses than to step out on the stage alongside of that black imp of hell—Jimmy.

"And as he says these things he walks up and down in his dressing room, cursing Jimmy and glowering at him like a maniac. They're having an out-and-out bust-up, like a team. Calling each other hams, among other less repeatable things.

"The house manager and all the actors were frightened silly at the noise. But I was used to Gabbo by this time, and began trying to calm him down. But I got no chance to get in a word edgewise—what with the way these two were going after each other. Gabbo thundering in his baritone and that damned dummy squealing back at him in his falsetto.

"I saw at once that Gabbo had really sort of gone over the edge. This time there was a murderous rage in his voice. And in Jimmy's, too.

"I got so mixed up I began to worry—for Gabbo. Dummy or no dummy, I began to think that . . .

"Well, anyway, it appears that Rubina, his adored, the light of his life, has flown. And Gabbo's idea, nutty as it sounds, is that Jimmy knows where she is. That she and Jimmy have framed against him. That Jimmy, the dirty hound, has stolen her love. Can you beat it?

"There's no use trying to reason under such circumstances. Any more than getting logical with a man who has the D. T.'s. Gabbo won't go on with the act. And he don't. He's through. And I stand still, and say nothing, and watch him hurl Jimmy into his black case, grab it under his arm, and start out with it.

"And I follow him out of the theater. He starts walking peculiarly, like a man half stewed. Then I see that he's doubling on his tracks, trying to elude somebody. Me, I figured. But I kept on. Finally he goes into a store, and I watch him through the window. It's a hardware store, and he stays in there for five minutes, and then comes out and makes a beeline for the hotel.

"I got to his room almost as soon as he did. But the door was locked. I stood there listening, and all of a sudden I hear screaming. In English, French, and several other languages. I swear to you, it scared me silly.

"I started banging on the door. But it's no use. Finally I beat it down after the manager. We're back in five minutes. And we open the door.

"Well, the room is silent and empty.

"I stood staring for a minute. Then I saw something. The floor is covered with pieces of wood. Splinters, sticks. It's Jimmy. Chopped to pieces, cut to smithereens. He'd murdered Jimmy, honest to God.

"We looked all around the room, and found the ax he'd bought in the hardware store. And then found that he'd lit out through the window. Made his getaway down the fire-escape.

"And that's the last trace we could pick up of him. We hunted high and low. I had two men scouring the town. But he was gone, leaving everything behind him. Fled—like a murderer, a murderer fleeing from justice, so help me.

"I'd gathered Jimmy up and put him in a piece of wrapping paper. That's how confused I was. And I carried him to the office and finally threw him in the wastebasket. And then I went home, and was unable to sleep for six nights.

"That's almost the end of the story. Except that two years ago I come in here one night after the show, and I see somebody familiar sitting at a table. I can't place him for a few minutes, and then all of a sudden I see it's Gabbo—Gabbo the Great—with a gray toupée and the mustache shaved.

"I rush over to him and begin talking. And he stared at me—highty-tighty like.

" 'My name,' he says, 'is Mr. Lawrence. I am sorry you make a mistake.'

"Well, I'm not unusually dense, and as I stood there it dawned on me that Gabbo didn't want to be known. That he'd come back after fleeing from justice for eight years—come back disguised and with a different name, so that the police wouldn't pick him up for his great crime.

"And here he sits." Ferris looked at me with a mirthless smile. "Everybody knows his story in this place, and we all kid him along, calling him Mr. Lawrence and keeping his secret. Yeah, and when we get funny we call him the Ax Murderer. You know, just a gag among ourselves.

"Wait till he leaves"—Ferris picked up his glass—"and I'll take you over to the table where he's sitting."

This struck me as a rather empty offer.

"What for?" I inquired.

"So you can see what Jimmy looked like."

Ferris suddenly laughed. "He always draws a picture of that damned idiotic dummy on the tablecloth—every night."

# *The Adventures of Professor Emmett*

THERE WAS a certain moodiness to Gifford Emmett which he had picked up somehow while acquiring human shape in his mother's belly and which caused him to enter the world with a special lack of equipment for living in it. What he lacked chiefly was the desire to become a human being. Life sometimes produces these reluctant bloodstreams which, like backwaters without beat or destination, remain morbidly outside the traffic of existence.

Gifford Emmett spent his thirty-six years of life in a subtle campaign to return to his mother's womb. Though he matured physically, and his mind developed far enough beyond its fetal stage to earn him a full professorship at a university, Gifford actually never existed. He merely imitated the ways of life as one might the manners of a repugnant country. Like an exile in an undesired land, his soul retained nostalgic recollections. It yearned for its larval state, and all its subsequent stages seemed full of alarms and discomforts.

You will understand this matter better, perhaps, if you look back on your own birthday. Few of us arrive in the world with any real conviction or even positive attitude. We are inclined to squander our time in the womb, only to be dislodged at the last moment, and in many cases evicted. And with many of us, thus driven from our only Eden, there is a tendency to turn our tiny, half-simian backs on the world into which we are ejected. Even the best of us who later grow to assertive manhood come out protesting furiously at the miserable change of fortunes the forceps have to offer. Once out, we signal our despair with heartbreaking noise, or we lie stunned and unbelieving of the nasty trick that has been played on us by our mother's suddenly hostile muscles.

Our infancy is as much a time of readjustment as of education. During the first wretched months of our existence, we must inure ourselves to the repulsive oddity of a cradle vastly too large for us. We have been dethroned and our soul is full of complaints. As the days pass, however, we are wooed and purred into certain revaluations. We are kissed and fondled and made the focal point of this new and inferior existence into which we have blundered. A new if lesser ego is offered us. We are loaded with despot scepters and bedazzled with tyrant crowns. Whereupon, slowly and with many a night of sad weeping, which I myself can well remember, we reconcile ourselves to our second nests, and say farewell forever to our original dream of perfect living.

No such time of reconciliation or farewell, however, came to Gifford Emmett. The reasons for this I shall do my best to reveal.

Little Gifford was born on a December morning of the year 1902, in an old brick house that stood in the second nicest residential section of a small Wisconsin town. At the moment, the town was covered with snow, and in its streets lonely figures, booted and mittened, were prowling about in a blizzard. Under the cold beat of the wind, the Emmett house stood quilted and turreted with snow, its windows and doors half obliterated. In a bedroom too cold either for amour or for its public sequel, Mrs. Emmett lay doing her best to persuade little Gifford to take his place in a larger world.

After some seven violent hours, Mrs. Emmett finally triumphed, and little Gifford appeared, refusing to breathe or offer any tell-tale signs of life. His efforts to outwit the new and the horrible by a possum-like unconsciousness availed him nothing. The family doctor, a canny old gentleman aware of the ruses of the newborn, belabored little Gifford's bottom with a stout palm. Then he shook and rattled him about as if he were no more than a dollar alarm clock to be jarred into ticking. Eventually a tiny moan rewarded the scientist's work, and Gifford Emmett was declared officially in the land of the living.

At this vital and sensitive moment, a disastrous thing happened. The street door of the Emmett house was flung open, and eleven adolescents ranging in age from twelve to sixteen entered as if they were the spirit of the blizzard outside. They came in howling and prancing and fell to rolling on the floor and assaulting each other with snowballs scraped from each other's shoes and hair. Five of these arrivals were the moaning little Gifford's brothers and sisters. The other six were a species of local self-elected orphans who preferred the Emmett home to their own as an arena for feats of strength and budding musical talents.

The opening of the Emmett street door let in a wintry blast that scampered icily up the stairs and into the accouchement chamber. And since none of the eleven arrivals could find time to close the door, the wintry blast grew wintrier. It swirled and steamed up the stairs, and little Gifford, but recently induced to breathe, found himself swept by such frigid currents that he turned instantly blue and began to shake as if with palsy. He wailed once and then fell into that stoical, powerless silence that marked his demeanor for life.

There is no doubt but that little Gifford's aversion to life was fully developed when the forceps seized him. The opening of the door, the wintry blasts, the horrifying shouts of laughter, and the sounds of furniture toppling were merely details that instantly and forever verified his already full-blown conviction that he had been cast out of the best of all possible worlds into a nowhere.

Biologically, the facts are that little Gifford was the fruit of an unexpected and autumnal flicker of parenthood. Mrs. Emmett had conceived in her forty-third year, to the disquiet of her husband, himself nearing sixty. And though little Gifford had emerged a fine infant, with a full quota of appendages, it is fairly good science to conclude that he had been put together a little tiredly. The elderly genes and chromosomes laboring at his fashioning had sighed at their work. And that cymbal crash of life that inspires the newborn to shed its larval soul fell on tired ears with little Gifford, if he heard it at all.

Whatever world he had been born into, it is likely that Gifford would have bloomed as a psychosis rather than a sultan. Still the Emmett home did have its share in the non-development of little Gifford's human side. There was no room or role for this laggard little guest in the firmly established hullabaloo of mixed quarters, juvenile sports, and endless riotings that were the routine of this Wisconsin ménage. Gifford had arrived too late to be of any use or interest to anybody. For his mother, no new activities focused on his crib. His father instituted no new regime for his sake. Nobody breathed or kissed or fondled an ego into his consciousness. His brothers and sisters regarded him with the perfunctory interest they had for all creatures who fitted into neither football squads nor wrestling tournaments, to say nothing of moonlight singing.

And from his first weeks little Gifford exhibited the detachment of one who knows himself an interloper. He allowed himself quietly to be stowed away in attics and back bedrooms and other distant culs-de-sac where the banjo and piano banging and other alarums of adolescence could not reach to break his hypothetical slumbers. He suffered sudden drafts, hunger, and terror, without even the little comment at his command. And during such naps as he was able to steal amid the hurly-burly of the household, he dreamed happily of that land of warmth and plenty from which, like a peri, he had been expelled.

And so Gifford grew into a sober and unprotesting infant, well shapen but enigmatic. Soon he shuffled about on hands and knees, doing his best to avoid flying missiles, charging feet, and other hazards of life. He had no interest in living, but his intelligence had not yet encompassed the idea of suicide. In his second winter, he seemed to all the Emmetts but one a model child. He had by that time completely abandoned his small struggle to become part of life. No music or laughter could lure him now from his seclusion. He haunted the unwanted corners of the house, sitting on the floor and staring tirelessly into space with a sort of Oriental calm. When summer came, he crawled into the currant patch behind the house, and lay in the cool dirt under the bushes. His mother, busy with stretching Mr. Emmett's weekly pay check (he was a chemist in the town's bottle works) over the seven days, smiled gratefully on his seeming ability to amuse himself. She misunderstood entirely the moods that sent him crawling under beds and into airless closets. There were times, however, when Gifford's eyes, looking intently at her, startled her and made her wonder if anything was wrong with him. It appeared to her then that the child Gifford looked at her with a most curious and desperate concentration, as if he were weaving a spell. Drawing him to her, she would ask kindly at such times what her little man wanted. But Gifford kept his secret.

The lone Emmett to whom Gifford seemed something less than a model child was Edward, the father. When Gifford was a few weeks old, Edward Emmett perceived that his son hated him. Mr. Emmett said nothing about it. He had long ago been elbowed out of any vital existence by his brood and their satellites, and converted into a fluttering, negligible shade of parenthood who continued to drop lamb chops and fried potatoes on the Emmett table from his little perch as a bottle maker. This history had conditioned him to keep his thoughts to himself.

When the curious fact that Gifford fell into a fit whenever his father approached him began to be generally noticed, a number of theories sprang up as to its cause. Mr. Emmett defended himself vigorously against charges of clumsiness and unfriendliness. But Mrs. Emmett had still another theory that left him silent. His wife was of the opinion that the little creature objected to the smell of chemicals always arising from Mr. Emmett's person. And her husband recalled that Lily, as a bride, had once burst into tears over some chlorine gas lingering in his mustache, and concluded that Gifford had inherited from his mother this unreasonable distaste for antiseptic odors. Mr. Emmett took to bathing and cologning himself like a stage beauty, but, sweetened though he was, his effect on his son remained unchanged. The otherwise placid infant continued to have convulsions at the sight of him.

Such, without going any further into the matter, was Professor Emmett's childhood. Ignored by his brothers and sisters, misunderstood by his mother, and mysteriously outraged by the male collaborator of his being, Gifford tottered about at the age of three like a little ghost whom every dawn threatened to dissipate. At four he took to running away from home and hiding beneath neighborhood verandas, from under which he was dragged weeping at the frustration of his plans. At five he became a moody survivor of a vanished era, for his brothers and sisters and their hallooing intimates were then scattering to work and to college. Gifford haunted the once gay household like a little beggar poking around in the wake of a carnival. In the summertime, shooed out of the house to get some air, he spent long hours under the currant bushes, inert and moody.

It was in this retreat that Gifford, at six, discovered surprisingly a world that fascinated him. This was the world of insects. His child eyes became aware of ants and spiders, wasps, butterflies, grasshoppers, and earthworms. Lying on his stomach, chin cupped in his hands, Gifford would remain absorbed for hours by the busy ways of this wonderfully unhuman population. He began to see in the seemingly aimless careenings of these, his first friends, certain patterns of conduct. These minute creatures, in whose midst he sprawled like a Gulliver, became significant and interesting to him as human beings had never been, and he watched them as if they were tiny letters spelling out a new and breathless tale.

Through long summer hours he would lie this way, and sometimes, lured by these Pied Pipers of the garden, he followed them to sit like a guest on the thresholds of their curious homes. He learned many things. He became aware of the mother love of the beetle, of the precision and cruelty of the spider, and of the marauderies of the wasps. He grew to know the little wind lanterns of the glow-worm. The large head of the grasshopper, like that of a tissue-paper horse, became as familiar to him as if it spoke. The beetle, senile and saucer-eyed, and the paunchy spider, with its crown of legs, waiting owlishly in its hazy net, were his comrades. None of these diminutive ogres frightened him. Their ominous caricature of human limb and feature pleased him like a set of strange toys. He never tired of watching this little universe crawl and fly and dart, weave its homes and struggle murderously for its food.

Unguided by books, he created for himself a childish version of all he saw. The dark leafy tunnels of the overhanging currant bushes became a fairyland where eccentric-looking heroes performed for him. Dragons and helmeted knights battled on their twig arenas. Hobgoblins hung by invisible threads. Miniature witches leaped through the air, and the eyes of genii gleamed out of tiny holes in the ground. Troubadours, transported by summer, played their violins, and little scarecrow kings teetered on the berry clusters. The ants seemed to him like beaded acrobats of the grass blades. And over the bushes the darning needles fired arrows at the sun, and the butterflies swayed like tiny flags.

Like his friends, Gifford prepared himself for the winter months. He erected an insect zoo in his room. Glass jars containing ants and spiders, wasps, beetles, and flies, crowded his bureau top and his window sills. When the cold days came, Gifford tended his charges anxiously. He fed them and invented diversions for their welfare. He constructed exercise yards for them out of shoe boxes and built rickety mansions of mosquito netting. For the ants he modeled special hills of dirt so that they might not grow homesick.

It seemed unnatural to Mrs. Emmett that anyone should be interested exclusively in bugs. But her efforts to lure her child away were unavailing. It was the despised Mr. Emmett, whom Gifford still hated, but in an inactive fashion now, who rescued his son from the shadows of ignorance that seemed to be permanently enclosing him. Mr. Emmett understood that Gifford was a scientist. He was proud to have handed on to his son his own interest in this profound side of life. Diffidently, Mr. Emmett sat with his son and imparted to him his own theory of education.

"If you will go to Bible class and pay attention to your teacher in school," he said, "you will be allowed to study what you like when you grow up. I can't explain why it is, but you must study about angels and presidents before you can study about bugs. But I can promise you that after you've gone to school a long time, you'll be able to return to insects, and nobody will bother you."

Lured by the promise of this reward, Gifford submitted himself to the educational system. And long after Mr. Emmett's death, the prophecy he had made came true. At thirty-four, Gifford Emmett was raised to a full professorship in the university he had entered as a gloomy, gangling youth. Jars filled with insects, and elaborate cages teeming with his beloved coleoptera and arachnids, crowded his bachelor apartment just as they had his childhood bedroom. And for several hours a week, as Professor of Entomology, he lectured happily on the secrets of that Kingdom of the Little which he had first discovered under the currant bushes.

In leaping thus from the seven-year-old Gifford to the tall, thin, dark-haired, and goggle-eyed savant of thirty-four, I have omitted little of his life that calls for chronicling. During these missing decades Gifford was engaged chiefly in the moody but ungraphic business of receding from the world. He continued to hold himself like a bystander on the outskirts of its charms, its follies, and its adventures. He read tirelessly and studied deeply, and his mind evolved within the egg of inaction. It was a curious mind full of wit and learning. But it revealed itself to no one.

He had matured without tasting anything of life. Now he thrived like some specimen in a bottle, detached from his species and forgetful of them. Only one thing occasionally disturbed him. This was a periodic lapse into melancholia. The desire to die seized him each year of his life, and stretched him weeping and inanimate in his bed. These melancholic fits lasted usually through the week of his birthday. He suffered then from a sense of suffocation. The chill and contemptuous wit of his mind turned to fog. He lay staring at unbearable walls and listening to sounds of a life that tortured him. However, he always recovered quickly, and resumed his reading and his friendless ways of living as if nothing had interrupted them.

There are some of us, many more than are usually counted, who do not grow up at all. Life is unable to alter these little ones among us despite the plant-like increase of their bodies. In them the child persists not as a dim imprisoned ghost, but as a face always visible. All the trappings of age, its wrinkles, its wisdom, and its very largeness, seem like misfit clothes in which these children must stagger grotesquely about. And no matter what their lives or passions may be, there remains stamped on their reluctant adulthood the bewitched and pathetic contour of innocence.

Professor Emmett was one of these nursery lingerers. His face glowed as if it were a shell that had never known wind or sun. So gentle and disarming did the smallest of his gestures seem that there was hardly a female student but felt an impulse to mother him. Men were equally charmed by his staccato wit and child-like simplicity. But Professor Emmett, who, if you looked closely, was still the little Gifford busy with his currant-bush comrades, evaded any intimacies.

In his thirty-fifth year, however, an adventure and a relationship befell him. And with it my tale of Professor Emmett's Homeric adventures in a sense begins.

Myra McKillup entered Gifford Emmett's life at that precise moment when he had decided to quit it. The melancholia that had assailed Gifford since his boyhood had subsided in his thirties. Now as he was approaching thirty-five it returned. Animation once more left him. Mysterious tears coursed out of his soul and overran his cheeks.

Of the diseases that touch the hearts of others, those of the subconscious are certainly the least. It is difficult to take seriously the nightmares which these oddly afflicted ones seem to parade as pets. We are inclined to regard them as impostors rather than martyrs. The fact that these impostors frequently leap from windows, hurl themselves under trains, thrust their heads into gas ovens, or blow out their brains is not enough to convince us of their reality. Their deaths come too late to impress us with their diseases. Even those who weep at the bier of the neurotic are inclined to withhold their sympathy for the secret agony that sent him to the undertaker's.

Thus, though I have come to a moment in my hero's life that might well call for a little tenderness from any reader, I feel it better to deal unemotionally with the matter. Of objective griefs such as we fancy drive folk to their deaths Gifford had no more than any of the grasshoppers he tended in their bottles. No amorous or professional entanglements beset him. No frustrations sawed at his nerves. Around him lay a little world of flattery, and he had no dreaded tomorrows awaiting him. Yet with all this well-being at his fingertips, Gifford sat ready to die. And if the reader will not cry over the fact he must at least believe it, and not assert that Gifford was behaving absurdly, as wives have been known to remark of husbands just before the latter leaped out of windows.

For a half-hour Professor Emmett sat inert and befogged. He held in his hand a small bottle of chemical which he was about to drink. Outside, it was a lavish spring morning. The windows of his study were open and through them came the shout of early vernal winds, colors, and odors. But this lean, goggle-eyed man remained insensible. Insensible, too, he stayed before another phenomenon. His spiders, hatched on this spring morning, had climbed the towering bamboo stalks provided for them and were escaping through the open windows, afloat on their silken rockets. Unmindful of this long-awaited spectacle, Professor Emmett blankly regarded the poison in his hand. Like any of his brothers in their bottles, he too sat separated from life by walls that obscured its breath. No tragic thoughts were in his head, and his reason for dying was no more than an oppression that called for death as thirst calls for water.

Occupied thus with the vague gesture which in a moment would bring about his dissolution, Gifford was unaware of a visitor until she had come close to him and removed the open bottle from his mouth. He looked up and saw dimly a dark-haired young woman with large, trembling eyes. And at this moment Gifford was overcome with a misunderstanding of Myra McKillup that precipitated his first romance.

He saw her, this sad man pulled back to life, as a creature full of calm, beauty, and goddess-like radiance. A measure of his misunderstanding may be seen in the fact that Miss McKillup was a thin girl, undersized and meatless except for her breasts. These were not large, but, landscaped as they were by famine, they seemed plenty.

Because Gifford's desire to die had been only a temporary one he felt a surge of gratitude for this student who had entered his study by mistake, as she explained. Part of the need he immediately felt for her was probably due to her seeming to his bewitched senses a maternal figure. She had brought him to life, like a secondary mother, and Gifford's long campaign to re-enter his mother's womb transferred itself, a little more practically, to Miss McKillup. He stared at her from that first day with timorous, incestuous eyes, and she seemed to him a human being cast in a tender and superior mold.

This concept too was as completely unrelated to any image of the young woman as his first physical estimate. In addition to being as unmotherly as a hop-toad, Miss McKillup was actually a flibberty nerve-racking creature with a touch of pituitary emaciation. She owned a mind much like a sieve, through which her twenty-five years of life had passed leaving behind a froth of hysteria. She was an unstable and muddle-headed girl. She had a thin, forward-thrusting face like a bird's, bony hands, and a talent for breathlessness. She considered herself a superior person, for no reason that I can determine. It may be she fancied herself more sensitive than most people, and regarded her inability to talk rationally on any subject as a measure of some kind of mysticism rather than stupidity. She inhabited every cliché like an Archimedes yelling "Eureka." She was a-swoon with economics, art, and a bit of biology. There are whole continents of such women, who seem to feel that they master any subject they take up merely by sighing on it. Attracted by an idea, they belabor it with gasps and tremors as if they were coaxing it into bed with them. Usually, to do them justice, there is some sort of male attached to the idea.

Miss McKillup was of this inarticulate and oracular run of femininity. She was enrolled in a post-graduate journalism course under the not entirely erroneous impression that she belonged on a newspaper—as some kind of critic. Perhaps there was nothing more the matter with her than a need for seeming more intelligent than she was, which so often turns people into fools. Or perhaps she sought to reveal a beauty of soul as a lure for the opposite sex, there being little other bait at her disposal. Unsavory-looking girls often go in for this sort of spiritual cosmetics and flit about with over-rouged ideas and insane-looking mental coiffures.

I intend, however, to run no magnifying glass over Myra. That Gifford should have fallen in love with this lady at first sight and beheld her as a Demeter full blown with the blessings of the earth is a matter between him and his subconscious. My hero, who had never once felt the stirring of libido, was overcome suddenly by a mating instinct as implacable as it was mistaken. This movement of sap in Gifford, however, expressed itself only in a desire to talk. And the professor's many admirers looked on with surprise as their good savant devoted himself to addressing incessantly on the most abstruse of topics a young woman whom they knew to be as rattle-brained as a mongoose.

The curious couple was to be seen haunting all the lonely places that neighbored the university. Pale with long confinement in its bottle, the soul of Professor Emmett emerged and fluttered moth-like before the light it fancied lay in Miss McKillup's eyes. It filled the night with the colors of its wit and wisdom, for it is the habit of long-locked-away lovers to create themselves first before they fall to sighing for another.

It would be cruel to say that Myra understood nothing of what Gifford revealed to her during these trysts. Women usually understand what is said to them in courtship, but their listening has so much more coquetry than scholarship in it that the most Socratic of dialogues turn to valentines under their applause. Yet it is only fair to point out that if Myra listened with other organs than were meant for words to the wisdom of Professor Emmett, the latter was, in a sense, not speaking to her at all. She had accidentally removed the top of the bottle and the professor was emerging genie-fashion.

Gifford began his love-making with an attack on life. His aversion for living had spun many dark ideas in his head. His wooing of Miss McKillup consisted, to the end, of an effort to convince her of the infamy and absurdity of human existence.

For their first tryst, Miss McKillup had guided the professor to a little hilltop overgrown with tall grasses. This was the evening of Gifford's rescue from death. He had clung all day to Miss McKillup, allowing her to cool his head with icy towels and to induce him to eat. Still shaken by the double experience of attempting death and of discovering the first woman he had ever found tolerable, Gifford sat moodily on the hilltop. Now his melancholia thawed into phrase. The shawl of pain lifted from his senses and he spoke coolly and lucidly to his companion.

"I have always hated life," said Gifford, "and have found human existence a sort of calamity."

"You say human existence," said Miss McKillup with the air of a philosopher. "Is there any other?"

Gifford's romance almost collapsed under this insensate question. He looked coldly at the young woman.

"Human existence," he said, "is the least of the phenomena of Nature. The most rudimentary thinker must see us as a needle in a haystack. The history of the human race from its first grunt to its last sigh will be hardly more than a footnote to the story of life. We are less than a chirp in Bedlam."

"I know," said Miss McKillup sadly, "but don't you think there's some God who is aware of us, or some force?"

"God is aware of us only if He is a microscope," said Gifford, "or unbalanced. Our species will have come and gone too quickly to interest any sane Super-Intelligence."

Miss McKillup sighed and her face became full of compassion for the littleness of man.

"I've often wondered," she said, "what the end of our race would be. Whether the insects would finally vanquish us—or what?"

"The insects are not interested in us," said Gifford irritably. "We are too vague and unimportant in the scheme of things to attract their attention. They bite us purely by accident. As for vanquishing us, nothing could be further from their thoughts. It is rarely that one species vanquishes another. The mind of the earth which we call Nature is so exquisitely balanced a pendulum of creation and destruction that even the most foolish of its children are able to survive."

Miss McKillup looked wistfully at the stars as if she were saying farewell to them.

"It is not the insects who will nibble our species into extinction," announced Gifford. "Our fate is more tragic than that. Man will be one of the few suicides in Evolution."

After a silence during which he continued to stare abstractedly at her knees, Gifford informed Miss McKillup that the dissolution of the human race already cast its shadow into our day. Thought, like a Walpurgis Night, was descending on man and the time was nearing when he would vanish on all the broomsticks of his philosophies. Luckily Miss McKillup was more stirred by his attentions than his assertions, or she might have become sincerely depressed.

Gifford launched into his first courtship essay. The human mind, he said, began very slowly. It took a long time to improve on its first growls. Why it began at all is a mystery. All we can be sure of is that it was intended as a serviceable bit of plasm. Let us say a sixth sense—a sense of knowing. Nature is full of similar compensating gifts for those of her children unable to run, fly, dig, smell, see, or hear too well. Each of these possesses the gift of some ruse by which it can outwit its enemies sufficiently for survival, like the spider's sting, or the glue arrows of the soldier ant.

Miss McKillup, listening, was surprised to find so much violence in this gentle and child-like man. Nevertheless, it pleased her, for it gave her a duty. She would make this morbid but delightful scholar change his opinions about life, which she was certain he would do under the influence of a little sweetness.

"For a long time," Gifford spoke up again, "the human mind fulfilled its simple destiny. It enabled us to outwit our better-equipped enemies. Primitive man was a very fortunate animal. But we are in no way related to him. We have been whisked out of Nature into the Alice-in-Wonderland realm of thought. Our mind has hatched a universe. It has projected a world of phantoms on the screen of our senses. We inhabit this world. We crawl on our animal legs into a mirror."

"Please go on," said Miss McKillup throatily.

Gifford remained silent.

After a pause Miss McKillup added wistfully, "I want to hear."

"I think you will understand me better," he resumed, "if I discuss the human mind merely as a parasite."

"Yes," said Miss McKillup breathlessly, "oh, yes. It will be much easier for me. Although everything you say is marvelously clear. Marvelously!"

Gifford nodded and waited for her to find a more comfortable piece of ground. She selected a place near his ankles and, lying down again, this time on her stomach, raised her face eagerly.

"The parasite mind," said Gifford, "is already nibbling at the biologic sanity of the species. Most of modern medicine is the record of the mind's ability to cripple the body. Modern history also has become a record of mental aberration on a grand scale. Intellectual quibbles now breed our wars. It's not difficult to foresee a world locked in a death struggle over theories for its improvement.

"But," mused Gifford, "I don't think the species will destroy itself in this coming struggle of Tweedledee and Tweedledum."

Miss McKillup sighed like a harp that is being plucked. All the same, the dissolution of the race disturbed her much less than the appearance of a slight flush in the professor's cheeks.

"It's so warm," she said softly. "Wouldn't you rather take your coat off?"

"Thank you," said Gifford mechanically and removed it.

"And your waistcoat," Miss McKillup insisted. This too was removed.

"No," Gifford resumed as she loosened his tie, "it will not be the war of man against man that will bury us in the grave of the dodo bird. Man against himself will be our finish. Not an honorable death, mind you, on the field of battle, but a gruesome suicide in the loneliness of the night, is the fate that awaits us. This suicide has begun. Thought has already crippled our nature. Our efforts to live by our ideas as if they were our bloodstream have rotted away half our health.

"Just look at us today," Gifford cried out to the seemingly fascinated young woman beside him, "us creatures who call ourselves the top of Evolution. Lords of the world, indeed! Why, the humblest beetle might laugh at us if it had time for the study of nonsense."

Gifford paused and stared at the night over the hilltop. How pleasant it was to speak thoughts, even the sullenest! He breathed excitedly. A new and exhilarating argument against life had just occurred to him.

"Our senses," he announced, "are caught in a net of reason. There's hardly a single thing we feel but we must busy ourselves misunderstanding or improving it. All our animal desires must crawl around on the flypaper of our mind and either die there or drag out an enfeebled existence breathing the poison of our ideals. All the magnificent functions of Nature are becoming confused in us. We can't sleep. Eating gets to be more and more complicated. Sex has become full of hazards and confusions. Morality and poetry have so bewildered the spinal cord that it has forgotten how to signal for a blood supply.

"Yes," cried Gifford triumphantly, "our search for the Ideal has converted our glandular system into a rubbish heap! Unable to transmute us into angels, our minds have turned us into invalids. Our last stand will be in the laboratories—as patients. Our scientists will toil away desperately at extricating our organs from the octopus of the mind. But I'm certain they won't succeed."

After a pause, during which he noticed with some surprise that Miss McKillup's head was now resting in his lap, Gifford continued.

"Have you ever noticed how the spider captures and destroys the powerful locust that leaps accidentally into its net?" he asked.

"No," Miss McKillup said, and sighed.

"The legs of the locust," explained Gifford, "are strong enough to kick the silken snare to shreds. But, as the spider stays out of reach, invisible to the procrastinating locust, it remains busy at work. It envelops the struggling bit of life in a flow of almost invisible thread. Round and round the locust the spider spins its delicate strait-jacket. Finally the locust is unable to move. Then our spider leisurely drains it of its blood, and the locust shell is left hanging in a net to rattle in the wind. We will end in a similar way. Enveloped by thought spun around us, our species will finally wither away to a few last neurotic husks, and then hang motionless in the web."

A little later the two strolled down the hill to the university, Miss McKillup clinging to Gifford's arm. She was pleased with what she called their first heart to heart talk, for she saw that it had made Professor Emmett extremely happy. He smiled when he said good-night to her, and she watched him walk off with a youthful spring in his long legs, trailing his coat and vest like a workman come home from a picnic.

A number of similar trysts followed, which I might report. But I shall hold myself down to the account of only one more. This took place a week later.

After they had dined together one evening, Miss McKillup—she was known to Professor Emmett as Myra now—guided him to a new rostrum, a little wooded river bank remembered from a previous love affair with a member of the university rowing crew. But Gifford ignored the loveliness of the spot, as he did for the most part the presence of his companion. For he was still too selfish in his pleasure to notice any contributing factors.

Just the same, he spent the first few minutes fidgeting and silent. This was because he suffered as always from the result of too much expectation. It takes time to adjust oneself to the reality of a Miss McKillup when one has walked with Dante's Beatrice all day.

Miss McKillup—Myra—did not allow herself to become discouraged by this ominous beginning. She smiled breathlessly as they sat in the little grotto once sacred to Venus and an oarsman.

"I've been looking forward so all day to this," she said. "I've lost interest in everything else in the world—except listening to you."

Gifford blushed, being unused to such bouquets. He remained silent and listened to the frogs and crickets singing everywhere in the spring night.

"I feel," went on Myra, "I feel as if we had known each other a long time. A terribly long time. I suppose that's because I can't remember ever having had any thoughts except those you've given me."

"The frogs sound very musical, don't they?" said Gifford.

"Divine," said Myra quickly.

"But it's a horrible music to others," Gifford said.

"Others?" cried Myra and looked around in alarm.

"I mean the insects," said Gifford. "Whenever I hear a frog I can almost feel the terror of the coleoptera and arachnids."

"Nature," said Myra, "is cruel, isn't it?"

"No," said Gifford. "That's a most ridiculous misconception. There's no cruelty in Nature. There are only necessity and precision. No animal tortures another animal. The frog devouring the spider acts out of an instinct shared by the spider. It is their stomachs and not their souls that are thrilled by murder."

"I hadn't thought of that," said Myra soothingly.

"Nature," said Gifford, "is a banquet board at which the feasters and the feast are one. This was shown to me once when I watched a praying mantis eat a grasshopper. The grasshopper had caught a caterpillar a moment before. It continued undisturbed to eat this caterpillar while the praying mantis munched on its own legs. Not until the mantis sank its teeth into the grasshopper's digestive organs did the latter abandon its own feast."

"It's all so frightening." Myra shivered.

"To me," said Gifford, "it is merely sane. I find our own species vastly more terrible than the mantis, the spider, and the humble caterpillar. Our mind is supposed to have improved on the manners of Nature. But if you examine our activities you will find that the mind has done little more with our animal criminality than rationalize its crimes. It has added to the simple murder-politic inherent in Nature the genius for depriving the victim not only of his life but of his good repute. There's no monster, in Nature, whose fangs are as cruel as our ideas."

"We are all animals in exile," said Myra with a shiver.

Gifford thought it astonishing that she should not only understand him but share his point of view. He was also surprised that this young woman's head in his lap failed to check the flow of his thought, but somehow increased his desire to communicate his ideas to her. Despite a slight numbness in his thigh, he permitted her to remain pillowed there.

"I'm afraid it's going to rain," said Gifford.

"Oh, no," Myra sighed, "I'm sure it won't."

"There's no question of it," said Gifford firmly. "I've been watching that spider." He pointed to a bush overhead. "She refuses to repair her web. When the spider refuses to reweave her web at night it's always a sign of rain."

"And yet," sighed Myra, "man believes himself the only thinking animal."

"He is," Gifford corrected her. "Spiders don't think. Nor do the bees or the ants. It's true some entomologists presume to see in the precision of insect life human motivations such as love, hate, ambition, or sacrifice. This is ridiculous. Take the case of the Clotho moth. This moth, who sews so wonderful a nest for her children, fills it also with materials out of which they will be able to weave their first spring frocks. Without these they would die of cold. Having laid out this wardrobe, the Clotho moth finishes her work of nest building by plugging up the last little hole in it with her own body. She dies with her wings spread as a barrier against her children's enemies. She might seem to be the most infatuated of Nature's mothers. Yet to call her a mother at all is to libel her. For the moth is unaware of what is in her eggs. She never lives to see them hatch. It is absurd to imagine that love for these never-to-be-seen moth infants animates her. They are, in fact, not her children but her ghosts. They are her future shapes. It is life she perpetuates. She is as devoid of personality as the wind that rocks her tiny body. Her loving and thinking are both done for her by a never-blundering hypnosis we must call instinct."

Gifford paused and looked lovingly at the night, and Myra wondered why he was trembling.

"How wise the insects are," he said softly. "Their learning is so great and their joy of life so intense it seems almost inconceivable that they have not evolved that foolish talent for comment which would destroy their Eden. How enviable their world is. . . . The bee, for instance, so industrious, and yet as devoted to capering and singing as any drunken troubadour. You might," he added wistfully, "call the bee a hymn to life."

He addressed the girl tenderly.

"You never see an insect becoming irrational or insane, do you, Myra? The reason for this, you see, is that her talent is not her own. It belongs to her species, and she can neither improve on it nor discard it. She feels the pleasure of living, but she has no ego with which to distort or exaggerate it. And so she doesn't confuse either herself or her species.

"For instance, the cicada is like some wonderful fiddler. When it emerges from the earth in the spring, it is overcome by the marvel of sun and air, and it strikes up a tune, playing on its wing with its saw-toothed right leg. But luckily it is stone deaf and doesn't hear its own paean to the spring. If it did, it might become a musician and cease to be an insect. It would devote all its instincts to music and disintegrate as a cicada."

Myra opened her eyes and smiled.

"You know," she said, "you have made me realize how much greater our spirit is than our so-called intelligence."

Gifford hoped she was using the word "spirit" in the right sense, but was fearful of inquiring. In a moment, however, he forgot completely the presence of his companion despite the fact that both his legs had now turned numb under the weight of her head. He sat looking happily at the scenery of the night. The rain was coming. Its smell arrived first. He smiled at the wise spider idling on the verbena leaf. The dark about him trembled as if awaiting a visitor. The leaves were stirring with the new pressure of the air. The night was full of microscopic traffic as his old friends fled for shelter or emerged to flit and dive in the film of moisture hanging everywhere. He remembered that in his childhood he had lain often under the bushes waiting for the soft explosion of the rain.

"It's amazing," said Myra, who had reached the collaborative stage of female pursuit, "but sometimes when you talk I almost feel that you're not really a member of our species, but an ant or a beetle or something."

Afraid that she had disparaged her admirer, Myra presently amended this.

"I mean with a soul of course."

But Gifford was flattered.

"It's hard to tell what we are," he smiled. "We have only our mind to figure with—and it's difficult to think out any of the mysteries of which we are only so small a part."

Myra had no such difficulty.

"I believe in the transmigration of souls," she said, throwing back her head.

"Fairytales," said Gifford, after a pause, "are likely to contain just as much truth as science. For, whatever Truth is, it seems to express itself as much in fantasies as in facts. Every movement of our mind is inspired by the Truth that exists forever outside it. Who knows but we will yet discover that our myths are the real science and that science is the only myth?"

"Then you do believe in soul transmigration!" Myra cried. "You do! Please don't deny it!"

"I never deny anything," Gifford said patiently. "All thought is the shadow of some truth we cannot understand. And since we can't ever see the Truth, I think it wise to study all the shadows it casts and to discount none of them."

"How wonderful that we should both believe in soul transmigration!" Myra chanted.

This was too much for Gifford.

"I don't know anything about soul transmigration," he said a little angrily. Then he added, more for the sake of politeness:

"However, Nature is so economical, it may be she uses her forces over and over. Perhaps she does this with the spirit of life, and perhaps this life force continues like a never-broken thread on which she strings the endless little brittle beads of our bodies."

"Oh, to come back to life again as a bird!" cried Myra, carried away by what she felt to be their mutual understanding. "Oh, to fly, to sing, to—"

"It would be terrible for the bird," Gifford interrupted in alarm. "A bird with a human soul in it, even the remains of such a soul, would be a most ridiculous and incompetent fowl. I can't bear to think of anything in Nature so handicapped."

The rain came. A mist and an odor trickled into the little clearing. The roof of leaves resounded with the rain clamor.

Gifford was silent. It occurred to Myra that he was a very strange man. She sat up and looked at him. He was sitting, ears cocked to the wild hum of the rain. She watched his dark unflickering eyes and wondered what they were seeking in the night. He seemed to have fallen into a trance. She touched his hand to waken him, but his curious expression remained unchanged. The round black eyes protruded, empty and sage-like. The thin lips were curled inward over the teeth. The entire face glistened with so mad a preoccupation that Myra shivered. Gifford's face seemed for an instant like something brittle rising out of the grass and regarding the night with an ominous and secret understanding.

"What are you thinking?" Myra asked softly.

"Nothing," Gifford answered. "I wasn't thinking."

Myra drew nearer to his side.

"How foolish people seem in the rain," said Gifford suddenly, "as if rain were no longer meant for them. They've left the breast of Nature."

"Is there no way back for us?" asked Myra. "I mean, for those who understand?"

"No," said Gifford, "we're on our way somewhere else."

After its first gusts, the rain dwindled. Myra decided that the climax of their tryst had been passed.

They walked back arm in arm to the university. On this night Gifford was too preoccupied to smile when he left her.

After Myra McKillup had listened to Professor Emmett for a month she put an end to his talk by marrying him. There is no need to go into the tender and unscrupulous progressions at the end of which our hero found himself before the altar. He was a little amazed and considerably bewildered. After having been blessed by the minister and kissed by the bride, Gifford suddenly asserted himself. He refused to go on a honeymoon.

He announced, a little tardily, that he had been looking forward to these three summer months as a perfect time to investigate the stomach of the termite. He was determined, Gifford firmly told his bride on their way home, to solve the riddle of the parasites that inhabited this wood-devouring insect's stomach. It was these parasites that provided the termite, to Gifford's never-ending amazement, with a digestive apparatus omitted by Nature in its construction.

Seated in his apartment, now newly curtained and groomed out of recognition, Gifford did his best to explain the intricacies of the problem to his bride. And technical though this problem was, I feel its details are entitled to the precedence given them by the bridegroom. His investigations into the termite's digestive phenomena, started on the day of his marriage, were to mean more to him than the pathetic relationship into which he had been whisked. They were to outlast this union and even himself, and they were—in these pages at least—to place his name on the small scroll of heroes. I shall therefore join Gifford Emmett in elbowing aside his marital duties in favor of the colony of termites to which he hurried right after the wedding ceremony.

Gifford's interest in the parasites that served the termite in the place of digestive organs antedated by many years his wooing of Myra McKillup. He had, as he explained soothingly to Myra, often watched these microscopic mills at work. The parasites and not the insect converted into a nutritive pulp the otherwise fatal wood cellulose it consumed. It was indeed odd that the termite, considered by scientists the most essential mouth in Nature, should be lacking in its own digestive equipment. For it was the termite whose unique and diminutive jaws were the pestles that ground death into life. They transmuted the cadavers of trees into that womb of nitrate which is earth. Without this spectacular work done by the termites, as Gifford had often informed his students, the world would have hardened into a vitrified and unproductive crust long ago. The mundane detail that in their heroic task as earth-makers the termites also nibbled away a few wooden houses seemed to Gifford hardly worthy of consideration. The termites were of vastly more importance to the world than the handful of people they inconvenienced. Yet for this vast and scientific task, Nature had devised an incomplete tool. The stomach of the termite was incapable of the miracle assigned it. Its labor was contracted out to parasites.

Concerning this, Gifford had a theory which he admitted (to his petulant bride) was more romantic than scientific. He sometimes thought that the very importance of the task had inspired Nature to divide its execution so mysteriously. Thus, if something disastrous happened to the termites as a species, the parasites, much more invulnerable, would survive to seek out another ally within which to carry on the great work.

But the greatest riddle to him (Gifford also confided to Myra) was that of the parasite's genesis in the insect's stomach. For the termite was born innocent of them. They showed up later, a work-crew arriving as if by magic to take up the business of converting the earth's dead wood into life-giving soil. On the death of the termite they departed. Gifford was determined to uncover the secret of the parasites' arrival.

Two theories attracted him. Either the newly born termites acquired their work-crew from the excrement of their older fellows, on which they fed and which served as a transport service for the parasites; or the termites were part of a double birth phenomenon truly unique in Nature. It was possible that they were born with parasite eggs already in their useless stomachs and that these eggs contained their supplementary selves.

Myra was left during the long days of her honeymoon to contemplate these matters and a few others even more disturbing. But for Gifford his parasite hunt was the happier side of marriage. He secured the help of Professor Gerald Canning, an accomplished biological chemist, with whom he spent the greater part of his honeymoon.

But Gifford's home life can no longer be ignored. Even Gifford was becoming aware of certain challenging factors in it. The first and most disturbing of these was that in marrying the provocative Miss McKillup he had suddenly found himself locked away with a companion to whom he was totally unable to talk.

The explanation for this evaded our confused bridegroom. Like so many men Gifford had been lured into wedlock not by a woman but by a superior version of himself risen genie-fashion out of his bottled existence. It was, in a sense, himself he had married. He had taken a witty and exuberant Professor Emmett to the altar, and apparently left him there.

This hidden and evanescent self, which the most unlikely of women are able to evoke in us, is one of the chief causes of marital disaster. Its disappearance at the first breakfast table gives the groom the uneasy impression that he is bewitched. The phenomenon occurs most often to unsexual men in whom the mating instinct gives birth to personality rather than desire. Enchanted by their vivified personalities, these bridegrooms collapse like a jack-in-the-box at the first conjugal caress. The superiority born during their courtship is almost instantly deflated in the marriage bed. The former lover full of dreams and rhetoric vanishes like an impostor. There is left an inferior and useless husband.

Gifford was thus stranded. The situation of the incompetent male has long been a comic fixture. But it inspires less laughter today than in heartier times. There is a phase of sex of which the world is becoming sadly more and more aware. It is the fact that the generative organs have a deeper capacity for giving pain than pleasure. Normality, pleasing and diverting though it be, rarely lifts the soul higher than the bedposts. Abnormality, however, can plunge it down into Hell.

It is perhaps to insure our survival as a species—as Gifford might have explained it—that Nature places such a penalty on the absence of sex in us, and invests its lack with such irrational agonies and confusions. Though love, to the male, is usually a minor diversion, his inability to love becomes an entire career. It became, and quickly, the whole consideration of the loveless Emmett household.

The issue, at the beginning, was not of Gifford's making. Although cast down by his lack as a husband, Gifford was inclined to regard the matter in its perspective. It had no bearing on his labors of dissecting the termite stomach, which he considered his real lifework. The absence of any sensual interest in Miss McKillup came as no surprise to him. Neither she nor any other woman had stirred even so much as curiosity in his head. He would have been as much astounded at any evidence of passion in himself as if he had grown horns. Accordingly he had weathered the first nights with more distaste than panic and hurried off to his termite colony with the childish hope that his incompetence would soon turn his bride's attention to other matters.

Although innocent, he had brought to his nuptial couch a curious sex lore gained from watching through a magnifying glass the libidinous moments in the lives of his spiders, beetles, and ants. His shyness before the swooning Myra was a little complicated by these memories of cohabitings studied since his boyhood. The hundred fierce little dramas of insect amour, whose details he had fully recorded in notebooks, bewildered him on his own bridal night as much as the memories of any rake. There was one scene in particular that kept recurring to him during his first days as a groom. It was the mating of a praying mantis observed seven times enlarged under his glass.

He had come upon the affaire mantis just as the female, lean and spectral, had permitted the woefully lesser male on her back. He had watched the tall and dreadful bride turn her serpent head and begin slowly munching on the passionately employed lover. The Romeo's head, wings, legs,. and torso had disappeared under the razor-edged jaws of his mate. Yet this headless, legless, armless, but still enfevered swain had continued at his devotions. There had remained of him finally little more than a sexual organ. This, still alert and full of lubricity had concluded by itself the act of love.

Gifford's imagination fastened on this spectacle the moment Myra emerged from her dressing-room in a creamy, green-dappled negligee with flaring sleeves, and held out her arms to him. The costume had instantly reminded Gifford of the hieratic and macabre wings of the mantis used by that ogress to bewitch her prey. He had said nothing of this to Myra. He felt during the following days, however, that he would be unable to embrace her as his wife as long as she reminded him, by coloration and gesture, of that cannibal insect.

On the fifth day of his marriage Gifford stopped on his way home from Professor Canning's laboratory to buy Myra a blue unpatterned negligee with tight sleeves. Myra, whose sex lore had not been acquired through a magnifying glass, accepted the gift without understanding. She kissed her husband gratefully, but appeared that night in the creamy, green-dappled, mandarin-sleeved transparency which she believed to be extremely seductive. Gifford shuddered, broke into a cold sweat, and clung fearfully to his own bed. After some minor caresses Myra retired to her pillows. She lay for a long time considering the various courses open to her in this combat with Gifford's virginity.

Left alone during the day, Myra preoccupied herself with what now appeared to her a tragic matter. She went over in her mind her own experiences. Though limited to the oarsman and a youthful cousin seduced during her own adolescence, these had left her with a workman-like knowledge of sex. She was also well read on the subject. Her thirst for wisdom of every sort had led her to devour numerous books on sexual abnormalities. Like most young women of the time she had substituted Freud for Browning and was as versed in the horrors of love-making as her sisters had once been in its poetry. But Myra's mind being a sieve, neither her experience nor her reading availed her. Her therapy was reduced to clumsy attempts at rape. All this rough-and-tumble wantonness failed to help the bridegroom. The impression only deepened in Gifford that if there ever was a praying mantis, here was one in his bed.

My attitude toward Myra is, perhaps, unfair. It occurs to me that the ex-Miss McKillup was a young woman lacking in malice or any of the villainies of temperament that wives so often bring as their sole dowries to marriage. She was neither possessive nor given to that home-wrecking preoccupation with her mirror which vainer faces, or prettier ones, adopt as a career. Her heart was kind, and her delusions of being a superior woman were for the most part harmless and inarticulate. She felt deeply on the subject of the professor's prestige and future, and was awed, as she should have been, by his talents. And no one could have asked of Gifford's wife a more hopeful scientific prognosis for his single but vital failing.

Yet with all these qualities I am inclined to accept Gifford's first nuptial glimpse of her as a praying mantis. She would devour him a little more subtly than that rapier-bodied, balloon-winged horror of the insect world. But devour him in the end she would. Stupidity is the cannibalism of the female. It is able, no less than razor-edged teeth, to devour men of talent.

Gifford Emmett did not live long enough to be either devoured or uncolored by the commonplaceness of the woman he had married. He underwent, however, some preliminary fading, just as Myra exhibited that first blossoming of a vocabulary enlarged by his phrases which would have resulted in time in that pathetic common denominator that Strindberg has named "the marriage likeness."

During this first and only year, however, Myra was too busy in other spell-weaving directions to have any influence on Gifford as a mind and an entomologist. She had fallen to work during the first flush of their honeymoon on turning Gifford into a male—which, by the way, is about the only thing women can't turn us into. They can clip our wings and turn us into barnyard companions. Or dip our sandals in the glue of their devotion and turn us into domestic statuary. But men they cannot make of us. It seems a pity, too, that the alchemists who are able to transmute us into the gold of husbandhood can do so little about the simple backwardness of our glands. But the truth is that perhaps the only medicine that fails utterly as a cure for male impotence is a woman. Exercise, a change of diet, an ocean trip, diathermy, a confession to the police, a rise in the stock market—these are among the numerous therapies for a shy libido. At least they are harmless. But the female rampant as a panacea is not only useless but as menacing as the unrestricted sale of arsenic. In her avid arms, impotency, a minor disease if there ever was one, turns into lunacy.

Not that there was any hope for Gifford's insufficiency. My poor hero was as lost to the joys of sex as any parthenogenic worm. His spinal cord was as detached from the signaling female as if it were a-flutter in the wind.

Yet, there is this point—before his marriage Gifford had not suffered from his missing libido. He had been, I admit, the victim of a melancholia that had led him unassisted to the portals of death. But it was a poetical and uncrystallized melancholia. Neither a doting wife nor, later, medical science, had stripped him of his toga as a philosopher. Had he died at that time he would have been buried with his soul intact. It was a serpent's trick to give him of the apple to eat and to send him cowering and outcast to his grave.

Gifford's cowering began in the third month of his marriage. Before that time he worked feverishly over his termites. He filled scores of notebooks. He sought to hide his unserviceable masculinity in other industries. But there is no concealment for a man who has found a part of himself ridiculous. The canker will eat away his conquests, and his one little useless organ, like a worm, will devour his greatness.

Finding himself night after night stretched beside a woman, and always as futile and absurd as if he were a bit of rotten cork, Gifford began to lose his character. The mornings found him more and more morose. He arrived at the laboratory with a clouded eye. Week by week the talents he had developed came to seem less than those he had been born without.

His impotence finally spread to the ants. He was as unable to deal satisfactorily with the termites as with Myra. Soon he was no longer able to eat properly. A tremor made his delicate research work impossible. Sleep withheld itself. Nightmares rode his bed. He grew gaunt and a little stooped. A harried look gleamed from his eyes. His desire to become a male, and his increasing psychic efforts toward that end, had been received apparently as a declaration of war by his well-armed subconscious. A conflict had started in Gifford, and his organs became a befogged battleground. He sat around twitching and bedeviled with the echoes of this hidden warfare.

In the fourth month Myra insisted that he consult a psychoanalyst. It was only fair to both of them, Myra argued, that he turn to science, since love had failed. Gifford resisted. His soul rebelled against this picture of itself being stripped like an onion in an analyst's office. His wisdom shuddered before the thought of being treated as if it were the layers of a disease. How foolish it seemed to him then to reduce the jewels of the mind and all its talents to the symptomatology of inert glands, to make of himself an enemy and harry himself like a traitor. But, as Myra pointed out, he *was* his enemy. His mind, brilliant though it was, must be regarded as the foe of Nature. And Gifford hung his head as his theories came home to roost. He saw himself as among the pioneers of disintegration. He was tasting the future of the species which must end, as he had prophesied, in the laboratory as patients. And so Gifford Emmett and all his wisdom and talents went to the doctor.

There has been in my generation such a blathering on the subject of psychiatry and its capricious twin—psychoanalysis—that I hesitate before this last phase of Gifford's life. I have no desire to reshuffle those new terminologies by which medicine has crept another millimeter into the vast dark of the human being. But this is hardly a time to desert my hero. And if we both sound a little befuddled, there is no help for it. The science of charting our subconscious—that secondary bloodstream that flows through us without arteries or tissues to mark its course—is a work so in its infancy that all who discuss it must sound in some way infantile.

The notion that it is possible to reshape our souls and play shoemaker to our tattered egos is perhaps the most ambitious project since the Tower of Babel. And at present at least its success looks as dubious. Its artisans are already screaming at one another in languages nobody can understand. But this may be only the disorder that attends the launching of all great tasks and not the confusion that marks their collapse.

I am not certain but, standing beside my hero in his travail, I am inclined to believe the former as the truth. In a time to come these Maestros of the Spirit Ducts may be able to reset a psychosis as easily as they do a bone. Chants, rituals, sesames may be discovered which, better than the scourges of our ancestors, will be able to drive the unwanted devils of Neurosis from their lurking places. A race of Mood Surgeons will attend our gall bladders, and medical Dostoievskys will operate on our dreams to cure us of such ills as stem from them. It may even become known and proved in the time that I foresee that all ailments, including the ravages of bacteria, and the accidents by which we break our necks, are no more than visitations hatched by our wills. And it may even be that on that day when Disease and Death have been identified as the effluvia of disordered Thought, we will seek for immortality on the analyst's couch.

There is of course nothing new to this theory except that it has come to be regarded by organized medicine a little more as science than imbecility. How sensible this change of attitude is, only the layman will eventually be able to say, for he is, in medicine as in politics, ultimately the proof of the pudding. The prognostications that doctors have to make concerning their own business, their judgments of what is science and what is quackery, can be more or less dismissed, historically.

In fact one would think that, confronted by a history so dubious as their own, so full of greed, bigotry, and organized outcries against every bit of medical fact that has been uncovered, its present custodians might feel hesitant about coming again to final conclusions. They have only to look in the dusty corners of the centuries to see them full of pale savants groping for mysteries beyond the purgatives and operating tables of their day, and discovering these mysteries, only to be ridiculed and cast out by Contemporary Medicine.

The biologist and his little umbrella-carrier, the doctor, have always been slow to yield the small ground they have won for the ever-befogged and uncharted spaces of the New—first asepsis, then endocrinology, now psychiatry. The sons of Hippocrates struggled violently enough against their elevation from barbers to medicos. How much more will they battle against a fate that now asks of them that they be geniuses!

The case of Gifford Emmett will, in a way, bear out what sanity there is in their aversion to psychoanalysis, and mine—not to mention the cases of my friends, who, with the aid of these present-day soul searchers, are committing everywhere around me a sort of intellectual hara-kiri in their efforts to outwit their ills. The condition of these friends—my contemporary neurotics—seems to me truly as pathetic as was that of the ancient lepers whom science sought to cure by the application of hot irons to the afflicted parts.

Our current lepers have their attention now scientifically directed to the obscene and idiotic waywardness of their souls. The rubbish heaps of their subconscious are turned over for their dazed inspection. Their wounds thus uncovered, and their hideous diseases thus exposed, they are handed diplomas that entitle them to cure themselves. Having given them a bad name, the scientist in charge washes his hands of them. It is presumed that, once a patient has located the sickening part of himself, he will vomit it out or rid himself of it elsewhere by virtue of some spiritual physic of which the doctor has no knowledge, but which he is sure exists in the pharmacopoeia of the patient. Thus the new therapy is placed in the hands of quacks and amateurs, for what else is a layman and particularly a diseased one? It is no wonder that most of these pathetically combined doctor-patients are bundled off to asylums to scream away their convalescence, or, more therapeutically, to put a bullet through their brains.

Dr. Oliver Jerome, the soul searcher into whose office Gifford was piloted by Myra, was an extremely talented man with an instinct for spiritual anatomy that soon won his patients. Gifford was immediately attracted by this new lens under which he was placed. His own keenness grasped quickly the manner of its operation. And instead of the repugnance he had anticipated, he felt himself being drawn into that friendship for the dark-eyed, placid-faced Dr. Jerome which is the first step of the "cure."

The human being has a remarkable and tireless gift for loving himself, or at least for being fascinated by himself, and he will fasten his gratitude on anyone who assists him in this direction. Within a week Gifford felt deeply attached to his ally—the analyst. The quiet-spoken, unemotional questioner seemed to him both guide and matchmaker. The analyst's eye that looked on human sins as if they were blood cells removed Gifford's social sensitiveness. He was able to experience the thrill of encountering the unknown in himself without embarrassment. He became oddly pleased to discover that his soul was as full of intrigue as a nest of spies and that the Gifford Emmett he had known was a sort of Character-President who had achieved office through the political chicanery of his subconscious.

This first uncovering of self is usually a delight to the neurotic. He embraces with elation the new features revealed, and sees in their often horrid and despicable aspect the mystic charm of kinship that our own always has for us. For a time he is actually happy to meet the disheveled Cromwells of his underworld, and he feels himself, giddily, as full of local color as a slum. Later, when this colony of gangsters and perverts on whom he opened a door loses its novelty, his elation is likely to give way to disgust. On his return to his capitol, the patient grows haunted by the chicanery and lawlessness of his own government. And sometimes in his disgust he abdicates.

This, briefly, was the history of Gifford's analysis. During the first days spent with the analyst, he fumbled nervously with his memories. In the second week, Gifford was in full cry after his past. Dr. Jerome, delighted by the eagerness and intelligence of his patient, explained they were trying to discover the origin of his aversion to sex. It was necessary to locate the exact moment in which the patient had decided on the criminal career of impotency.

Gifford offered his theory of the praying mantis, and related excitedly the many points in common which he had detected between that baleful insect and his wife. Dr. Jerome listened patiently to these somewhat lyric comparisons and then informed Gifford that the mantis religiosa was only a ruse to distract him from the deeper, darker truth of his ailment. Guiding him past the mantis, Dr. Jerome led his patient inexorably back to the scene of his crime. This turned out to be the wind-swept room in the Wisconsin home in which Gifford Emmett had been born. On the way back to this room poor Gifford ran the gamut of father-hatred and mother-fixation and a score of other criminal selves. Each day he was whisked along these byways and sent stumbling further into his past, until he arrived before the true and implacable enemy of his life. This was the tiny emerging infant that had, after a fashion, gladdened the Emmett home one snow-bound morning.

Dr. Jerome, aided by Gifford's memory of family tales, discovered that the little visitor had wanted none of this world. Spanked into existence, the indignant tot had devoted the rest of his life to a kind of suicide. Unable to get back into the womb for whose warmth he yearned, little Gifford had compromised on an aversion to all life outside it. Dr. Jerome was certain that if not for the currant bushes his patient would have willed himself into some form of idiocy. Gifford pathetically agreed that his learning was no more than a ruse by which he had evaded the world of reality. He agreed that his philosophy of hatred of humanity was the flowering of his original aversion to the doctor's forceps. As for his sexual impotence, Gifford saw that it was part of his fixed decision to remain, as much as was possible under the adverse conditions of maturity, a child in the womb. He was a little confused by Dr. Jerome's added hint that his frigidity toward Myra involved also a fear of committing incest.

In the seventh month of the analysis, Gifford was in full possession of his criminal history. His elation over his unknown selves had long since left him. He had returned to his capitol, and there he sat brooding and helpless. He mastered the conception of himself as an intricate and tireless suicide, and there he halted. He understood that his cure lay in his ability to dispatch his infant nemesis with some mystic *coup de grâce*. But how does one destroy one's oldest self? And with what weapons can one attack that which is deeper than the mind?

Gifford retired into himself and remained there with a futile, moody smile signaling defeat from his lips. His wisdom, silent since the first hour of his marriage, reasserted itself. It considered the quality and strength of his enemy. It measured him by all the science at his command and it came to certain conclusions.

I shall report Gifford's words on this subject because they were the last movement of his human-bound mind. Myra heard them excitedly, for she hoped that the analysis was bearing fruit. She was unaware that Gifford had risen finally from his analyst's couch only to speak his epitaph.

"I should like to believe," said Gifford, sitting with Myra in their lonely home, "that it is possible to re-educate the human soul. But I doubt whether even Dr. Jerome has been able to convince himself of this. For how can one re-educate the soul when it is obvious that it is impossible to educate it at all in the first place? The womb, alas, is the only university from which we may graduate with honors. The rest of our schooling adds hardly a credit to our standing. For the life particles of which we have been compounded have completed their studies before Nature entrusts us to the world. They have even completed our particular design. Our glands contain the full album of our photographs. The amount of our hair, its situation and duration, our height, weight, and coloring; our capacities for love and hate and even the nature of those who are to stir our emotions—all these are written in our embryos. The strength of our muscles and length of our bones, the very bent of our talents—whether we shall sing or be mute, whether we shall think brilliantly or dully or not at all; our politics and hobbies, in fact, are assigned us in the womb. Our thousand moods as well as many of our physical mannerisms are all predetermined for us by the quality of our thyroid, pituitary, adrenal, pineal, and other bits of tissue. We can move only in the directions charted for us in these glands. The distances we may cover are also fixed. We are, in the main, as predetermined as the insects—but less perfectly so. For there is left for us a small margin of chance and an even smaller one of effort. Within this little margin we are permitted to rattle around like peas in a pod. It is this pathetic movement we call our individualism, free will, divine independence, and so on.

"Seeing ourselves complete this way when we are born, with our destiny inscribed in every gland, I can't understand Dr. Jerome's theory that we are capable of rewriting our fate—that is, if he has such a theory.

"I am afraid," said Gifford, "that my cure lies in a more practical rebirth than our psychiatrist has to offer."

A look of torment came into his eyes and he muttered almost inaudibly: "It's not pleasant to be a human being."

Myra squeezed his hand tenderly, but Gifford continued to look fixedly at his shoes.

"Dr. Jerome's science is not impressive," he said at length. "But for that matter no science is very impressive. If you look back on what the Mind has thought since its first known statement, there's only one thing worth noting. This is the fact that its thinking invariably turns out to have been comic. Today's truth becomes tomorrow's jest. The Mind is always a hero to its own generation and usually a clown to the following. It is well to remember that we are in the midst of a constant yesterday of folly.

"The tale of who and what we are," Gifford said sadly, "is the tale told by a Peeping Tom flitting from one keyhole to another. Our knowledge is full of scandal and rumor, but none of it has seen the face of life or looked even for an instant into its eyes."

Gifford finished and stood up. He smiled for a moment on the alien woman whom he had married, and then went to his room. In the morning Gifford Emmett was found dead. Beside him was the bottle which Myra had taken a year before from his lips. It was empty. Myra, who had come into the room to waken Gifford, stood looking at his body with more amazement than grief. It was curled up, the knees clutched against the chin, and the head tucked down in a sightless and yet pleasant-seeming sleep.

II

Now that we know that the spirit of the tree returns to the earth, to be born again as loam, mushroom, or forget-me-not; now that we have discovered that when sea-water dies, algae appear to breathe back to it those very chemicals that had fled its dead and mighty cheek; now that we have mastered, however vaguely, the fact that all matter is a transitory display of eternal energy, and that there is no destruction but only renewal, it will be an aborigine of a reader, indeed, who sneers with incredulity at the bewildering fate that turned Gifford Emmett into an ant.

I say bewildering because, despite the assurances of science, there are some things I don't understand about it. I understand fully that the human spirit is chemically related to the sap of the vegetable and the whinny of the Unicorn and shares their fate. All that lives must ride and bob along on the same curving but unbroken seminal river. The headwaters of this eternal stream are unknown, and the Sea of Death into which it empties is another vast and unknown place. We know only the little landscape between that we call Nature. Having completed our brief excursion on this bright river, we very likely become part of some piece of legerdemain such as the sun performs on the sea. We, too, are probably lifted out of the Sea of Death and precipitated again into the hidden headwaters. And I can understand fully that this evaporation must be a fine democratic sight—that a man, a crocodile, and a gnat all evaporate, as it were, together into one great mystic cloud. And out of this far-away womb we come tumbling out again in an anonymous and intermingled cloudburst, hailstorm, or drizzle. We are returned to life as capriciously as weather. And out of this reservoir of vibrations or, at best, a sort of laboratory mist, we must not expect to emerge in the guise we entered. This would indeed be preposterous. We are re-costumed for our new excursions out of a most chaotic wardrobe. And it is our fate that any cap fits, whether it be a rooster's comb or a bishop's miter.

Of these matters I am fully cognizant and I can thus understand Gifford's reappearance as an ant. I could, if I wished to devote more space to the problem, explain it in considerable detail. But still one phase of it bewilders me. This bewilderment does not lie in the fact that Gifford became an ant but that he remained a human being. There I am a little at sea as an explainer.

I can only state categorically that Gifford's soul passed unchanged into the newly laid egg of a termite in the low Sierras to the southwest of the Republic. What the psychic and intellectual points were that made the new-laid termite still Professor Emmett, I shall eschew for the time being. Also, if there is something more mysterious in Gifford's appearance as a California termite than as a Wisconsin infant—in itself a very mysterious matter if you stop to think of it—it is an increase of mystery on which we had all better turn our backs if we wish to avoid too much confusion.

The egg out of which Gifford emerged was one of some fifty thousand that waited constantly, mob-fashion, for egress from the belly of the termite Queen. It was the habit of this ovarian monster to pump some five to ten thousand of her children daily into the royal bed. Each of these remarkable litters contained, in a ratio deemed proper, supplies of workers, nurses, agriculturalists, soldiers, and lovers. (Since Darwin and all the succeeding biologists have failed to explain the phenomenon of an ant hatching a social system, I shall also ignore the explanation. It is obvious that Nature is not only a scientist but a magician too, and, if she chose, cows would give birth to guinea-hens and Minervas to tree-toads.)

Gifford arrived in the contingent of lovers. He was born a male with the single destiny of cohabitation. All other insect learning would be denied him. He would be unable to forage for food. He would lack all equipment for toiling and fighting. Sex would be his lone talent, his delirious and solitary objective.

In the beginning the Gifford Emmett who lay curled in this tiny egg was scarcely any more related in character than in size to his preceding status. There was no more in this egg than a flickering consciousness of previous human estate.

For many days after he was born the new Gifford lay sightless, tiny, and content to be a grub. His human intelligence was the most delicate of obstructions to the perfect passage of time as the insect knows it. It existed like a bubble against which the great chemical currents of insect life swept and whirled. But, bubble though it was, they failed to dislodge or shatter it. The bubble persisted and within it, as within a secondary body, Gifford's human soul grew stronger.

When he had reached his third instar, having shed his chitinous exterior three times, and acquired the wings that identified him as one of the male reproductives of the kingdom, the human Gifford awoke sufficiently to become aware of his status and surroundings. But he experienced no shock, for what his mind saw appeared to him only the most fascinating of dreams. And, as one accepts in a dream the strange clothing and abortive geographies of the wandering Personality, Gifford accepted with no sense of panic his dwindled guise and amazing habitat. His dream of being an ant pleased him—though not entirely. He would have preferred in his dream to have been an early paleontologic insect with a wing-spread of two feet, and he made an effort to re-transform himself into such a redoubtable coleopteran. But while he could see himself as an elephantine gnat of some sort, the dream ant remained.

By the time of his fourth instar, Gifford had given up his efforts to alter the time and condition of his dream self. He devoted himself amiably to the study of this little phantom. Yet if it were an escape dream, why had he invented himself as a sexual ant? Here, Gifford thought, was something that would tax the psychiatrist's dream-book lore a bit.

He contemplated other things, among them the lineage of his dream figure. It had descended unchanged from lower Oligocene Tertiary times—as was evidenced by its identical amber-imbedded ancestors still in his college laboratory. It stood to reason, likewise, that the activities of the colony in which he lay maturing had also never changed since that far-away time. The government of which he was now a subject had not found it necessary to pass a new law for a million or more years. It had achieved social perfection when man was still lost in the anarchy-ridden debut of his evolution. This pleased Gifford and he was proud to be a member of a kingdom so hoary and glamorous.

In his sixth instar, curiosity beset Gifford. His dream seemed to him too static. He desired adventures. He was accordingly pleased to notice that his termite self was moving about. But even as he nodded with approval (an inward nod which the nonvertebrate termite in no way shared) he became aware of dangers now besetting this sightless and winged dream self. He recalled with a touch of fright that the status of the alate in the termite colony was a most precarious one. For this alate, who alone of all the castes in the kingdom was designed for love, inspired revulsion and rage wherever he appeared. Unequipped for foraging for food himself, he was ignored by the busy workers, who seemed intent on providing food for all mouths but his own. In fact these toilers seemed full of contempt for him and for all his sexual brothers, who lay about dreaming of their coming hour of love in the spring. And the soldiers too exhibited toward him the warrior's distaste for the sybarite. They were constantly decapitating and dismembering the defenseless, half-starved Romeos of his caste, tearing off their wings in what seemed to Gifford nothing more than the sadism of morality.

Wisely, Gifford accepted the fate of his kind in the kingdom, a sort of leper's fate. He must hide away from every one of his fellows, steal his food at the risk of his life, tremble before every clanking troop of warriors that passed, and lead a bedeviled existence that was truly heartbreaking—all this because for one hour in spring he was to enjoy the pleasures of love. It would seem that the State, jealous of its metronomic soul, resented even that exercise of individualism which insured its continuance.

Undeterred by the dangers that beset him, Gifford continued to study the swarming life around him. He saw the workers toiling at their thousand tasks, keeping the ventilator corridors in repair, hurrying down the spiral roads with food for the combination store- and furnace-rooms. He could feel the warmth rising from the decomposing provisions and calculated quickly that winter lay outside.

In addition to the multiple domestic tasks of feeding, cleaning, airing, heating, storing, nursing, and all that occupied the kingdom, there was the constant work of battle. Troops of soldiers were continually a-rush to the outer gates of the kingdom, for here the enemy everlastingly threatened. The black and red ants, scenting the stores of foodstuffs and hungering for the soft bellies of the termites, were forever hurling themselves into the kingdom and advancing down the ventilator roads.

Gifford watched a number of battles. He saw the warrior ants march in formation to meet the enemy, and take their stand like a praetorian guard barring the way of conquest. These armored bullies, whom Gifford had come to hate because of their wanton and vicious manner toward his own daydreaming caste, now became heroes whom even the alates must admire.

He had watched angrily these idling guardsmen standing about so overarmored that they were unable to feed themselves. A sycophantic worker class not only brought them viands but stuffed them in their mouths while these robots stood glowering like visored knights with iron-gloved hands clutching halberds that could never be laid down. But when the tocsin sounded in the termite land, and the alarm of the enemy at the gates was spread through the kingdom by the soldiers, and the corridors echoed with the beating of warrior helmets against enameled walls, Gifford, flattened against a ceiling, would see a rally and a march forward that were unforgettable.

The several battles Gifford witnessed were beyond anything he knew in the history of human heroism. He learned now that the courage of the termite warriors actually modeled their figures from birth, for they wore no armor on their backs. Since they would never turn tail to the enemy, no wasteful protection covered their rears, which were as vulnerable as the bellies of moths.

Calmly and precisely the soldiers advanced to meet the dreaded enemy now streaming down a ventilator corridor. Arrived in one of the vast chambers through which the zigzagging roads of the kingdom ran, the halberdiers would spread into a double-rank formation. Thus they stood barring the way into the interior. The enemy, usually sharp-fanged black ants, came rushing forward. They charged like a mass of little black bulls. Swifter than the termites, their armor more supple, they came in a deadly rain upon the defenders, whom they often outnumbered a thousand to one. Motionless against this tide of shields and sabers, the termite soldiers stood swinging their mace-like claws into the bodies of the swarming enemy. They fought erect. As long as possible, with their legs interlocked, they stood barring the way into the heart of the kingdom. On their courage depended all that was termite. Once past this barrier, the enemy would swarm triumphantly down all the roads of the kingdom, devouring the stores, the workers, and bursting into the royal chamber in murderous waves. Here, with the last of the royal guardsmen destroyed, the feast of the King and Queen would end their conquest. And the vandals who had found a kingdom would leave behind them a tomb in which not a tentacle was left moving.

This knowledge was in the halberds of the termite warriors. They fought on fiercely, piling the dead around them in great heaps. But from the top of these heaps, as from a thousand towers, the enemy continued to hurl himself in ever-increasing numbers. Losing ground, the beleaguered warriors sounded the signal for the reserves. The signal, like a high bugle note, drifted down all the roads of the kingdom, and in answer to it the waiting reservists moved forward. This signal was not only the warriors' cry for help but also their swan song. The reserves arrived, rank on rank of unarmored workers. With their arrival the termite warriors moved forward into the charging enemy. They had saved for this moment their last store of prowess. Erect and implacable, they held off the fanged host, and behind them the reserves worked desperately. They sealed the passage into the kingdom.

Pumping glue and plaster out of their bodies, they walled off the battlefield. The road to life thus cut off for them, the termite warriors gathered themselves into a last phalanx. Left sealed in with the enemy, they were torn to bits by the thwarted hordes.

Gifford watched and admired these constant Thermopylaes. He grew to feel a regard for the clanking militarists in whom burned this great mood of valor and sacrifice which seemed to him a little nobler than his own dream of a spring cohabitation.

And still the half-delusion that these were all fantasies parading in his human sleep held Gifford's mind calm. The delusion remained until his seventh instar. On that day, full grown and finally winged, Gifford tasted for the first time the whole horror of finding himself an ant. His awakening occurred in the following manner. Moving furtively along the deep corridors, he had made his way through encampments of warriors and caravans of workers toward the place he knew existed somewhere in the kingdom and which he had not sufficiently observed in his first metamorphosis. This was the royal chamber of the Queen, where he discovered himself standing presently.

At first his human mind was fascinated by what he saw. But as he stood watching the hailstorm of termite life heroically brought forth in her bed, realization smote him. He became wildly aware that he was not dreaming this sight, that he lay in no bed of his own, hatching fantasies out of his subconscious. This tiny deviled termite standing on the Queen's threshold was himself. These pin-point features, this drop of matter was Gifford Emmett. His human mind was attached like some incredible fungus to an insect. It existed within its tiny structure. It was he, Gifford, who was the dream. And it was the ant who was reality.

With this knowledge, horror streamed through Gifford's mind. Despair erased for a time all his thought. His soul sought to hurl itself out of this minute and suffocating world in which it was trapped. But the insect in which it had its spurious seat clung to it with the clutch of doom. He sought to cry out and like some insect Samson to wreck the pillars of his prison and bring the kingdom crashing down on him and all its subjects. But no sound came from him and, though his mind vaulted, his midge of a body remained motionless. And he realized that he had no powers of expression other than those of an alate. His soul, complete with all its human senses, was not only without face but without talent of utterance.

Recovering slowly from this shock, Gifford found himself clinging to the wall of the great royal gallery and, philosopher that he was, he presently concluded that his condition and new environment were of minor importance.

There were many dead thinkers, mused Gifford, shaken but heroic, who occupied an even smaller space in the world than he did at this moment. And what, he argued, was the human body compared to the operation of reason but a cloud to the sun?

From this it will be seen that Gifford's former notions about the horror of Thought underwent a most thoughtless change no sooner than he had discovered that it was his only human possession. He clung to reason now like a survivor to a wrecked homeland. Despite his former infatuation for bugs of all kinds he refused to consider himself one, now that so ideal an opportunity offered. It was no doubt odd that Gifford, having become one of Nature's superior children this way, should cast his lot so loyally with a species he had always derided. But we are, perhaps, none of us ever ready to be what we dream.

His mind careening in the rapids of these revelations, Gifford opened his eyes again to the monster mother on her couch. Monster was a poor word, he mused, shuddering at what he saw. The termite Queen was no new sight to him, but it was one thing to have studied her as a scientist and another to look on her as one's progenitor. This new view held Gifford spellbound and nauseated. Two thousand times bulkier than any of her children, for she was six inches long, three inches tall, and as many thick, the Queen lay motionless like the figure of Mother Earth at the core of the world. Her great saucer eyes were sightless. Her legs hung from her as useless as feather fans. She was neither animal nor insect but a fount of life—a God-like ovary that hatched by itself an entire race. For there were no other mothers in her world. Within the great clay ball swarming with myriads of her progeny, she alone gave birth.

In the chamber all about her, several thousand soldiers stood guard. They were picked troops, taller and more unwieldy-looking than those of the corridor encampments. They stood immobile, as the workers fed them. A stream of caterers also attended the Queen. Her gigantic face, gray and bloated and lost in a spermatic dream, swarmed with subjects bearing food. These kept her mouth constantly filled, stuffing its monster jaws with cellulose pulp, dung, and the mangled bodies of her own children. She munched constantly as she lay. Another stream of attendants presided over her continuous accouchements. As the eggs issued from her in an unbroken larval ribbon, the medical caste hurried them off to the nurseries of the kingdom.

And Gifford, watching the horrid manner of his birth, saw too the ugly mechanics of his conception. He saw the pallid King, half the size of his consort, come dragging himself like some sack of concupiscence to the royal bed. The movement of this gouty Lothario made him more horrible-seeming than his inert mate. This, like the Queen, was no longer an insect but a mass of seed, an ugly and bloated servant of Nature, servile with lust. His very eyes were distended with sperm. Pale, crippled, and unrecognizable as one of his family, he dragged his volcanic loins toward his immobile bride. Slowly he mounted her and Gifford beheld the disemboweling deed of creation.

The cordon of warriors also looked on. Dwarfed by the occupants of the royal bed, they seemed like homunculi defending a throne. They watched the deed with awe, for it was the holiness of the kingdom, the chant to creation. There was no other sire in the land and no other such deed anywhere. The writhing Monarch astride the Queen was her single lover. From his loins poured the immortality of the colony.

The thought came to Gifford that this ritual before him was his own future. He had been born to breast the thousands of hazards of death that lay on the way to the insect throne. If he survived them, he too would become a king. Even now these were the precarious hours of his apprenticeship. And hours even more laden with death awaited him. He would be among the thousands of kingly aspirants who swarmed out of the termite fortress into the world of spring. There in the open, he would seize on a mate. Around the multitude of bedazzled lovers that coupled in the maddening light of life, all Nature would be waiting, ready to devour. Lizards, spiders, black ants, frogs, everything that crawled or leaped or flew, would swoop upon the orgiastic nuptials and dine on them.

But there would be a few who survived. These would drag themselves wingless and exhausted into some burrow to found a new kingdom, to copulate endlessly, to hatch new myriads of workers, lovers, and soldiers, to grow into twin monsters of lubricity. Gifford, watching the bloated Monarch and his insatiable Queen, turned his thought coldly against such a future. His human aversion to sex was multiplied a thousandfold.

He left the royal chamber. Weak with hunger, he crept through a crack into an abandoned room recently the scene of some mighty battle. Around him he saw the disfigured warrior bodies all fallen forward on their faces, and the enemy dead. Gifford paused and feasted.

When it had gorged itself with its first full meal in weeks, Gifford's alate self started forward. It moved slowly, for it was burdened with food. Gifford's mind grew alarmed. He knew the fate that awaited the lethargic insect, and he turned his thought for the first time to the control of the alate's movements. For several minutes Gifford saw that both he and the alate continued to crawl slowly toward the distant corridors filled with clanking soldiers and inimical workers. But as he exerted what he hoped were hypnotic powers, the insect stopped moving. He remained uncertain whether his will had curbed the termite, or some tropism. Nevertheless, a sense of triumph came over him as the insect crept into a niche, where, safe from all dangers, it fell asleep.

At least, he exulted, he, Gifford, would not have to submit to being dragged about willy-nilly by an ant. He could bend it, evidently, to his own desires, even though the process by which he was able to dominate the insect seemed not only mysterious to Gifford but at variance with his learning as an entomologist. But whatever the situation was between himself and his ant self, he would soon determine it, Gifford assured himself. No entomologist had ever been so ideally equipped and situated for research.

Now there were other, more pressing, matters. These were his Thoughts. Like Robinson Crusoe's few possessions salvaged from the shipwreck, they must first be put in order.

He had just learned that he was an ant, and had survived the shock. Now he had to admit he was Gifford. For proof, he had been calling himself by that name. And otherwise, too, as far as he could make out, he was everything he had been before, even, he sighed mentally, to the point of being Myra's husband. Regarded externally, it is true, he seemed no more than an ant, but, observed from within, his learning, sense of personality, and human consciousness were intact as Gifford Emmett.

This raised the question—and one that might fascinate any psychologist, Gifford thought—of what constituted a man. Were he to crawl in his present guise before any group of scientists and address them to the effect that the human body was an unwieldy and superfluous masquerade, Gifford doubted whether a single one of the scientists would remain long enough to hear him out. And those who didn't bolt would identify him as a mass hallucination perhaps, and hurry off to some other scientist, maybe Dr. Jerome, to be cured of delusions.

On the whole, after musing for some time, Gifford was glad that the structure of the termite was too rudimentary to permit of speech.

Not that he feared he would drive any of his former colleagues into any serious aberrations. Considering the shocks he himself had just survived, the sanity of his former species seemed to him well-nigh indomitable. Besides, Gifford was too well aware of the propensity of orthodox science for ruling out unruly facts from their organized learning—thus making man's reason doubly safe.

But why, mused Gifford, when they had so much prettier theologies, should he attempt to substitute the promise of anthood for that of Heaven, if indeed such a metempsychosis as his own were the rule, and not the exception? (Since his courtship, Gifford disliked the word transmigration.)

This left him all alone with his immediate problem. This problem was to ponder, first, the generality of man's survival, then its relation to his own specific rebirth, and, finally, to compute, if possible, the various eventualities before him.

He eliminated as unimportant any question of the generality of rebirth. The immortality of the human soul was, after all, the most ancient of theories, and, *ipso facto*, he considered it proven.

As for his own rising from the grave as an ant rather than an angel, this was a more intricate idea. For one thing, it left him at least no closer to the bosom of God than he had been as a university professor. Then, it had not enlarged his wisdom according to the popular theory, but neither had it removed such enlightenment as he had, for which he found himself now wonderfully grateful.

In fact, closing his mind to any disputation for a moment, Gifford for the first time in his two lives repeated slowly and gently the words of a voluntary prayer. He pleaded with the Lord to accept a humble ant and open His arms to its wandering soul. And from this deed he learned the power of prayer as a bulwark against the extremely unusual.

At this point, although it was a far cry from his own Bible school Deity to the Hindu, his scientific mind obliged Gifford to take such a leap. He recognized in this older myth of the genus Homo a perfectly serviceable theory, according to which he was now scheduled for numerous incarnations. Death after death would probably be his, and also life after life. He would persist through these as Vishnu, Krishna . . . or, far more likely, he corrected himself, once he was through with the ant, as a moth, a lizard, and so on.

And here the disquieting question offered itself to Professor Emmett in all its darkness and bedevilment. Why, *why*, had he survived as Gifford Emmett? What possible purpose could Nature have had in fashioning an ant man?

The answer was inescapable. Professor Emmett found himself with no choice but to admit that something must have gone amiss with his death and the mechanics of his survival. He was no soul at all pursuing its normal orbit after death. He was a mistake. Owing to some aberration of Nature, he had entered this termite stage as Professor Emmett instead of arriving incognito as the pure spirit of life. Death had obviously blundered and forgotten to strip him of his useless human consciousness. He was at large in the Unknown as an interloper.

And now he faced the prospect of being doomed to exist—as a Professor Emmett forgotten by Nature—through an eternity of anthills and birds' nests and fish hatcheries. He might even find himself meditating amid the electrons of inorganic matter and forced to lie about for aeons as a stone. This thought that he was ordained to travel through the wonders of Nature like some perpetual tourist grew stronger in Gifford. Just as he had been born unfit for his former world, he had been reborn unfit for the Unknown. Gifford asked himself sadly if there was any profound and secret reason for his having been appointed eternal freak. Perhaps there was some pattern in his mismaking, some plot of which he was a mysterious part?

At this point, remarkable doings aroused Gifford from his scientific inquiry. A great commotion filled the kingdom. Gifford entered the senses of his termite self, now astir, the better to understand what was going on. A series of astonishing impressions smote him. Although blind, the alate was capable of a curious kind of sight. It saw reality as an inward dream. No objects existed for it, but it was as full of visions as a saint. Gifford applied himself eagerly to its sensory fibers as to a series of microscopes. Although still unable to translate most of its sensations into human understanding, he knew enough now to realize that the tiny body in which he resided was leaping about in a state of mingled exultation and panic.

A great noise filled the kingdom. From everywhere came the whistle of ants and a ghostly shout of song. The towering corridors were full of rout and revelry. Masses of ants appeared singing and leaping and rolling wantonly over each other. The once orderly roads had become the arenas of a Bacchanal.

Gifford moved forward into the hullabaloo. He saw the alate was no longer in any danger. Its status had changed. Bedeviled since birth, it was suddenly cock-o'-the-walk. And Gifford knew that the festival of Priapus had begun in the dark of the termite kingdom. The dreaded warriors greeted him with whistles of joy. They beat their helmets against the walls, and their cruel halberds had become castanets and tambourines. They had become an orchestra playing for his delight. Above the chant pouring from a million ant throats they sounded their delirious and compelling drum-beats. Gifford stood on his hindmost legs and danced.

Everywhere crowding all the roads the termites were dancing. They stood upright, swaying to the banging of the soldier drums. Now another wilder element entered the festival. A wind appeared, swirling and beating against the walls. Gifford perceived that the wind came from the swiftly moving wings of the alates. Above the heads of the mobs these males and females were now fluttering and leaping, heedless of everything but the joy of flight. They spun and dived into the press of orchestras and dancers, overturning whole ranks of them and scattering them fearlessly. And as he danced and hurtled with the rest, Gifford became aware that he was being fed. Honey-tasting morsels were being pushed into his mouth, and his head was covered with tidbits as with garlands. Food rained down on him from everywhere. The armored bullies ran beside him, clearing the way for him. Garlanded and serenaded and preceded by hordes of dancers, the males and females were being escorted to their hour of love.

Swaying, chanting, and with a bullet-like urge in his heart, Gifford reeled along as part of the insect hallelujah. The writhing and screaming processions were moving toward some holy place that signaled from somewhere, and the subterranean kingdom was a single cry and its myriads were a single wave.

Suddenly the whirling spokes of some magical illumination overwhelmed Gifford. The chant around him was drowned by roars of light and sound that lifted him on their reverberations and tossed him headlong. The rush of the lovers out of the bowels of the kingdom to the couch of the sun was on. The exultation of air and light swept away all the memories of that dark termite land, and the alates, wings spread, were flashing toward its gates.

Gifford's mind removed itself from his insect self. He went to work again as a hypnotist. Desperately he exerted his will. He had set his mind implacably against any future that led to the royal bedroom. His human aversion to sex now gripped his insect self with a violence not to be denied. As he neared the little disk of sky at the end of the termite road, he struggled to command the clamorous instincts of his tiny body. Violently his mind proclaimed that he was not destined to couple with any of these million Myras, or to expire, still throbbing with pleasure, on a lizard's tongue.

The moment of exodus arrived. As out of a thousand rifle mouths the alates vaulted into space. Puff after puff of wings burst from the kingdom and remained like madly waving ribbons of smoke. Gifford was among them. He guided his insect self, however, to a leaf-shadowed twig. He knew that there would be neither bride nor enemy in the dark. And from his perch, he witnessed the prenuptial flight of his fellows. He saw that even the soldiers and workers had emerged to watch the spectacle. These stood thronged about the many gates of the kingdom, as the once despised lovers filled the bright spring air with the fiery prelude of their passion. Gifford's insect self trembled, but Gifford held it firmly in the shadow.

Looking at the world above him, he perceived a mass of forms whirling around as if caught in some overwhelming spout of sun and air. And from these insect jets came the bellow of bulls and the bugles of the chanticleer. The dance in the sun and air continued for a long time. Then, having saluted the mystery of space, the lovers sought out one another. They embraced in mid-air. Gently they exchanged caresses, as yet too overcome by this first taste of pleasure to dream of more. Clinging together, legs and wings locked in a first innocent kiss, the lovers drifted downward, seeking a couch. And Gifford saw that their couch was the frog's toothless mouth and the spider's glue-dipped web.

Blinded to all but their dream of pleasure, the lovers died in droves. Shining-backed bugs leaped at the double morsels. The air and the earth became thick with murderers come to the carnival. Here and there a pair of lovers escaped for a moment the gulp of the wedding guests. They lay coupled and creating. And when the moment dreamed of through the dark year was done, they threw aside their wings and started off for immortality. But the locust and the cicada came to bar their way. The killer flies swooped into the grass jungles after them. The snails and the earthworms closed the roads.

Gifford watched this scene of bliss and death until the grass grew still and the hum of slaughter was ended. Seemingly all the lovers had been destroyed. But he knew that somewhere the road to immortality had been left open. He thought of the two or three royal couples, attended by the souls of the slain multitude, crawling into the earth to continue the everlasting kingdom of the termites. And his one-time admiration for the nobility and cunning of the insect cosmos fell from Gifford as if only now that he was an ant had he become a man alive with human ego.

A contempt came to him for the manner in which Nature had just now handed on the termite scepter. The few alates who had survived to become Kings and Queens had earned their royalty neither by merit of their own nor by the operation of any law. Caprice alone had planted the crown of survival on them. And though he had always been aware of this lack of individuality in Nature, the fact seemed now outrageous to Gifford's mind.

Gifford recalled that in his human days he had been full of admiration for the Perfect State in which the termites and so many other insect species existed. But viewed now from within, this Perfect State seemed to Gifford a challenging and empty structure. There was, he mused, something revolting about the egomania of Nature, who, like some tireless dictator, demanded a kingdom of sleepwalkers to hymn her glories and never their own.

The perfection of Nature, thought Gifford, is made out of the imperfection of her subjects. The lower the slave the finer the state, was the secret of her ideality. The beautiful government of which he had been a part existed at the expense of a million individuals who had no existence at all. Their life and death were a command performance. And he thought of his termite brothers as somnambulists trapped in a monotonous dream. All experience was denied them, even that of age. They were permitted to learn nothing, for the wisdom of the tiniest grub and that of the hoariest grandfather were identical. They lived and died under a hypnosis that prevented them from ever changing or bettering the world into which they had been summoned. Their valor, industry, sacrifice, and even love-making were grimaces of obedience, and submission was their only genius.

It was a form of genius that occurred often among men, as a degenerative process. Whole nations of humans became capable of stripping their minds of all individual existence. Unquestioning and prostrate before Authority, their souls, identical and callous as so many beetle backs, offered the rhythm of their servitude as their greatness.

Those human groups like the Germans, the Italians, and the Japanese, thought Gifford, who seek for strength in the destruction of the individual, are operated by some dark and ancient ideal of Nature's. The lust for mass power is stronger in them than the dream of human development. By depriving the individual of a soul they are able to create an external and hypnotic soul called the State. Neither truth nor justice nor the graces of intellect become then the goal of the individual in it. But an ant-like metronomic existence allures these citizens. Their glory lies in being able to become by the surrender of self something more powerful and glamorous than lay in these scattered and struggling selves. These ego-castraters are the turncoats of evolution and they betray humanity back to its pathetic beginnings.

"I wish," added Gifford sadly, "that I had concerned myself a little more with the politics of the world when I was a human part of it. For I see now that politics is not the history of governments but the broad currents of biology. I was extremely stupid in admiring the spider and the termite above Lucifer and Prometheus."

In the midst of his musings Gifford became aware that he was crawling somewhat uncertainly down the tree in which he had been roosting. He quickly placed his Thought within his alate self and looked on the outdoors for the first time as an insect. What he saw bewildered him. He was plunging through ravines and craters which he recognized, after some hesitation, as the bark of a tree trunk. Monsters beset his way and, holding his breath, Gifford careened to the ground. Arrived at the foot of the tree, Gifford felt that he had been suddenly translated to the dead and awesome caverns of the moon. Around him loomed shapes of infernal size and strangeness. Monstrous scimitars waved over his head which, with difficulty, he remembered were grass blades. Above the grass, the leaves of bushes floated like vast domes. As from the floor of an abyss, Gifford looked up at a gargoyle world.

Around him, as he crawled, rose the scream and roar of enemy figures too gigantic for his vision to encompass. Disaster echoed everywhere. Every bit of stone was a mountain inhabited by ogres and every hollow was a chamber of death. Of all that moved, he alone was without size. And Gifford perceived that to an ant Nature was a storm blowing and a sky falling. Weaving onward, Gifford held his breath as if in the midst of panic. No one thing threatened, no visible fate pursued, but he was part of some general rout going on all around him. His ant was fleeing aimlessly from life, scaling crags and tumbling into pits, scampering up waving roads that ended in nowhere and toppling from these spiraled highways, moving ever without destination like some pilgrim lost in chaos.

Then suddenly Gifford halted. He felt a warmth within his body. And his ant self remained motionless in this bedlam as if before a friendly hearthstone. The warmth was some sort of signal. Gifford recognized it presently as the rays of the termite kingdom beckoning. Flattened against the earth, Gifford refused to move. The belly of a spider like a great cloud passed over him. He watched the forest of its legs drift away. Huge and jagged shapes leaped from the abyss with the noise of thunderclaps. Meteor bodies flashed beyond the leaf domes and vanished. He beheld horned creatures of incalculable lengths sliding down mountainsides toward him. Great heads protruded hissing and slimy from the earth, and Gifford stared into the chimera faces of the worms. In the midst of this paean of destruction the ant remained crouched as at some fireside.

Then it resumed its movement. But now it had discovered a road. Gifford realized that it had located the rays of the termite kingdom. He thought, rushing forward now, that here lay the secret of the homing instinct in nature's children. The air was honeycombed with radio-active currents. Placing themselves on these as on invisible rails, the unerring travelers of the sea, land, and air were able to return to their homes and homelands. It was obvious, mused Gifford, that this electric spoor was exuded by every species and that the seemingly trackless wastes of air contained a wonderfully organized system of vibrating streets. But this problem, which would have fascinated him in his human guise, occupied him only a moment in his present travels. He thought instead of the fate that awaited him on re-entering the termite kingdom. The warriors were undoubtedly still hovering about its gates, for it was their custom to assassinate such useless stragglers as returned unwedded from the field of love. Exerting his will, Gifford halted the termite and led it to the top of a vast stone. Here, he reasoned, it would be safe from its subterranean enemies. On this stone, with the warmth no longer in its body, Gifford's alate self submitted to his commands and lay motionless.

When he had rested on this stone for a long time, Gifford heard a sound different from all the noises around him. It was a muffled and continuous note, rhythmic as a purr. As he listened, Gifford grew frightened. This surprised him, for, being ringed everywhere as he was with the faces of death, why should he conceive of a sound coming from somewhere within the earth as unusually terrible? Surely there were no gradations to doom, argued Gifford against the terror-inspiring purr that filled his senses.

"It is not the ant who is frightened, but I," continued Gifford. "It lies with its wings folded like the toga of a Stoic. No hero was ever so calm in the face of disaster or so unperturbed before its many hideous heralds. Surely, I am as good a philosopher as an ant."

Thus, gathering courage from the termite's example, Gifford's mind grew calmer, though the horrible sound continued to come from somewhere in the earth.

"And of what," pursued Gifford, "have I to be frightened? If I am to be slain as an alate, I shall obviously make my reappearance in some other form. And no guise into which I am translated could be so distasteful and unflattering as this over-sexed little somnambulist I now inhabit. My efforts to keep this priapic midge alive are absurd and short-sighted. Certainly there must be something more for me in Infinity than a post-graduate course in entomology."

Now entirely calmed by his musings, Gifford settled himself to wait for whatever doom lay in this ominous sound beneath him. But no monster came protruding from the earth or creeping over the edge of the rock. And as the sound continued, Gifford tried to locate and identify it.

"It is evidently something in the earth," he thought, "some monster of terrific proportions creeping along. Its eyes will be white, for it will be earth-blind. It will have a remarkably long and armored snout with which to dig and it will be possessed of countless shovel-like claws. And like all subterranean creatures it will smell disgustingly. But what monster is there," Gifford pondered, "that can creep through stone? For this noise is immediately under me. I can feel the vibrations of the creature's travels in this rock. I know of no animal or ogre who can crawl through the interior of rocks."

An enormous shape suddenly appeared and loomed on the stone. A vulture had alighted beside the professor. He stared at the arrival, pleased to be a morsel too insignificant for its powerful beak. The vulture was evidently resting, for its lidless eyes seemed full of weariness. Then, without warning, something astonishing happened to Professor Emmett's winged rock-mate. Gifford saw its legs disappear into the rock, and a moment later it had vanished entirely. It had fallen into the stone as if into a drum. There was a wild flapping of wings, and after some moments the vulture lifted itself out of this unexpected trap in a billow of dust. Without pausing to examine anything, the bird beat its way off toward the clouds.

Professor Emmett looked bewilderedly at the place where the vulture had stood, asking himself what sort of stone was this that collapsed under a bird's weight. Moving toward the hole, which was still smoking with dust, he beheld a sight incredible to his human senses. A multitude of termites was in the heart of the rock. Spread symmetrically before him like the spokes of a wheel, the insects were feasting. He watched the wheel turn and the stone disappear slowly before it, vanishing grain by grain into the bellies of the termites. They were eating their way into the rocky core of a mountainside, and Gifford realized that this was the monster at whose purring he had been eavesdropping.

Looking further into the stone he saw that this wheel was only a segment of the monster. There were other wheels turning. A series of circular tapeworms was moving like cogs of destruction within the flinty mountain base. Gifford looked up at the mountainside. The thought came to him that this whole towering and bouldered landscape was a shell similar to the rock through which the vulture's feet had plunged. And he remained for some time lost in wonder.

"I have come on a new species of termite," he reasoned, "that is able to penetrate rock as easily as its brothers penetrate wood. It is evident that these rock-eaters have evolved a new race of parasites as their digestive equipment, and that these hardier occupants of their stomachs are able to convert particles of stone into a nutritive pulp. Since nothing is impossible to the chemical genius of the insects, I must accept without further quibble the fact that they have mastered the secret of extracting nitrogen from a completely inorganic form of matter. As Newton said, one must not ask unfair questions of Nature. One must study her secrets not as if they were miracles but as the simple, visible links of a hidden chain."

Fortunately Gifford was able to bolster up his unbelievable observation with the memory that there were certain ants that had always been able to penetrate but not digest limestone. These ants were equipped with small tanks of formic acid that acted as a solvent. However, no species of ant had ever before been able to turn a whole mountain into a shell from top to bottom—a soufflé of earth and granite whose very existence would presently be threatened.

If this were to be the case—and he feared it would be—Gifford knew that it was a climax which was to be postponed. In the first place the ants were not likely to reveal their presence to their enemies, and in the second place they would be sure to devour the landscape completely before allowing any avalanche to interfere with their meal.

Pleased to be the first man in the field to view such a phenomenon, Gifford started on a tour of inspection.

"One can't help admiring the little beggars," he mused to himself as he toiled upward from rock to rock, listening always to the purr beneath him. "They know to a fraction the amount of material to remove without collapsing the structure they disembowel. This ability to calculate swiftly and with the most delicate precision the various stresses of a mountainside, the different pressures of its boulders, forests, and rivers, is an instinct containing in it information beyond all the engineering data known to man. Such a talent would be comparable in man to the ability for measuring the weights, distances, and constituents of the stars merely by looking on them with the naked eye."

This was backsliding toward his older attitudes, and Gifford knew it. And he knew, even in the midst of that vacillation so comically typical of the scholar, that there were greater duties before him than that problematical report to a scientific commission with which his fancy kept toying. What this tremendous adventure was to be, he did not know as yet.

Here, half-way up the mountain, he made another scientific discovery. He was resting from his labors on a high rock covered with frost, but the alate was apparently undisturbed by the chill of his lofty roost. Gifford couldn't help marveling, for the termites of every known species perished in a temperature below fifty degrees. This astounding fact, and his present certainty that the whole mountain, from peak to base, was alive with the insects, led to only one conclusion. The termites were engaged in some sudden evolutionary spurt. They had not only acquired new talents—for eating stone, resisting cold, and so on—but they had obviously increased fantastically their rate of reproduction. (Any numerical estimate was impracticable.)

Gifford paused at this point in his musings and observed that a storm was gathering around the mountain peak. He noted also that the purring within its heart had ceased. Full of apprehension, Gifford watched the black clouds massing and hurrying forward like armadas. Great gusts of wind came from their careening hulls and then the rain leaped down. Thunder crashed and the lightning brandished its quicksilver knives over the mountain peak and hurled its broken spears into its forests.

Gifford waited wretchedly. The mountain was quivering all about him. With each thundercrash it seemed to breathe and swell as if it were coming to life. Under the beat of wind and rain its sides shivered like rattled drumtops, and a rumble issued from its heart that drowned the noises of the storm. The din from the earth increased and the pulsing of the mountain grew wilder.

Then Gifford saw the mountain vanish. Bellowing and screaming, the great hill turned to dust. Its boulders exploded, its ravines and gullies opened into great umbrellas of dust. The mountain roared in the darkness. Cavernous night filled the air. Through the darkness Gifford beheld the forests raining out of the sky. Trees were shooting past him. Like a great rocket that had burst in midair, the mountain plunged out in every direction and collapsed in a thousand avalanches. Gifford leaped to a falling bush. Tossed far into the air by winds and gases, the bush parachuted to the earth. It lay on the edge of the smoking shattered mountain base.

Gifford looked out at the disaster. The rain had ceased. A cloud of vultures was drifting toward the mountain corpse. Looking into the great pile of wreckage extending for miles, Gifford saw that all that had lived in this mountain had been destroyed. The fish in its streams, the animals, large and small, who had haunted its forests, and great colonies of birds had all perished. All had been crushed and entombed, all but the voracious little wheels that had devoured the great hill. These still lived. Gifford saw the termite regiments racing undisturbed through the mountain remains, like vandals abandoning a razed and alien house.

Then suddenly Gifford realized the full import of what he had beheld. He had seen a new war lord launch a world conquest. The vision of all the cities of the earth devoured by termites came to Gifford as he lay staring at the mountain corpse. It was the insects who had conquered the Greeks (despite his argument to Myra), for that valiant race had degenerated through malaria. But how much greater a conquest this would be than all the plagues and epidemics of the past! These termites, whose numbers were already incalculable, would multiply within a year into great moving deserts of destruction. They would spread like a quicksand. As the mountain had fallen, so would all the steel and stone towers, all the homes and factories topple. The structures of the world would become a dust drifting away.

Gifford pondered the vision of civilization ravaged. Man would be stripped of all his inventions. All his refuges, instruments and machines, all his books and his seven-league boots would end in the bellies of the termites, ground to dung by a horde of parasites. The great human house of toys would be devoured and man would be left like an infant, naked and resourceless, on the inhospitable doorstep of Nature.

For a time Gifford lay motionless with his vision. He thought of the shout of panic as the first great structure toppled in the cities, carrying millions to their deaths. He imagined then the next inevitable downfall—civilization collapsing like a row of dominoes; art, beauty, and achievement vanishing in a rain of dust and splinters.

How long, he wondered, would it be before all man's systems of philosophy were swept from his soul as he returned again to the caves and campfires? How long before all wisdom and delicacy of spirit would be outlawed as incompetence? A month, a year, at most a handful of years, and power would be seized by sinew and sadism. And would the spectacle of man struggling in the savage state for which he had so vaingloriously unfitted himself be his final deathbed scene? Would he be able to repeat the great conquest of his near ape ancestors and come marching triumphantly out of the jungle mists once more? No, thought Gifford, he is a poor creature now, incapable of defending himself against the climate alone. The sun, moon, wind, rain, and snow would do for him without any other enemy's helping.

And Gifford thought of what a tragic little rabble of bad spearsmen all the politicians, preachers, industrialists, poets, and philosophers would make. How quickly Nature would close in on this child who had bartered his animal birthright for a fragment of soul.

There would be a battle against the ants, of course, before all this came to pass, for the human species was not without weapons and courage. It would mobilize all the chemicals in the world, and fall upon the termites with poison and fire. But all this would be futile against the overwhelming numbers of termites that Gifford foresaw at their present rate of increase. Also, the chemicals would give out, for the manufacturing plants would be destroyed. And, courageous though man might be, the ant was possessed of a heroism beyond his. Death had no meaning for the ant, for it was only a cell that died. The termites would attack as a single monster, invulnerable and immortal. Villages, farms, and cities would disappear—a scattered rubble heap of a decomposing species.

Here the thought that had been haunting him came into Gifford's mind like a thunderclap. It occurred to him that he could save the world. He could carry news of the coming conquerors to the scientific outposts of the race, and give man time to prepare for the termite raid. He could, somehow or other, guide an army into this unpopulated land where the conquerors were still hatching. Attacked quickly here in the desert, the termites could be destroyed. The entire mountain range which they now inhabited could be blown up, the surrounding desert irrigated with poisons, and the human race saved.

"I could save the world," Gifford repeated to himself, and lay staring as if under a spell. Then he began irrationally to move. For several minutes he darted about, climbing through the branches of a tree.

"I could save the world," he kept repeating as he climbed the tall tree. Arrived on its uppermost leaf, he hung from its pointed tip and was silent as he looked at the sky.

"I could save the world," he resumed finally. "I can save the entire world of Thought. It is something I must consider. A few hours ago I was full of sentimental memories of the human race. I felt indignant at Nature and her hordes of somnambulistic children. But let me think now of man. Where is his worth? For instance, is there a single thought worth saving? Is there one dream or scheme that has not brought misery to the species? Where in all its history is there an idea that, once launched, has not crippled and tormented it? What have its philosophies and religions been in the end but the means for the creation of new victims? And what is the mind of man, seen as a whole, other than the ghost of his fangs still tearing at the throat of life?"

And, looking back into the world, Gifford denounced it from his high leaf as an ugly place.

"Ah," he said, "if only thought were perfect, or half as perfect as anti-thought; if the human mind were not so eager to surrender its little handful of questing words to every charlatan who crossed its path!

"Unreasoning, malformed world," he cried, "world that fills its governments with witless, howling tyrants, that is forever driving reason into caves and placing ogres on its thrones, what is there in such a world to save?

"Remorseless and inhuman world, that postures like a parson and roars like a beast, wherefore save this world? Intolerant, cowardly world, that mangles its weak and spits upon its poor, what is there in such a world worth preserving?

"Wherefore save this world," Gifford cried to himself, "that has from age to age torn at its brother's face? This mocking, gall-souled race that denies solace to itself, that allows itself to be everlastingly conscripted into the vile armies of unreason, what is there in its soul worth the preserving? Stupid and clamorous race that can be bled of all honor so easily by any mountebank and brought crawling on its belly to cheer at every crucifixion—it will be well for itself to end. For what is there to rescue," demanded Gifford, "what is there to man but a little mask, a bit of silly lace that covers the tiger's eyes, a dainty little glove that hangs tattered from tiger claws?

"I shall stay here," pronounced Gifford, "and wait till all the pretense and vileness that has come to be called civilization shall have achieved the honest pattern of termite dung. And from some place astride a grain of sand I shall witness the extinction of the human race with the equanimity that befits an ant."

Gifford was silent. The matter was ended. Within the body of this termite high up in a tree, the fate of man had been decided. Let the termites multiply and devour man—his soul and his works. Gifford would not move from his leaf.

A little awed by the situation, Gifford decided to put the whole matter out of his mind and devote himself to the business of being an ant. And returning to his termite's senses, Gifford observed the scene. He noted that the sky and the leaf were of equal size, and that the tree in which he roosted was like a limitless sea whose waves roared and tumbled beyond the rim of the world. Thus occupied with the cosmos of an ant, Gifford suddenly heard a faint voice, a little sound of words that rose from his innermost self. It was his own voice, coming out of a buried self, that spoke. The humanity he had condemned was speaking in him, as if lingering in the court of his mind to whisper against the verdict it had heard.

We have not done so badly, it said, not if you care to look at us a little more closely. Considering everything, we have not done so badly. Before you condemn us, look on us again. Not on our pomp and murder, not on our governments and gibbets, nor racks nor righteousness. But look deeper and beyond these. The list of human evils is long and humanity's record of honor is small and scattered. But it is worthy of survival.

Gifford listened to the voice of the world he had found intolerable during his residence in it, and a sadness overcame him.

Consider, it went on softly, consider who we are, and the darkness out of which our mind was born. Consider how ancient the beast is beside the little furrow of thought that has come to mark its brow. Though we have in our ignorance spilled a great deal of blood, we have also wrested a little wisdom out of the dark. In the midst of our lusts and bigotries we have found time to draw maps of the heavens, to examine the roots of plants, to peer through microscopes at our bacterial forefathers, and to pry open a fraction or two the doors of mystery.

And listening to this cajoling voice in him, Gifford beheld slowly another vision of humanity. He looked at its science. Behind the political diseases of its centuries, hidden in the ugly shadows of its religions and conquests, he beheld the isolate mind of man—a never-dying light that gleamed through the ogreish history of the race. How valiantly it twinkled even in the darkest corners, how steadfastly it shone out of the ever-dreadful shadows! No wind had ever blown it out. No tyrant with whip and sword and exile but had left it glowing more brightly.

Consider, he mused, how great was the ignorance with which we were born and how many priests and captains have held us forever chained in this ignorance. Though we have come forward only a small way, it is a noble inch we have moved.

There are a few, continued Gifford, who do not merit my judgment. They are those who have preferred the search for truth to the banners of tyrants. They are the few who devoted themselves to something other than the making of crowns for bigotry and hysteria. Amid all the great hunger for applause and power which has wrecked each age, there have been always these humble ones.

And Gifford thought of the scientists, of the eyes that had kept everlastingly peering out of the human shambles at the ways of the moon, the sun, the stars, winds, birds, beasts, and all the elements and exudations of Nature. Even in the day when piety was feeding infants to the god Moloch there had been eyes to look beyond the fires of sacrifice at the meaning of the heavens.

And Gifford recalled these immemorial heroes of the mind whose names were written on the small scroll of wisdom. Where the many others had butchered and lusted and left behind the gaudy, vanishing tracks of conquest, these few had toiled and died and left only some tiny fact to mark the small road of learning. But how much brighter this little way shone than all the tracks of glory. And how much sweeter was the fame of these everlasting little plodders than that written on the arches of Triumph. Their names were inscribed on bugs and insects, on the skeletons of sea monsters and on the petals of flowers and the sacs, vesicles, and fibers of all physiology. Atoms and gases kept their memory green, and in every chemical and computation their laurels bloomed. They had striven for truth and not for greatness; died in poverty but bequeathed riches. And their honest names, unknown to the changing crowd, had found immortality in a spider's genus or a bit of human tissue.

And how far and tirelessly, Gifford thought, these had journeyed in their quest of truth, dissecting the eyes of butterflies and weighing the flaming bodies of the stars, ever a-tinker with mice and lichens, sea bottoms and cloud tops, and pursuing God or Nature into the invisible and marching on with their mathematical lanterns where there was neither light nor matter to guide them.

These are the mind of man, thought Gifford; these are the lawgivers and the rulers of the world. These are the soul of the race. All the rest is a froth of hunger and ego, lust and lies and actors sick with the need of applause. The light of these remains to deny the most abominable darkness. I have judged wrongly. That grim and suffering face of humanity that finds solace in torturing its fellows is not to be judged, for it is only the rudimentary face of man. The list of human evils is long and the record of human honor small and scattered. But it is worthy of survival.

Having come to this conclusion, Gifford trembled on his leaf and began to glow with excitement.

It is possible, he thought, that I am not a freak but a Messiah and that I have been appointed to save the human race from extinction.

That is, if there is a God it may well be that I am a Saviour, and that . . . But here Gifford paused and frowned at his own musings.

Such a theory is nonsense, he resumed coldly. It would seem that whoever allies himself too fully on any side, be it even that of reason, becomes forthwith full of the rankest delusions in its behalf. Obviously, if there was a God who had selected me to be His Saviour, He would now invest me with some sort of divine power, or some sense of His existence other than this worrisome quibble at present in my mind. At least He would not rely on an ant to rescue Mankind, if such a rescue was His intention.

Perhaps, added Gifford, I should pray. Whether I am a Saviour or not, it can do no harm.

And Gifford prayed for some metamorphosis which would enable him to speak and enlighten the race as to its impending doom. Trembling within his ant body, he tried to make the prayer sound as unselfish as he could. He murmured humbly that he was content to be an ant but that his desire to serve God's will made him long for increased measurements and some means, denied to the hymenoptera, of expressing God's word to the human race. Nothing came of his prayers, and Gifford found himself convinced neither one way nor the other by their failure.

The history of God, Gifford remembered, as written by His most infatuated admirers, reveals Him as too busy to give more than a glance at any of His problems. He has never asserted Himself in other than an incalculable way. He smiles out of Infinity like a coquette, and turns His back on anyone smitten by His light. As a result His messiahs usually end up in bonfires, crucifixions, or as mince-meat.

"Whether or not I am part of some divine pattern for the saving of mankind," Gifford smiled, "of all messiahs, false or true, I am surely the most pitiful and futile to look at."

These confusions finally passed from Gifford's mind, and the decision he had made sent him helter-skelter down the tree. During his descent he kept looking about him with his human senses and wondering where he was.

"It is going to be very difficult fulfilling my mission," thought Gifford, "with or without divine assistance. And until I receive some revelation I will approach the career of Saviour as scientifically as I can. This desert around me may be part of Africa, Asia, or America. It is too bad I am such a poor geologist. Professor Wallachek could have told at a glance where he was. My ignorance is unbecoming both to a scientist and to a Messiah. However, I will not waste time bemoaning it. My first problem, wherever I am, is to find some human habitation and then figure out some means of attracting human attention and imparting my Message to human intelligence." And without further debate Gifford started forth.

For forty days and forty nights he continued to dart aimlessly over desert sand and hills. The bewildered but obedient ant plunged about this way and that, and no Saviour of mankind ever turned so many circles as did this termite. During this time Gifford was tempted often to give up his search and abandon the human race to its doom.

"It would be so much easier to be a Messiah," he mused wearily as he pursued his desperate journeyings, "if there were a God." And he paused time and again to pray, excusing the vagueness of his supplication by thinking: "If my piety is uncertain, it is not nearly so uncertain as God's interest in me. However, I should be a fool if I ignored altogether the possibility that I am a Messiah. In the midst of so many miraculous events as have befallen me, prayer is not entirely out of place.

"It will be easier to persuade Americans to save humanity than it would be to interest other nations in such a project," mused Gifford, "for Americans are about the only people left still amiable enough to be interested in preserving the race rather than in exterminating it."

On the fortieth morning Gifford emerged from the wilderness. He came upon a road. Urging the bedraggled ant to its edge, he surveyed the enormous stretch of concrete. The perfection of this road, the symmetry of its seams and smoothness of its surface, gave him a feeling that he was in his native land. A few minutes later an automobile swept by and he recognized it as American. At least his mission lay in a familiar country.

For several hours Gifford remained thus at the edge of the road, while a half-dozen dust-caked American automobiles appeared and vanished. The sight of the doomed but heedless human beings in them filled him with a sense of compassion. Gone now were all the doubts that had assailed him during his wanderings in the desert. Instead, his mind was full of plans. Foremost was the decision to go to Washington and reveal his news. Since the destruction of the termites would undoubtedly be a Federal project, much time would be saved in bringing the menace to the attention of the White House itself.

Gifford thought hopefully of the Chief Executive, famed for having surrounded himself with men of vision. Surely, he jested to keep his courage up, there would be no difficulty in adding an ant to the Cabinet, particularly in these times of social experiment. As each car passed, he looked desperately up at it.

"It is too much to expect," he decided presently, "that any of them will stop to give me a lift." And he began to crawl along the road.

Hour after hour he crawled, until, finding himself lying flattened against the hot concrete and no longer moving, Gifford realized that the inevitable had happened. His ant body had collapsed. Gifford remembered its hysterical scramble through the desert with death everlastingly looming and roaring around it, and was not astonished at its exhaustion. The termite, like a toy wound up, had run its course. His will was no longer able to budge that spent creature.

"How pathetic it seems," thought Gifford, "that the fate of the human species should depend on the fragile legs of an ant. For without its body to transport me I am powerless."

Studying his alate self closely, he saw it still breathed. The only thing left to do, he thought, was to signal some passing car. And Gifford's soul took its position on the road's edge and fell to sending out thought waves at each speeding vehicle. Toward nightfall the miracle happened. The despairing ant saw a car come to a halt in front of him. It was a lowly and battered conveyance, snorting as if in the last stages of mechanical existence. Smoke poured from its hood, and its doors were tied shut with pieces of cord. It had broken down, and its driver had alighted and started repairing the engine. There were two elderly women in the back seat. Gifford crawled slowly toward the car, mounted the hot wheels, and deposited himself on one of the four shoes. Here he lay listening eagerly to the conversation of the travelers. He learned that he was in the State of California, route 9, spur 52; and that the mountains some thirty miles to the south were called the Navajo range.

As these were the hills in which the termite hordes were toiling, Gifford memorized the information carefully. Eventually he heard the sound of the motor and the rush of wind and knew his journey of salvation had begun again.

During this journey Gifford changed automobiles a number of times. Hitch-hiking from tourist camp to tourist camp, he remained loyal to his mission. Daily he listened to groups of mindless people debating the ways of the world, and in the nights, as he lay tiny in the dark, he was shaken with doubts as to this civilization he was so desperately intent on saving from the termites' bellies. And though he saw that his fellow-travelers were as untouched by the three thousand years of science, art, and philosophy to which they were the heirs as if they had doffed only yesterday their nose rings and skirt feathers, and that if every statue, painting, book, idea, and instrument of learning were to disappear from the earth overnight these people would experience no more sense of loss than a backward child for a school that had burned down, he kept alive his ideal.

"I am riding to the rescue not of humanity but of a few of its dreams," thought Gifford. "I must bear this in mind lest everything I see and hear disillusion me and turn me back. It is a pity in a way that to save so little that is good so much that is stupid must be allowed to flourish. But a Messiah cannot afford to be critical."

On the afternoon of the eleventh day Gifford arrived in the city of Washington, which he found full of alarums. Crawling to a newsstand, he learned that the hysterical aspect of the capital was due to five recent attempts on the life of the President, all within the past ten days. The government, as a result, was full of panic, and the press was lucratively occupied with the horrors of the would-be assassinations. Gifford read a more or less cool account of the events in a Republican (anti-administration) newspaper. The criminals, this gazette reported, had all been captured. Four of them were men, and the fifth a scullery maid in the White House. The latter had poured a bottle of arsenic into the President's soup, endangering not only his life but the lives of his entire family. The others had concentrated on shooting and hurling bombs.

Under questioning, the five were revealed to be suffering from what several psychiatrists (Republican) identified as a New Deal psychosis. All five of them considered themselves in the light of saviours. The scullery maid submitted in defense of her action that she had heard on excellent authority that the President intended to close all the churches and banish all the priests, as had been done in Russia. She had acted solely in the interests of the Church, and felt certain that if she were executed for her so-called crime God would receive her with grateful arms as a valiant foe of the present administration.

One of the bomb throwers, a professor of economics at a boys' prep school, had acted out of the delusion that the President had tried several times to break into his study and set fire to it. And on two different occasions he had, in the nick of time, discovered fires lighted by the President in the main dormitory. He regarded his deed not only as one of self-defense but one in defense of many thousands of lives.

"I have nothing more to say," he declared, "except to express my regret that the pyromaniac President is still alive, and, what is worse, at large."

The third would-be murderer, a sergeant of police, appeared to be suffering from a misinterpretation of the finest Republican thought. He had read hundreds of editorials proclaiming that the President was seeking unscrupulously to retain his power by drugging the lower classes. The sergeant had conceived the idea that the nation's Chief Executive was head of a gigantic dope ring and engaged in distributing narcotics to a demoralized Republic. He had accordingly sought to remove him. From his cell this zealot called indignantly on other patriots to rally to the rescue of their country. Otherwise, he announced, the United States was doomed to share the fate of a drug-ridden China.

The other two assailants refused to give any reason for their attempts to shoot down the Chief Executive. Informed that they would be tried for high treason, the penalty for which might be death, they answered proudly that Germans knew how to die in defense of their Fatherland.

Gifford digested these matters and all their sidelights from the journals. He realized he had come to Washington at a difficult time, for with all these attempts on his life the President was bound to feel a certain prejudice against any Saviour, however authentic. Just the same, that afternoon Gifford crawled down the policed and deserted street leading to the White House. Undeterred, he scurried up the wide steps and entered the Mansion. The vestibule too was crowded with Secret Service men. Lingering among them, he learned that the President was in his study upstairs preparing his message to Congress. Gifford zigzagged up the steps, located the study door by the presence of four armed guards, and entered through a tiny space over the threshold. A few minutes later, Gifford, from behind a towering inkwell, looked out upon the face of the Chief Executive, who sat in his shirtsleeves. He had a faraway look in his eyes and was chewing on a pencil.

Gifford observed that there were three other figures in the study. Two were obviously guards, for they remained stiffly looking out of the windows. The third was evidently someone very close to the President, for, like his Chief, he also was in shirtsleeves. After a period of silence, this friend of the President spoke.

"It isn't necessary to finish the message today," he said. "You've got a whole week."

The Chief Executive nodded. He addressed the two guards and Gifford was surprised by his whimsical tones.

"Any more assassins lurking about?" he inquired.

The guards answered solemnly that the coast was clear.

"It's damned hard trying to write with a lot of hecklers around," pursued the President.

"Hecklers!" cried his friend. "That's a fine name for those murderers."

"They didn't murder anybody," said the President amiably. "I guess, along with my other shortcomings, I'm a pretty bad target."

"Listen," said the friend, "I'm dead set against joking on this subject. And, what's more, I'm not going to let you pull any grandstand plays about those assassins. There's going to be no humorous attitude or official clemency. If you let them off easy, it'll just encourage every poisoned mind in the country to take a shot at you."

"That would be a lot of shooting," the President chuckled. Then he added: "How do you like this paragraph?" And he started reading from the penciled manuscript on his desk.

"We must bear in mind," he read, "when we listen to our great industrialists proclaim that they are motivated only by an interest in the welfare of the working classes, that these same gentlemen achieved their high estates by a complete indifference to the welfare of these same working classes." The President smiled apologetically. "That's all I wrote today," he said. "And I guess we better get fixed up for dinner."

"O.K.," said the friend, and turning to the guards at the windows he ordered them to remain at their posts until they were relieved in the morning.

"I don't think that's necessary," the President objected.

"There's no telling what some poisoned mind will do next," his friend insisted. "One of them might hide himself in your study and lay for you."

"Take it easy, boys," the President said.

Gifford watched the President and his friend leave. He had long before decided on his method of communicating his information, but he waited now patiently behind the inkwell. Knowing the literary obsession of the President, Gifford was fearful that he might return for another bout with his Congressional message. Accordingly he allowed hours to pass.

At one o'clock Gifford moved. He crawled quickly up the inkwell. On its edge the ant paused. Gifford urged it on but it remained obdurate. It refused to plunge into the ink. This unexpected mutiny delayed Gifford a half-hour. At the end of that time his will overcame the termite's reluctance and the insect, quivering for a last second on the edge of the inkwell, dropped into its black contents. A moment later Gifford came crawling out of the well. He moved with difficulty, being half choked and blinded with the ink. Down the side of the inkstand he crept and on toward the President's message. Here Gifford pressed his belly firmly against the paper and began to write. The writing required a score of trips to the inkwell and constant use of his human will. At the end of his labors, however, he had completed the first of a series of carefully contemplated messages to the President. In a wavering thick script, full of erratic deviation caused by the termite's inability to move in a straight line, Gifford had spelled out with his belly the first words of his Message: *Beware the Ants!* The warning covered the entire page of the manuscript.

When it was done the ant sank into a stupor, and Gifford waited for the dawn. He was not worried, for he felt that with practice his ant body would improve as an amanuensis. He felt certain, too, that despite its present exhaustion the ant would survive the hardships of composition.

The President entered his study at eight o'clock in the morning. He greeted the guards amiably and sat down before his desk. Gifford, who had stationed himself under a blotter edge, watched eagerly. He saw the President glance at his manuscript and start to sharpen a pencil and then pause and stare.

"Mr. Sykes," said the President sharply. "Come here, please."

Mr. Sykes came to the desk.

"Who wrote this on my manuscript?" the President asked quietly.

"I don't know." Mr. Sykes frowned. "There's been nobody in this room since you left."

The other guard came to the desk.

"Are you sure of that?" asked the President.

"Absolutely," said both guards.

"If you didn't write this, and there's been nobody in this room since I left . . ." began the Chief Executive, but gave up the logic of his case with a thoughtful "Never mind."

"Thank you, just the same," he added abstractedly.

The incident made a small stir in the White House. The President's friend pointed out that there could be only two explanations: either the guards had dozed off, permitting some vandal to enter the room and deface the manuscript; or one of them or both of them had done it themselves in a fit of aberration.

"It goes to show," said the friend, "that we can't be too careful. Even the White House is overrun with poisoned minds. I'll have those two guards questioned by a psychiatrist at once."

The President worked until late on his manuscript. When he left, it remained on the desk. But four new figures stayed behind this time to watch the premises. They had been carefully selected from the Secret Service ranks by the friend himself. Their instructions were not to leave their posts at the windows and door for any reason, except to apprehend an intruder.

"Nobody moves," repeated the friend. "We don't want suspicion falling on any of you four. Just keep away from that desk and keep your eyes open."

The following morning there was a greater stir in the White House. For the President had found on sitting down to his desk that his manuscript had been defaced once more. Across its top page was a wavering scrawl as if some infant or idiot had trailed an ink-dipped match over it. The scrawl read: *Termites now eat stone.*

A number of officials were instantly summoned. The four guards were removed to military headquarters. Here they were grilled by the Secret Service head, flanked by two psychiatrists. They persisted, however, in their original statement. None of them had moved from his post and no intruder had entered the study.

This absurd but mysterious sabotaging of the President's manuscript appeared to all concerned as something sinister. It was regarded as the beginning of a sixth plot against the President's life. Investigations were started within the White House. Every inmate and every inch of space were gone over by squads of detectives. After several conferences, the President stated, late in the afternoon, that he had something more important to do than chase a will-o'-the-wisp. He settled down again to the writing of his Congressional message. It was eight o'clock when he quit his desk. Six men remained behind, among them the Secret Service chief himself. Guards had been placed outside the windows, and at every door of the Mansion. The garden shrubbery was jammed with detectives. The President himself took the further precaution of placing his unfinished manuscript in a desk drawer.

"I don't think," he smiled on the group guarding the room, "that we'll have any more trouble with that scribbler."

The next morning the Chief Executive entered his study at the unusual hour of six. He was accompanied by his friend and an unknown man whom Gifford designated as his Chief of Staff. The guards and their leader greeted the President with smiles, and the latter was pleased to be able to report that there had been no vandalism during the night. The President unlocked the drawer of his desk and removed his manuscript. A frown came over his face as, without comment, he pointed to the ruined top page.

Scrawled in smaller letters that wavered less than those of the previous messages were the startling words: *Civilization in danger. New ants coming. Eat stone. Trillions. If think mankind worth saving hurry up.*

Several hours later the President, his Chief of Staff, his Secret Service head, and various wise men from the Military Intelligence Department were still in conference. A clue had been discovered and the best analytic brains of the nation were wrestling with its significance. Traces of ink had been found in the keyhole of the drawer in which the manuscript had been locked.

The men confronted by the mystery were all agreed on one theory. This was that some mechanism involving perhaps radio-activity and controlled from some point outside the White House had been used. The motive, it was decided, was a plot against the sanity of the President.

"But I am not at all likely to go insane," the President protested. "And besides, most of the Opposition think I am already crazy."

"The Opposition," his friend answered, "has underestimated you for eight years. Let us not underestimate them."

"What's more," said the President, "I am convinced that no mechanism is being used."

Pressed for further opinions, the Chief Executive remained glum for a space.

"I would dislike this to get out," he finally offered with a sigh, "but there is such a thing as Revelation."

The friend was the first to speak in the silence that followed.

"Well," he said, "the plot is working."

"What plot?" demanded the President.

"You can see the effect of such a notion on the country," explained the friend firmly. "They're bound to crucify you for it."

"Me?" cried the President. "Crucify me for what?"

"For thinking that God is writing you letters," cried the friend.

"I have not referred to God or made any statement involving Him in this mystery," said the President coldly.

"Indeed," said the friend and lit a fresh cigar, "you said it was Revelation. And who else can make revelations besides God?"

"I don't know," said the President.

Although every effort was made to keep the bizarre events of the President's study hidden from the world, news of the White House mystery spread. It was garbled news, to be sure. The rumor that billowed through the nation concerned itself with the uncovering of some monstrous plot against the President's life.

In Republican circles, the tale ran that several members of his Cabinet had turned on the President, as in the case of Julius Caesar, and had tried to stab him as he was taking a walk. Another rumor swept through brokerage firms and other strongholds of conservative thought. This had it that the White House had been undermined, and numerous caches of dynamite discovered. These rumors and others reached the editorial desks of a thousand newspapers and set a thousand editors bristling with expectancy. By nightfall the reports had reached such proportions that a new and corollary whisper became current. This was that the President was dead. Oddly enough, gossip agreed he had been strangled by a close friend while in the White House study. The New Dealers, however, were in a plot to keep the news from the country in order to insure, for a while at least, the continuation of their policies.

Despite the absurdity of this last rumor, it had gained such circulation by midnight that the press took to clamoring through its representatives in Washington for the President to show himself and be photographed then and there—if he was alive.

This the President, ever ready to outwit the Republican press, was glad to do. At twelve-thirty he appeared in one of the larger drawing-rooms, and allowed a dozen photographers to take flashlight pictures of him. He was in evening dress, having been to a state dinner. Of the curious matters that had thrown the Secret Service and Military Intelligence into so obvious a panic, he refused, however, to make any explanation.

"If anything of any importance happens to me or to the country," the President smiled, "I or my survivors will inform the press immediately. Let me assure you, though, that nobody has shot at me, tried to poison me or blow me up for five whole days, and that if this armistice continues I shall have my message to Congress done on schedule."

The journalists were quick to note that the White House was a veritable encampment of generals, detectives, and bodyguards, and that the rugged face of the Executive was pale, and his large eyes far away. Leaving, they spoke to one another furtively of these impressions, and of the grave and ominous events that were obviously in the offing.

Some of them doubted that they would ever take the President's picture again, and decided secretly to save the plates of these "last" ones.

The President's mind, so apparently elsewhere, had actually been fastened on the scene in his study upstairs. Here some twenty-five officials, scientists, and Secret Service operatives were assembled. They were standing in a regularly spaced circle around the room and their eyes were intent on the President's still unfinished message to Congress, which lay exposed on the desk. There was no light in the room other than that of the moon in the windows.

The twenty-five vigilantes were armed with various devices as well as weapons. The army had brought over its most recent radio-activity detectors. Three of the scientists present were world-famous psychiatrists on the *qui vive* for evidence of mass hypnosis.

At last the President hurried upstairs. A dozen guards made way for him. He entered the study as smiling and eager as a boy finally arrived at a circus.

"Well, gentlemen," he blurted out, "any more messages?"

There was a stir in the unlit room. The officials in charge assured him nothing had happened and urged him to leave the premises. They hinted that danger lay in the room and that the conspirators had most obviously planned some final *coup* for this night.

"Well, if you don't want me to go insane," smiled the President, "you'd better let me hang around here. After all, it's my study and it's my writing that somebody is defacing and it's to me that the warning about those ants is being given. I'll just sit here and wait with the rest of you."

The Secret Service chief explained that they had decided to make everything as easy as possible for the villain controlling the radio writing, as the mysterious warnings were now termed. Therefore the vigil would be kept in the dark. All the conditions prevailing at the times of the previous defacements would be duplicated. No one was to go near the desk. The President's message was to lie exposed as it had on the first night. And nothing was to be done to prevent the scrawling of the gibberish. However, a new type of radio-active camera had been trained on the desk. This camera, able to photograph in the dark, was even now taking pictures of what was going on on the desk.

"We are remaining here until dawn," concluded the Secret Service chief.

"So am I," whispered the President, and there was a note of glee in his voice.

Silence had been agreed upon, and the occupants of the room remained without sound. The white page of the manuscript on the desk shone faintly in the dark. Every half-hour the President's friend tiptoed over to examine it, and returned to whisper that nothing had happened yet.

At five o'clock in the morning the Secret Service chief rose from his chair. Dawn was coming.

"Nothing," repeated the friend, after a trip to the desk. He moved toward the President, who had dozed off in his chair.

Alarm was in his voice as he asked: "Are you all right?"

Immediately five Secret Service men turned their flashlights on the Chief Executive. The silence became suddenly full of hissing breaths and a hum of awe and consternation. The voice of the President's friend rose sharply.

"Nobody move," it ordered. "Everybody stay just where they are. I'll take care of him!"

"Take care of whom?" muttered the President, opening his eyes.

"You," said the friend. "Be still, please."

"Lights!" the Chief of Staff demanded.

The study became bright with electricity. The twenty-five figures stood staring excitedly at the Chief Executive.

Rubbing his eyes, the President looked about him and demanded nervously: "What's happened?"

"It's on your shirt front," said the friend hoarsely.

"What's on my shirt front?" the President began, and looked down. "I'm sorry," he added after a pause, "I can't read at this angle."

"It's a message in ink scrawled on your shirt front," repeated the friend.

"I know that," the President answered irritably. "The point is, what does it say?"

The friend looked at him strangely.

"Don't you know?" he asked.

"I told you I can't read it," said the President. "I'm no contortionist."

"Do you have to read it?" said the friend meaningfully.

The President burst into a guffaw.

"Are you suggesting," he managed to say presently, "that I have been writing on my own shirt front?"

"You have had access to it," began the friend, but the President interrupted him.

"Listen," he said in a low but vibrant voice, "use your head. Why would I write a message on my shirt front? Why would I try to confuse the country with that kind of shenanigans?"

"There's some ink on your collar!" cried out the Secret Service chief, who had been examining the President closely during this discussion.

"There are some ink blots on the third bookshelf!" spoke a detective, who, among others, had been combing the room, inch by inch.

"Will somebody kindly read what is written on me," demanded the President, "or must I undress?"

The Chief of Staff stepped forward and saluted.

"It's the same general type of message, sir," he said. "It reads as follows: 'Hurry, hurry, Mt. Navajo, route 9-52, or world lost. Send ant expert. Hurry. Consult atlas.'"

"There's some more of it on the back of his collar," the Secret Service head spoke up.

The President grinned.

"Well, that exonerates me," he said. "I'm no good at writing with the back of my head. What does the collar say?"

"It reads," said the Secret Service chief, "'Can't keep this up much longer. Hurry, for God's sake.'"

"Well," said the President, "the whole thing sounds very impressive to me. This makes the fourth warning about ants. Did anybody ever hear of ants that could eat stone and steel?"

A psychiatrist present who had studied entomology smiled at this absurd layman's question.

"There is no such ant," he stated with scientific finality. "The thing is a hoax from beginning to end."

"I see," said the President and added: "Did anybody see anybody writing on me?"

The Secret Service chief replied nervously after a pause.

"No," he said, "but we expect a number of arrests within the next few hours."

"Mt. Navajo, Mt. Navajo," muttered the President. "Sounds like the Southwest."

He walked toward the bookshelves, where an officer guarded the new ink blots.

"Keep away from those books!" cried the friend and several others.

"Gentlemen," said the President, "if we are to be afraid of books, we may as well resign as human beings."

The room remained silent as the President removed an atlas.

The vigil keepers watched him as he turned the pages of the large, heavy volume. At length the President spoke.

"Here's a Navajo mountain range," he began and then paused, open-mouthed.

"Quick, somebody come here," he whispered.

"What is it?" cried the friend, and the Secret Service men drew out their revolvers and stood in a ring about the Chief Executive.

"An ant," said the President softly. "Somebody pick it up." Both his own hands were occupied. "Look. It's sitting on the Navajo mountains."

The Secret Service chief reached for the volume. By a slight miscalculation the President removed his hands from it before any others received it, and the book fell and slammed shut as it hit the floor. The Secret Service chief picked it up.

"Page two hundred and sixty," said the President.

The atlas was carried to the President's desk and opened. Page two hundred and sixty revealed a detail map of lower California.

And on the map near the Navajo mountain range lay splattered a blot of ink. The squashed remains of an insect protruded from it.

"Was that ink there when you looked at it first?" asked the Secret Service chief.

"No," said the President softly, "there was only an ant."

Two days later, the first telegraphed report from the Federal Mount Navajo Investigation Committee arrived on the President's desk. It read: "Fifty thousand men needed here at once to fight new species stone-eating termite. Termites already undermined several hills and moving northward in incalculable numbers. Will devour nation if not stopped here. Scientific survey of situation follows."

Of the remarkable battle that took place in the Navajo Hills between man and the termites I have little new to add. The two-thousand-mile ditch dug around the enemy's domain and filled with two-thirds of the nation's supply of petroleum appears to have checked, for the time at least, the termite conquest.

As for Gifford Emmett, of him there is no further record. After several conferences between the President and his advisers it was decided that no reference be made to the blot of ink on the atlas page. The President made a brief address to his Cabinet on his reasons for silence.

"Whoever that Saviour was who came to the rescue of mankind," said the President, "it will be best, I feel certain, to let him die unhonored and unsung. For history shows that only confusion arises from the worship of God's emissaries. We are in the midst of too much confusion today to add to our troubles the hysterias and dissensions which this miraculous ant would bring to our nation and perhaps to the world. If it is God who saved the race, let Him be content that it is saved. And if it is God who sent a Son to us in the guise of an ant, we may well believe He did it in order that we might ignore the Messiah. The Almighty could not very well have sent us a more inconsequential Saviour and one calling more for our indifference—if He desired any practical results. A gnat or a microbe would have been physically incapable of the Divine warning given us. I say, therefore, that we should continue to worship God's previous representatives without adding an ant to the galaxy."

Thus Gifford Emmett's cross was oblivion, which he may well have preferred. I am moved, however, to add an epitaph to the blot of ink that lies in the President's atlas. Of this little blot of ink I write:

Here lies one who hated life, who shuddered before the scurvy inhumanity of the world, who considered with revulsion the record of its endless injustice and triumphant cruelty.

Here lies one whose soul was wasted by the stupidity and barbarism of his fellows, and whose mind, looking out upon the earth, saw it overrun by the inane, the unscrupulous, the aberrant, and the sadistic children of the beast.

Yet here in this little blot of ink lies one who in all that he hated beheld the bright and beleaguered face of tomorrow and died full of hope.

# *Café Sinister*

Always in a cafe of elegance where the elite come to advertise their boredom I feel the promise of sinister events. My years as a newspaperman still make me think of the fashionable and the famous in terms of derogatory headlines. I never enter one of these hothouse roosts without feeling immediately that around me are the important scandals of tomorrow.

Here they sit—in the ornate anteroom of suicide, bankruptcy and blackmail—a-glitter with the spoils of life including that last most dangerous treasure—ennui. You would never fancy that these toy-faced heroes and heroines of the city's night were anything but what they seem—a group of beribboned insomnia victims come to stare at one another and exchange yawns. But this is a deception. For in these moribund huddles sit beauty, talent and wealth. And, however bored they seem, you may be sure that where such sit there is always devil's music playing nearby.

I have a friend, Dr. Mortimer Briggs, who is a Harun-al Rashid sort of psychiatrist. He is given to wandering the city after midnight and peering into its psychoses and, perhaps, looking for customers. This soul-gazer assures me that his favorite haunt, El Granada café, is the most clinical spot in town, and I have taken to haunting it with him. My interest is chiefly Morty, who is a witty and instructive companion and who has the gift of making the dullest people blossom into werewolves and moon monsters—a side of psychiatry that has always pleased me.

In El Granada after midnight, says Morty, assemble the daemon-driven of the town—the rich, the brilliant and the beautiful. The rich, he tells me, have warped souls—all of them—as a result of exercising their egos rather than their wits. As for their playfellows—the men and women of the arts—these are in an even worse situation. For only successful geniuses can afford to bask in El Granada, and medically, says Morty, there is nothing as troublesome to genius as success. It substitutes press notices for dreams and cocktail parties for the pursuit of beauty. Fame, holds Morty, is a sort of mummy case in which the creative talents of yesterday lie in state and glitter with mania.

As for beauty, my friend's theory is that all the lovely ladies who bloom nightly in El Granada are more phantom than female. They are, he says, shallow and dangerous. They are designed, like mirages, only to stir hunger and arouse the imagination and they have no food to offer either.

In the months we have been squatting almost nightly in El Granada, that ornamental cauldron has yielded the press four suicides, one murder, fifteen divorces and innumerable lesser items involving bigamy, treason and embezzlement. None of these events actually happened in El Granada, but its violent actors were all recruited from its yawning tables.

It was while sitting with Doctor Morty in this Pandora's box of a café one night that I witnessed the debut of the Baron Corfus, and with it the opening scene of a drama as fantastic as any in the Arabian Nights, and one that fulfilled in abundance its promise of sinister events.

There was no hint of macabre enterprise about the tall, pottery-faced gentleman who made his first entrance that night. It was midnight—an hour in which El Granada is so crowded with men and women of distinction that it is practically impossible for anyone to achieve the slightest attention.

The arrival of an elegant-looking elderly man wearing a camellia in his lapel and accompanied by a beautiful girl in camellia-studded furs is a matter of no more import to El Granada at midnight than the squeezing of two more shoppers into a subway train during the rush hour. The fact that Ganzo, the headwaiter, himself conducted the pair to a reserved table was no clue to the importance of the newcomers. It indicated that a $20 bill had changed hands. The presence at the newcomer's side of so fetching a companion was also an indication of nothing. Fetching companions in El Granada may mean anything from another $20 bill to a major disaster. You can tell nothing by looking at them. They are a bland and radiant lot who manage to exchange their characters for a coiffure when they come to El Granada.

Thus it was that the Baron Corfus and his companion created no ripples with their entrance. I remember well, however, that Morty was quick to bag the newcomer.

"Never saw him before," he said, "and the girl is new, too."

"Not bad looking," I said. You have to be modest in your opinions in front of Morty or he explodes. Psychiatry is basically the science of contradiction.

"Strip her, scrub her face and comb her hair out," said Morty, "and you have a slight case of pituitary emaciation plus a bit of Narcism."

"She still looks like Salome to me," I said. "Do you think that red hair is real?"

"The hair is real," the great scientist admitted grudgingly, "but the eyes are of glass. The man is vastly more interesting."

"He looks well preserved," I said.

"To the contrary," said Morty happily, "he is in the last stages of disintegration. A well-dressed case of cachexia always looks like a visiting diplomat." Morty mopped his face with one of his many handkerchiefs. Though not a fat man—as psychiatrists go—he was in a constant perspiration, and regardless of the temperature seemed always either to be choking to death or about to be laid low by the heat. He performed this mopping operation with quick and furtive gestures as if he expected nobody to notice the oddity.

"Besides," he went on, "that man has too much poise unless it's arteriosclerosis. By God"—Morty changed handkerchiefs—"a very curious fellow—that fellow."

I shall describe the new arrival as I saw him this first time. He was a man so imbedded in an attitude that his age seemed a mystery. The attitude was one of charm and aloofness. The gray face with its long jaws, its thin lips, its enamelled gloss, was raised as if it were in the midst of some performance. He had metallic gray hair that was curled tightly on his skull and seemed to have been polished rather than combed. But the man's eyes were his chief attraction. They were almost tightly shut. The eyelids were lowered as if against a glare and the eyes were reduced to two glittering lines—like the dashes in a code.

"I'd say he was almost blind," Morty went on slowly, "and the squint is a ruse for increasing his small vision. Or else—"

"Or else, what?" I asked, humbly.

"Or else," said Morty, happily, "he's as mad as a hatter. A man closes his eyes like that for one reason, usually. He doesn't want to be seen. I call them ostricho-maniacs." Morty considered this a joke.

"That's a hell of a theory about a gentleman who seeks out a spotlight like El Granada," I said.

"It's his soul, not his camellia, that's in hiding," Morty answered.

The music resumed. El Granada was filling up for the night, which meant that the fashionable and the famous were being reduced to sardine-like postures that made drinking, talking or eating well-nigh impossible. Dancers inched about on the small floor. The service grew panicky, breathing difficult; elbows sent glasses toppling; the crash of dishes sliding from overcrowded trays punctuated the South American melodies; table hoppers tripped over furs strewing the floor; the dancers, diners, waiters, bus boys and bandsmen became wedged together in an immovable mass. And in the midst of these intolerable discomforts the clientele of El Granada sat with mysterious satisfaction as if they had finally achieved the best of all possible worlds.

Baron Corfus had added himself to this ensemble as if it were his natural element. At one-thirty the newcomer rose to leave. Morty and I automatically called it a night. Together with some twenty other frolickers bored to a point of nervous collapse, we squeezed our way out of El Granada. I wondered idly as we stepped into the life-restoring street who the elderly glassy-faced dandy in front of us was and what type of insomnia had brought him to our roost.

An elegant automobile drew up to the curb. The Baron handed Ivan, the doorman, a five-dollar bill for his single bow and entered the car with his lovely redhead.

"A very strange fellow," said Morty. "I hope we see more of him."

We did. In the weeks that followed El Granada had produced a new diversion for us—a mystery man.

Mystery is not a thing that happens quickly. It is the negative side of events, the blank curtain concealing drama. You must look at this curtain a long time before even becoming aware that it is hanging in front of you. Having located it, however, you have a front seat at the greatest show on earth—the Unknown.

The Baron Corfus—headwaiter Ganzo had supplied his name—became our show—more Morty's than mine. For while I was content to enjoy knowing nothing and imagining everything, like any good mystery fan, Morty was busy with solutions. The trail, said Morty, after several weeks of studying furtively our camellia-tipped dandy, offered several scents. For one thing, the unvarying midnight entrance and the unvarying departure at exactly 1:30 A.M. was the sort of ceremonial behavior, said Morty, that revealed mania. Since my friend managed to discover lunacy in practically everybody who came under his scientific eye, I was not too impressed.

"The difference in this case," said Morty, "is that here we have lunacy in action. We are all lunatics, but inert ones. Psychic duds, so to speak. But the Baron's mania is up to something. It's performing for us. It's plotting away every night."

"Plotting what?" I asked modestly.

"That, I don't know," beamed my Sherlock, "but I will soon. All we know now is that the Baron arrives here with ceremonial regularity on the stroke of midnight with a beautiful young lady in whom he has no interest and we have also the fact that our Baron, a tireless exhibitionist, nevertheless refuses to commune with any of the customers here."

We had both observed that our mystery man had frozen off a dozen neighborly attempts at conversation. I attributed this to jealousy of his companion.

"Nonsense," Morty answered in a smacking voice that made me wonder if any of his neurotics ever jumped up from the analyst's couch and took a poke at him. "Definitely the Baron is not jealous. He's just busy and doesn't care to be interrupted."

"Busy doing what?" I asked, humbly.

"Hiding," said Morty, "and plotting."

It was I who first noticed, a few evenings later, that the Baron had a different young woman with him. This was not as easy an observation to make as it might seem. For the new siren was out of the same bandbox as her predecessor. In fact, all the young women who come to El Granada look sufficiently alike to line up at the sound of a music cue into a perfectly matched chorus. The Baron's new lady friend, in addition to wearing the same camellia-studded furs, the same fingernails and the same fixed glow of an enchanted window dummy—was also a redhead.

"Well, we've got a new clue," I said. "We've found out that the Baron has a redhead fetish."

"A putrid deduction," said Morty. "A man who keeps his eyes shut isn't going in for color fetishes. The redhead is a coincidence. Or perhaps a drug on the market." But I could see that Morty was not too impressed by this notion.

A young naval lieutenant squeezed into a chair at our table. This was Dickie Malchen, one of our night-life alumni who had wheedled his way into the landlocked sector of the Navy.

"Hiya," said Dickie, "I'm on leave again. First free breath in five weeks. Ever been in Washington in the summer?" The young mariner shuddered. "There's nothing worse on earth than that Navy Building."

"War is war," I offered. I had never liked Dickie. He was of the tribe of rich young men who go in for a career of billboard love affairs. El Granada has a large complement of these Romeos who, lacking all other enterprise, devote themselves to the pursuit of ladies. The pursuit seldom goes beyond a jog-trot but even at this pace the night club Isoldes are easily lassoed. The goal of both sexes being identical—to achieve mention in the gossip columns as often as possible—little time is wasted outside the limelight.

There was actually nothing objectionable about Dickie, but for that matter there is nothing objectionable about stewed calf eyes, a delicacy also on tap at El Granada. As for the amount of damage he did as a Don Juan, I imagine that Dickie was as harmless in his amours as in his new calling of war.

"The old hunting grounds," our lieutenant said sentimentally, turning a flaccid face on the clientele.

"How do they look after the terrors of Washington?" I asked. Dickie always appreciated minor insults.

"Better than ever," he laughed, still sweeping the horizon with an expert eye. His attention came to halt. "At least," he went on, "I know now what I'm fighting for."

"And what's that?" I asked.

"That redhead," said Dickie softly. "Holy hat! That's an item! Who is the graveyard with her?"

I gave the Baron's name.

"Never heard of him," said Dickie. Since Dickie had heard of every dubious character in the world, this was flat ostracism. "Corfus—Corfus," he repeated. "A phony."

Morty beamed and was about to say, "Out of the mouths of babes," but I forestalled him.

"Ever seen the girl?" I asked.

Dickie sipped his drink and was thoughtful. One had the impression of a young man peering into a myriad of hotel rooms.

"Uh, uh," he said moodily, "but it's my dish. I think I'll go over and cheer the poor little thing up. I never could stand to see redheads wasted."

"You won't get very far," I said. "The Baron is a seclusive type. He shuns people."

"My dish," Dickie repeated softly and stood up. "Watch me. The Navy never misses."

We watched and were astonished. Lieutenant Malchen stood in front of the Baron's table smiling and speaking easily. The Baron arose, smiled and bowed. Whereupon the beautiful redhead stepped from behind the table and in a twinkling our lieutenant and the Baron's prize were on the dance floor locked in a sort of rigor mortis. I watched Dickie and noted that he had not lost his cunning as a ballroom artist. He still favored the strangle hold for waltzes and the bear hug for all other rhythms.

Morty nudged me.

"That bears it out," he said.

"Bears what out, oracle?" I asked.

"My first diagnosis—that the Baron doesn't give a hoot in hell about redheads." Morty mopped his seething brows. "He hasn't opened his eyes, turned his head or stolen a single peek at the blitzkrieg on the dance floor."

Twenty minutes later, Dickie returned the rumpled beauty to her perch beside the Baron, and sat down next to her. There was a small group of tax-tortured citizens at our own table discussing the future of the world. This vital topic, however, failed to hold my attention. I waited for the Navy to bring us tidings of Baron Corfus. And while waiting, I noted with some surprise that our Don Juan apparently had lost interest in his redheaded quarry. Both he and the "dish" sat unaware of each other, listening open-mouthed to the elegant Baron.

At 1:35 Dickie returned from the vestibule and joined us. The tax-debating society had moved on to the Stock Club for inspiration and Morty and I were alone.

"Holy hat!" said Dickie. "What a guy! The most exciting old pollywog I ever listened to."

"How'd you get in?" I asked.

"Oh, that," Dickie grinned. "Just pulled the old gag. Introduced myself and told the old boy I'd made a fifty-dollar bet with you gentlemen that I could prevail on him to let me dance with the lovely young lady at his side. It worked like a charm. The thing that helped was that the old boy knows you and doesn't like you. Uh, uh—not for apples."

"Knows who?" I asked.

"The doctor," said Dickie. Morty beamed. "He hates psychiatry," Dickie went on, "if that's of any interest to you."

"Of the deepest," said Morty.

"What did he talk about?" I asked as Dickie sunk his nose into a wine glass.

"Terrific." He looked up. "Biggest authority on Nazis in the world. He knows them all—Goebbels, Goering, Hitler. All the big shots. He's been at their homes. My God, I never heard anything so fascinating."

"As for instance," I prodded.

"Oh, well," said Dickie, "an absolutely inside track on all those boys. Don't you think that's pretty interesting? By God, I do. You know—who loves who and what those goddamn Nazis say when they let their hair down."

Here at least was an answer to the Baron's fascination for the two redheads. Our mystery man was full of intimate tidbits concerning the nature of the enemy and apparently had bowled over Dickie as well with tales of the home life of Germany's boogiemen.

"Holy hat!" Dickie jumped up suddenly. "I forgot to get her telephone number. I'm slipping."

"Sit down; she'll be back tomorrow night," I promised. "What did she have to say about his nibs while you were dancing?"

"Not a talking type," said Dickie, with a soulful look toward the vestibule, "but quite a dish, eh? Looks a little like Evie, wouldn't you say?"

"Which one was Evie?" I asked.

"That beautiful redhead that ditched me for the movies last year," said Dickie, "just as I was recovering from the big thing with Miss Colligan. God, I had a terrible time. I find 'em and Hollywood grabs 'em."

"Was Miss Colligan another of your conquests?" Morty asked, shyly.

"I was cut to ribbons," Dickie sighed. "God, I would have married that girl—if she'd waited."

"What was the color of Miss Colligan's hair?" Morty inquired, archly.

"Red," said Dickie. "Most beautiful redhead I ever met. Well, you can't have everything. Be seein' you." Dickie started squeezing his way toward another part of the room.

"Well," said Morty, "we've found out one impressive clue. The Baron knows who I am and dislikes me. I think that's vital information."

"For your press book, perhaps," I said. "Personally, I am more interested in his being so close to the great Nazis."

"Lies, all lies," said Morty. "He doesn't know any Nazis. He never met Goebbels or Hitler. He's merely taking advantage of the ingénue American interest in backstairs tittle-tattle to put something over. His dislike of me proves that absolutely."

"You're sending up bubbles," I said. "I don't follow you."

"My dear friend," Morty beamed, "the man's up to something and he's terrified I'll see through him. All lunatics feel that way about me."

Morty let his face drip in exultation.

"They're telepathic," he went on. "They can sense a brain piercing through their hocus-pocus. That's what ails the Baron. He knows I've got his compulsion neurosis by the tail and that I'm likely to see where it's going—any minute."

Highly pleased with himself, the moist thinker forgot it was his turn as guest at our table and picked up the check.

Thus our mystery remained for a week. The only progress made was by Dickie Malchen, whose relationship with the redhead had already borne fruit in the gossip columns. I had hoped the lieutenant would play go-between and get us a bid backstage of our mystery. Nothing of the sort happened. The only news that Dickie brought us of the Baron was of his remarkable collection of paintings and of his aversion for Morty.

"I suggested we all get together," said Dickie, "but he can't stand psychiatrists. You ain't mad, are you, Doc?" And Dickie winked at me.

"Not in the least." Morty also winked at me. "Nobody loves a nosey psychiatrist."

Dickie chortled and squeezed off toward the dance floor.

It was the next night that the curtain at which we had been staring so long began finally to rise. It did not rise far, but enough to give us our first glimpse of the design of the hidden stage. The design was Uncle Albert Malchen, Dickie's most renowned relative.

The honorable and disintegrating Albert was rarely seen in such gaudy dens as El Granada. He belonged to an era that had come to a full stop with the diabolic invention of the income tax; an era, also, that had regarded sin as a very important matter worthy of secret mansions, secret yachts and posthumous autobiographies. Uncle Albert, having squandered millions on amour, was averse surely to seeing it knocked down nightly in the open market for a single magnum of champagne, which may have accounted, in part, for his absence from such haunts as ours.

His appearance on this night sent a ripple through the blaring room, for Mr. Malchen was more than a celebrity come to be seen holding hands with another celebrity. He was a legend stepped out of ancient Wall Street deals and international love scandals—a gentleman as archaic as the Devil in red tights—and the flesh-pots curtsied nostalgically to him. Beholding him, the clientele of El Granada remembered tales of chateaus on beaches, mountain tops and boulevards, recalled Rembrandts and Raphaels showered on strumpets, wheat markets cornered and somebody shooting somebody else on the opening night of the Opera.

The lieutenant piloted this white-mustachioed, red-faced legend through the crowded room. He held it tenderly by the elbow and a look of extreme piety was on him as if he were guiding an abbot to his prayers. The two, uncle and nephew, stopped in front of the table of our camellia-studded Baron. Introductions took place and chairs were adjusted.

"Well, my friend," Morty scowled, "at least the first part of the mystery is cleared up. We can dismiss the Titian sirens from here in."

He mopped his face frantically.

"We're a pair of idiots," he resumed. "Good Lord, imagine my not seeing through the whole thing in a minute. It makes me sick."

"But you did see through it," I comforted the scientist.

"Only as far as Dickie," Morty frowned. "I saw that the redheads were a bait set out for our naval hero. And I saw that the Baron had gone to considerable research for a foreigner to establish the fact that Dickie had a fetish for red-haired ladies. But I didn't think beyond Dickie to Uncle Albert."

"You're quite right," I said. "It looks pretty obvious. Our Baron snagged Dickie with a redhead. And then used Dickie as bait for Uncle Albert. And Uncle Albert is now going to be taken for something neat and considerable."

The Baron and Mr. Malchen were conversing amiably against the padded satin wall. Mr. Malchen's red rubbery face was full of a sort of roguish good humor of the old school. He appeared to be urging something on the Baron and the Baron with much charm appeared to be refusing whatever it was.

"One thing confuses me," Morty spoke up suddenly. "There doesn't seem anything mad about the whole business. And there should be. There should be something very definitely maniacal going on. And there isn't. It's all too stupidly logical."

Morty glared at our Baron as at a mendacious patient.

"We are being misled," he sighed. "If that man's a swindler, I'm a chiropodist." And Morty sat glaring at the Baron indignantly.

Our mystery was being seated when we reached our El Granada roost the next night.

"I wonder what the next step is," I said as Ganzo with tip-dizzied tenderness guided the Baron and the redhead to the padded wall.

"The next step involves us," said Morty in a whisper; "the fellow is beaming at us like a brother Elk."

I turned and saw this remarkable sight. Baron Corfus was smiling unmistakably in our direction, and Ganzo was moving toward our table.

"The gentleman over there," said Ganzo, "Baron Corfus, asks if you care to join him as his guests."

"We'd be delighted," said Morty softly.

Ganzo bowed and smiled like a good fairy whose work is done.

We squeezed our way to the Baron's side.

His voice fitted him like another camellia. It was softly accented and full of good humor, the voice of a man of wit who has learned English where it is spoken only by the most elegant of people.

"I feel we are old friends," he said after the introductions to the red-haired Miss Annabella Wilkerson were done and we had all sat down. "Your faces have the quality of long companionship. I am certain that mine must be equally familiar to you."

This was not bad as a dig at our weeks of scrutiny.

"Yes," said Morty. "We've been interested in each other for some time. In fact, my friend and I have been happily mystified since your first appearance."

I thought this a little crude but the Baron was delighted.

"I didn't know psychiatrists were ever mystified," he said. "I thought people were an open book to them—a rather ugly book."

"Open," said Morty, kittenishly, "but hard to read halfway across a room."

The Baron nodded and failed to look wary. His eyes continued to glitter through their slits with a sort of gayety that confused me. But not Morty. Morty apparently understood this symptom thoroughly. He seemed, in fact, full of a friskiness that matched the Baron's and I was reminded of two fighters who square off with a grin on their mugs, each equally certain of himself. We ordered wine and I tackled the red-haired Miss Wilkerson with a few opening remarks about Dickie.

"Oh, really now," Miss Wilkerson answered in a swooning southern voice, "all Navy men are alike, don't you think? Ah don' mean anything disrespeckful tawed the Navy, but they ah so Navy, wouldn't you say?"

The Baron smiled at her without mockery.

"I find this place very interesting," he resumed, "and also a little sad."

"Why sad?" I asked and earned a mysterious kick under the table from Morty.

"It is sad when you see how little riches have come to mean," said the Baron. "And how small a thing luxury has become. Hardly more than this." He nodded wistfully at El Granada, and continued, "Luxury was once the goal of all intelligent human beings. Now we are all a little ashamed of it and actually frightened of its fine clothes and pleasant hours. It's a pity that the dream of luxury has been frightened out of the world."

"It will not be luxury that's removed from the world"—Morty

mopped his face and kept peeking like a schoolboy from behind his handkerchief—"but only its present formula—a great deal for a very few. This is being altered into another formula, a little for everybody."

"I wonder," said the Baron, "if useless things can be rationed or idleness evenly distributed. It is doubtful."

"Why did you ask us over?" Morty asked suddenly, and I was glad to see that the boys had come to an end of their sparring.

"The scientist is always direct," the Baron smiled. "Here is our wine. Shall we drink first?"

The lovely Miss Wilkerson cooed over the bubbles.

"Ah just adaw champagne," she said. "It relaxes yaw mind. It really does."

The Baron raised his glass to her.

"To you," he said, "for being so beautiful."

"Thank you." Miss Wilkerson widened her eyes at all of us.

Our host said, smiling at Morty, "I asked you over because your deep interest in me made me think you might enjoy the only small gift I have to offer—that of the raconteur."

"I knew that," said Morty smugly. "I knew you had something to tell us."

"Perhaps you even knew what it was," the Baron smiled.

"Whatever it is," beamed Morty, mopping his face and peeking excitedly, "I'm sure it will be very persuasive."

"You mean untruthful," the Baron said.

"I never discuss psychopathology with laymen," Morty lied pompously. "If you want to tell me a story, go ahead. I can take it."

A waiter appeared bearing a telephone instrument which he plugged in.

"We have your number now," the waiter said.

"Excuse me." The Baron smiled at us and spoke into the instrument. "Hello. Is that Emil? Emil, this is Corfus. Do you remember that time I told you I expected the gentlemen. . . . Ah. . . . They are? . . . Please, I will speak to the lieutenant."

The Baron sighed and looked at Morty.

"I have done a very stupid thing," he said. "I thought my appointment was for one-thirty rather than midnight. Isn't that what I told you, Miss Wilkerson?"

"Yes," she nodded earnestly. "Ah understood it was one-thirty. Ah remember distinctly. . . ."

"I'm afraid we are wrong," he smiled. "You must explain to me, Doctor, how it is that one's memory can be so accurate, so vivid and accurate about the past and so completely worthless on matters of the present."

"Perhaps the present is of no interest to you," Morty cooed. I knew he had spotted the shaking of the Baron's hand and the tension in the slitted eyes.

"Hello," our host spoke into the phone, "Lieutenant? . . . Oh, I'm so very sorry, Lieutenant. I had an impression that we were to meet after the café. . . . Oh, really? . . . Yes, I recall now. In fact, I've been uncertain for fifteen minutes. Please convey to your uncle my deepest regrets and ask him if he will be kind enough to look at the paintings. I will be over very soon. Tell him the data is on my desk. . . . Oh, he is? I am delighted."

The Baron's breath caught in a curious gasp and the shaking of the hand holding the instrument increased.

"Then there is no need for me to rush," he resumed. "And how are you, Lieutenant? We missed you this evening—in more ways than one. Yes, she is here. Would you care to speak to her?"

He handed the phone to Miss Wilkerson. Morty mopped away and peeked excitedly and I wondered if he would offer his handkerchief to the Baron, on whose temples a film of moisture had appeared.

"Hello tha," said Miss Wilkerson. "So sorry yaw not heah, Mr. Malchen. . . . Yes, tha's a wonderful crowd heah tonight. . . . Oh, just everybody. . . . You do? . . . Oh, that's very naughty, Mr. Malchen. . . . No, I won't call you Dickie ever if you talk like that." She laughed, as Dickie apparently stepped up his campaign, and tossed back a series of arch and ambiguous gurgles. The Baron sat listening with what seemed a breathless, dreamy air. A smile twitched his mouth and he took the instrument from Miss Wilkerson.

"Will you please ask the butler to fix you a drink, until I get there?" he said. "Oh, it's no trouble at all for him. And I'm sure he has some sandwiches ready. . . . He did? Well, I'm delighted. . . . No, no, no. . . . Please, say nothing about that till I get there. And give him all the time he wants. A great art connoisseur loves to be alone with his quarry. . . . And I'm sure he'll find the paintings quite worth his attention. . . . Yes. . . . We'll finish our drinks and be over. . . . And my apologies for forgetting the hour. . . ."

He hung the phone up and looked at his wrist watch. The moisture had spread from his temples to his chin and glistened now on his shaking fingers. His voice, however, was smooth enough as he said, "Mr. Albert Malchen is at my apartment looking at some paintings I own and am not averse to selling."

Morty stared at him blandly.

"It really upset me." The Baron removed his own handkerchief and mopped his face. "I cannot bear to be unpunctual. Punctuality is perhaps my defense against a completely disorganized mind. At least, I often think so. But no harm's been done. Shall we have another bottle of wine?"

"Ah don't think we ought to leave Mr. Malchen alone," Miss Wilkerson pouted.

"But I cannot desert our new friends here so abruptly." He smiled. "Particularly Dr. Briggs, who is still curious as to why I sought the honor of his company. I am an exile from a country that I once loved. There is nothing pleases me as much as to tell stories about that country. It is the same as one feels toward an old, old friend who has died. One loves to recall him and speak of him to others."

I had an impression the Baron was babbling and waited for Morty to say as much. But Morty had grown dreamy and I knew his mind was far away from the Baron's words. He was thinking like a steam engine.

Baron Corfus spoke for another five minutes, chiefly of a dinner party at which Mussolini had recited an ode to himself. He then ordered the check from Ganzo. He was still lingering over its payment and finishing another tale of Nazi intrigue in Warsaw—the details were reminiscent of a movie I had seen a few months ago—when the waiter appeared, bearing a telephone.

"For you, sir." He nodded at the Baron, as he plugged in the wire.

"Hello," the Baron spoke into the phone. "Yes. . . . What? . . . I don't understand. . . . Oh, I see. . . . Oh, I'm terribly sorry. . . . Yes, I have one in my pocket. . . . Yes. . . . Oh, I'm sure nothing has happened. . . . Yes, indeed, I'll be right over."

He hung up quickly and rose. Morty followed him to his feet.

"Has something happened?" he purred.

"You look awfully upset." Miss Wilkerson put her hand on the Baron's arm. "Is it something about Dickie?"

"I'm sure it's nothing," our host sighed, starting toward the vestibule. Morty was at his side and the Baron added, "Mr. Malchen says his uncle locked himself in my drawing room. The door has a spring lock and I have the only key."

"Why doesn't Uncle Albert open it?" Morty asked softly.

"Apparently he is so enthralled by my paintings," the Baron smiled, "that he cannot hear his nephew's outcries."

"I am a doctor," said Morty quietly, "and will go home with you. In case one is needed."

The Baron's apartment was five minutes away by taxi. The four of us rode there in silence. The most mystifying thing in the taxi was the fact that Morty had stopped perspiring. He was cool and contented.

The butler who opened the Corfus door for us looked like Voltaire—a puny and electric old gentleman. Dickie gathered Miss Wilkerson to him and begged her not to worry, because he had already sent for Dr. Kenneth O. Bishop, the heart specialist and his uncle's chief personal physician. Miss Wilkerson patted the mariner's cheek, and was certain everything would be all right.

In the meantime Corfus unlocked the door, at which we were all looking. We saw a large, softly lighted room with a number of paintings on the walls. At the far end of the room stood an easel with a large painting of a woman on it. The easel was an imposing affair with velvet drapes on each side.

A third look revealed Albert Malchen on the floor, his face flattened against the rug. The fabled Malchen was dead. In this room hung with too many paintings, he looked like a child collapsed amid its toys.

We stood like a little group of mummers who had not learned their lines for the death scene. Particularly Morty. Morty had turned his gaze away from the mighty Malchen crumpled on the rug. He was looking at another figure—the one on the easel. It was a full-length portrait of a woman of twenty. She was a proud and fragile lady done chiefly in greens.

Dr. Kenneth O. Bishop found us with highball glasses in our hands. He was tall, learned and expensive-looking, and obviously of the Supreme Court of medicine. No M.D. had taken his diplomate in cardiology or been elected to his academic society without appearing first before this haughty face. It was apparent at once that dead millionaires were no novelty to him. Mr. Malchen's death held no surprise. He had been treating the financier for a bad heart for a number of years, he said.

Dickie, removing his arm from the Wilkerson rib cage, explained the events preceding the demise. He had accompanied his uncle into the room, and they had just started looking about when Baron Corfus had telephoned. Dickie had followed the butler to the phone, which was in another room, and asked the old fellow to mix him a drink. The butler had prepared the drink while Dickie talked over the phone. Then he had sat drinking and giving the butler his favorite recipe for mint juleps. Going back to join his uncle, he had found the door locked. Mr. Malchen had closed the door himself, Dickie imagined, because he wanted to look at the paintings without interruption.

Morty, who had been listening blandly, added the question: "Were the drapes on the easel painting open or closed when you left the room to answer the phone?"

"They were closed," said Dickie, frowning.

Morty nodded agreeably.

The more expensive-looking scientist then made a curious statement. Some seven years ago Albert Malchen had specified that he should not be buried without an autopsy. This was a request not uncommon among his extremely wealthy patients, who were evidently haunted by a fear of foul play. Of course, this phobia did not mean anything, but he would let Dr. Briggs know any interesting findings, he added graciously, favoring the gleam in Morty's eye.

He paused and sighed.

"Mr. Malchen was a very dear friend. It's obvious that he became overexcited by these paintings, particularly the one on the easel."

"It is a beautiful thing," said Corfus.

"Well, it was too much for him," said Dr. Bishop. "Poor Albert, he always loved art above everything else in the world."

"A wonderful theory . . ." Morty whispered in my ear sarcastically. "That painting never excited anybody—except me."

I saw the Baron nod to the old butler as we started leaving the room. Voltaire remained behind and slowly drew together the drapes.

Morty telephoned me the next afternoon. I asked him if he had seen the Baron.

"No," he said, "but don't worry about him. We'll see him tonight at El Granada."

"You think he'll be there?" I asked.

"You *are* a babe in the woods," Morty chuckled. "He'll not only be there but he'll be alone."

I asked my Sherlock how he deduced that.

"Because he's expecting me," said Morty. "I hold a great fascination for him. Much greater than he ever held for me."

I assured Morty that I was completely baffled by the whole thing and asked about the autopsy.

"Mr. Malchen died of a bad heart," Morty said happily. "No contributing factors in the way of bullets, poisons or blows were found. It was a perfect crime. Twelve o'clock—and don't be late. I don't want to keep the Baron in suspense."

Baron Corfus was there, and alone, poised as a bit of old statuary, his steely hair polished, the long glazed face riveted in a grimace of charm, his eyes almost shut and looking more than ever like the dashes of a code, and the camellia flying. And, obviously, he was waiting for us.

I have always admired dandyism in distress—Charles of England removing the long curls from his neck and murmuring that there was no occasion for the ax man to disturb them since they had offended no one, the literary Prince of Paris listening to the pompous death warrant being read to him and interrupting wearily: "Tut-tut . . . the style of Diderot . . ."; and that Brooklyn boy swimming through the oil-flaming Coral Sea and calling out to the rescue boat: "Hey, buddy, here's a couple of hitch-hikers." The temperament that yields no whit of its style to calamity has always been my favorite, and on this night our Baron was an elegant member of its tribe. For if ever calamity signalled its presence and Nemesis bayed in the offing, it was Morty. He squinted at our host as if he were sighting a rifle on him, he perspired, leered and fidgeted like a June bride, and he gulped down tumblers of wine. But his gloat was that of the pedagogue in pursuit of truth rather than the Puritan laying evil by the heels, and I forgave him. It pleased me to know, however, that our Baron would sit unperturbed until doomsday, and that it would have to be Morty who first unmasked. It was Morty.

"Corfus," he said finally, "I'd like to tell you a story."

"That would be only fair," the Baron smiled. "You've listened to several of mine."

"Before I begin," said Morty, "I want to make it plain that I'm here not only as one who is going to accuse you of murder, but also as judge and jury."

"The court of El Granada," the Baron nodded smilingly, "a charming locale in which to be tried."

"I'll enter the evidence quickly," said Morty, "since, of course, it will offer no surprise to you. My only reason for boring you possibly with the details is to convince you they are in my possession."

"You will not bore me," the Baron said.

"I am pleased that you're not full of hostilities and contradictions," said Morty.

"I never contradict a guest who is enjoying himself," said the Baron. "Will you have some more wine?"

He refilled Morty's glass. Morty drank it absent-mindedly.

"I'll begin with the redheads," he said. "I couldn't satisfy myself about the significance of those damned redheads. I knew, of course, they were decoys for Dickie and I knew Dickie was a decoy for Uncle

Albert. But why should a man with such authentic paintings to sell go through such a hocus-pocus to meet the art-hungry Malchen? This question, of course, was among the several answered last night. You needed both Dickie *and* Uncle Albert on the scene. You, naturally, were going to be absent. And you wanted someone present at the scene of Malchen's death besides your butler. That old gentleman with the Heidelberg scar is hardly a character that would bear close questioning. And if the mighty Malchen were found dead on the premises of a stranger with nobody but that dubious creature on the scene, there would be considerable questioning. Dickie was perfect insurance against any such investigation. Hence Dickie. Hence all the hocus-pocus."

The Baron remained a picture of polite interest.

"The part I am grateful for," Morty resumed, "was that you called me over to your table last night to use me—as part of your alibi. That wasn't very nice . . . but I enjoyed it. It was fruitful. And now we come to your vital and slightly paranoiac adventure. I knew, of course, from the first that you were neither a crook nor swindler, but a man of hate."

"Hate," said the Baron, in the most amiable of tones, "is the sole diet of continents today."

Morty mopped his face and continued.

"Last night, when you spoke over the phone here, the basic nature of the adventure became clear to me. You lied. A lie, my dear fellow, is always the best signpost to the hidden. As long as a man doesn't lie, his secret is safe. My profession of psychoanalysis, as you know, is little more than a lie hunt. I'm always geared to spot a lie. When you said over the phone that you had forgotten the exact hour of your appointment with Uncle Albert, the gong sounded. A man who has devoted two months to bagging a Malchen isn't going to forget any detail of his appointment. It was also obvious, while you were talking on the phone, that you had been engaged for two months in establishing a public habit —an El Granada habit of attendance between midnight and one-thirty. This habit would serve as your alibi—this, and ourselves. Yes, indeed, El Granada had many uses for you."

The Baron glanced at his wrist watch humorously.

"It is almost one," he said, "and I am still in the grip of habit."

"We will be through in time," Morty beamed. "To return to this spectacle of you at the telephone. You showed all the signs of extreme strain. Your hands shook, and your face sweated. And I knew that the adventure—a seven-year adventure as we learned last night from Uncle Albert's long-standing fear of murder, had reached its climax. The murder of Malchen was taking place as you held Dickie on the phone."

The Baron sighed.

"I am confused," he said. "Whom are you accusing—my butler?"

"Heavens, no," Morty said indignantly, and added, "At any rate—only as a very minor performer. The thing was so clear that I was afraid that ass Kenneth O. Bishop—O for ossified—would see it."

Morty shook his head reprovingly at the Baron.

"You took a big chance killing Mr. Malchen with a Forain portrait," he said, "—a piece of painting that couldn't possibly affect his heart action—except to depress it."

"Forain is a much undervalued artist," said the Baron, and I felt that they were both mad.

"I could see you had great faith in him," Morty chuckled, "the minute I entered the room. Nevertheless, I wondered why an art connoisseur like yourself should honor a fifth-rate canvas with a draped easel. Once I had asked myself that question, my dear Corfus, I needed only to ask another to know all the details of the murder. Were the drapes on the easel closed when Uncle Albert entered the room? They were. The rest was simplicity itself."

Morty paused as if for a round of applause. "Having gorged himself on Memlings and Goyas," he continued, "an art lover like Malchen would turn eagerly to the obvious prima donna of the collection—the canvas honored by a draped easel. Now we arrive at the crime. When I left the room, I made a final observation. I saw the butler, so-called, pulling the heavy drapes closed with some difficulty. I noticed that the knob on the cord of the drape rode up to an unusual height when the curtains were closed—in fact, above Uncle Albert's head. Uncle Albert had to reach for this knob and pull hard, when he turned at last to gaze at the deadly Forain."

I felt like laughing.

"Do you mean that the extra exertion of opening the drapes ended the life of Mr. Malchen?" I asked.

"I mean nothing of the sort," said Morty. "The knob on the draw string killed him. There was a syringe in that knob, and when he grabbed hold of it, he received a deadly injection."

"Poison?" I looked at the imperturbable Baron.

"Obviously," said Morty. "But a special kind of poison, I realized, when Corfus didn't seem to be the least disturbed by the promise of an autopsy. I spent all night over a pharmaceutical volume refreshing my memory about poisons that leave no traces. Today, when that antediluvian medical freak, Dr. Bishop, phoned to assure me the results of the necropsy were entirely negative, I knew. There is only one such fooler. Insulin."

He looked at Corfus triumphantly.

"At least two hundred units of insulin were in the needle that was released into the hand of Mr. Malchen when he reached up for that knob and pulled greedily. It was perfect. Your victim received a staggering insulin shock, which nobody can distinguish from the last throes of a fatal coronary attack."

Our table became an oasis of silence in the blaring café. After several moments Morty said, rather appealingly to the Baron:

"It's your turn, Corfus."

The Baron seemed rather tired.

"An interesting story," he said softly, "but a little fanciful."

"I haven't gone to the trouble of digging up any proof," said Morty coldly, "but if the police were told to look at Uncle Albert's right palm, they would find a perforation. Also, an analysis of the draw cord on the easel would show insulin, and would also show, I am sure, that a new and more innocent knob has been substituted for the one I have described to you."

The Baron seemed to have fallen asleep. I realized with surprise that he was talking—quietly, and without emphasis.

"Perhaps it will satisfy the judge and jury of the court of El Granada if I reveal my true name. It is Count Eitel von Lichtenfels. This name is my only defense."

Morty beamed.

"Naturally I've heard the name. I studied in Berlin, you know. It was one of the big banking families of Germany. But it doesn't shed any light."

"I am sorry," said the Baron. "It would have saved us time. That portrait by Forain that you failed to admire was of my sister—Marie von Lichtenfels."

"Why, of course," said Morty. "Forain didn't do her justice at all. She was a famous beauty."

"Yes, the gods were lavish with her—too lavish. They added one gift too many around her cradle. They bestowed on her the honor of being part Jewess. I don't know the exact percentage but it was a sufficiently large part to aggravate Dr. Goebbels. And being perhaps the richest of the undesirables, our family fled Germany in 1935. We escaped without any casualties—except that laceration of the heart which the exile feels when he must choose the world instead of his native land.

I went to Russia. My father, brother and sister went to London. In London my sister, Marie, received a cable from the American financier, Albert Malchen. He was in Austria and wished to buy a castle she owned in Salzburg. My father knew Malchen. He had tried for many years to buy a Rembrandt that was the pride of the Lichtenfels collection."

The Baron sipped his wine and looked dreamily at the dance floor.

"It is a difficult story to tell," he resumed, "because it has lost none of its horror. Mr. Malchen's death has improved it only slightly. The death of one scoundrel does not lessen the inhumanity in the world. I am sure"—the Baron looked again at the dance floor—"that there are dozens of Albert Malchens enjoying themselves around us. But if I talk like that you will think I am mad, doctor. And that is untrue. I am world-poisoned, nothing more."

Morty nodded and we waited for Corfus to continue.

"Malchen asked my sister, Marie, to meet him in Austria," the Baron resumed. "But Austria was dangerous ground for her. It had not yet been gobbled up by the Nazis, but they were sitting at its banquet board, knives in hand. Marie arranged with Malchen to meet him in Zurich but Malchen failed to appear. He sent her a letter explaining that he was bedridden in a sanitarium just across the Austrian border and he begged her to visit him and close the deal for the castle there. My sister, who was brave and eager to improve the family fortune—for we had fled with little of our wealth—my sister crossed into Austria and arrived at the sanitarium. Mr. Malchen was not waiting for her. Instead a group of Gestapo agents seized her and took her to Berlin. You see, it was known to the Nazis that our family, on fleeing Germany, had buried the bulk of the Lichtenfels art collection somewhere in a forest in Saxony. We had left fifty paintings, very famous ones and worth millions, underground to await our return when the Nazis had finished their day."

Baron Corfus sighed.

"It is a long day," he said; "longer than we imagined."

He paused.

"In Berlin," the Baron resumed, "the Nazis tortured my sister for three months. They disfigured her face and broke her hands and legs. And they were able finally to learn from her the hiding place of the Lichtenfels collection. Mr. Malchen was rewarded immediately for his part in the affair. He was allowed to buy the Rembrandt he had so long coveted for a comparatively small sum. It hangs in his own collection now. Mr. Malchen had evidently heard that the remaining members of the Lichtenfels family had sworn to avenge Marie. My father was not among them. He shot himself after Marie died. Friends in Berlin were permitted to bury her. They wrote us that they were unable to recognize her. Last night my butler, who is my older brother, Frederick, and I were able to fulfill the vow."

The Baron sighed.

"Last night," he said, "my sister watched Mr. Malchen die at her feet. If you will pardon me now"—the Baron smiled faintly—"it is one-thirty."

He stood up.

"The check has been paid," he said, "and thank you for an interesting evening. I hope we shall see each other again."

"Good night," said Morty, "and don't forget to burn the cord on that drape."

Baron Corfus bowed and walked toward the vestibule.

"My conscience," said Morty, "doesn't bother me at all. Justice of a very high order has been done."

"It's still murder," I said.

"Murder, my eye," Morty mopped his face. "The whole thing was a fantasy of mine. You can forget about it. Very pleasant fellow, Corfus. Too bad he's not long for this world. I made a close study of his physical signs tonight. That cachexia. It can only mean an advanced and pretty well metastasized cancerous condition. The man is probably in constant pain. I give him six months listening to El Granada music. It's a great place. . . . Best in town." Morty beamed, and I followed his eyes around the crowded tables.

They were all there, all the toy faces of the city's night life. Fame, wealth and beauty sat huddled like a flock of bedizened sheep come in from a storm. Outside, the world was exploding on a hundred battle-fronts. Around us the God of Trivia was still in his heaven with his votaries yawning at their devotions.

And the most elegant and ennuied of them all was Baron Corfus, bowing his good night to Ganzo in the doorway.

# *The Pink Hussar*

THERE ARE many kinds of refugees in our land these days and, as is customary with people who carry too large a load of troubles, they are not among the most popular of folks. We Americans have hearts as open and unsnobbish as a drive-in frankfurter stand but we are, nevertheless, a cynical lot. We are gifted with a sort of national schizophrenia, or split personality. We will play Galahad but we know the fight is fixed.

After we have whooped with piety and brotherly love it is our habit to sit down and sneer at ourselves. And having gone to war to save Europe from losing its soul, it is natural for us, as schizos, that we should become full of carping attitudes toward this aforesaid soul of Europe.

There is, however, a tribe of refugees who are more or less unknown to our citizenry, which is unfortunate, for they are a truly charming lot and could do much to popularize the continental exiles.

These are the talents from Vienna and Budapest—the little world of song and play writers, actors, journalists and bon vivants—that has fled its beloved cafés and brought its intrigues and goulash pots intact to the U. S. A. They differ from all the other refugees because they are not refugees at all—since it is in their power to bring the best of their homeland to our shores—themselves. Their homeland is an ego surrounded by wit and good cooking. It is a Strauss Waltz and a handful of epigrams and a touch of gout. They were the hurdy-gurdy of art and letters that played in the last little charming corner of Europe, that favored anecdotes above panaceas and that, to the very end, sat polishing jests instead of sabers. Had there been enough of them, they might have laughed the Nazis out of countenance and conquest. But there were only a few cafés full and their tunes and witticisms were outnumbered by the Panzer cannon.

It is of these spritely folks I write—a task a little hazardous, for sitting among them I have heard a thousand and one tales, plots, jests and ironies—and do I put one of these on paper I will be sued for plagiarism instanter. For plagiarism suits are as firm a part of Magyar culture as double-decker pastries. In fact, the joke runs that in the golden days of Hungarian letters the first thing a Budapest playwright said to his valet on awakening with a Pilsener hangover was, "Well, Rudolph, whom do I sue today?"

Luckily the story I have to tell is one that actually happened under my nose, and do any of my Hungarian or Viennese admirers detect in it similarities to plays or novels they have themselves composed, I have a whole file of newspaper clippings to testify for me and I am certain I will escape with only a small fine plus court costs.

The most interesting thing that struck me about these famous exiles, when I first met them two years ago, was that I had never heard of them before. I had friends who sighed at the mention of their names and murmured, "Ah, Budapest—ah, Vienna." But not having been abroad since 1920 and having attended strictly to my American knitting, the galaxy of the Danube was unknown to me.

My introduction to this most amiable tribe of refugees was as unexpected and whimsical as if it had been written by one of them. I was engaged at the time in a sort of Desperate Desmond enterprise—that of raising money to produce a movie in New York. There is no reason to produce movies in New York, considering they can be done as easily as tossing cards into a hat in Hollywood. But a contrariness and a childlike fascination with high finance have urged me on several occasions into New York cinema production.

After several conferences with a bank president, I had been assured that the bank would put up half the finances needed were I able to lay hands on the other half. This is not such a bonanza as it sounds. It is exactly like being promised the Lackawanna Railroad, providing you can go out and buy the New York Central first. The sum involved, known as the second money, was $200,000 and no cents.

My delight at meeting Mr. Vinsey was thus deep and genuine. For it was Vinsey who, appearing out of the blue in my hotel-room money-raising headquarters, not only offered me $200,000 as casually as if he were proffering a bite out of an apple, but inducted me almost immediately into the ghost cities of Budapest and Vienna.

Mr. Vinsey had read my script, he told me after he had sat down and put his red-feathered green fedora on his knees, and he considered it a superb and lucrative piece of property. He begged to be allowed to place the $200,000 I needed in my hands.

I saw a smiling, relaxed man in his fifties, with a round face, a look of surprise to his fluff of grey hair, with a soothing, cynical voice and an air about him of a child playing hookey.

He sat looking at me over his green fedora as if he were at home among his oldest friends. I have seldom met a man so instantly likeable as Vinsey and, sensing he was someone of importance, I felt embarrassed never to have heard of him. Vinsey put me at my ease by reciting in an apologetic voice his list of achievements. They included the production of nine movies—three of which had won some sort of prizes—and thirty-seven plays in Hungary and Austria. I had never heard of the plays, the movies, the prizes, or of Vinsey.

"But my poor accomplishments are of no matter to you," he smiled. "What you want from me is $200,000. Am I right?"

I nodded.

"It will be very easy," said Vinsey. "We will be partners. I shall provide the money; you, the brains. It is for you an unfair arrangement. But one, alas, which the artist must always make in our mismanaged civilization."

"It's a very fine arrangement," I said happily, "and if we make it, you can have sixty per cent of the profits."

This was the statement that usually produced a snort and a string of morbid statistics from the potential second money to the effect that no New York movie production had ever grossed enough to return the hind end or second money part of the investment. Mr. Vinsey's answer was the opposite of such crudity.

"Oh, no," he said, "I could not allow that. Sixty per cent would make me your chief. I shall take only forty-nine per cent and be flattered to work under your talents in a most humble and advisory capacity."

There was an Alice in Wonderland sound to this interview, but honesty of a kind that cannot be simulated signalled from the Vinsey ego. Yet a man may be as honest as Abraham Lincoln and still not have $200,000 handy for a dubious investment.

Accordingly, I asked, "When do you think you can get the money?"

"By Monday afternoon," Mr. Vinsey smiled. "Over the week-end. You may forget about all financial problems from now on. Consider your work already in production. It is a beautiful thing and is certain to win a prize."

"Then I'll see you Monday," I said.

"Yes." Mr. Vinsey stood. "But let us have dinner tonight at a friend's house and become more acquainted."

I made inquiry before dinner time and learned that everything Vinsey had told me of himself was true. The only new fact I uncovered was that he had produced two plays since his arrival in New York and that they both had been immediate flops.

The dinner that night was in the home of Gita Lengel, the Bernhardt of Budapest and the Duse of Vienna. None of these things I knew about Gita when I met her. My first impression was that she was related in some way to Vinsey—probably his sister. The same witty smile widened her mouth, the same relaxed and good-natured tones issued from it and the same graceful buzz of personality surrounded her. She was a woman of thirty-eight and I would have called her beautiful if she had had less charm. As it was I called her delightful.

We were joined for dinner by a third refugee, a handsome and boyish man of forty. He, too, struck me as a relative, both of Vinsey and Miss Lengel.

Vinsey introduced the new dinner guest.

"My favorite dramatic critic, Janos Fulka," he said.

"Oh, no," said Gita, "novelist, essayist, and philosopher."

"He is my favorite dramatic critic," Vinsey said, "because he has given up that profession."

Fulka bowed slightly and looked very cynical as he smiled.

"I have given up none of my professions," he said. "I am improving myself secretly in all of them."

"Janos and Vinsey once fought a duel over an adjective," said Gita, "but it turned out to have been a printer's error. Something like the word compatible being changed to contemptible."

We ate chicken paprikash and Vinsey broke the news to his friends of our partnership. A great surge of excitement swept the table. Kisses were exchanged. A fresh bottle of wine was opened. I was treated for a few minutes to the joyous finale of a Viennese operetta.

When the huzzahs had subsided, Vinsey looked tenderly at our hostess and said, "It is too bad we have no part for Europe's greatest actress." Fulka immediately seized one of her hands and kissed it.

"I still live on the memory of your Nora," he sighed.

"And of Julie," Vinsey cried, "and the Princess Rividavia. You put over *The Sofa*."

I didn't know *The Sofa* was in capital letters and looked a little startled.

"Turay's *The Sofa*," Fulka explained. There was a pause and they all looked at me. "You have heard of Turay?" Vinsey inquired.

"Good Lord, yes," I said, "one of the best playwrights left in the world."

The three sighed. Their faces glowed and they nodded in unison as at a prayer meeting.

"Gita's second-act curtain in *The Sofa* was one of the greatest laughs in the history of the theater," said Fulka.

"For two seasons," Vinsey cooed. "I watched her every night."

The partnership was for the moment forgotten and both men looked at Gita with such homage as might have been given the queen of an ancient realm.

"There is nothing for me in your script," said Gita—I was to find that this delightful woman had read every unproduced script on Broadway—"but, truly, the pleasure of reading it was as great as acting in it. Believe me—and have some more wine."

"The theater of New York," said Fulka, "may be measured by this fact that Gita Lengel is not on its stage. This is exactly the same as if the United States decided to win the present war by immobilizing its fleet."

"My accent," said Gita, "and my stubbornness."

"Quite right," said Vinsey. "She has turned down excellent parts."

"A maid with a duster," said Gita, "who turns out to be the head of a gang of black marketeers. And a mother who begs the governor to pardon her son from the electric chair." Gita looked pathetically at me. "Those are the two parts that have been offered—with salaries. I am not silly. I would have played them. I would play a cabbage or the hind legs of a horse—just to be on the stage again. But those plays! My dear—unbearable!"

"One of them is still running," Vinsey sighed.

"So is the war," said Gita. "Duration is no virtue for calamities."

"Tell me"—Fulka glared at me as he patted her arm—"how is it that in a city like New York with seven million adults you have a theater only for children?"

"It is the critics!" Vinsey smiled. "They are in a plot to keep the theater inferior to themselves. They like to look down instead of up—because if they look up there is too far to look."

"Worse than that," said Fulka, "the critics of New York are so old and so fat that they usually collapse before the final curtain. As a result, they do not report the play but their own symptoms."

"Schopenhauer wrote the perfect line about critics," said Vinsey moodily. " 'When a jackass looks into a mirror you must not expect an apostle to look out.' "

"Poor Janos," Gita sighed, "you will never be a critic in New York.

You always admired plays that were either too deep for your understanding or too brilliant to make jokes about."

Guests began arriving as we were finishing our dinner—and as the room filled I felt as if a land of charm and curious customs was coming to life around us. I met Dr. Alper-Mayer, a portly dark-haired gentleman with a short square beard and a useless medical fame in his bow; and Stephan Holz, a thin-faced tight-mouthed painter with an overdeveloped sense of courtesy. Fulka whispered to me that his was the most vitriolic brush in Austria. A jowled and beaming playwright named Herzog appeared, and a tense young lady in a sort of peasant dress who looked as dedicated to something as an Ibsen heroine. There arrived a fragile brunette with white lace at her throat and a delicious voice that seemed to be produced by a zither and who turned out, on a second inspection, to be not twenty years old, but sixty. She was Lili Marisca, a musical comedy star with the names of Friml, Lehar, and Strauss in her diadem. And lastly, a gentleman named Lazlo with a paunch full of laughter. He announced joyfully that he was ready for a second dinner.

"Lazlo begins eating at seven o'clock," Vinsey explained to me, "and continues until after midnight. It is a difficult career in wartime. Luckily he is highly in demand at dinner parties."

"Play your new waltz, Lazlo darling," said Gita, "and I'll see if there is any chicken left."

Lazlo played and the company listened like a group of doting relatives. I heard a lilting gallant bit of music that seemed to say, "Dance with me, love with me, and forget how old and far away we are."

This was my first of many evenings in the ghost land of Budapest and Vienna. But during these original hours I learned all I was ever to know about its witty citizens. I was never to know how they kept alive, what mysterious means made possible the chicken paprikash, the wine bottles, and the pleasant apartments. Nor was I to learn until the day of the Unbelievable Plot whether failure had secretly embittered them or the memory of vanished fame left them with hidden wounds. For they apparently had only one face for life, the face of talent that remains intact whatever else has crumbled.

Vinsey spent a month trying to raise the $200,000 for our movie and kept assuring me daily that the project was a few hours from completion. I assured him in return that the delay was of no consequence and that I would not be ready to shoot the movie until the Fall.

"Ah, by that time," Vinsey smiled, "we will have twice that much in the bank. In the meantime, we remain partners without capital—but a future," he sighed. "It would have been so simple once in Budapest. I had only to pick up my telephone, and wagons full of gold drew up to my office. Here the telephone is not such a magic instrument."

The Unbelievable Plot began a few nights later with the arrival of a startling Vinsey at my hotel.

"I am very upset," he said, after downing three beakers of beer in silence, "and I have come to you to talk because I love and trust you."

"Just what is it?" I asked.

"Turay," said Vinsey in a voice of doom. "Turay is coming to America. He leaves Lisbon today. He will be in New York in no time."

I looked at Vinsey with some surprise. Turay, as the greatest living Hungarian, and perhaps European, playwright, seemed hardly a visitor to wring such groans from a fellow refugee.

"Why, that's marvelous," I said. "I'm glad to hear that Turay is alive and bringing his greatness to our city."

Vinsey groaned again.

"What's the trouble?" I asked. "Is he an enemy of yours?"

"I adore him," said Vinsey softly. "He was my God for thirty years. Since I am a boy I have sat at his feet—as have all the writers and actors and critics of Budapest and Vienna. Turay"—Vinsey's eyes grew misty—"ah, if there is a graceful soul and a fountain of wit left in the world, it wears that name. You have had many charming talents in this country. Put them all together, all the poets and lovers and brilliant playwrights and happy story-tellers—and you have, perhaps, Turay. No, not a full Turay. Such a one could only exist in Budapest."

"Then why are you beating your bosom over his arrival here?" I asked.

"Because," said Vinsey softly, "he must not come. It is wrong for him to come. He must not do what we have all done—on a smaller scale—change from a man of fame into an eccentric nobody. Dear friend," Vinsey's voice throbbed, "we all admire your country. And New York—ah, it is the last of the Ali Baba cities. But it is a curious robber—the new world. It robs the old of its glitter, its meaning, its importance. My friends whom you have met. Myself. We were all great men. The press was filled with our achievements. The public adored us. That was in Budapest, in Vienna. Here in New York, what are we?

Nobodies. We make jokes, we write plays, we paint pictures, we hold salons, we do everything we ever did—and we are still nobodies. The ear of your country is not for our jokes. Our wit dies at your feet."

Vinsey paused and handed me a cablegram. It was no climax to his eloquence. It read only, "Arrive, Dodo."

"That is the first word of English he has written," Vinsey groaned.

"Are your friends as upset as you?" I asked.

"Oh, completely," said Vinsey. "Even Dr. Alper-Mayer. Dr. Alper-Mayer is a great intellect. He was the very leading physician of Vienna. Turay's own doctor. And Schuschnigg's. The most expensive and complicated diseases sought him out. And here he is able to find neither patients nor even an office and is mistaken by everybody for a vaudevillian out of work. I spoke to him before I came to you. Turay, he said, must not come to New York. He must not be defeated here as we have been. As a result of such a thing we may all end up by committing suicide. Not Turay, mind you. But us. People, you must know, can suffer a great deal as long as a symbol of their success remains somewhere alive. Turay has been such a symbol for us. To see him fail, as we have—that would be the unbearable thing for us."

"But why must he fail?" I asked.

"Ah," Vinsey sighed, burying his nose in a fourth beaker, "the critics!"

I waited at Gita's home for the great entrance. The party was in honor of Turay and the ghost cities were assembled in full. The three rooms—including the dining room—were packed with celebrities who had lost their names.

The playwright had arrived in New York in the afternoon. This was his welcoming party, his safe-from-home-coming. During the hour I waited I learned a number of surprising things about my friends Gita, Fulka, Andri, Marisca, Holz, Dr. Alper-Mayer, and Vinsey. I learned them from strangers who, finding me in their midst, imagined I knew everything that was known to them.

Gita had been Turay's wife some fifteen years ago. Marisca had once been married to Turay thirty years ago. And Andri, the young Ibsen heroine, had been Madam Turay five years ago. Fulka had left his own wife twelve years ago and stolen Gita from Turay. And twenty-five years ago Vinsey had stolen Marisca from the great playwright. On the other hand, Turay had lured away Vinsey's three later wives from his keep. As of today, the grey-tufted Vinsey was desperately in love with Gita, who, however, had given her oath to Fulka that she would marry him—as soon as she got a job; although it was the opinion of several of the guests that it was not the job that stood between Gita and Fulka but the ghost of Turay, whom she had never ceased to love during the twelve years despite her two subsequent marriages and present betrothal.

This all seemed a little confusing but what most confused me was the fact that I had been dining almost nightly with these fanatic wife and husband snatchers and had never detected anything but an innocent camaraderie among them.

I was talking to the Countess Graudenz, a former opera star whose beauty was now a little dimmed by overeating.

"What about Dr. Alper-Mayer and Holz, the painter?" I asked. "Are they related to, let us say, Turay?"

"Dr. Alper-Mayer was married to Gita after she ran off with Fulka," said the diva, "and Holz—my God, Holz is the father of the two children Turay raised in Paris. He supported them for twenty years. But I thought you knew that."

"No, I didn't," I confessed to the Countess, and the silence of a curtain-raising came over the room. It was Turay. He stood in the doorway and smiled on the ghostland before him. And this moment of silence was like a salvo of ghostly applause. The eyes of those around me—eyes that were the connoisseurs of mockery—grew misty. And though no one wept, there was the smile of tears as if, not a man of fame, but a beloved child had returned to them.

This was true. The thing that distinguished this great man in the doorway was a quality of childishness. Or he might have been a wide-mouthed, gentle-eyed clown come to amuse other children. He was tall and plump about the waist and the sleeves of his rumpled coat were a bit too long. His grey hair slanted in a boyish mop across his forehead and his face was pink. Looking at this smiling and abstracted face, full of innocence and mockery, I realized where Vinsey, Fulka, Gita, Lazlo, and all my new friends had got their expression. They had borrowed it from Turay—for he resembled all of them except that he looked a little dreamier.

The silence was now over and there was talk and laughter as if nothing had happened. There was no rush of handshaking and no crowding of admirers around a hero. He had sat down at a table in a corner with four friends and was nibbling at a platter of cheese. The rest of the company occupied itself with the business of gossip and jest; but, though they seemed to ignore the arrival, there was a verve that had not been in their manner before. Sitting quietly in a corner, eating his cheese, Turay was among them—and all was now right in their ghostland.

Vinsey brought me to the table. Turay was telling a story, and Dr. Alper-Mayer, Fulka, Gita, and the hungry Lazlo were listening to him as attentively as if they were seated in a schoolroom.

"I was young at the time," the pink face and the grey hair were saying, "nineteen years old. I had been in the country on a vacation for three weeks and now I come running back to Budapest because my heart is breaking and I cannot endure to be away from the lady I worship. Ah, if I could only remember her name now, the story would sound a little better. I come, out of breath, to the house, the magic house where she lives. I ring the bell. I wait and I die of suspense.

"Then the door opens and a strange young woman is standing there. She has just moved in with her family. My adored one has just moved out, leaving no address. I stand looking at the young woman and I am so unhappy I begin to cry. That night I figure for the first time in my life that I will commit suicide. And I go back to say goodbye to the magic house. Here I meet the strange young woman again. And I do not commit suicide but, instead, I marry her a month later. And this is the theme of my new play—that marriage is a search for somebody who has disappeared when you are young."

Vinsey asked softly, "The new play, is it done, Dodo?"

"Yes, I finished it on the plane," Turay smiled. "You do not expect a playwright to come to market without a basket of fresh eggs."

"You have a title for it?" Vinsey sighed.

"I call it *The Pink Hussar*," said Turay, and added with an apologetic smile, "Do you think it sounds a little old-fashioned?"

"My dear friend," Fulka spoke up loyally, "Turay makes his own fashions. Is that right, Gita?"

"Yes, always, always," Gita laughed, and Turay's eyes widened innocently at the drama in her voice. Then with a smile he took her hand and, looking around the room said, gently, "We are all here. All except Immelmans, the waiter. I miss his dirty apron."

"What a play that was," Fulka cried, and explained for my sake, "a one-acter. Immelmans was the hero. Ah, his exit with the coffeepot spilling! You remember, Gita?"

Fulka laughed, overcome, and Lazlo interrupted.

"Do you remember the waltz in *A Handful of Isoldes*?" He began to hum.

"There was no music in the 'Isoldes,'" Gita said.

"Off-stage, off-stage!" Lazlo cried. "The waltz when you were dying.

During that long speech—when the little orchestra in the café downstairs drowns you out. My God, such is fame!"

"I will never forget the night you lost your voice," Dr. Alper-Mayer smiled. "The opening night of *The Sofa* when I gave you the electric shock in the larynx. It was the first time in Europe this treatment was ever used."

"She could only speak in a whisper," said Vinsey, "and I chased all over Budapest looking for Turay to make him write in the line, 'The Princess Rividavia has a cold.'"

"What a characterization that was!" Fulka sighed and added, "Of course, it was a great play."

"They were all great plays," said Vinsey. "Masterpieces."

"*The Pink Hussar* is much better," said Turay slyly, "at least so it seems to me."

I had decided to see if money could be raised in Hollywood for a New York movie production and spent the next three weeks shaking futilely at the Hollywood Christmas tree. Nothing fell from it but advice. But there was still Vinsey. Vinsey was waiting for me on my return but not with $200,000. He was in a state of shock and apparently had forgotten entirely the matter of our partnership.

"The very worst thing has happened," he told me at dinner. "No. Order for yourself. I cannot eat. Even Lazlo cannot eat. We are all very, very upset."

"About Turay," I said.

"Naturally," said Vinsey. "He has sold his play. It is going into production. It is like waiting for a massacre."

"I'd like to read the script," I said.

"It is not necessary," Vinsey sighed. "I will tell you all you have to know. It is beautifully written. Very tender. Extremely cynical. In short, Turay. And it is also as full of failure as a broken-down old actor. My God, the critics will kill it!"

"You can't always tell," I said.

"You can tell about *The Pink Hussar*," Vinsey groaned. "Four plays exactly like it—all stolen from Turay—were produced last year. By four of our best Hungarians. Did you happen to see them? They were cut to ribbons by the critics. One of the playwrights—Fodor—is still in bed moaning. Believe me, *The Pink Hussar* has even less chance. It is half fantasy. It has one speech three pages long. Guess who recites it? God. And He is not even on the stage. The stage is empty for three pages. No, there is no chance. The critics will have a feast. Turay *en brochette.* When I tell you that thirty people who love Turay better than their own fathers and mothers have read *The Pink Hussar* and all said the same thing—you will understand how there is nothing but doom ahead. Even Gita. She cried for two nights after Turay sold it. He has not sold a play, she said. He has arranged for his funeral."

"Who's producing it?" I asked.

"Jock Kane," Vinsey said, "the final black wreath on top of the hearse."

I knew Jock. He had once produced a play of mine. In those days he had been a puissant man of the Broadway theater, and hailed to the ends of the earth as a wizard. In the space of five years he had been demoted by the critics from wizardhood to oblivion, which, on Broadway, is not so far a throw as it sounds. The critics run an elevator service between these two points—with no stop-overs.

At his peak as a wizard, Mr. Kane had produced nine flops in a row. There was this, however, to say for him: Disaster had not tempered the man. In clover or in limbo, there was never a more nerve-wracking, macaw-souled figure connected with the Broadway scene than Jock Kane. With his talents and his gold petals fallen from him, and the maniacal bloom of his certainties and wizardries gone to dust, he remained a noxious weed-like fellow sticking in your eye.

"Jock used to be quite a genius," I said. "He may have a rebirth."

"When Jock Kane is reborn," said Vinsey, "it will be as a tarantula. He is a vicious, greedy, and unscrupulous man who knows nothing and has the quality of a murderer."

Vinsey watched me eat for a spell and then went on: "On top of his faults, he has a virtue which is even worse. He loves Turay. He sits around listening to Dodo and rolling his eyes like a little girl up to her neck in art. And already he has swindled him. Five per cent less royalties. A pitiful advance, only. And no say by Turay in the casting. He begged, practically on his knees, that Gita should play the lead. She would be perfect. But Mr. Kane, who loves him like a brother and Gita like an uncle, would not even consider it. Also, Mr. Kane has taken an extra twenty-five per cent from Turay out of the movie rights. But this matters nothing. There will be no royalties, no movie sale. There will be only a funeral."

Vinsey drew a deep breath and repeated his cry of a month ago, "It must not be. We must save Turay from becoming one of us—another broken-down genius from Budapest who eats chicken paprikash and tries to remember who he was. Dear friend, I have a mission. I am going to prevent the New York critics from wiping out the last bit of glory that belongs to Budapest. Gita Lengel is a bum, Fulka is a bum. Lazlo, Holz, Dr. Alper-Mayer, Fodor, Marisca, Litauer, Vinsey —we are all bums. But Turay is going to stay Turay."

Vinsey's eyes were glowing and he leaned forward with the air of a conspirator under a pier.

"Will you help in our cause and be a member of our committee?" he whispered.

I nodded.

"Then I will call for you tomorrow at seven," said Vinsey. "The producer is giving the celebration for the opening of rehearsals at Gita's home. Mr. Jock Kane dislikes public restaurants where the check interferes with the camaraderie."

I joined Vinsey and Fulka in the hotel lobby at seven.

"We are an hour early," Vinsey greeted me. "The dinner is at eight. We will spend the hour here, discussing the plot."

Fulka looked around, nervously.

"I think I saw the critic for the *Journal* in the dining room," he said. "He might afterward get suspicious."

"A creature who is deaf, dumb, and blind is immune to suspiciousness," said Vinsey.

"Let me recite the plot," said Fulka.

"By all means," Vinsey said. "I will not interrupt."

"The critics of New York," said Fulka, "once loved Turay. Twenty years ago, even twelve years ago, they considered him one of the world's greatest. Even today they are willing to admire him as a museum piece. What we are going to do"—Fulka stared at me—"is arrange for the critics to hail *The Pink Hussar* when it opens, and fill the city with their love of Turay."

I stared back at Fulka and then at Vinsey. It seemed odd that two such witty men should take leave of reason together.

"What are you going to do?" I asked. "Bribe the critics?"

"In a way, yes," said Fulka. "Tonight Turay is going to be taken ill. Desperately ill."

"Dying," said Vinsey, happily.

"He is going to be rushed to the hospital," Fulka went on. "Dr. Alper-Mayer will attend him. In the morning the papers will be full."

"Turay stricken as his last and finest play goes into rehearsal," sighed Vinsey.

"And then," continued Fulka, "he will remain unconscious. His death will be assured. A matter of days. Perhaps hours."

"Wait a minute," I said. "Does Turay know about this?"

"Good heavens, no!" said Fulka. "We are not consulting him in any way."

"Then how is he going to get sick?" I asked.

Vinsey drew a small bottle out of his coat pocket.

"In his coffee tonight," he said quietly. "It is tasteless."

"What's in it?" I asked.

"I don't know the name," said Vinsey. "Dr. Alper-Mayer prepared it. Two spoonfuls will produce a heavy perspiration and also unconsciousness."

"He will have the seizure after he drinks the coffee," said Fulka. "Tomorrow when he wakes up in the hospital, we will give him another spoonful at noon. There is no danger. It is entirely harmless and even good for the nerves."

"That part of the whole thing is in Dr. Alper-Mayer's hands," said Vinsey. "We will work in another direction. The publicity."

"On the night of the opening of *The Pink Hussar*," Fulka said, "Turay will be in his last coma. Imagine the effect this will have on the critics. And the first-nighters as well. They will be listening not to a play but a swan song. Turay dying will be like an orchestra playing sweetly in the wings. The reviews will be simply sensational. And then Turay will recover slowly."

"And retire," said Vinsey. "Another deathbed would give the show away."

"You need worry about nothing," Vinsey whispered as we rang Gita's bell. "Everybody has been assigned a part to play."

"How about Kane?" I asked. "Is he in on it?"

"My God, no!" said Vinsey. "I would not trust a crook like Kane with an old shoe."

"We have saved the best news for you as a surprise," Fulka whispered. "There will be two critics at the dinner. Two big ones."

"That's a little dangerous," I protested.

"My dear friend," Vinsey smiled, "have no worry. We are the best actors in the world."

The room was filled. There were three aliens in ghostland—Jock Kane and two of the leading drama savants of the press. Fourteen of us sat at the table. Laughter rang. Witticisms bounced about like ping-pong balls. I looked nervously at the two captive critics, fearful that they recognize all this gaiety as that of a cast performing. But, no. They sat smiling politely through the great scene, hiding the discomfort of their wallflower souls in an air of tolerance and superiority. Their manner spoke that it was a noisy old-fashioned evening worthy of the museum piece who sat pensively at the head of the table. I wondered at this pensiveness and thought several times that I noted a frown on the child-like pink face.

Vinsey explained to me in a whisper as we left the table and scattered about the room for our coffee.

"Dodo is angry," he said. "He thinks we are trying too much to impress the critics with how gay and witty we are. He has an excellent sense of the theater. How he would enjoy the scene, if he only knew what it was."

Lazlo went to the piano.

"Dear ladies and gentlemen," he announced, puffing with four helpings of goulash, "I have arranged especially in honor of Mr. Turay a medley of his favorite songs—going back to when we were both boys together and in the cafes of Budapest they were singing——"

Lazlo began to play and the contralto of the Countess Graudenz sounded softly.

"Is it not beautiful?" Fulka whispered at my side. "He is going to die—with the music of his youth playing in his ears."

I looked at Turay who was frowning abstractedly over a coffee cup. The song ended and another tune was begun and then, suddenly—although I had been expecting it—Gita's voice cried out in fright.

Turay had dropped the coffee cup. He was swaying in his chair, his head rolling from side to side. Then, with a sigh, audible in the silenced room, the pink face and the grey hair slid to the rug.

The morrow found the committee gaping at victory. The newspapers showered manna. We convened in my room, behind locked doors.

"Look at this one," said Vinsey and read aloud in a lover's voice, " 'The stricken Turay's position in the theater is a high one. With G. Bernard Shaw he is the last of the Great Contemporaries.' "

"This one is better," said Fulka, and read, " 'For the past twenty-five years Turay has been regarded as one of the theater's pillars of wit and ideas.' "

"Perfect, perfect," Vinsey beamed. "We have, without question, scored a triumph."

I asked after Turay's condition.

"He was just recovering consciousness when we left the hospital," said Fulka. "Gita is with him, being very brave—for the photographers."

"She should never have gone to the hairdresser's," Fulka frowned.

"Nonsense," said Vinsey; "she is giving a magnificent performance. Tomorrow Marisca will do even better. And Wednesday, Andri. I am coaching her."

"On the whole, we have nothing to worry about," said Fulka. "Dr. Alper-Mayer remains at the bedside. At four o'clock he will administer a second dose. And the thing will grow by itself."

Vinsey read from another paper, "—a heart condition that holds small hope for recovery. As the brilliant dramatist himself has so often written—the final curtain falls slowly."

The old showman looked up.

"It is like the old days," he sighed. "Everything happens just as we dreamed."

For four days the committee sat on top of the world. The Unbelievable Plot was surpassing all their dreams of it. The press had taken the bit in its teeth and there was no need for publicity spurs. It offered interviews with Gita, Andri and Marisca, the three lovely ex-wives of Turay, and all at his bedside weeping in exotic unison—a scene the gifted playwright himself might have written. It told of messages from kings and coachmen, from big and little celebrities all over the world. It carried stories of the actors rehearsing in *The Pink Hussar* who had sent the dying dramatist a great box of flowers and saluted him with the words, "Master, whatever happens, we will make the world gay once more with your wit." Under their photograph one paper printed, "Turay's Last Cast. While the playwright lies dying, the theater he loved answers with its tender battle cry, 'The show goes on.' "

By Sunday the style of all the leading dramatic critics had undergone a change. They wheeled out whimsicalities and greeted the Grim Reaper hovering over the Hungarian genius as if they were Turays all, sprightly and wistful before disaster and never forgetting that life was a Waltz. It was all highly wonderful and the committee reeled about in its cups, giddy with the Hungarian renaissance that had smote the town—until the fifth day.

Vinsey brought me the news. He was white, his eyes were bloodshot, his hands fluttered like fans. He entered, collapsed on the couch and sat moaning.

"Something gone wrong?" I said.

He nodded.

I asked what it was.

"It is too terrible to think about," Vinsey groaned. I poured him a large drink, which he swallowed abstractedly.

"Turay is sick," he said hoarsely.

"I know that," I said; "he's dying."

"Please, no!" Vinsey cried. "Don't say that! Don't!" He clapped both hands to his head and weaved as his eyes overran. "We have done something awful. It is the judgment of God."

"I'm waiting to hear," I said.

"I am telling you," Vinsey cried. "Turay is ill. He is unconscious. He cannot talk."

"You mean honestly ill?" I said.

"Honestly unconscious," Vinsey groaned. "Dr. Alper-Mayer did not give him the medicine yesterday. We were skipping a day. The committee had agreed that Turay should regain consciousness so he could make a little statement for the press. For his sake, you understand. He would never forgive us if we did not give him a little speaking part in his death scene."

Vinsey shuddered and I handed him another drink.

"Dr. Alper-Mayer telephoned me at nine," he whispered. "I flew to the hospital. There he was. Lying there, unconscious. Turay in a coma. A real coma."

"What does the doctor think it is?" I asked.

"He doesn't know." Vinsey wiped his eyes. "He examined him for two hours. The heart is beating—but that is all. I tell you we have killed him"—he raised his voice—"the greatest mind in Europe."

"The medicine was harmless," I assured him. "I took some myself for a sleeping dose."

"It is not the medicine," Vinsey said. "It is the shock. Turay found out he was dying. Somebody must have left a newspaper by the bed. He read it while he was only half drugged. A sensitive soul like his. A mind so delicate, so open to phenomena! It reads it is dying. And it dies. It is psychological murder. We are a committee of murderers."

"What's being done?" I asked.

"Gita and Marisca have gone to church to pray," Vinsey whispered. "Fulka wants to give himself up to the police. Dr. Alper-Mayer has ordered some kind of a life-saving apparatus. And Lazlo and I have agreed to be buried on the same day with him—one on each side." Vinsey held out his empty glass and murmured, "A few last drops."

The committee crowded the hospital waiting room. Lazlo arrived last with all the afternoon papers. We listened as he read in a husky voice, " 'The scene around the dying playwright is a page out of Murget's *La Vie de Bohème*. It is a wake of wit. Each of his old cronies vies with the other in gay reminiscences of Turay's spicy sixty-two years. Jests fly and chuckles sound, but behind the mirth is the tear of a waltz ending.' "

"That was yesterday," Fulka groaned.

" 'The waltzes of Budapest play on,' " Lazlo continued reading.

"Shut up about waltzes," Gita cried from the chair. The committee breathed heavily and avoided looking at one another.

Dr. Alper-Mayer appeared. His beard glistened but his voice was calm. He bowed in front of me and said, "Mr. Turay wishes to speak to you, sir."

"He is alive!" Gita cried.

"We have rallied him slightly," said Dr. Alper-Mayer. "Ice packs. Adrenalin. The mass drip. Electricity. We have overlooked nothing."

"Is there hope?" Vinsey trembled.

"We are struggling with a hypnotic state," Dr. Alper-Mayer said. "The life force is gone."

"Think of it," Fulka moaned, "Turay should become a zombi!"

"Not quite," Dr. Alper-Mayer said. "There are left a few organs that have not become cataleptic. We are working on these."

"But if he can speak," Lazlo cried, "that means—"

"Nothing." Dr. Alper-Mayer interrupted firmly. "He will go under in a few minutes. It is only a flicker. Please remember I have had many similar cases in Vienna and Berlin. Hurry, please."

I followed him to the sickroom. He opened the door.

"I will wait outside," he said. "He wishes to see you alone. At such a time we humor the aberration."

He closed the door behind me and I was alone with the dying Turay. I stared down at the wasted face on the pillow and a distaste for Hungarian plots overcame me.

"Get me two bars of chocolate, please," the playwright whispered without opening his eyes, "and, if possible, a liverwurst sandwich. Soon as you can."

I stared.

"And be so kind to break the needle on that damn machine." The blue eyes opened and scowled sleepily at the intravenous drip apparatus. "I need a collaborator," he sighed. "It is too big a production to handle by myself."

"Your friends outside," I began, "I'll call them."

"My God, no—please!" Turay whispered. "I will explain. I am

nearly dead—but only from hunger. I have been living for five days on dew. Maybe you can bring a chicken leg back in your pocket. No. Too dangerous. I could not swallow the bones. Sit down, please. As my collaborator, you will hear everything."

I sat down and stared.

"When I woke up the first morning in the hospital," the wasted face resumed, "I knew right away what had happened. It is an old plot. Fulka and Vinsey may even be sued for using it. They were going to make *The Pink Hussar* a success by having me on my deathbed. The coffee was drugged, like in *The Juggler's Return*. I wake up. I read the papers and I understand everything. It is not a bad idea. But on the second day I begin to worry."

"You were unconscious." I stared at the child-like face. "I was here. I saw you."

"I saw you, too," Turay smiled. "I was unconscious part of the time. The rest of the time I worried. You cannot play a death scene with epigrams and gypsy waltzes. My friends were behaving like an 1890 operetta. Did you read Fulka's interview about death is like a Pierrot in a black ruffle? Very bad dialogue. It is the Hungarian failing. He writes with rouge." The voice grew fainter. "Do you know how I became famous? By not putting any jokes in my plays. I was the first Hungarian to write without epigrams. The whole world embraced me —with relief."

Turay sighed and rallied himself.

"You will bring some cheese with the liverwurst," he said.

"What kind?" I asked.

"A pocketful," he said weakly; "I am not particular. I will finish the plot for you. Yesterday, when that idiot Alper-Mayer— My God! He has been freezing and electrocuting me for thirty-six hours." Turay's voice brightened as if he were only now waking up. "Yesterday he gave me no drug. I understood at once he was going to let me regain consciousness so the public would have some hope. And then I am drugged again and the grief is greater. This type of suspense is ridiculous. It is good only in the movies. Did you see the picture *Little Women*? Very sickening. As soon as I understand, I see it is my opportunity to take over the whole plot myself. I have a bottle of sleeping pills in my pocket. Very powerful ones—from Budapest yet. I hide the bottle under the mattress and I take three. You saw the improvement in the situation immediately. Vinsey, Fulka, Gita—all of them. Now they are acting with conviction. No more epigrams. And that idiot Alper-Mayer. He is behaving like a doctor. He is confused, desperate and knows nothing."

"A sort of revenge on your friends," I said. "I can see its charm."

"No, please." Turay smiled. "It is not revenge. It is Act Two—*my* act—with a new plot turn. You will help me?" he asked eagerly. "Please, I need you."

I nodded and Turay removed a bottle from under the mattress. He spilled three pills into his hand.

"I have learned to swallow them without water," he said. "It is quite a trick." He put the pills in his mouth. "In an hour I will be unconscious. You cannot wake me up with a hammer. In the meantime, here are the principal points of Act Two. With a hint of the theme of Act Three."

Five minutes later I joined the Committee in the waiting room. They rushed toward me.

"His play," I said. "He's worried about it. He wants to see Jock Kane at once."

Dr. Alper-Mayer, followed by a nurse carrying three large ice bags, hurried to the sickroom.

"Did you tell him he wasn't dying?" Fulka asked tensely.

"He only smiled," I said. "The hypnosis is very deep."

"His soul is exiting on a wrong cue," Vinsey moaned. "I am going in there and scream in his ears. The truth! The whole truth!"

"He will only think you are treating him like a child," I said. "Call up Jock Kane. It may be wise to humor him."

Jock Kane arrived from rehearsal in a half hour. He was left alone in the sickroom. The committee discussed him grimly for fifteen minutes. One and all were agreed that he was the greatest swindler and rogue in the history of the theater, and its lowest intellect. Jock finally came out. He was oddly changed. His dark, avid face with its scorpion-like glitter looked toward us with the gentleness of a Madonna. The unscrupulous eyes were wet with tears. He sat down beside Gita and took her hand.

"You are going to play the lead in *The Pink Hussar*," he said softly. "Report for rehearsal tomorrow morning."

Gita stared.

"He asked for it," Jock continued in a purring voice. "It was wonderful. If I live to be a thousand I'll never forget that scene. A human soul stripped bare. He could hardly speak. He sounded just like a little child whispering in the dark. He took my hand like this and said softly, simply—that God was good to him because He had provided a great producer for the epilogue. Then he said to me, 'You were right about Gita. She is not ideal for the part. But with your genius as a director, she will be perfect. You will remove from her that phony Hungarian foolishness. You will breathe reality into her.' Then he smiled and said, 'When I am in my box on opening night—in my little box with the satin lining—I will feel closer to heaven if Gita is behind the footlights again.' "

Jock paused and looked far away.

"Those were his last words," he whispered.

A sob came from the window where Andri sat with two newspaper reporters. Gita's head drooped, and Jock put an arm around her.

"You must be a soldier," he said, "and forget everything. Forget your grief, your heartbreak and your Hungarian tricks. And turn in the wittiest performance of your life."

Gita nodded, and a flashlight exploded.

I returned to the hospital at midnight. Dr. Alper-Mayer was in the corridor with two internes. He seemed to have aged. The three were grouped around a large apparatus.

"I was going to try electric shock tonight," Dr. Alper-Mayer muttered sleepily, "but this *verdamte* machine is broke again. That is American equipment for you!"

I entered the sick room and slid a bag full of dainties on the closet shelf. It was dangerous but the plot called for it.

For a week I played blockade runner and my hat went off to Hungarian courage. Bedevilled by Dr. Alper-Mayer and his ice bags, electric shocks and mass drips, Turay kept heroically to his six sleeping pills a day—three in the morning and three at midnight. This allowed him a few hours of fuzzy articulation. It was during these hours that he performed his wonders.

Vinsey brought me the news of them. A second deathbed scene with Jock Kane had resulted in Vinsey receiving a ten per cent cut of *The Pink Hussar* as a gift. Turay had offered to buy this for his old friend but Jock had refused to accept any money. Three newspapermen had been present to applaud this scene of largesse. And on the following day Andri was announced as having joined the cast of *The Pink Hussar* in the important part as The Young Ghost. The afternoon papers carried news of a third substitution. Madam Marisca had been coaxed into playing The Old Ghost, another vital role in the eagerly awaited fantasy. And all three substitutions had brought only gallant phrases from the actresses who had yielded their places. Two of them had even gone so far as to tear up their run-of-the-play contracts. This was all in deference to Turay. What more fitting than that the dying dramatist should have his last play performed by the three women he had loved and made famous?

But Vinsey, Gita, Marisca, and Andri were only part of the achievements of the wily possum of Hungarian letters. One of the more emotional gazettes offered on Wednesday the opening chapter of a serial entitled, "Turay—The Last Smile of Europe." It was written by Janos Fulka, identified as the most renowned and cleverest critic in Europe. And it was illustrated by Stephan Holz, identified as the foremost caricaturist of the Continent. Fulka had launched a sprightly tale of Budapest's art life. There were enough epigrams in the first installment to stun any salon. None of them, however, were about critics. And there was, lastly, the wonder that befell Lazlo, the unemployed waltz king and mighty eater. An ent'racte score was being specially composed by him for *The Pink Hussar,* a score destined to jingle for months over the air waves.

Of how these amazing things had happened, I received only bewildered and hysterical accounts from Vinsey.

"He held the editor's hand in his coma," Vinsey reported, "and he was barely able to talk. We all thought it was the final scene. 'If I live,' he said—I never cried so much, I swear to you. Gita and Andri, too. It was unbearable. 'If I live,' he said, 'I would like to write my life for your paper. It is the perfect paper for my life. But I would be cheating your paper. Because it would not be as well written as if Janos Fulka wrote it. For drama, me. For prose, Fulka. He is our greatest genius.' " Vinsey sighed. "The same way with Holz and Lazlo. A few words he speaks. Then his eyes become glazed. His voice disappears. And the coma comes back. Death is beside him again. We hear only phrases out of a tomb—a living tomb."

I listened to Vinsey daily, read the paper, smuggled in the cheese and chocolate bars, and watched the second act unfold. The master dramatist, soggy with sleeping pills, recoiling under Dr. Alper-Mayer's scientific assaults, operated without falter.

We had a last whispered conference in the sickroom the night before the opening of *The Pink Hussar*. I suggested to Turay that he begin his recovery and so lighten the spirit of his cast.

"The girls sit and cry between scenes," I told him.

He looked at me wearily and his voice was blurred.

"No," he said, "it is better this way. They will give a wretched performance. They will overact. They will frighten the audience with their gaiety. But this hysteria will be mistaken by the critics for genius. Thank God, I will not be there to see it." The voice weakened. "My last five pills," he murmured. "I am taking them all at once in the morning." He opened his palm and looked dully at the five pellets. "I assure you I will not be nervous on this opening night," he smiled and dozed off.

The great triumph of *The Pink Hussar* is theatrical history. The three new dramatic stars, Gita Lengel, Madame Marisca, and Luba Andri are also theatrical history. The names Janos Fulka and Stephan Holz are loud in the gossip columns, dinner parties and fancy barrooms where the arts still find precarious haven. Lazlo, the new Lehar, is the toast of all radio lovers. These matters need no further comment.

The triumph of Dr. Alper-Mayer is, however, a little less known. His great work in pulling Turay back from the very brink of the grave, has resulted in medical recognition unprecedented among refugee doctors. He has not only an office crowded with adoring patients, but is busy almost nightly lecturing to psychiatric and neurological societies. The Alper-Mayer treatment for narcolepsy, so successfully practised on Turay, is certain to win the hyphenated scientist world renown.

I sat with Turay alone in his new apartment a month after the opening. It was Sunday and the dramatic sections of the morning papers were scattered around his bed. The playwright was still weak but the pinkness was returning to his dreamy face. Each time I saw him I was bowled over anew by his continued modesty, for he had revealed to none of his friends the manner in which he had toiled and suffered to reinstate them in the arts.

"The critics continue to be very kind to me," he grinned. "Did you read them today? I am the spirit of the waltz. I am the spirit of democracy. I am the spirit of the ages." He smiled. "I will tell you something secret. *The Pink Hussar* is not a very good play. I sneaked in and saw it for the first time last night. My God, the direction! It is like a ballet under water. That Jock Kane is a complete imbecile. And the acting! Even Gita. Abominable. And the play is no better. Those speeches by the ghosts and God. They are absolutely without meaning. Why didn't somebody have sense enough to cut them out? Yet everybody raves—the critics, the audience. Imagine standing room only for a Hungarian play! They applaud. They weep and laugh. It is things like that that make me love the theater. Everywhere else people see only what is before them. In the theater they see what is inside them. I am happy to be the spirit of the ages for them."

Vinsey came in.

"Ah." He embraced me. "I am glad you are here. Tonight we are having a party. Everybody will be there—including an old friend of Turay's. Did you tell him yet, Dodo?"

Turay shook his head.

"Mr. Mangriff," said Vinsey, "the munitions maker who is a refugee. But a special kind of refugee. A refugee with millions. Turay read him your script. He's mad to be the second money. Tomorrow morning he puts $200,000 in the bank. Tomorrow, also, Gita marries Fulka and Andri marries Lazlo. That is why the party. And tomorrow I am a producer again. Everybody is famous and everybody has money. How can such things happen?"

I looked at Turay sitting on his throne of Sunday dramatic columns. The pink hussar who had ridden single-handed to the rescue of Budapest's ghostland winked at me like a happy child.

# *The Wistful Blackguard*

IT WAS FIVE O'CLOCK of a February afternoon in 1919 and Harry Gruenwall, of the *London Express*, and I were standing in the snow-covered Potsdamer Platz, Berlin, full of doubt and excitement. One of those things which belong to the day-dreaming side of newspaper reporting had actually happened to us. As a matter of fact it had only happened to me, but Mr. Gruenwall, an alert and suspicious fellow, had been looking over my shoulder at the moment of its occurrence. The letter which Mr. Gruenwall had helped me read was in my pocket now. I had found it among my mail at the Adlon Hotel. It read:

> "Honored Sir,
>
> "The undersigned begs one of the Representatives of the Entente Press to meet him at the corner of the Potsdamer Platz, side entrance, Palast Café, at five o'clock on Friday afternoon. The matter is one of the utmost importance to both parties. If the Sinn Fein influence in Ireland is to be fought in a successful manner, I am the man who will supply the material."
>
> It was signed: "One of the Irish Brigade."
>
> "P.S. Writer will be standing opposite the Palast Café door and will be whistling the refrain of 'It's a Long Way to Tipperary.'"

I had heard of the Irish Brigade—macabre legends relating how five thousand Irishmen had deserted from the English army in 1915 and fought alongside the Germans; and of how Sir Roger Casement had been executed for his part in this wholesale treason. The thing had been one of the most tragic and colorful of the early war incidents. I had been in Germany two months, however, and had been able to find neither hide nor hair of one of these Irish traitors.

The Germans I had talked to were invariably silent on the subject. General Hoffman, who signed the Brest-Litovsk treaty, had shrugged his shoulders and answered, "Yes, I know Sir Roger. A very fine man. But don't talk to me about those Irish scoundrels of his. Damn all their souls, is all I can tell you."

Mr. Gruenwall and I stood waiting. There was much excitement in the Platz. Sparticusten—German Reds—were bombinating from improvised street platforms. Herr Noske's government troopers were dashing about with swinging rifles. A putsch was going on—one of those nose-thumbing encounters between the gabby left wingers of Berlin and the well-fed, well-armed retainers of Herren Ebert and Scheidemann, enthroned in Bismarck's Wilhelmstrasse as heads of the new Socialist Republic. Snow fell. Figures scurried. Battle cries sounded. Hoch this and Hoch that. And Mr. Gruenwall and I, veteran observers of scores of these embryonic Bastille days in this same Platz, waited with our minds on other matters.

"It's a wild-goose chase," said Gruenwall.

"We'll stand right here till six," I insisted.

"Unless these idiots start shooting," said Gruenwall.

Reason counseled me that I was as likely to encounter one of Caesar's legionnaires whistling the latest New York fox trot as I was to come upon my musical Irish traitor. As a reporter I had kept such trysts a score of times and they had always fizzled into adventures with ambitious panhandlers.

At 5:30 Gruenwall grabbed my arm and pointed carefully. Standing a few yards from us in the midst of a street-corner argument was a tall, clean-shaven man. He wore the German uniform and over it the long gray military overcoat. He was topped by an under-officer's cap and sported the bit of black and white ribbon which identified him as having been in the Kaiser's active service. On the cuff of his coat, however, was sewn a shamrock and with an immobile face he was whistling "It's a Long Way to Tipperary"; whistling it softly, with his eyes far away and a bantering smile in them.

"That's a nice song you're whistling," I said to him in English.

He continued the tune without looking at us.

"It's an odd song for you to be whistling here," said Gruenwall.

"It is that," said the whistler in a gentle Irish voice. "Let's go over to the café yonder."

The three of us walked into the Palast Café. A waiter with a shaved head pounced on us.

"We'll take another table," said the Irishman. "I don't like the fellow.

He spotted the shamrock on my coat when I came in. They watch us pretty close now in this God-forsaken city of swine."

We moved to another table in the rear. I asked him what he would drink.

"So you'll drink with me," he said, smiling. "Well, you're an American and an American will drink with the devil, the liquor being good. But how about your friend? He's English. I can tell by the supercilious way he holds his nose. The English can do a lot with the nose, denied to lesser peoples."

"We are three men doing business," said Gruenwall and smiled. "What's your order?"

The Irishman looked at him amiably. This was a few months after the Armistice and patriotism was still a major matter in the world.

"A strange people, the English," said our guest. "Well, if you'll drink with me, the both of you, that's encouragin'. Even though the liquor's no good. Nothing's worth a damn in this hell-hole of a place."

We gave our order. Shots sounded in the Platz.

"Do you hear 'em?" said our guest and chuckled. "Poppin' away at each other like a lot o' ducks in a shootin' gallery. God aim all their guns straight and keep 'em from wasting good ammunition."

Our drinks arrived.

"Well, to begin at the beginning," said our guest, "my name is Quinn Lusk. And here's luck to you and me. I see," he turned to Gruenwall, "you're studyin' my uniform. Yes, take a good look at it. There it is. It's the sort of uniform that fits a traitor and a blackguard, eh? That's what you're thinkin' now. Well, I don't usually parade around in it. But I put on my full regimentals for the rendezvous. Gentlemen, you are studyin' the uniform of the Irish Brigade, that bunch of high-minded cut-throats who fought for old Ireland in the war—on the Kaiser's side."

Gruenwall sputtered.

"I told you the liquor was no good," said Quinn Lusk. "Or is the business not to your likin', sir?"

"Go on," said Gruenwall.

"If it's not to his liking," said I, "there's always the door and a droshky back to the Adlon."

Gruenwall grinned at me.

"I'm a newspaper man first," he said.

"That's fine," said Quinn Lusk.

"Go on about the Irish Brigade," I said. "And I'll order some more drinks."

"Oh, we were a fine lot, we were," said Quinn Lusk, "and so were the ladies and gentlemen who enlisted us in the holy cause of Irish freedom, damn their souls, under the Hun flag, the dirty swine."

Gruenwall, grinning like a Chessy cat, was fumbling with a pencil stub.

"Never mind taking the notes now," said Quinn Lusk. "I'll write it all out in a formal document myself. I'm a pretty good writer. And I'll get you legal documents, letters to Roger Casement and letters from Sir Roger; and I'll load you down with all the existin' data there is on the famous Irish conspiracy, I will. And all that for a paltry few hundred dollars."

He paused to smile at the machine gun trilling a few blocks away.

"'Tis music," said Quinn Lusk. "It rocks me to sleep every night. Do you suppose there's any likelihood of them blowin' the whole town to bits, swine and all?"

"I doubt it," said I.

"Before we can get down to prices," said Gruenwall, "we'll have to hear a sample of your story."

"Here's lookin' into the bright eyes of the future," said Quinn Lusk, raising his glass, "and here's the sample of the story without any doodads thrown in. First, I'll tell you that I was a member of the Royal Irish Regiment stationed at Raglan Banks, Davenport, England, when the war broke out. And that for six months I fought beside my comrades against the Huns. And if you'll come to my room I'll show you my real uniform, the uniform, sir, of the Royal Irish Regiment that I've kept like a mother keeps her baby's shoes."

Quinn Lusk swallowed another drink—we had ordered a bottle brought to our table—and turned his bantering eyes to the snowfall outside the windows of the Palast Café.

"The liquor, bad though it is, makes me mellow," he said. "I'm sittin' here thinkin' that there was only one rotten low-down trick left for me to do that I haven't done; and that was to sell out the people who have kept me fed and clothed for the last year. But that's what I'm doin' now or goin' to be doin' so it's perfectly all right. Me character is intact. If you'll pay me money, I'll give you the story of the Irish Brigade. I've stolen a lot of letters and documents incriminatin' everybody that's been good or bad to me."

"How much?" said Gruenwall.

"Well," said Quinn Lusk, "I'll leave it to you and your conscience."

I suggested five hundred dollars. Gruenwall frowned.

"Your friend is right," said Quinn Lusk, "that's too big a sum to pay for anything except my appearance on the gallows."

"Three hundred is plenty," said Gruenwall.

"I'm in no position to haggle," said Quinn Lusk. "I'll trust you for the amount in case you haven't got it on you. I know you newspaper men, English or American. You'll buy drinks for blackguards and deal honestly with the devil for the sake of a story. You're a fine sort and here's to you. So that's settled. Three hundred dollars, American coin, it is."

We waited while Quinn Lusk indulged himself in a reverie.

"I don't feel just right about it," he said, "for even a scoundrel like myself has his fine feelings and his better moments."

"You'd better forget them," said I.

"Not a hard thing to do," said Quinn Lusk. "I'll tell you somethin'. I'm a traitor and I turned traitor because I believed a lot of lies. Or, to be honest, maybe I didn't believe 'em so much. I'm wastin' my breath exoneratin' myself and I know it.

"You're English, Mr. Gruenwall, as I saw at once from your supercilious nose, and you'll maybe get red under the collar. But the English have always been dirty dogs to me. They turned my grandmother out of her home in Ireland and they've ridden my country for a century like she was a spavined nag fit only to be whipped. Ha, listen to me wave the green flag! Me, a dirty louse in a turncoat."

Gruenwall continued to nod amiably and sip his brandy.

"Well," said Quinn Lusk, "when the opportunity came, if you wish to call it by that fine name, I was ready to meet the Hun halfway. I'll tell you all about that as soon as I have swallowed me next drink. You've got to be used to this cognac to drink it for it ain't fit to wash the feet of a pig in. Now you lads keep sober and let me do the drinkin' for it's a small bottle, be damned to you. First, gentlemen, I wish to say that if I had it to do over again, I wouldn't be doin' it for a fortune nor would any of the boys—the worst of them—not that there were any good ones, I assure you.

"Some of us joined because of the wine and women they gave us and the high-class food; and some of us went over because we were dirty scoundrels. But we all had something in us that made it seem right—when we got enough liquor under our belts—a love for old Ireland and a hate for England."

Quinn Lusk leaned back in his chair and whistled softly his theme song, "It's a Long Way to Tipperary," and we waited patiently for the end of this musical interlude.

"Well," said Quinn Lusk, "I was thinkin' this while whistling. When you come to write the story be sure you make one fact certain and outstanding—that there were only forty-nine Irishmen in the Irish Brigade. That with all the thousands of marks the boches spent, with all the women they dragged into our beds, with all the fine, dirty promises they made, they could only get forty-nine of us. Not another soul. Just a damned forty-nine. They claimed one thousand and five thousand, but damn their eyes, forty-nine is the number; forty-nine creatures like meself.

"Oh, it was a black day for me when I listened to Casement. But Sir Roger was a man. Don't mistake that. A fine man with a big soul. The only man in the whole lot of swine who was working for Ireland at German expense. Working for Ireland, indeed! A lot they cared about Ireland. A lot they cared about freedom and all the fine words they talked. A pack of double-dealing swine they were, with nary a spark of soul in them, makin' traitors out of half-starved Irishmen in German prison barracks. Lyin' to them and cheatin' them worse than any English landlord. All except Sir Roger. Nary a word against Sir Roger from me. I was a boy of twenty when I joined. And it wasn't till later that I saw that poor Sir Roger was bein' played with, cheated and lied to by the Huns. He was never a scoundrel was Sir Roger, but a gentleman and a patriot with a silly head on him. I'll drink his health now and damnation to all the rest of the Irish Brigade, meself included, and every man and woman who had their dirty fingers in the mess."

By himself Quinn Lusk drank his bitter toast and then grinned at us.

"It's an old story to me," he said, "rattlin' around in my head for four years. But it gives me a queer feelin' to be tellin' it to gentlemen like yourselves. You see, I was one of the first to succumb to the Hun blarney. I was in prison barracks and when they come after me I thought they were the salt of the earth with their Kultur and their fine manners and their words of love for Ireland. And recognizin' my merit, they made me recruiting sergeant among the Irish prisoners in Germany and gave me my pick of a dozen gals for me escort. I was the silver-tongued little flag-waver who talked Ireland to the boys. And to help me along in their conversion, my polite friends, the Huns, held up their rations and beat them when I wasn't looking. And when they were rollin' on their beds with pain and hunger I would come marchin' in spruce as a Darby winner and begin promisin' them countesses and duchesses and feather beds the like of which they'd never even seen, let alone slept in with their dirty hides. 'Kisses and wine, money and victuals,' said I to them, 'and a noble cause to fight for.'

"And they only got forty-nine of us, with all of it. Forty-nine of the blackest-souled scapegoats in the army, including your humble servant, meself. By God, we'll drink to old Ireland that had only forty-nine traitors in her ranks—silly, empty-headed blackguards though they were."

Again Quinn Lusk drank his toast alone. He continued seemingly none the worst for the half-bottle he had swallowed.

"Well," he said, "we cost the Huns a pretty penny and we killed more of them back of their lines than we ever did fighting them from the Allies' front. We gave them plenty, I tell you, even though we did march up and down Unter den Linden like a lot of geese under an Irish-German flag. There was Malone who broke the neck of Unter-Offizier Baumgarten in the football game at the stadium. And Paddy who cut the throats of two sentries in the Danzig guard house. And Tim who knocked the life out of a Prussian Hauptmann with a monocle and a lisp. And our Sergeant-Major who stole the wife of a Bavarian Colonel and then finished the irate fellow off with a club. The Colonel's lady was a wild one and before we got through with her she was havin' fits at the sight of a green blade of grass.

"Oh, we've done our bit back of the Hun lines, fighting everybody, including ourselves. For we were a fine pack of patriots after Sir Roger left us—drinkin' and ravishin' and murderin' up and down the country."

Gruenwall interrupted.

"Did they put you in the trenches?" he asked, softly.

"Put us in the trenches," Quinn Lusk laughed. "Eh, now you should know better than to be askin' that. They knew better than to be askin' us that, they did. No, they didn't stick us in their lousy trenches, nary once. They knew what we thought of them and there wasn't a man in the Brigade who wouldn't have sold what was left of his soul for the chance of emptying a brace of guns into a Hun dugout. No, they paraded us in our fine uniforms with the shamrock starin' woefully from our sleeves and the poor flag of Ireland over our heads. They used us as propaganda. And the girls leaned out of the windows to cheer us and pelt us with roses. There were forty-nine of us in the propaganda and there were forty-nine hundred who got paid for the job—Americans among them: Irishmen livin' on the fat of the land while we starved in our traitor barracks—after Sir Roger left us.

"Yes, sir, a lot of fat rogues collectin' their thousand marks a month as the price of our shame while we had to knock a man down in an alley to pick up the price of a drink. That's how the thing turned out, you see. We sold our souls to the devil and he double-crossed us."

We ordered another bottle of the raw cognac and our guest shook his head to clarify it and agreed he would eat some eggs.

"I feel better now," he said, "about sellin' them out. When I come to think of it in the full light of me reason it's not so bad a deal I'm doin'. Perhaps I'm doin' Ireland a good turn after all, by handin' them over, names, letters, documents, and all kinds of fancy proof. And that was all I wished for once when I listened to poor Sir Roger. Here. I brought one of the letters—as a credential of me villainy. I'll read it to you before I go on with the story. But another drink. Because I'm sellin' out one of the few women that was good to me. A very fine Irish lady and a traitor like meself. Mrs. Fannie G—— of Munich. A lovely woman and a traitor but she meant well and she was an honest friend to Sir Roger."

Our guest removed the letter from a wallet and read it.

"Dear Sir Roger,

"Just a line to cheer you up with the news that thanks to the generous assistance of Mrs. R——, Mrs. T—— and Mrs. S—— where you dined one evening, I will be able to send a very nice Christmas present to each of your Irish volunteers.

"I wish you could see the things because I am so pleased with the result myself. Each one gets a green satin bag filled with some cakes and candies—a tiny sample of tea tied up in green. A box of fifty cigarettes and what else remains to be decided tomorrow, but I thought best to let you know lest you might be getting things in Berlin when they are provided here."

"I repeat," said Quinn Lusk, "I have a room full of papers and documents and such. It is the whole history of the Sinn Feiners and their connection with the German Irish plot."

"We've settled for three hundred dollars," said Gruenwall.

"That we have but I've changed my mind," said Quinn Lusk.

"For instance?" I inquired.

"You'll be surprised," said Quinn Lusk, "but I'm for giving it all away free. Not a shilling asked or taken."

"Don't be a fool," said Gruenwall.

Quinn Lusk's eyes, a bit reddened with the liquor, grinned at the two of us.

"I'm not that," he said. "Never that. Do you happen to know the British Colonel stationed in Berlin?"

"Yes," said Gruenwall.

"Then I'm a lucky man," said Quinn Lusk. "For if you'll arrange for me to meet that gentleman I'll give him all the evidence I got against the traitors of England—free without a shilling changin' hands."

"To square yourself for going Hun?" asked Gruenwall.

"To Hell with that and with the British, all of them," said Quinn Lusk. "I'm feeling this moment like I always have for the British. A pack of lyin' tyrants that have ruined my country, if I can be said to have a country, which I doubt. I bear them no love, mind you. And I hate the Huns, mind you. And I hate the Sinn Feiners for gettin' me into this mess. I hate them all impartially. But if you'll arrange the matter I'll hand the documents over to this Colonel providin' he agrees to let me go back."

"Where to?" asked Gruenwall.

"Dublin," said Quinn Lusk.

"No other perquisites?" asked Gruenwall.

"None but that," said Quinn Lusk. "I would like to walk on God's earth again in Dublin, daffy though it sounds. I would like to sit in an Irish pub and get drunk again with Irishmen. And I would sell out me own grandmother for the privilege. Take me over to his nobs the Colonel after you have spoken with him and he can have everything I've got. Enough evidence to jail a thousand Irishmen and hang as many if he wants. And all I'm asking him is safe passage back to Dublin and he wash his hands of me once I land there."

We made the pact, interviewed the Colonel and waited for word from Quinn Lusk. We learned after a week that he had been arrested in Riga for drunkenness and fighting. And while he was languishing in some Baltic jail the March revolution broke out in Berlin. This interfered with our using the Quinn Lusk story. And in the excitement of workingmen fighting behind barricades, of aeroplanes bombing our hotel and of rumors that Trotzky and his Red Hordes were about to sweep westward across Europe, Gruenwall and I almost forgot our Irish traitor.

He appeared late in March, bleary-eyed and in tatters.

"I broke jail," he said after we had taken him to my room. "I thought sure they would be makin' an end of me. I was in for two years and I was almost tired enough to stay there. But I gave me promise to the British Colonel and I'm here to keep it. I've moved the documents to a place outside the city. Come along and I'll get them. And trust to the honor of an Englishman to keep his side o' the bargain."

At this point I was pushed into the background of the negotiations. British officers appeared. There was considerable palaver and scurrying and Quinn Lusk, in a new suit of civilian clothes, seemed a busy man. A week passed and he arrived again with Gruenwall in my room.

"I'm for saying good-by," said Quinn Lusk. He was half drunk and beaming. "My friend Mr. Gruenwall and the British factotums, God bless their dirty souls, have arranged for my returnin' to Dublin. Only I have had to promise the Colonel and so has Mr. Gruenwall that we will not be using the story I told you—for some time."

Gruenwall rather sheepishly corroborated this.

"I've given my word," he explained, "not to use the yarn until the British intelligence department gives me permission. I'm in rather a fix. You have half-rights in the story and it's up to you. If you want to print it go ahead and Quinn stays here in Berlin. If you care to hold off publication Quinn goes to Dublin."

"Sure you'll hold off," grinned Quinn Lusk. "What is a story more or less to you, you havin' the fine brain you have for figurin' out so many o' them. It'll be as good tomorrow for printing as it is today. Hold off," he stared intently at me, "and I'll drink to you every night wherever I am, in good Irish whiskey. And to you, too," he turned to Gruenwall. "I'll toast the both of you from one end o' Dublin to the other. What's more it'll only be a question of months. A few of them, I tell you. The Sinn Feiners, who are a nosey lot, will be finding out what I've done and be after me. I'll have an alias and take care but they'll come on me when I'm least expecting them, the filthy dogs, and make an end of me. And once I'm out of the way you can print the story as long and as wide as you please."

I succumbed to the sentimental project of preserving the worthless life of Quinn Lusk. Gruenwall gave me my share of the documents, although the cream of them had gone to the British Colonel. Two days later Quinn Lusk came to say a final good-by and drunker than ever.

"God damn their dirty green souls," he cried. "I'm goin' to Dublin tomorrow and there's no race as cruel and vengeful as the Irish. Swine they are but me own kind. They'll cut me to pieces as soon as they find out who and what I am. But I'll drink enough of their liquor and listen to enough of their talk to last me for a long time in Hell, before they rend me to bits."

Quinn Lusk left Berlin and the subject was dropped. Gruenwall and I commiserated with each other one evening on the sentimental trap into which we had fallen and went about our business for our papers.

I returned a year later to New York. Quinn Lusk went out of my head along with other curious anecdotes that had occupied me in post-war Germany. Another year passed and then the story received its ending. A letter from Gruenwall arrived containing a short clipping from the *London Express.*

"Maybe this will interest you," wrote Gruenwall.

The clipping read:

> "The body of a man riddled with bullets and outrageously beaten was found on the West Road outside of Dublin. A hint of mystery was aroused by the discovery of the crime when it was learned that the dead man was one Quinn Lusk, active for some time in the Sinn Fein movement. Lusk had been living in Dublin for two years under the name of Timothy Frees and leading a disorderly life. No clue to his murderers has been found by the police."

# *Actor's Blood*

THE DEATH of a famous actress is the signal, as a rule, for a great deal of maudlin excitement. The world that knew her rushes up on that last stage where she lies with her eyes sincerely closed and joins, as it were, in her death scene, posturing and poetizing around her bier like a pack of amateur mummers. For a few days everyone who knew her is a road company Marc Antony burying her with bad oratory. The stage is a respectable and important institution, what with its enormous real estate holdings, but we still patronize an actress, particularly a dead one.

Marcia Tillayou's death let loose an unusual amount of "Alas, poor Yorick" poses among the laity because she was found in her apartment one summer morning with three bullets, all of them through her heart. This struck everybody as almost too rich a scenario to believe, that so glamorous, beautiful and witty a woman should add murder to the excitement of her dying.

We who were her friends were not exactly delighted. But there's no denying the thrill that lay in that dénouement. Even to her intimates the whole business of mystery surrounding that dead and beautiful body seemed more dramatic than real, seemed more a performance than the ending of a life. Not Marcia lay in this bed of death, but another of those exotic and witty characterizations for which she was famous.

As for the Press, it was honestly and naïvely grateful. It is seldom that an interesting, let alone famous, woman gets murdered. Our murder victims are in the main the dullest and most depressing of stooges. The best that tragedy has to offer the city editors is an occasional chorus girl and more rarely someone sufficiently well dressed to warrant the word Society in the headlines.

Marcia's exit kept the presses roaring. There was inexhaustible color to the mystery, and there was more bad writing and idiotic sleuthing than had distinguished the news columns for some time—a month at least. A life-sized portrait of Marcia as Pierrette hanging over the "murder bed" had been slashed across the middle. The furniture of the gaudy room had been smashed. Her satin-hung dressing table with its glass top and hundred perfume bottles had been demolished. All in all it looked as if Marcia had been done to death by a herd of bison. But the police and the newspapers chose to regard the attendant ravages as the work of a Love Fiend.

Since these matters and all the clues and surmises of that first week came to nothing there's no point in dwelling on them. My story of the Marcia Tillayou mystery is, as a matter of fact, not part of any police record nor is it to be found in the newspaper files.

At the time of Marcia's death there was one who wept more than all the rest, who ranted more, postured more and seemed more humanly objectionable than any of the mourners who carried spears to her funeral. This one was her father, Maurice Tillayou, a Thespian hero of other days, an ancient theatrical windbag with a soul still full of grease paint and obsolete bravado.

Old actors are perhaps the greatest bores in the world, particularly old actors whose day is past and whose very agents no longer carry their telephone numbers in their records. Tillayou was of this tribe, and so much the actor still that he could never seem the man again on the stage or off.

This rubbery-faced son of bombast had had his heyday at the turn of the century. He had strutted his little hour as one of those barrel-voiced, fur-collared, blue-skinned tragedians of whom our fathers, forgetting their names, still mumble with pretended delight.

Unlike many of his generation, old Tillayou had never adjusted himself to the growing realism of the theater, never tried to soothe his grandiloquent antics to fit the more prosaic tempo of the modern stage. As a result, at fifty, he had almost vanished from the boards; at sixty, he had become one of those myths who cling to some dimly-lighted corner of a theatrical club drinking bitterly to the death of art and the venality of managers.

He who had played all the Great Rôles—Hamlet, Lear, Romeo, Jekyll, Monte Cristo, Richelieu, Ben Hur, St. Elmo and Quo Vadis among them—sat in the shadows without a part, as if not he alone but all the swaggering, thundering heroes in whose shoes he had paraded shared his exile. He was given, because of this quaint delusion, to rolling his eyes, working his shaggy brows with mystery and wrapping himself in a peculiar sort of phantom dignity. He spent the day in sonorous complaints against destiny and like all discarded actors was full of an offensive and useless egoism.

There was nonetheless a slightly exciting air about Tillayou, soiled and musty though he was. His wispy gray and yellowish hair rose from his mottled scalp like the whiskers of a cat. He wore an old-fashioned stand-up collar into which he could have retreated turtle fashion had he so desired. His clothes were as ill-fitting as a waiter's or perhaps a philosopher's. His massive face seemed in repose to be folded up and able to open like an accordion. But bore though he was, didactic and misinformed on almost every human topic, his mind as disheveled as his garments, he had about him the charm of authenticity. He seemed more "theater" than a hundred electric signs. He seemed with his tiresome boasts, his rumbling voice, his pompous mannerisms and over-plastic face like some lost puppet playing truant from those theatrical storage houses in which the thousand and one forgotten kingdoms of the stage are stacked away.

During the years I knew him I saw him in harness but three times. A restoration drama revival brought him before the public for a few weeks and once, under the wing of a profit-sharing actors' enterprise, he blossomed briefly and rather foolishly as Richelieu. For, removed from under its bushel, the old Thespian's genius, alas, set no rivers afire. Tillayou emerging from the shadows of exile brought with him all his retinue and was never content with the mere acting of the rôle on the program. He sought to dazzle as well with a dozen other remarkable characterizations of which he was equally master.

The third time I witnessed his performance was the occasion of the anecdote I've set out to relate.

Marcia Tillayou became a star when she was twenty-five. This means a great deal in the theater. It is, as a rule, the reward more of personality than of talent. You must be distinctive and have a new pattern of vocables and gestures to offer. You must have a peculiar voice, it may be inaudible as a conspirator's or incoherent as a train announcer's, but this matters very little providing it has any peculiarity at all—barring adenoids. You must have a set of mannerisms to keep you from being submerged in any characterization, and a certain high-handed way of playing all your parts alike, whatever the dramatist has written or the director demanded.

Marcia had been playing Marcia Tillayou for some eight years, most of them on Broadway, playing this peculiar young lady consistently and with infatuation, when rather abruptly one evening her persistence was rewarded. She had stumbled upon a part even more Marcia Tillayouish than herself—a waspish-tongued, brittle-spirited creature of disillusion invented by Alfred O'Shea—a woman whose green eyes shone with wit and despair, whose gestures were tense with ennui and who, in the play, loved, jested and died like a glass of champagne going stale.

Through the medium of that particular drama which was called *The Forgotten Lady,* audience and critics beheld Marcia Tillayou for the first time as dozens of intimates already knew her, and this enlarged recognition of her personality made her a star. It was a tremendous début and all who witnessed it knew that ever after, whatever fortunes befell, however many bad plays and adverse criticisms came her way, her stardom was fixed, she would always be one of that handful of women of the stage who are an Electric Sign in fair weather or foul.

Marcia Tillayou's emergence as a star was not the only dramatic event of that evening. There was also Maurice Tillayou's emergence as a father. This happened shortly after the last curtain fell.

There was a reception in Marcia's dressing room. Nobody in the world, except perhaps nursery dolls, receives such concentrated and overwhelming flattery as does an actress on the night of a Great Success. The theater touches off the facile emotions and its heroes and heroines come in for blasts of adulation which would terrify more realistic souls.

Maurice Tillayou was present at this backstage coronation in Marcia's dressing room. He stood in a corner, a soiled and musty unknown, his eyes glittering at the sight of the make-up boxes, the mirrors, hangings, strewn finery and heaped floral offerings; his ears tingling with the praises showering the head of his daughter. He lurked silently in the corner until the ecstasies had subsided and the last of the bandwagon soloists drifted out of the room. Then he came forward and, for the first time in the memory of either, kissed his daughter. He pressed her hands. His eyes shone with tears and he added his gift to the triumph of that evening.

"You are a great artist," he said in capitals, "you have taken your place tonight in the great tradition of the stage beside the immortal figures of Rachel, Siddons, Bernhardt and Modjeska. May I have the honor to congratulate you, my child?"

He said this all very glibly and sonorously as was his habit, but in a strange way this pronouncement of her hitherto boring and negligible parent excited Marcia. Regarding the old windbag with her tired but always witty eyes, she felt the deeper meaning of his words. He had come offering her his egoism, that battered, offensive and useless egoism which had sustained and applauded him when all other palms had grown silent. He too had undergone a transformation this night. He was no longer Maurice Tillayou, the star, albeit in temporary eclipse;

but old Tillayou, father of a star newly risen. Holding her hands and kissing her, the old gentleman seemed to Marcia to be letting go forever his treasured career and passing on to her, twenty-five years after her birth, some gaudy, hereditary talisman of genius.

The story of Marcia's nine years of stardom is a tale that wants a longer telling than this. It was the career of a high heart in a higher mind. To those who kept pace with her or contributed to her life she seemed as complicated as music by Stravinsky, as troublesome as a handful of fine but broken glass. She owned an acidulous mind and a schoolgirl's heart. She was ironic and disillusioned, yet ineptly romantic. She was always beautiful. Her hair shone as if a light were concealed in her coiffure. Her green eyes were never without comment—amusement, derision. Her skin was pale, her mouth wide and mobile, with restless lips. And, as in women of personality, her face seemed bolder, more strongly modelled than suited her taut, slender body. Her crisp voice was an instrument for wit rather than sighs, and her beauty, despite her reputation, was a thing of which men seldom thought lightly. There was too much character and epigram behind it. Clever people have a way of seeming always gay and this was Marcia's manner—to jest at scars, her own or others'. Her sprightliness, however, was disconcerting, not only because of the cruelty it contained but for the fact that in her very laughter lurked always the antonym of weariness. She was like one of those fragile chemicals that burn too sharply, giving off a curious and vicious light.

Throughout the nine years of her stardom Maurice Tillayou hovered in the background of her affluence, intrigues and follies. He lived elsewhere but was to be seen often at her dinner table, drinking his wine with a faraway happy stare at the Maestros, Savants, Journalists and Heroes of the Pen and Stage who graced his daughter's board. He was still a musty old dodo but full of punctilio and reticence.

What there could be in common between this ghost of the theater and the glamorous daughter whom he haunted no one was able to make out, except that she obviously supported him and that he doted on running errands. Marcia's life seemed hardly fit for such continual parental observation, but there he was peering continually from behind his high, stand-up collar at this legendary world of which he had always dreamed. He lingered in the background, saying nothing that anyone heard, through Marcia's hysterical marriage with Alfred O'Shea, author of her first success, *The Forgotten Lady,* and through that scoundrel's subsequent hegira with Reena Kraznoff, the dancer; and through a dozen liaisons and entanglements, all of them full of heartbreak and hysteria. For Marcia was one whose heart clung to illusions that had no place in her bedroom, and who bought her counterfeit pleasures with genuine coin. Like many of the stage she bargained desperately for beauty and took home tinsel.

Old Tillayou was somehow involved in all these unfortunate doings of his daughter. And though Marcia suffered no social blemish from her wanton antics, her father seemed to lose caste, to become a sort of paternal gigolo.

Yet however bedevilled by her wit, reduced by her sins or made the butt of her reminiscences maliciously remembered from childhood, Tillayou remained always charmed by her presence. She treated him as if he were some eccentric toy to which she was playfully attached. Yet this once most touchy of Hamlets seemed immune to her belittlements. He would smile at her sallies and add a bit of trenchant data to her tales and remain, in a way that touched the hearts of those inclined to notice him at all, respectful and idolatrous. He was, in short, a musty old spectator basking in a corner of his daughter's glamour.

The year and a half which preceded her mysterious death had been a troublesome time for Marcia. A reverberating set-to between herself and Phil Murry, her producer, had resulted in the closing of the play she was in. There had followed a shortsighted jump to a rival producer, a hasty production under his banner and an equally hasty flop. A second appearance under the management of the gifted Morrie Stein had resulted in another failure. And Marcia found herself verging toward that second stage of stardom in which the star, unexpectedly and as if bedevilled by witches, develops play trouble. Still glamorous, still a great box office draw, she floundered through productions that set critical teeth on edge, her colors flying valiantly above a bog of theatrical bilge.

That alchemistic combination which makes for success on Broadway is a tenuous one. Its secret often evaporates, leaving no visible change in the ingredients, except that the gold is gone. And sadly there rises for these stars confronted with empty seats the first bewildering breath of limbo. All this was beginning to happen to Marcia. There was no belittlement of the name Tillayou. It was still an Electric Sign but growing ghostly, slipping, still aglow, into the side streets of fame.

At this time, too, Marcia's finances came in for ill luck. Yet with a falling market and diminishing salary checks, her extravagances continued. Credit took the place of money. To the clamor of friends and lovers on the telephone were added the appeals of tradesmen, dressmakers, bootleggers, landlords and even servants. It was a stormy period and full of those thunders and lightnings with which temperament, thwarted, manages to circle its head as an antidote.

During these months old Tillayou's importance increased. It was he who led the talk in the dressing rooms after each new disastrous first night. He was an encyclopedia of alibis. Where, he wanted to know, had they got such a Leading Man, so horrible and unpractised a fellow? He had, said Tillayou, ruined the two major scenes. And where, he wanted to know again, had they discovered the Character Woman? How could a play mount with such a bungling amateur hanging on to it? The set, he was quick to point out, had killed the third act completely. And the rain, he was certain, had depressed the audience. The lighting in the love scene had been atrocious; the director had garbled the first act curtain. But Marcia had been and was always wonderful, superb as ever, giving the best performance he had ever seen any woman offer on the stage. Moreover, he was quick with that final solace —that it was weak plays such as this which made the best vehicles for great stars, that it was in such as these that they personally triumphed.

Papa Tillayou stood at the pass like some valorous Old Guard. He knew, alas, all the thousand and one excuses for failure, all the quaint, smug, fantastic box-office circumlocutions which in the theater deaden the sting of defeat. And his voice rumbling, his eyes glowing with their best Hamlet fires, he fought these dressing room Thermopylaes, a veteran forsooth.

In the excitement of Marcia Tillayou's murder, Maurice Tillayou lapsed into complete shadowiness. He had been observed at the funeral carrying on like a Comanche, bellowing with grief and collapsing on the wet ground not once but a dozen times. He had ridden back alone to his bailiwick in Washington Square. And here Maurice Tillayou had remained in seclusion while sleuths and journalists played bloodhound through Marcia's life in quest of the villain who had sent three bullets through her heart.

This made fascinating reading and sophisticated dinner-table talk for the Broadway cognoscenti. Theories were as plentiful as jackrabbits in May and as elusive. We who had known Marcia felt the thrill of tragedy and mystery on our doorstep and we spoke guardedly of the matter, for there seemed always present, or closely represented, some one on whom our choicest suspicion was for the moment centered.

Although the police were baffled, God knew and so did some hundreds of New Yorkers who are nearly as omniscient, that there had been material enow in Marcia's life for a whole series of murders. Marcia's career had been interwoven with the careers of equally electric names, names which live in a sort of fidgety half-public undress and seem always but a jump ahead of the thunderclap of scandal. We waited excitedly for the hand of the law to fall on one of these—for who could have murdered Marcia more logically than one of those who had been part of her life?

First in our suspicion was Alfred O'Shea, who had married her once and who at her death was still legally her husband. This tall, dark, prankish chevalier, Don Juan, playwright, wit, over-charming and malicious, full of grins, bon mots and moody withal as a beggar on a rainy day, was a most obvious suspect to us, his friends. His strong Irish-Castilian face held a jester's nose, pointed and a bit awry, held cold, centered eyes and a gaunt muscular mouth and a promise of high deeds—murder among them. We knew his story well enough. Absurdly infatuated with his Reena, a dancer with a lithographic face and an accent full of charm and faraway places, he had abandoned Marcia and set up a clamor for divorce. Marcia had refused, loathing, she said, to hand him over to so belittling a successor, and we remembered hearing of times this over-charming Celt, drunken and vicious, had broken into Marcia's bedroom threatening to have her heart out unless she released him. What bourgeois trait, what subterranean wiliness inspired Marcia to step so out of character and thwart this man whom she had so desperately loved, I could never make out. She had only jests for answers.

But O'Shea was in a goodly company of suspects, those first weeks of the mystery. There was also Phil Murry, the producer—cool, round-faced, paunchy with a homely chuckle and a little piping voice, all very deceptive qualities, for Mr. Murry was as treacherous as a cocklebur to wrestle with. He was a maestro as famous for his unscrupulousness with women as for his hits.

Marcia had been his mistress until supplanted by Emily Duane, long considered her closest friend. La Duane, an Electric Sign in her own right and a vest-pocket edition of Duse, cello-voiced and full of a deceptive ingénue wholesomeness, had jockeyed Marcia completely out of Murry's life—his theater as well as his arms. We remembered poor Marcia's to-do over Murry's faithlessness, her involved campaign of retaliation—a matter of social ragging and continuous public baiting which had driven that paunchy maestro out of his mind on a number of occasions and reduced Emily to a sort of humorous female Judas in our eyes. How these two had hated Marcia and what vengeance they had sworn against her poor, sad wit!

There was also the grayish, Punchinello-faced Felix Meyer, theatrical lawyer de luxe as he called himself—glib and of the old school as his redundant phrases and ancient cravat testified. This elderly bravo was a species of liaison officer between Broadway and a mysterious world of reality called the Law. But to that world he found it seldom necessary to resort. For, immersed in the thousand and one secrets of the theater, his practice was in the main a species of affable blackmail and counter-blackmail—his activities as arbiter, backer, judge and Don Juan being only dimly sensed by his intimates, and not at all by his wife.

His affair with Marcia had been an unusually gritty one, based on her inability to pay him an exorbitant legal fee for services rendered. It had lasted several months and left both of them with a horror of each other. Lawyer Felix went about in terror lest Marcia, out of spite, betray him to his wife, to whose name he had with foolhardy caution transferred all his holdings. And Marcia, aware of his craven fidgets, had time and again promised to do just that. How relieved this glib and accomplished fellow must have felt that first moment reading of her death, and how full of disquiet he must have sat while the bloodhounds scurried through Marcia's life sniffing for clues.

There was also Fritz von Klauber, who had painted Marcia as Pierrette, a dapper gentleman of the arts with a mandarin mustache and a monocle to help him intimidate the less fortunately born theatrical producers (a rather numerous set) for whom he devised unusually expensive scenery. Von Klauber's relations with Marcia had ended more unprettily than most. We knew that he had borrowed thousands of dollars from her while her lover and refused to recognize the debt after discovering or pretending to discover her in the arms of Morrie Stein. Mr. Stein, a purring, monkish Semite with over-red lips, upturned eyes, a grasshopper's body and a prodigious sneer flying, flag like, from his lips, had been Marcia's last substitute for love. We knew little of this adventure, but our suspicions of Morrie were quickened by an aversion which all his intimates seemingly held for him.

There was slightly down on the list of suspects, but still qualifying for our gossip, Percy Locksley, a Pickwickian fellow minus, however, all hint of simplicity or innocence—a journalist with a facetious but blood-curdling cruelty to his style who had figured disturbingly in Marcia's life. He had been rumored as her possible husband, which rumor Marcia had scotched with great public cries of outrage and epigram at Locksley's expense. And though this might seem small motive for murder, to know Locksley was to suspect him of anything, from homicide to genius.

And there was also Emil Wallerstein, the poet, who had hounded

Marcia's doorsill for a year, smitten, drunken, vicious, bawling for her favors and threatening to hang himself with her garter (like Gerard de Nerval) if she refused; who had made quite a show of going to the dogs (at his friends' expense) as a result of her coldness; and whom Marcia, for reasons hidden from us, had thoroughly and always cleverly despised.

Also further down the list was Clyde Veering, a charming, faded roué, once a font of learning and now a fat little Silenus in oxford glasses clinging to a perpetual cocktail. Veering was known amusingly as a connoisseur of decadence. His tasteful bachelor apartment was at the service of his friends of both sexes provided their intentions were sufficiently abnormal or dishonorable. It was a bit difficult to conceive of Veering as a murderer, but like a number of others we held suspect, it was more his possible secret knowledge of the crime than participation in it which excited us.

However, none of these, nor anyone else, came under the hand of the law. There was some surreptitious questioning, a great deal of libel-cautious hints in the news columns, but no arrests. Nothing happened despite the baying of the bloodhounds. A peculiarly gallant reticence seemed to surround Marcia, dead. No letters were found among her effects, no voice from the grave gave direction to the hunt. And the mysterious ending of this charming and famous woman slowly embedded itself behind other local excitements.

It was four weeks after the murder, when its mystery had subsided to an occasional paragraph, that Maurice Tillayou emerged from the shadows and in a spectacular manner.

We who had known Marcia well, or too well, received an invitation from the old gentleman. It was strangely worded. It read: "May I have the honor of your company at a dinner Friday evening which I am giving in memory of my daughter, Marcia? I strongly urge you to attend, for matters vital to yourself as well as to the mystery surrounding my daughter's murder are to be revealed in my house. I am asking you in all fairness to be present—or represented."

A few of us were amused and touched by the old actor's melodramatic summons. But there were almost a score of others whom I found to be filled with disquiet. The matter was guardedly discussed over a number of telephones. Efforts to reach old Tillayou in advance for further information availed nothing.

It rained on that Friday night. Thunder rolled in the sky and the streets were full of that picnic-like confusion which storm brings to the city. I rang the bell of the Tillayou roost and waited in the unfamiliar old hallway until the door was opened by an amazingly senile fellow, stooped, cackling and practically mummified. He was obviously the servant and obviously in a state of complete mental paralysis. For behind him in a large studio-like room, buzzing, clattering, laughing, was as browbeating a coterie of celebrities as the theater had to offer. They had arrived, and this was odd for these chronic dinner wreckers, on time. I noticed that a number were already on their third cocktail and that the babble which greeted me was completely lacking in those overtones of ennui, disdain and bad manners which usually marked their get-togethers.

I looked vainly for a glimpse of Tillayou and learned from several sources that the old windjammer was still lurking in the wings, building up his entrance. It was a familiar enough group, a rather morbid round-up it seemed, of men and women who had loved Marcia Tillayou, cheated her, quarreled with her, lied to her, drunk with her, amused and betrayed her and been part of that strident, characterless treadmill which is the Broadway Parnassus. So reminiscent were they all of Marcia that she seemed almost present, almost certain to appear and join them, as they stood about maliciously guillotining absent comrades and exchanging those tireless reminiscences which Celebrities always have for each other.

I was rather thrilled at the spectacle, for old Tillayou's intention was plain. He had assembled a company of suspects and was obviously going to climax the evening by some formal accusation of guilt. There was a handful, like myself, who could look forward to no such distinction, but who knew what the old actor had got into his addled head. We had all been part of Marcia's world and we might all be presumed to have had some insight into the mystery that had climaxed her life.

This little world Tillayou had summoned out of its orbit into his humble old actor lodgings made a uniform picture. Its members were as alike as the decorations on a Christmas tree. There was about them an identical air, a similarity of inner and outer tailoring as if they had all been finished off on the same loom. Success was in their names and New York, the New York of the roman-candle signs, of Ballyhoo and Ego, Merry-go-round Achievement and Overnight-Fortune hung like a tag from their words and manners. They were the cream of a certain electric-lighted firmament—its satraps and its nobles—and if you liked this world you liked them; if you revered this world, as old Tillayou once had, these were gods for your genuflections. A swift and glittering world it was, a bauble of a planet, out of which were hatched nightly the ephemera of art, the fireflies that masqueraded as beacons for an hour.

I joined Veering, always a source of rich information. He was pouting childishly over his fifth cocktail, cackling that he was much too bored by old Tillayou's banality to talk about it and regretting he had wasted an evening, when so few (virile) ones remained. I moved toward Locksley and fell to studying the half-hundred costume photographs of Tillayou in his heyday that decorated the wall.

"He played all the parts," I said. "He could illustrate a full edition of the Bard."

"Yes," said Locksley, "he had that talent for bad acting which made him a natural and tireless Shakesperean."

Von Klauber, joining us, remarked, "Marcia always called him that Old Davil Ham."

"We saw him once as Richelieu," O'Shea said, coming up to us. "I'll never forget Marcia's delight when he went up in his lines in the third act. She said it saved the play."

Wallerstein, the poet, not yet drunk, stood glowering at von Klauber.

"The destruction of your Pierrette painting of Marcia," he veered, "was a great blow to the world of art."

"Thank you," said von Klauber, "I didn't know you had ever had the good fortune to see that painting."

Veering chuckled.

"Marcia always loathed it," he said, winking at everybody. He had, mysteriously, a distaste for artists.

"It was painted under handicaps," said von Klauber calmly.

"Miss Tillayou must have been a very difficult subject."

Lawyer Felix had joined us.

"Not difficult to paint," said von Klauber, "but difficult to please."

"And very ungrateful," Locksley chuckled. "She always secretly believed that the portrait had been painted with a cake of laundry soap. Or so she said."

Veering stared morosely toward the door of an adjoining room.

"That," he said, "is presumably the old gentleman's lair. Do you think if we applauded violently, he would come out for a bow, at least? I'm slowly perishing of hunger."

The rain rattled on the windows, the thunder rolled, our babble grew tense and nastier with a growing undercurrent of mutiny, a large contingent beginning to murmur of bolting the entire farcical business, and then Tillayou appeared. He was dressed in a combination of evening clothes and a black velvet jacket and looked surprisingly younger. None of us had ever seen or dreamed of so vibrant a Tillayou, or fancied so dominant a figure would crawl out of that old cocoon.

We stopped talking and listened to Tillayou as if the lights had gone out around us and he alone stood in brightness. He had brought a stranger into the room. He introduced this new guest, identifying each of us unctuously by calling and achievement. The guest was Carl Scheuttler which was a name as striking to us at the moment as Sherlock Holmes. Mr. Scheuttler was from the District Attorney's office. He had led the futile hunt for Marcia's murderer and had promised, in the news columns from day to day, "important developments before nightfall." His presence in this room surrounded by this round-up promised definite entertainment. Marcia's murderer was among us, or at least so Tillayou thought, and was going to be served us for dessert.

We started for the dining room, all grown very formal. A long, improvised banquet table was set for us. Tillayou ordered us to find our place cards and under no circumstances change them. Mr. Scheuttler was eyeing us professionally, at least so it seemed, holding himself aloof from our sallies and making no compromising friendships which might embarrass him when the great moment of accusation and arrest arrived.

As we seated ourselves we noted a number of odd things, which then dropped at least out of my mind because of what happened immediately. Locksley was the first to speak after the chairs had stopped scraping and we were all in our places.

"Who," inquired Locksley feelingly and pointing at the empty chair at the foot of the table, "who is that miserable miscreant?"

From the other end of the table where old Tillayou and his velvet jacket were presiding came a slow sonorous answer.

"That is for my guest of honor, sir."

Locksley reached over and examined the place card.

"Well, well," he chuckled, "this seat has been reserved for one not entirely unknown to all of us."

"Who?" inquired Morrie Stein.

"Marcia Tillayou," said Locksley, "who has gone out for the moment to fetch her harp."

"Serve the dinner, Mr. Harvey," said our host to the old mummy, "we are all here."

Kraznoff, the dancer, who was seated rather near the empty chair, rose nervously.

"Please, I like change my plaze," she announced.

There was laughter.

"Come, come, sit down," Morrie Stein grinned. "Marcia was much too sensible to turn into a ghost."

Locksley was beaming at our host.

"This is marvelous," he said. "Mr. Tillayou, bless his old heart, will turn out the lights and little Marcia will dance for us with a tambourine."

"It's an insult to Marcia," said Emily Duane.

"You're mistaken," von Klauber smiled at her, "the insult is to us. But a very stupid one. So it doesn't matter."

Lawyer Felix, sensing troubled waters, grew oily.

"Perhaps Mr. Tillayou isn't serious," he said. "It may be just a sentimental gesture. You do not really believe she is here, Mr. Tillayou?"

To this Tillayou answered softly, "There are more things in Heaven and earth, Horatio, than are dreamed of in your philosophy."

"Very good," said Locksley.

O'Shea, who had been staring sadly at the empty chair, suddenly leaned across the table and addressed it.

"Hello, darling," he said softly. "You look quite stunning tonight. Who gave you those beautiful lilies?"

The thunder rolled outside. Emily Duane gasped. But Locksley, not to be outdone in sallies by thunder or screams, cooed politely.

"Pass the olives, will you, Veering," he said, "before Marcia makes a pig of herself."

There being no olives and since there was no Marcia, this struck us as doubly droll. We laughed. Von Klauber turned his monocle on the "Representative from Scotland Yard."

"Do you believe in ghosts, Mr. Scheuttler?" he asked.

"I'm sure they're out of his jurisdiction," said Veering.

The elderly Mr. Harvey was tottering around the table filling wine glasses. Wallerstein, his dark, angry face intent on the empty chair, announced abruptly:

"Death is not a final word. We do not die so quickly. Marcia was never more alive than she is in this room tonight. Her innermost secrets are at this table. We are a compendium of Marcia."

"That's quite right," said O'Shea moodily. "We all loved her, in our varied fashions."

Tillayou, silent and queerly aglow, repeated under his breath the words, "loved her," and stared around the table, his eyes flooding with tears.

"Now that's rotten taste," Veering murmured, "calling us here to stage an exhibition of table rapping—and tears."

"A little grief over Marcia's death wouldn't be so amiss," said O'Shea, "particularly among her friends."

The aged Mr. Harvey, who, Locksley had been quick to decide, was the famous Santa Fé provisioner, was bringing in soup plates, sparsely filled and almost cold, and clattering them down one at a time in front of the guests. Indignant requests for spoons rising from one end of the table confused him and brought him to a standstill, shivering in his tracks and regarding his master unhappily. Tillayou nodded reassuringly at him, dried his eyes, beamed, pushed his chair from the table and stood up. This unexpected gesture brought quiet. I noticed that Mr. Scheuttler had lowered his head and was frowning severely at the tablecloth.

"I am an old actor," Tillayou began in measured tones, "and with the audience seated and the curtain up, I find it hard to wait."

He favored us with an engaging, almost cringing smile.

"'Art is long but time is fleeting,'" he continued, "and there is one who bids me speak." However, he didn't speak, but fell once more into quotation. It was a poem this time.

> "Love, hear thou! How desolate the heart is, ever calling,
> Ever unanswered, and the dark rain falling,
> Then as now. . . ."

This mystic invocation done with, Tillayou struck a pose that showed the oration itself was about to begin. But how describe such an oration! How bad it was, and how illumined afterwards with a grandeur we never knew was in it. Yet to betray its climax would be somehow to deprive it of the quality belonging to it during its delivery, the bravado with which he spoke it into the sharpened teeth of perhaps the city's most finicky raconteurs, the clownish humors which it achieved unconsciously as it went on, the boredom, the suspense which seemed to promise only the cruel laughter of the audience.

There were, alas, sad lapses of logic in his speech, when the old actor's mind failed to provide the correct transition, ironies which would have seemed far-fetched and inexplicable were they not so obviously borrowed from Marc Antony's funeral address; and there would have been more pauses in it even than there were, had Tillayou not helped himself to the language of the Bard. We heard *King Lear,* and *Macbeth* and *Romeo,* in whispers and inflections that sounded to our kind like rather hilarious caricatures. We listened with distaste, sneers, and apprehension for what might still follow, to Shylock's unctuous tones, and the cries of Spartacus before the Roman populace. Altogether, it was a performance that would have required more than a little indulgence on the part of the politest audience, and one which only O'Shea among us, his head leaning on his hand in one of his idle postures, seemed mysteriously to enjoy.

"You are my guests," it went, "very distinguished guests, and if I offend by what I am going to say, I ask your indulgence as the father of one who was admirable to you. I am the ghost of Banquo come to trouble your feasting.

"These, Mr. Scheuttler, are all very honorable and distinguished citizens who have gone out of their way to gratify the whim of an old actor by supping in his home. They are the great names of that world I have so long served with my humble talents.

"You asked, sirs, if I believed my daughter Marcia was present in this galaxy of her friends. It may be the wandering wits of an old man but I see her there, sitting tragic and beautiful, about her the sound of rain and of sweet bells jangling out of tune. Smiling at those who loved her. Yet she looks with cold eyes at one who sits here, with accusing eyes at one whose heart shouts, 'Avaunt and quit my sight! Let the earth hide thee!'

"Sweet and fair she was, the brightness of her cheek did shame the stars as daylight doth the lamp. But I won't bore you by asking you to recall those charms you once admired so, those virtues you once held so highly, almost as highly as myself.

"You have not come here tonight to hear a doting father spread his miseries before you, but for sterner business which from your courtesy and attentiveness I feel sure you have guessed.

"Mr. Scheuttler asked me to tell him this matter privately but I refused. For you were all her friends, her honorable friends, and I wanted you present.

"Who killed my daughter? Who took her life? There's the question. I have the answer. But I'll not merely give a name and cry 'murderer!' No, I have the proofs.

"You all loved her and admired her, helped her through the years of struggle, made life sweet for her with your tenderness and understanding and unselfishness. Yet one of you murdered her. Murdered her!

"He is here. He came to my humble house, fancying himself too clever for detection. He sits now at my table. Mr. Harvey, close the doors! Lock them! So he can't escape. Lock us in! The windows, too.

Ha—good man, Harvey. He has served me well. He was with me through those years when I too, like my daughter, was a star; not as bright or shining as she. But Maurice Tillayou was a name, sirs, that belonged to the grand days of the theater. Thank you, Harvey. You may go to bed now and sleep sweetly, and may angels guard thy dreams.

"Where was I, Mr. Scheuttler? Oh, yes, the doors are locked. Is this not like a play? Your faces waiting for the name—the name of Judas. All of you waiting, each edging from his neighbor. I keep my promise, Mr. Scheuttler. I have the proofs, all of them, enough to send that one from this table to the gallows. The man who killed Marcia, who murdered my Marcia, is looking at me. Ah, the terror in his eyes. His name is——"

Thunder had been rolling through the last of his words. Now it crashed outside, drowning out his voice. And at the same time the room in which we sat turned black. The entire scene disappeared as in a dream. The lights had gone out. The women screamed. Chairs toppled over. There was a moment of mysterious confusion, consternation, with cries and even laughter in the dark. But we were riveted by a voice calling wildly in the black room. It was Tillayou.

"Let me go! He's killing me! Help! Help! Oh, my God! He's killing —killing——"

The voice shut off as if hands were choking its sound. There was a flash of lightning and in the phosphorescent glare that lay in the room for a moment we seemed to see something mad—Tillayou sinking to the floor in a corner, his hands over his heart, and blood flowing over them. The tableau vanished.

An awkward, nightmarish and foolishly restrained commotion followed. We seemed to think it was something unreal we were witnessing and we were not a crowd to scream, to throw down chairs or believe in murder at a lightning glance. Reality is a far cry from those forever writing about it. Emily Duane inquired in a polite voice for lights.

O'Shea was the first to hold a cigarette lighter over the old man in the corner. On his knees, gasping, one hand on the floor and trying to crawl somewhere, we made out Tillayou. In the same moment Mr. Scheuttler, who obviously knew his way about in such dilemmas, was on O'Shea with a flashlight and apparently convinced he was the murderer. Now at last there were screams from the women and a rather hysterical calling for lights from the men and over it all the groans and gasps of a dying man whom Mr. Scheuttler was hounding professionally for a dying statement.

In fact we, Mr. Scheuttler and Tillayou seemed to be acting in a play—one of those Broadway melodramas full of darkness, murder, suspects and all the unconvincing trappings of theatricalized mystery. Some of us lit matches, others cigarette lighters, others searched for lights or joined in hounding the dying man alongside the frantic and barking Mr. Scheuttler. O'Shea provided a minute's extra excitement by kicking in the door and reappearing in the face of Mr. Scheuttler's drawn gun, this official having forbidden anyone to leave the premises, with a candelabra. This he lit and the candelabra illumined with its mellow beam a scene that seemed as operatic as *Tosca.*

"It's dark," Old Tillayou was moaning. "Marcia, where are you? My little bright-haired girl. Marcia, my child."

Now we all leaned over him, urging him, like a mob of earnest supers, to tell who had killed him, and eyeing each other the while askance. Mr. Scheuttler, in particular, convinced that the old man was about to name his murderer, waited with his gun still drawn.

But the old actor was raving.

"Blood," he said, lifting his hands and staring at them. "My blood." And again asked to speak out, he started crying for Marcia. "Listen," he said, "listen to her. Ever calling . . . ever unanswered." There was more of it, heartbreaking and somehow unreal.

Then there was the awful moment when the old man seemed to search for someone. Now his eyes were calm. He recognized Mr. Scheuttler.

"Let me whisper the name," he murmured eagerly, and so faintly we could hardly hear. "He—he mustn't escape. Closer, my friends. Lend me your ears. . . ."

"Who was it?" someone couldn't help saying desperately.

Mr. Scheuttler roared for quiet, only to repeat the question himself in the next moment.

"Ah," said Tillayou, "it was . . . it was . . ." and lapsed into a silence. There was a babble of questioning as the silence grew prolonged, and then hysterical. Mr. Scheuttler no longer seemed to be watching his suspects. He was looking at the old man who appeared to be quietly crying. Some tears rolled down his cheeks. And then an incredible thing happened. Tillayou died.

There had been some coughing, the rattle that is so unmistakable even to those who have never heard it. But no one somehow had expected death.

An even more melodramatic pandemonium followed Tillayou's passing. Police were called for. We were ordered about. Mr. Scheuttler flourished his gun. Mr. Harvey was sent for from his sleep guarded by angels and, as he stood moaning over his master's body, questioned about the switch for the lights which hadn't worked all this time. O'Shea took a lead in this questioning, despite Mr. Scheuttler's violent orders addressed to one whom he now regarded firmly as a murderer. Mr. Harvey was incapable of any answers but O'Shea suddenly went down on his hands and knees and began crawling under the table while Mr. Scheuttler, fancying this an effort to escape, threatened loudly he would never get out of the room alive. But suddenly, in the midst of these threats, as O'Shea fumbled under the carpet at the table's edge, the lights went on.

"If you will allow me to be a bit oracular and put that gun away," O'Shea said, poking his head up from under the table, "the mystery is a very simple one. Tillayou turned out the lights himself. The switch was right under his foot. And then he killed himself."

It was dawn when Locksley, O'Shea and I entered O'Shea's rooms. We had spent an active and rather noisy evening as guests of Mr. Scheuttler and two police officials. Mr. Harvey had finally told his story. Tillayou had had the switch under the table installed the day before and this vital clue had been quickly verified from the electricians who had done the work. Mr. Harvey related that Tillayou had ordered him not to cook any food for our banquet, saying it wouldn't be necessary, and had also said that dishes and silverware would not be needed at his dinner. The absence of these items had been one of the odd things we noticed when we had first entered the dining room. Mr. Harvey also identified the dagger removed from Tillayou's body as one that had seen service in an ancient production of *Macbeth* and one which his master had spent the hours before the arrival of his guests sharpening in his bedroom.

There was no doubt that Tillayou had killed himself. But Mr. Scheuttler and the two police officials remained confused by the manner of his suicide. O'Shea persuaded them, aided by Mr. Harvey's tears and tattle, that the old actor's mind had been unhinged by grief over Marcia's death, and that the whole matter could be explained only by the poor man's insanity. We were all allowed finally to go, after assuring the officials we would appear any time they desired us for further questioning.

In O'Shea's rooms, Locksley and I waited patiently while that moody Celt opened bottles and prepared us drinks. After he had accomplished these rites he went to a drawer in a desk.

"I'll let you read this letter," he said. "It's from Marcia. It was mailed the night she was found dead."

He handed us a scrawled piece of note paper. We read:

> "Alfred, I'm bored, tired, hurt, sick, full of nasty things. You were always the nicest. So take care of my father, like a good boy, will you? I'd stay a while longer but death seems easier and simpler than life. What are a few pills more or less to one who has swallowed so much? Good-by and do you remember the first night of *The Forgotten Lady*? For the last time,
>
> "MARCIA."

O'Shea smiled at us moodily as we finished.

"That's the truth," he said. "She committed suicide."

"What about the bullets?" I asked.

"Guess," said O'Shea.

"Tillayou," said Locksley.

"Right," said O'Shea. "He found her dead with the poison still in her hand, very likely. And he couldn't bear that."

"I hate to think of it, too," said Locksley.

"He worshipped her," said O'Shea. "She was his star. But stars don't commit suicide. Only failures do that. Only very miserable and defeated people do that. He tried to keep her a star. So he set about slashing the painting and wrecking the place. It was all done very bravely so that the world might never guess that Marcia had died so ingloriously.

"At least," said O'Shea, "that's what I thought it was at first. And I decided to say nothing. What we saw tonight has got me all excited." He smiled and drank again.

"It was terrible," said Locksley.

"It was marvelous," O'Shea grinned at him. His gaunt, muscular mouth trembled with the mood of eloquence. "I read the signs wrong," he said. "Do you know what happened?"

"No," said Locksley, "except that the old boy was madder than a Hatter, poor soul."

"He wasn't mad," said O'Shea, "he was sane. You see, my lads, the old polliwog never thought of Marcia as having killed herself. He found her dead by her own hand. But that didn't mean anything. He saw her as murdered—by all of us. Murdered, gadzooks, by all the lying, cheating, faking rabble of friends that had danced around her including your humble servant, Alfred O'Shea. We'd killed her," he said dourly.

"Do you remember what he called us—all honorable and distinguished friends, all full of sweetness and unselfishness toward her? That was cute of the old windbag. Looking at us whom he hated so and rolling those juicy sentences at us. We were a flock of vampires that had fed off her. That's how he saw us, all of us. When he found her dead he thought of her as murdered, by us, by Broadway. It was all our hands that had lifted the poison glass to her mouth. And he went cracked with the curious idea of somehow bringing all these phantom murderers to justice."

We nodded. O'Shea drank again.

"That was a great performance tonight at the table," he said. "And a cold house. But he went over big."

"What made you think of another switch?" I asked.

"I knew that something strange was on the boards," O'Shea grinned. "I wanted to interrupt. But I hated to break up his show, whatever it was going to be. I'm kind of glad I didn't, aren't you?"

We said we were, but looked blandly at our host for further explanation. O'Shea drank again, grinned, his eyes filling with admiration.

"Do you realize," he said softly, "that the old barnstormer was playing his death scene from the moment he came into the room, with Sherlock Holmes in tow? He had the dagger in his pocket. He'd figured it out, rehearsed it in his bedroom for days, sharpening away at Macbeth's old toad stabber. He had his lines down pat. He'd planned to kill himself with the name of the supposedly guilty party almost on his lips. He was going to go as far as saying who it was that had murdered Marcia and then, out with the lights and the dagger in his heart. Suspicion would be turned on all of us. We'd all of us be clapped into jail and raked over the coals, not for his murder alone, but for Marcia's. That was the main thing. Whoever had killed Marcia had snapped out the lights and done him in, just as he was about to reveal the name. That was the plot. What a grand old boy! I'll never forget his dying."

"Nor I," I agreed.

"Dying and remembering his lines to the last," said O'Shea. "What a memory. That was my favorite poem he kept quoting—*Rain on Rahoun,* by Joyce. He heard me recite it once—on my honeymoon. You remember when he lay in the corner with the knife in him—acting, by God. All that waiting and mumbling about Marcia—do you know what he was doing? Ad libbing, like the good old trouper he was, filling in because death had missed its cue. Lend me your ears—it was the grand manner—grease paint and blood. And do you remember how he gurgled finally in that old ham voice of his—'It was . . . it was . . .' and died exactly at the right moment? What timing!"

"I remember how he said good-by to Mr. Harvey," said Locksley, "that was pretty."

We sat silent, overcome by the memory of old Tillayou's oration, hearing it anew with the mystery out of it.

"None of us will die as gallantly," said O'Shea, "and so much in the full sanctity of love—and art."

Locksley rose and shivered. A wry smile came into his Pickwickian face.

"A lovely piece of old-fashioned miming," he said, "but as fruitless a drama as I ever had the misfortune to witness."

"You're right," O'Shea said, "the plot was full of holes. I could have helped him a lot with the construction. But—it was a great Last Night."

# *My Literary Harem*

DURING MY FLING as a television oracle, I offered on an evening's program a list of fifty books I had most admired during my life, and I made brief comment on each of them. To the astonishment of my producer, Ted Yates, and of myself, some ten thousand letters arrived overnight at our WABC station pleading for copies of this list.

Our small secretarial staff, Miss Rita Quinn and Miss Jeanie Sims, started mailing out mimeographed copies of the broadcast. But what with their other multiple duties, such as remembering where I had mislaid my glasses, typing my new novel, bagging celebrities for Producer Yates, cooling off cranks on the telephone, et cetera, our doughty staff was unable to sate the public hunger for the list. Thousands of copies were mailed out, but a multitude of requests continued to arrive.

Therefore this epilogue to my book—a transcript of my November 11, 1958, TV program. It will not only save further secretarial travail, but it may divert, harass, educate, confuse, or outrage thousands of readers who managed to live through the year 1958 without encountering me on their television screens.

The broadcast was a duologue between me and my bright program associate, Miss Lynn Merrill, whom I addressed as Missy during our nightly confabs. I have removed a few of my ad lib stutters and added a phrase or two.

TRANSCRIPT

THE BEN HECHT SHOW

WABC-TV

November 11, 1958

MISSY. Ben Hecht is on the air. Author, playwright, and iconoclast, Ben tonight outlines how you can achieve a do-it-yourself Ph.D. by reading fifty books which he will describe and discuss. (MISS MERRILL *sits down behind a battered desk rescued from some scenery junk pile which is the main prop of our program.*) Before we get to the list of fifty books that our viewers have been curious about, I would like to know how important books are to you personally.

*There had been some curiosity. A dozen or more viewers had written in asking for literary guidance.*

MYSELF. I quote from myself: "Villiers de L'Isle-Adam, the Parisian writer who lived like an alley cat, ate stale fish, went threadbare through fifty years of penury—who wrote with frostbitten fingers on cigarette papers—spoke from his hovel when dying: 'Farewell! I have lived the richest and most magnificent of men.' We who read books can die with a similar boast."

MISSY. How did you arrive at these fifty books? What are their particular qualifications?

MYSELF. It is a rather sad process, picking fifty favorite books. You have to discard at least a hundred books that are every bit as good—sometimes better. And you mourn their absence. You feel unfaithful, unfair, even untruthful. The fifty I selected are not necessarily the fifty best books I have read, but the fifty books that stirred me most when I read them, and gave me a lively look into the mind of man.

MISSY. Your list starts with eight books on history. Why does history head the list?

MYSELF. History is the merry and amoral gossip column of the arts. It babbles brightly the tale of the endless disasters we call civilization, of the unending lunacy we call politics, and its attending mass murder we call war. And it lists gleefully the ever present handful of egomaniacs whose whims and talents provide devastation and entertainment for the world.

MISSY. With that we come to Plutarch's *Lives*. Tell me why.

MYSELF. Plutarch was one of the sprightliest of the gossips. His anecdotes of Roman and Greek heroes keep the past alive and forever intimate.

MISSY. Next you have Suetonius, and Gibbons *Decline and Fall of the Roman Empire*. These sound a bit highbrow and possibly on the dull side. (MISSY *is obviously a modernist for whom history goes no further back than Mr. Stanislavsky's treatise on acting.*)

MYSELF. Neither highbrow nor dull. Suetonius was an early Walter Winchell. He wrote of the pre-Christian neurotics who once ran the world. His account of their lunacies and depravities makes us realize how "modern" the ancients were. Gibbon was a fine English gentleman of letters whose witty tale of the fall of the Roman Empire and of the subsequent centuries offers a fine picture of Europe as a teen-ager —delinquent, gaudy, bloody, and half-mad.

MISSY. I'm sure people will wonder why you pick Thomas Carlyle's *French Revolution* and nothing at all about our American Revolution.

MYSELF. I've never read a book about the American Revolution that was interesting. The writers who report the American revolt write a sort of pious thank-you letter. Whereas the French Revolution, like the Russian Revolution, is a much more rewarding topic as literature. The French and Russian revolutions produced the sort of government in which the loser lost everything, including his head. The American Revolution produced the sort of government in which the loser gets a rematch. This makes for finer government but not nearly as good reading.

MISSY. Why is Prescott's *Conquest of Mexico* important enough to be on your list?

MYSELF. Prescott left us one of the goriest and most vicious accounts of human greed, bigotry, and gallantry to be found between book covers. After reading Prescott in my teens I was ashamed for some time to utter the word "God," because of the abuses and horrors committed in His name. Later, I transferred a little of my shame to the word "Man."

MISSY. Next you list Graetz's *History of the Jews.*

MYSELF. There's an even bloodier and more hair-raising work than Prescott's. It is the two-thousand-year story of the Jew who has not yet got down off the Cross.

MISSY. We have a rather serious omission that just occurs to me. Why haven't you included the Bible?

MYSELF. Because it is a book I have never been able to read. In the first volume I read about Job and also some spicy pages called "The Song of Songs." Due to my respect for my parents, I never got around to reading the companion volume. So I omit what I do not know.

MISSY. Today Africa has come into sharp focus. It is even on the best-seller list. John Gunther has been identified as the Bard of Africa. But you list a book called *Prelude to Africa*—a book we can't find listed in the New York Public Library.

MYSELF. That's my deficiency as a scholar. I have less memory for names and titles than for my own enthusiasm. This book was written some fifteen years ago by a midwestern lady schoolteacher who lived twenty-five years in Africa. Perhaps some of our viewers will help me remember her name and the correct title of her magnificent book.

MISSY. Let's hope we have a literary detective listening. You list next

Will Durant's *Age of Faith.* What area of knowledge does this illumine?

MYSELF. The book is a tale of the Dark Ages written with the brightest historical pen we have today. It recounts the almost forgotten story of the great and brilliant Arab civilization that for centuries dominated the world.

MISSY. That ends your history course, and omits about two-thirds of the world. Don't you think it's a little incomplete?

MYSELF. It is, theoretically. But, factually, no. For when you read these eight books, you will encounter footnotes, indices, references bristling with the names of hundreds of other enticing volumes. If you read these eight books, you are in the position of a drug addict who has been told where all the cocaine is hidden—free.

MISSY. Now we come to the science department. I notice you favor the insects. There are two books on bees, spiders, ants, flies, et cetera, by Imms and by Fabre: *History of Entomology* and *Bees and Spiders.* Why the stress on insects?

MYSELF. To me, insects are the most spiritual and religious sermonizers in the world. When you read about these little clockwork children of nature, you get more of a sense of the miraculous than the reading of all the saints and theologians can give you. To me, the most convincing priest in the world is a spider. He teaches you the inevitability of a planned universe, because bugs are God or nature, minus any egoism of their own. Unlike human beings, there are no doubts, defiances, or misinformation in them. Bugs are God.

MISSY. You list *The Expanding Universe* by Eddington. What marvels does that reveal?

MYSELF. Eddington is one of the hundreds of lucid physicists and astronomers who have sent the mind of man leaping into space like a rocket—and landed it almost at the feet of God. Our scientists today are our Shakespeares and Miltons—our poets with refreshed information of earth, sky, and nature.

MISSY. Next you list Raynor Johnson's *The Imprisoned Splendour.* What manner of tome is this?

MYSELF. Johnson is an Australian university professor, a sort of combination of Einstein, Keats, and a spiritualist seance. *The Imprisoned Splendour* is a bacchanal of chemistry, physics, astronomy, mysticism, and ghost-hunting.

MISSY. Now we come to three really heavy-sounding books. *In Search of Adam* by Dr. Wendt, *Gods, Graves and Scholars* by C. W.

Ceram, and Frazer's *Golden Bough*. Which ends our science seminar. Are these books for children?

MYSELF. All people who read are children—full of never sated curiosity. I read Frazer when I was a boy. He was the father of modern anthropology. His great work is an account of the emergence of the human family from semi-idiot cannibals to our present status of semi-idiot vegetarians.

MISSY. And *In Search of Adam*—?

MYSELF. —is about fossils: the story of the uncovering of the primordial footprints of man and his pets. Dr. Wendt writes the story with wit and a bit of derision. The nineteenth-century religious world and its passions and priests considered the discovery and identification of fossils a vile, sacrilegious business. For religious authorities had it that the world was around six thousand years old. How then could there be human and animal fossils a hundred thousand or a half-million years old? The first paleontologists and "evolutionists" were considered by the outraged spokesmen of God to be as bad as witches. However, both spokesmen and fossil fanciers are in good standing today.

MISSY. What of *Gods, Graves and Scholars*?

MYSELF. My favorite history of the recent science of archaeology. It tells of the forgotten civilizations uncovered by scientific pick-and-shovel men.

MISSY. Now we come to the thinkers. First on your list is François Rabelais.

MYSELF. I've tried to pick the few philosophers who didn't give me a mental cramp when I read them. Rabelais was among the first of the brickbat-hurling philosophers. He thought of people rather than of ideas, and illustrated his findings with tales of sex, gluttony, bigotry and mendacity.

MISSY. And Mr. Spinoza?

MYSELF. Spinoza was a different sort of philosopher. He hid from life and its echoes. He grappled with the mythomania and bigotry which our forebears called "thinking." He was the first modern to wipe the Christian and Judaic cobwebs from the European mind.

MISSY. You list next Montaigne's *Essays*. Isn't he too ancient for our modern appetites?

MYSELF. Montaigne wrote some three hundred years ago, but he remains, nevertheless, one of the most modern and lucid minds to be found in print. He is the sort of one-man civilization that is achieved when one human being thinks honestly.

MISSY. You have a German on your list—Schopenhauer's *Essays*.

MYSELF. Schopenhauer is one of the few Germans I know able to write bright and intelligible prose. He made cantankerous and witty answer to the ugliness of existence. He lived in Germany at the time.

MISSY. Next is Wyndham Lewis's *Time and Western Man.*

MYSELF. That's a personal choice. I knew Wyndham Lewis and liked him very much. He was a London lad. He was one of the few men who wrote of the mysteries of biology and astrology and all the high and mighty things, in journalese.

MISSY. I'm surprised to see Nietzsche listed, since he was the favorite writer of the modern Germans.

MYSELF. Poor old Nietzsche is one of the most misunderstood of all the writers. He was full of more hate for Germans and Germanism than almost any writer I know of. In fact, if Nietzsche had been believed and listened to in his accurate and lyrical attacks on Germany, we might have saved our century from being wrecked. I choose *Ecce Homo* as his book . . . it is a wonderful hymn of human anarchy.

MISSY. Next we have H. L. Mencken's *Prejudices.* Is this a serious work?

MYSELF. Mencken was never serious. He was a salty fellow with a shillelagh for sham and platitude. He put a brighter face on the Republic and unthroned (for a time) its "Booboisie."

MISSY. And next is Professor Sigmund Freud's *Selected Writings.* Are you a Freudian?

MYSELF. I have never enrolled as a disciple of any man or philosophy. Nietzsche wrote, "He who wishes to follow me must first forget me." Which may be an invitation to unconscious plagiarism. We are all that, toward Freud. Sigmund Freud discovered the second brain of man—the one that people don't like, but live by.

MISSY. Is there any religious bias in your listing of Bertrand Russell's book *Why I Am Not a Christian?*

MYSELF. No bias. Merely delight in Lord Russell, who is a wittier man than Bernard Shaw. Russell doesn't attack human faith or any spiritual belief. He reveals neatly, however, the fact that human beings do not worship God but rather their own bad thinking. And that the greatest sin there is, is to give the name of God to the stupidity, inanity, and infantilism of human misreason.

MISSY. Ernest Jones's *Essays?*

MYSELF. Dr. Jones is an Englishman who died recently. He's sort of a Cook's Tour of erudition and the subconscious.

MISSY. Now we come to people—writers—who loved people as much as thoughts. You begin with Georg Brandes's *Creative Spirits.*

MYSELF. Brandes is a Dane who wrote one of the most enchanting series of literary giants' lives. He's a sort of real biographical champagne.

MISSY. Now we have a shocker. It's illegal to bring it into the country. *Memoirs* of the Marquis de Sade. What help does that give anyone?

MYSELF. This is sort of a source book for all of the modern psychiatrists. He wrote a blueprint of all the sexual depravities and abnormalities there are in the human race. He wrote it in prison. It is an evil book, but we are, in part, an evil species.

MISSY. Next we have a *History of Art* by Elie Faure.

MYSELF. If you read this work you can walk around the campus as smart as any professor.

MISSY. Casanova's *Memoirs* . . . ?

MYSELF. Casanova wrote the finest hymn to sensuality and irresponsibility that a grateful human has ever put to paper.

MISSY. Now we have a list of novelists and poets. I'll read the title and you tell me why. First Herman Melville's *Moby Dick*.

MYSELF. He was the human being a-roar. . . .

MISSY. Anatole France's *Sign of the Reine Pédauque* . . . ?

MYSELF. Anatole taught me how to smile at error rather than snarl at it and I have always been thankful to him.

MISSY. Gogol's *Dead Souls* . . . ?

MYSELF. God, if the Russians had only remained like that—a troupe of wistful and hilarious butterfingers . . . !

MISSY. Turgenev's *Sportsman's Sketches* . . . ?

MYSELF. The *Sportsman's Sketches* by Turgenev is the best book of short stories in any language.

MISSY. Joris-Karl Huysmans' *À Rebours* . . . ?

MYSELF. He was a Frenchman whose works taught us adjectives in Chicago. He was possibly the best epithetician and stylist the French ever developed.

MISSY. Saki's *The Unbearable Bassington* . . . ?

MYSELF. The wittiest, smallest, and least-known of the English classic novels.

MISSY. Marcel Proust?

MYSELF. He was a sickly French homosexualist who nevertheless wrote the most elegant account of the nineteenth century that we have.

MISSY. Flaubert's *Salammbô* . . . ?

MYSELF. Historical caviar.

MISSY. Dickens' *Pickwick Papers* . . . ?

MYSELF. Dickens was a sort of British Museum for jokes.

MISSY. Dostoevski's *House of the Dead . . . ?*

MYSELF. A phosphorescent account of the criminal side of the human soul.

MISSY. Sholom Aleichem's *Tevye . . . ?*

MYSELF. A Jewish author who stands beside Gogol and Dickens and tells of people in the midst of misfortune hailing life with a grin.

MISSY. Theodore Dreiser's *The Genius . . . ?*

MYSELF. That's all the "new" novels in one.

MISSY. Joyce Cary's *The Horse's Mouth . . . ?*

MYSELF. An Englishman who wrote the best account of a non-conformist at bay before a conformity-demanding world.

MISSY. Ring Lardner's *Short Stories . . . ?*

MYSELF. I'd match Ring against Chekhov and de Maupassant.

MISSY. Peter Finley Dunne's *Mr. Dooley . . . ?*

MYSELF. This was the high noon of American cynicism and healthy disrespect for authority. Send copies to your congressmen and senators.

MISSY. John Steinbeck's *Grapes of Wrath . . . ?*

MYSELF. That was the first investigation of the fact that the American way of life was a death trap for many who shared it.

MISSY. Walter Pater's *Marius the Epicurean . . . ?*

MYSELF. A personal fancy of mine. History in a dress suit.

MISSY. Shakespeare's *Hamlet, Othello,* and *King Lear . . . ?*

MYSELF. The world's greatest march of words.

MISSY. Walt Whitman's *Leaves of Grass . . . ?*

MYSELF. That was our country's first lyrical cry that we were a new land with new people.

MISSY. Carl Sandburg's *Chicago Poems . . . ?*

MYSELF. That's a continuation of that cry—that we are still a new land with new people. (*A slip of paper was handed me at this point. It contained a telephone message from Rabbi Wohlgelernter, a friend of mine to whom I had once given a book entitled* North African Prelude *written by Galbraith Welch, thus putting an authentic title to my African entry.*) Thank you—and good night.

In my TV broadcast, I listed only forty-nine books, modestly leaving an opening for my viewers to fill. I have added the fiftieth myself in this printed version. It is Edgar Snow's *Red Star Over China.*